NAKED CAME THE

Florida Man

NAKED CAME THE
Florida Man

Tim Dorsey

wm
WILLIAM MORROW
An Imprint of HarperCollins*Publishers*

NAKED CAME THE FLORIDA MAN. Copyright © 2020 by Tim Dorsey. All rights reserved. Printed in the United States of America. No part of this book may be used or reproduced in any manner whatsoever without written permission except in the case of brief quotations embodied in critical articles and reviews. For information, address HarperCollins Publishers, 195 Broadway, New York, NY 10007.

HarperCollins books may be purchased for educational, business, or sales promotional use. For information, please email the Special Markets Department at SPsales@harpercollins.com.

FIRST EDITION

Library of Congress Cataloging-in-Publication Data has been applied for.

ISBN 978-0-06-279600-4

20 21 22 23 24   LSC   10 9 8 7 6 5 4 3 2

For Larry "Montana" Fletcher

NAKED CAME THE

Florida Man

Prologue

Don't shoot guns into the hurricane."

Elsewhere this would go without saying, but Floridians need to be told.

This was an actual warning issued by the Pasco County Sheriff's Office just north of Tampa Bay as a major storm approached. After all, a local man had just been arrested for DUI when he tried to order a taco in a Bank of America drive-through.

The alert was a reaction to people posting plans on the Internet for a party to shoot at the hurricane and make it turn away. The sheriff's notice even included a scientific diagram showing how the vortex of the core could curve bullet paths to come back and hit the shooter.

"Shooting at a hurricane!" said Serge. "That's the most brainless thing I've ever heard!"

Coleman looked out the rear window of their muscle car racing over a bridge. "Why is everyone else driving the other way?"

"Because they're evacuating. It's the smart move."

"Then shouldn't we be evacuating?"

"Absolutely not," said Serge, turning on tactical silicone windshield wipers. "They have to flee because they don't know what they're doing. We're professionals."

"How's that?"

"Everyone else gets ready for storms according to the official instructions." Serge reached under his seat. "Which is fine if you want to survive. But if you're taking it to the next level, all that jazz will just slow you down. Hurricanes are the marrow of Florida history, and my history always goes bone-deep. That's why I prepare for storms with an encyclopedic set of state guidebooks, every conceivable new gadget, and bags of provisions exclusively from the candy and snack aisles. Think about it: Little kids are programmed to thrive and that's the first place they go. That's how a pro has to think."

"I'm still not sure." Coleman flicked a Bic. "We're like the only car heading this direction."

"I've taken every conceivable precaution," said Serge, absentmindedly waving a pistol out the window as Coleman did a bong hit. "What can possibly go wrong?"

1928

The bloated, decaying body rolled into the ditch.

It fell onto its back, cloudy eyes still wide open, creating a frozen expression that bookmarked the last thoughts from a long, brutal life of hardship, hunger, harrow and few complaints. The final thought in those eyes: *What kind of shit* now?

"It creeps me out the way he's staring like that," said a voice at the top of the ditch.

"He's staring at God," said someone else, grabbing a pair of lifeless ankles.

Another body tumbled down the dirt embankment, and another, and so forth. The dead were all African American, just like the dozens of perspiring, shirtless men laboring with shovels.

The shovel gang most likely would have pitched in anyway, out of a sense of community, but this time they didn't have a choice. They occasionally glanced back at the white lawmen with shotguns propped against their shoulders and pools of tobacco spit at their feet.

"What are you looking at—!" The next word was impolite.

It actually should have been quite a nice day in late September. The sky was clear as a dream, and a cooling breeze swept over the fields covered with thousands of tulip-shaped orange wildflowers. The wind made the acres of bright petals sway as one, back and forth, like an immense school of tropical fish. Then the sun rose higher, and the breeze left. The air became stubbornly still, baking in that Central Florida humidity so thick it seemed to have weight. But worst of all:

It stank.

Blame history. It doesn't bother to knock. It doesn't even come in the front door. It's like those newspaper articles about a car that crashes through the wall of a bedroom in the middle of the night. This was before storms had alphabetical names, and it was called the Great Hurricane of 1928. Later it would become the forgotten storm. The victims didn't have money.

It began the afternoon of September 15. All the fancy weather instruments that now give residents a head start on hurricanes had yet to be invented. You'd be chopping carrots for a stew, and then a hurricane was just *there*. But if you were really paying attention over the years, there was one early-warning system. The Seminoles.

Something about pollen and a rapid blooming of the sawgrass. The Indians watched the plants down in the swamp, and when a low haze in front of the setting sun got that weird color, they seemed to know the exact moment to make for high ground. Many scientists have looked into the phenomenon and scoffed at the notion. But the Seminoles were always dependably on the move before each Big Wind, so they'd figured something out.

This time, the tribe had come up out of the Everglades on trails leading to the ramshackle towns of South Bay and Belle Glade, then made a right turn toward West Palm Beach. There was no panic in their march. Simply a parade of native families out for a very long stroll. Some of the townsfolk remembered a similar migration two years earlier, before a lesser hurricane, and decided to follow the Indians out. But most stayed put.

On the morning of September 17, the storm that had peaked at category five made landfall at the Jupiter Inlet lighthouse in northern Palm Beach County. More than a thousand homes were destroyed along the coast before it continued churning inland, unimpressed . . .

Now, a few days later, the digging of massive, macabre pits continued with a sense of urgency. Fear of disease swept the survivors, and in the immediate aftermath the locals were on their own. Many of them were about halfway up the east side of the big lake, which would be Okeechobee, in an empty place that would soon become known for its mass grave, which would be Port Mayaca.

The same frantic scene was replaying itself miles away, in opposite directions, at two other South Florida locations. Even as mass graves go, there wasn't remotely enough room. At least two and a half thousand dead by most accounts. Some said more than three. The nation's worst toll ever, save for the Galveston storm in 1900.

Here was the problem with the hurricane of '28: the storm surge. That's often the case, and almost without exception, the deadly waves come from the ocean. But this time around, death didn't come from the sea; one of the strongest hurricanes in recorded history made a direct hit on the nation's largest fresh-water lake sitting within a state. Who saw that coming? There was no dike, and the storm's rotation easily shoved much of the lake's contents south, in an inescapable ten-to-twenty-foot wall of water that blanketed hundreds of square miles.

In the following hours and days, the water began to recede, and then came the snakes, but that's another story.

As the overwhelming scale of death became clear, they started digging a second grave pit on the other side of the lake in some unknown place called Ortona, and then a third in West Palm Beach, just off Tamarind Avenue. It was back-numbing work for all those residents pressed into service. But here's what really pissed them off: The bodies of black victims filled the pits as fast as they could be thrown in on top of one another. Each white person got their own private pine box.

Then those boxes were loaded onto wagons and taken to the nearby Woodlawn Cemetery for proper burial.

A shotgun man stuck two fingers in his mouth for a shrill whistle that got everyone's attention. Shovels stopped.

"You three! Over there!" The shotgun waved east. "They need more help!"

A trio of drained men trudged toward a separate pile of work, and stared down at a pale corpse.

"Great. The pine boxes," said one of the larger men, named Goat. "I don't mind burying our own, but this is bullshit."

"Just grab him," said a stubby but deceptively strong neighbor. He went by "Stub."

The first worker began lifting the body by the armpits, then suddenly dropped him and jumped back.

"What the hell's gotten into you?" said Stub.

Goat just pointed with a quivering arm. "He's got a bullet hole!"

"Where?"

"In the forehead."

"Jesus, you're right!"

They composed themselves and lifted him into a box, providing a better view. "Wait a minute, I know this guy. It's Mr. Fakakta."

"Who's that?"

"Sugar man," said Goat. "Lived in that big colonial house out past the bend by the ice plant."

"That big place in Pahokee was his?"

"Ain't doing him no good now."

They grabbed the next body, a woman, and just as promptly dropped it.

"She's got a bullet hole, too," said Stub.

"That's his wife," said Goat.

"What on earth is going on?"

The pair quickly scanned nearby bodies. "There's his son. Head almost blown off . . ."

Stub was Catholic, made the sign of the cross. "*Ave Maria.*"

Goat glanced back twenty yards and watched a stream of brown juice shoot from between gapped teeth. "Think we should tell the deputy?"

"Definitely," said Goat. "Some monster murdered this whole poor family—"

A shotgun blast went skyward.

Everyone froze.

"Shut up over there and get back to work!" barked the lawman.

The pair nodded respectfully, then began hammering penny nails into the lid of a pine box. "Screw 'em."

Part One

Chapter 1

2017

"Help me!" yelled Coleman. "I'm trapped again!"

"Hold on. I've got my own problems." Serge pushed away a piece of plywood and crawled out from under a debris pile of dresser drawers, chunks of ceiling and a toilet lid. He stood to examine all his scratches and bruises, but saw nothing major. He looked around. "Okay, Coleman, where are you?"

"I don't have a clue."

"No, I mean just keep talking and I'll follow your voice."

"Okay," said Coleman. "Hey, Serge, I just realized that 'slow up' and 'slow down' mean the same thing. That's fucked. I'm still stoned."

Serge cleared a path, pushing aside fractured furniture. "Keep talking."

"Have you seen my weed anywhere out there?"

Serge cast aside a torn-down kitchen cabinet and lifted a soaked mattress. "There you are."

Coleman sat up, and his face suddenly reddened as a cord from mangled window blinds tightened around his neck.

Serge flicked open a pocketknife and sliced the thin rope. "Don't you know that's a choking hazard?"

"I didn't have a choice." Coleman rubbed his neck. "It just got me."

Serge stood again and stared thoughtfully at the bright, panoramic view out the front of the building where the wall used to be. "It got everyone."

Coleman checked his own bruises. "Is it over?"

"All over but the shouting," said Serge.

Coleman joined him, looking out across the calm waters of Bogie Channel. "So that was the big Hurricane Irma everyone was talking about?"

Serge would have opened the door, but there wasn't one. He hopped down from the building and walked toward the street. The only sound was the crunch of gravel and broken glass under his sneakers. The air had turned mild and comfortable, nothing to betray what had come before.

Serge placed hands on his hips as he surveyed what had recently been a historic row of quaint old fishing cottages in the backcountry of the Florida Keys. All had been knocked off their foundations, lying helter-skelter practically on top of each other.

Unless you've seen the aftermath of a major hurricane, you wouldn't realize how much of the damage appears to be the result of high explosives. Little pieces of shrapnel everywhere. Slivers and confetti. Most of the other cottages were missing their front walls as well, allowing the wind to go to work inside like sticks of dynamite. Cabin number 7 had no walls at all, just a roof lying on the ground, which had been pushed against the base of a palm tree that neatly cut it open like a jigsaw. The cabin with the least damage, still barely clinging together and listing like a floundering ship off the edge of its concrete slab, was number 5.

Serge looked the other way, toward the landmark two-story clapboard office and bait store at the Old Wooden Bridge Fishing Camp. It had stood apart from the cabins, alone, unprotected, with no trees to shield it on the edge of the channel. Now there was little evidence there had ever been an office, except for the matchbook-size pieces that littered the ground and floated in the water like another bomb had gone off.

Serge wiped his eyes.

"Are you starting to cry?" asked Coleman.

"Why couldn't it have taken out a Starbucks or some shit? We keep losing all our best places." He blew his nose. "I'd bet the bat tower on Sugarloaf is gone, too."

It was.

One of the island's endangered miniature Key deer sprang from the brush and bounded through the debris like an antelope.

"I've never seen one run that fast," said Coleman.

"I'm sure it has a lot on its mind."

Coleman turned back around toward their cottage. "Jesus, we could have been killed! Why did you want to stay here and ride out that hurricane? Didn't you realize it would be this hairy?"

Another doe darted by.

"I knew it would be strong," said Serge. "But these little deer always figure out how to make it through storms, so I figured how hard can it be? Second, I love cabin number five."

"It's your favorite," said Coleman. "You always kiss the number by the door when you first arrive."

"I knew that if God would allow just a single cottage to survive relatively intact, it would be Five. I figured this island would get pretty much torn up, so I wanted to spend a final night in that special place. And last but not least, I seriously miscalculated."

"Wait. Stop," said Coleman. "You mean we really could have been killed? But you promised me I'd be safe."

Serge pulled car keys from his pocket. "What was I thinking?"

"Hey, where are you going?"

They don't call it Big Pine Key for nothing. The day before, Serge had found a spot where he was able to back his car about twenty yards into the woods, surrounded by thick pine trees. The kind of place where the little deer hide.

"It barely has a mark on her," said Coleman. "So we're heading out of here now?"

Serge shook his head and opened the trunk. "It will take a few days for workers to clear the roads, so we'll be camping until then. Help me with this gear."

They pitched a tent with sleeping bags behind the row of battered cabins. A small campfire began to glow in a little pit surrounded by rocks. Bottled water and beer cans bobbed in the melted ice of a cooler. Serge returned to the car for a last item and brought it back to the fire.

"What's that thing?" asked Coleman.

"The beginning of my latest science project." Serge sat down with a clear plastic storage bin in his lap. He opened his pocketknife again and poked a six-inch grid of tiny holes on the end. Then he taped a small, battery-powered fan over it. Then another grid on the opposite end. "This project has an extremely long gestation, and I don't know when it'll come into play, so we might as well use this downtime to get a head start."

Serge grabbed a soggy package from the cooler. He took the lid off the bin and began evenly arranging the bag's contents across the bottom.

"Bacon?" asked Coleman.

"Your universal food group."

"It's the only thing that goes great with everything," said Coleman. "Eggs, pickles, ice cream, Twinkies, other bacon. It's just impossible to go wrong."

"You can with this pack. It seriously spoiled overnight." Serge held out a slimy, uncooked strip. "Unless you dig trichinosis."

"I'll stick to beer," said Coleman. "But why are you putting it in that bin?"

"Read it in a medical journal," Serge said. "In our advanced world of modern medicine, sometimes the best treatment is still low-tech."

"Treatment for what?"

"I'm not treating anything, just using the principle for my experiment," said Serge. "All will be revealed in due time."

Serge finished his task and picked up the bin. He walked over to the edge of the woods, setting it down behind his car . . .

TWO DAYS LATER

Serge listened to the morning news on his emergency radio. He reached inside their small dome tent and began shaking Coleman to no avail. "Come on, wake up! The road's clear. It's time to go."

Serge shook harder and harder until he heard primitive groans. Then Coleman woke up all at once. He had somehow managed to turn himself around in his sleeping bag during the night.

"Help! Help! Something's got me again."

"It's just your sleeping bag. Hold still."

But Coleman had the reasoning ability of someone drowning. "Help! Help!" He thrashed around like a giant caterpillar trying to molt. Then he jumped up and dislodged the tent's poles, and soon he was wrapped up in that, too, rolling left and right.

Serge watched without expression until his pal wore himself out. A piled entanglement of nylon heaved as he panted.

"You finished?" asked Serge. "Because the tent isn't completely wrecked yet."

"Just get me out of this."

Serge extricated his friend and they began breaking camp.

When everything was stowed in the car, Serge walked over to his science project. "Well, I'll be. It worked." He sealed the lid on the storage bin, started the battery-powered fan and stuck the whole business in the back seat.

A gold 1969 Plymouth Satellite emerged from the trees and drove away from the Old Wooden Bridge Fishing Camp. Soon, they were almost out of the Lower Keys, approaching the bridge to Bahia Honda. The debris piles that had been pushed aside by heavy equipment appeared like small mountain ranges down each side of the highway.

"Discussion time. Where were we?"

"When?" asked Coleman.

"I don't know. The hurricane destroyed our train of thought," said Serge. "Which is a plus because a train of thought is just another one of society's cages."

"Why don't we talk about society?" asked Coleman. "Your thoughts?"

"These are dark times." Serge tapped fingers on the steering wheel. "The decline of society can be boiled down to the culture of airline flights."

"I've seen the videos on the Internet."

"You take a couple hundred people from our savagely polarized nation, cram them cheek by jowl in a metal tube and send them up to altitudes where there's no oxygen. Then people read the headlines: 'Wow, I didn't see *that* coming,'" said Serge. "Plane travel used to be glamorous, people getting dressed up, wearing hats. But now it's devolved into a subway in the sky, cursing, shoving, public urination, removing socks from smelly feet."

Coleman popped a can of Schlitz. "Preach."

"It starts before you're even off the ground," said Serge. "Especially if you're in one of those planes where the coach passengers have to walk through first class to get to their seats. It trends Darwin in a serious hurry. First-class passengers watch the coach people walking past them in the aisle and they're like, 'Yeah, you lazy losers, this is what you get for being assholes: inadequate legroom.' . . . Simultaneously, all the coach passengers are checking out the elite in their giant, comfy seats: 'That one clearly doesn't deserve to be up here.' 'What has this guy ever brought to the table?' 'There's another cosmic mistake of seating assignment.' 'Don't even get me started on this prick.' . . . Then on the next flight, for whatever reason, some of the first-class people have to fly coach and vice versa, and they all immediately switch teams: 'God, I hate those fuckers.'"

"Then the plane takes off and the fun really begins," said Coleman.

"Something about flying makes people lose their freaking minds," said Serge. "And I'm not talking about getting grumpy over the food or a kid kicking the back of your seat. I recently spoke with some flight attendants, and the true stories of psychotic breaks at thirty thousand feet would send you screaming for Amtrak. They said the public would be amazed at the number of people who freak out and try to open the doors."

"It's a senseless crime," said Coleman.

"That's why flight crews have to carry so many handcuffs nowadays," said Serge. "One woman was refused alcohol, so she drank liquid soap and bit a stewardess. Two groups of football fans had a brawl from rows seventeen to twenty-eight. During night flights, passengers ask for blankets and then leave spent condoms in seat pockets. Guys take off their shirts, try to light cigarettes, sleep on the floor."

"Sounds like every traffic intersection in Florida."

"And I swear this one's true: Another dude jumped up on the serving cart, dropped his pants and took a dump in the peanut basket. I think you lose frequent flier points for that one."

"It's just not right," said Coleman, pointing out the window at a jet overhead. "There's one now."

"Take a pass on the peanuts."

They were four miles into the Seven Mile Bridge. "Oh man!" said Serge. "Irma whacked Pigeon Key!"

"What's that?"

"Coleman, you've asked the same question the last fifty times we've driven over this bridge!"

"Was I here?"

"Under the old Seven Mile, it's all deep water, except partway across there's a single peculiar little island under the piers, with a steep ramp rolling down to it. Very popular with postcard photographers," said Serge. "Tourists driving down to Key West on the new bridge can't miss it. They all look over and go: 'Aw, how cute.'"

"Like a puppy?"

"Roughly the same level of low-grade gratification. But then puzzlement sets in, especially when they see the ramp. 'What the hell is its deal?'"

"Serge, please tell us."

"I cannot deny the public!" He leaned toward the window for a closer look. "A bunch of Henry Flagler's people lived there when they were working on the oil baron's Overseas Railroad, which opened in 1912 and at one point had four thousand employees toiling under the sun to erect it."

"You said 'erect.'" Coleman giggled. "I see a bunch of wooden buildings that got clobbered."

"Some of the most beautiful examples of old Keys wooden construction. You'll find verandas and gables and tin roofs. Tin is key to my roofing pleasure . . . Damn, it even hit the Honeymoon Cottage."

"They look kind of familiar."

"That's because back in Key West I've dragged you through every art gallery on Duval Street."

"I hate that!"

"I've noticed," said Serge. "Might have something to do with the galleries being sandwiched between the bars."

"So close and yet so far," said Coleman. "I also hate it because whenever we go in galleries it means you're going to get me in a headlock."

"You won't look at the paintings otherwise. You just keep pointing out the door with a trembling arm: '*Beer,*'" said Serge. "Culturing you up requires wrestling moves."

"But then they always throw us out."

"It's so unfair," said Serge. "Doesn't opening a gallery mean they want people to admire art? And that's what we're doing, minding our own business looking at paintings with you in a full nelson. But no, they want us to do it *their* way. I try to explain that the whole concept of art is about individual expression, and I haven't seen any signs that say 'No Wrestling.' They just fixate and respond that all your thrashing to get free is driving away the others."

A burp. "And breaking vases."

"That's on them. They distracted me and your arms got loose."

A fresh can of Schlitz popped. "What were we talking about?"

"The buildings that look familiar to you on Pigeon Key," said Serge. "Before we got eighty-sixed from those galleries of shame, you'd seen dozens of killer paintings depicting quaint pastel cottages with fiery azaleas under vibrant coconut palms. A disproportionate number are from that little island under the bridge, because artists are always setting up easels down there to feel the muse. My favorites are the watercolors. Nothing captures the palette of the Keys like that medium, and I always get pumped visiting Pigeon Key and watching them work. They seem so happy. So I point out that the best art is spawned from a tortured soul, and offer to help. But here's the thing I've learned about these art types: They're highly sensitive, and as a general rule they don't like their easels knocked over when you wrestle."

The Plymouth came off the Seven Mile Bridge into Marathon.

Coleman hung out the window. "Man, there's a whole lot less trash on the sides of the road."

"It's amazing what a difference twenty miles one way or the other makes when the eye comes ashore."

Coleman pulled himself back inside the window and shotgunned the Schlitz. "Where to now?"

"Where we were going before the hurricane interrupted us," said Serge. "Continuing our cemetery tour of Florida."

"Is that what we were doing?"

"Cemeteries rock! They're portals to our roots with all the obvious history, not to mention upbeat landscaping and bitchin' statuary," said Serge. "The perfect places for a picnic, except I always seem to be the only one with a basket and checkered blanket."

"And playing a kazoo," said Coleman. "Remember the one time they were lowering that guy into the ground?"

"I thought the music would cheer them up."

"Instead they stomped your picnic basket."

"That's the downside of cemeteries," said Serge. "The only occasions most people go is when there's a lot of hysterical crying and they drag a dead body along. I don't have room for that kind of negativity."

The Plymouth crossed a couple of small bridges onto Grassy Key. Serge made a left turn near mile marker 58.

Coleman's head was back out the window, staring at a round, blue-and-yellow sign.

DOLPHIN RESEARCH CENTER.

"This doesn't look like a cemetery."

"It's not *technically* one," said Serge. "But I'm including famous individual grave sites. My tour, my rules."

"So who's buried here?"

Serge parked. "Follow and find out."

Moments later, the pair stood solemnly in a secluded corner of the property near the water, crowded by mangroves and other lush vegetation. In the middle of the plants was a statue. There was a marker below it. Serge knelt with a large sheet of paper and a block of colored wax, making a grave rubbing.

Coleman scratched his head and squinted at the statue of a tail-walking dolphin. "I thought you were taking me to where some scientist or soldier was buried."

Serge continued lightly rubbing. "Back in the day, this majestic creature was arguably the most famous Floridian in the whole country."

Coleman read over Serge's shoulder. "Flipper?"

"The iconic dolphin was introduced to the world in 1963, but few viewers realized the star was actually a female dolphin named Mitzi. And even fewer know that this is her final resting place."

"But why here?"

"Before becoming the research center in 1984, this place opened in 1958 as a roadside attraction named Santini's Porpoise School, and Hollywood came calling. Mitzi trained and resided here until passing away in 1972." Serge stood with his wax rubbing in hand and sniffled.

Coleman put a hand on his shoulder. "You okay, buddy?"

"We're in the presence of gentle greatness," said Serge. "Mitzi was a genius in the industry, able to pop out of the water and make clicking sounds that caused humans to respond: 'What is it, Flipper? You say that an evil research scientist trying to poach rare tropical fish is trapped in his personal submarine near the coral reef surrounded by unexploded mines from World War Two training exercises?'"

"Wow," said Coleman. "Next to that, 'Timmy fell in the well' makes Lassie look like an idiot."

Chapter 2

J ust before dawn. The horizon was on fire.

Literally.

Across hundreds of distant acres, bright orange flames whipped violently in the wind.

The sky began to lighten, revealing dozens of columns of black smoke rising hundreds of feet along the rim of the Everglades.

A rusty 1968 Ford pickup truck raced down a lonely dirt road, kicking up a dust plume. The truck was dark red, and the Florida outdoors had made the metal rough like sandpaper. The dirt road stretched through uninhabited miles of open fields. The road was elevated like a causeway, and on each side were canals. Water flowed broadly from Lake Okeechobee down into the Everglades, giving it the nickname River of Grass. The canals had been dug to divert the water and create hundreds of square miles of arable farmland. The canals were deep, and vehicles regularly sank in them. Drownings weren't rare. The pickup truck stayed in the center of the bumpy road, bouncing on old springs. Its bumper was held on by twisted coat hangers and rope. It was doing fifty. The bed of the truck was full of children.

Most of the children held empty canvas sacks and pillowcases. Their clothing was hand-me-down-and-down-again. Striped pullover shirts and ripped denim shorts and even a pair of swim trunks. The ones who had shoes didn't have shoelaces. There was a lot of chatter and laughing in the back of the truck. Bragging. Who had been champions in the past, and who would do even better today. Then the merriment trailed off. They were getting close.

The pickup sped straight toward the nearest fire. It approached upwind, but smoke still wafted over the truck. Some of the kids pulled the necks of their shirts up over their noses and mouths . . .

Palm Beach is the largest of the state's sixty-seven counties, and this was the *other* Palm Beach, the unknown one. Along the Atlantic shore: Worth Avenue, the Breakers Hotel, Rolls-Royce and Mar-a-Lago. On the opposite side, along Lake Okeechobee: boarded-up buildings, empty streets, burglar bars and poverty so corrosive that even the local prison moved out.

The area is now oddly known for only two things: sugar and football players.

These burning fields are where they meet.

From October to April, the harvest is on, and some of the nation's largest sugar growers set fire to their fields in controlled burns that remove leaves and weeds, making way for the mechanical harvesters. The procedure is done with straight lines and right angles. There will be a giant, perfectly square patch of flat, jet-black land where the last burn took place, right next to a thriving green square of waving cane stalks. From the air it looks like a checkerboard. When the fire and smoke start, the children head out, from Pahokee to Belle Glade to South Bay and Harlem.

The '68 pickup skidded to a stop on the dirt road, and the kids in the back hopped out over both sides like troops jumping down from a combat helicopter. They took off running full speed across a black square, their sacks flapping by their sides. Ahead, a wall of cane. The far half of the field was already on fire. They charged into rows of stalks that would soon also be ablaze.

It was a decades-old tradition.

They were hunting rabbits. By hand.

But this wasn't some thrill sport like running with the bulls in Pamplona. It was economic. Each pelt brought a few dollars, and what was left was dinner. Only if you lived around here could you realize how much of a difference that made. From years of experience passed down by word of mouth, even the youngest kids knew how to approach a burning field and head off the rabbits being flushed out.

The kids continued sprinting with all they had, smoke getting thicker. Then they saw them. The first child planted his foot and cut sharply left, diving through a row of stalks and pouncing. A cottontail went into his pillowcase. Then another child cut right, diving on another rabbit. Then another child, and so on as sacks filled.

The cottontails weren't exactly easy to grab, but the jackrabbits were another matter entirely. Almost nobody could lay a hand on them. Almost. Some of those who had accomplished the feat . . . well, everyone knew where they were now.

Amazingly, this short strip of tiny towns along the bottom of Lake Okeechobee has produced more than sixty players in the National Football League. A number so insane that there must be a catch. Word got around, and soon, each fall at high school games, there were almost as many college football scouts in the stands as parents. At first the scouts couldn't believe what they saw. But seeing was believing. These kids were *fast*. Except how was it possible, so many players from such a small area?

The legend began.

Chasing rabbits.

It didn't lead down to Alice's Wonderland, but turned them into professional football players. It even reached a point where ESPN sent journalists down to cover the hunts in the cane fields, reporting how the kids could nimbly cut, change direction and speed up again as the rabbits required. It was a heartwarming myth, but the real reason was more sobering: The kids had been dealt such a cruel hand of hardship at birth that it cultivated a fierce drive to succeed.

And on this particular day, instinct kicked in again. The children knew in their blood exactly when they had pushed it to the last second toward the advancing fire. Then they retreated as fast as they had charged in, regrouping joyously in the safety of the adjacent blackened field, peeking down into their sacks and comparing their hauls. One had four cottontails and proclaimed himself champion of the day, until a heated dispute and a recount. Another sack actually contained a fifth bunny. Hooray!

Then on to the next burning field. Young, lanky boys who had just experienced a growth spurt raced into the cane stalks, dashing and darting with stunning speed. Behind them came the younger kids from grade school, who idolized the older boys and tried to be just like them. They weren't nearly as fast but getting there. They caught the occasional cottontail, but most of the quarry eluded their grasp as they fell facedown in the dirt, and the older boys laughed. Then there was one final youth, the scrawniest of all. Named Chris. But lack of weight didn't affect this child's velocity; in fact it seemed to help. Chris ran on tiptoes. And was surprisingly consistent, nabbing at least one rabbit per field. Then, just as consistently, an older boy would snatch the animal away. "Give me that!" And shove Chris to the ground. "Now go play with your Barbie dolls."

Poverty prevented a lot of things, but not bullying.

They reached the next field and the mad hunt was on again. This time Chris actually came up with *two* rabbits, one in each hand, grinning ear to ear, until getting slammed to the ground again. The critters went in older boys' sacks. Chris just jumped up and took off after another cottontail.

The pickup truck arrived at the last field of the day. This time the haul was so bountiful that the kids pushed the time envelope beyond good judgment. Most were coughing on smoke, feeling the heat of nearby burning stalks, eyes watering as they dove for one more bunny.

Moments later, they burst out of the cane field, initially stunned silent by their own success, then celebrating. As the joy died down and the stinging in their eyes cleared, an odd sensation arrived. Something seemed off. Just a vague gut feeling.

"Is someone not here?"

"Where's Chris?"

"Shit!"

Three of the older boys dashed back into different rows on the edge of the cane field that was rapidly reaching full burn. After only ten yards in, one of the boys found a much younger, skinny kid with a big grin and a bigger jackrabbit.

"Gimme that thing!"

The grin left town. "No! It's mine! I caught him!"

The older boy seized the rabbit by the scruff of the neck, and used his other hand to shove the smaller child down into the dirt and smoke. The child clawed in the soil and fought for breath.

"Now get the fuck up and follow me," said the larger youth. "And don't tell anyone about the jackrabbit or I'll kick your fucking ass! I know where you live!"

The rest of the gang was waiting in the harmless black square, watching nervously as flames grew higher and nearer.

Finally someone pointed. "They're coming out!"

The older boy raised his trophy in triumph.

"Look!"

"James caught a *jack*rabbit!"

"He's going to play college ball for sure!"

On the ride back to Pahokee, the bed of the pickup was much louder than usual. Laughter and tall tales. Everyone had rabbits in their sack. Except one.

Chris just sulked with chin down, the way most of these trips ended.

The others wondered why Chris even bothered to come along. After all, she was a girl.

Chapter 3

Piles of hurricane debris continued to appear down the sides of the road as if snowplows had been at work. Branches, dresser drawers, broken mirrors, toilets, tires, ceiling fans, cans of food, ripped shirts, rolls of carpet, a deflated basketball and a cuckoo clock.

A Plymouth Satellite raced east.

"Stop the car!" yelled Coleman. "Stop the car!"

Serge screeched the brakes and skidded off the side of the highway.

"Jesus! What is it?"

"Wait here." Coleman jumped out and waddled fifty yards before reaching into the trash. He returned and climbed back in the passenger seat.

Serge pulled back onto the highway. "What have you got there?"

"Check it out!" Coleman thrust his arm an inch from Serge's eyes.

Serge swatted it away. "I'm driving over here."

Coleman cradled his find and brushed off dirt. "It's a squeeze bottle for Florida honey. I remember these from when I was a kid. See? It's a cute smiling alligator from one of those roadside places."

"The old citrus stands," said Serge. "The kind that sold tourists boxes of navel oranges that got crushed by baggage handlers and leaked on the luggage belts, leaving sticky slicks that contaminated other people's suitcases in our state's way of saying, 'Please visit!'"

Coleman twisted off the top and stuck an eyeball in the hole. "I'd been watching the road for something like this."

"You're kidding." Serge looked quickly toward the passenger side. "You were seriously looking for a cool vintage souvenir?"

"Oh, sure. It's just what I wanted."

Serge turned back toward the road and shook his head with a smile. "Well, I'll be. There's hope for you yet . . ."

A half hour later, the gold Satellite sat on the side of the road near mile marker 82 in Islamorada.

Serge glared across the front seat.

"What?" said Coleman.

Serge shook his head again, but with different import. "Hope with you is a fool's errand."

Coleman shrugged and stuck the alligator's head in his mouth, taking a hit from his new honey-bottle bong. He exhaled and pointed. "What's that on the edge of the street? The thing with orange lightbulbs?"

"Temporary highway sign to alert motorists," said Serge. "Don't bother me right now."

"I know it's a road sign," said Coleman. "But they usually say something like 'Detour Ahead.' Why does that one say 'Screw Worm Inspection Station Mile 106'?"

Serge was trying to concentrate on a file folder in his lap. "Because they inspect for screw worms. Probably not now because of the storm. But they'll be back up and running soon."

"I don't even know what a screw worm is," said Coleman. "And why would they need to inspect?"

"It doesn't concern you. Leave me alone." Serge intently flipped through the file.

"I just wanted to know. You're not the only curious one." Then Coleman lapsed into his stoner pastime of playing with the sound of words. "Screw *worm* . . . *screw* worm . . . *screwwwwwwwww* worm . . . screw *wormmmmmmmm* . . . screw wormy-worm . . ."

Serge slowly raised his reddening face and stared out the windshield.

". . . Screwy-screw worm . . . Worm screwy worm . . ."

"Fuck it!" Serge emitted a deep sigh and closed the file. He grabbed a thermos of coffee and chugged. "Okay, most flies—like houseflies—lay eggs in dead stuff. But there's this nasty other fly from Central American called *Cochliomyia hominivorax*. It needs living flesh and deposits eggs in open animal wounds. To up the gross-out factor, the larvae burrow into the meat as they feed, using a screw-like anchor that is so strong it can penetrate bone. It gets pretty ugly and is often fatal. You don't want to see the photos."

"Maybe," said Coleman. "But what's that got to do with the Keys? Why do we need that sign here if it's in Central America?"

"The United States eradicated screw worm flies in the early 1980s, but somehow they got back in and caused the current outbreak that is confined for now to the Florida Keys. That's why they need the signs. Any tourists who bring pets with them on vacation must have them inspected before returning to the mainland."

"They're eating poodles and stuff?"

"Not yet, but the outbreak has already caused much sadness down here." Serge pointed back over his shoulder. "You know those cute little miniature Key deer back on Big Pine that are found nowhere else in the world?"

A pot exhale. "Know 'em and love 'em."

"They seem all sweet and everything, but they're still wild creatures, and during mating season all bets are off. The males have these tiny antlers and they start butting heads for primacy. To watch these little suckers go at it, it's actually kind of funny."

"Kind of like babies fighting."

Serge paused. "When do babies ever fight?"

Coleman puffed and shrugged. "They can't all be nice."

"Whatever. So all this head crashing leaves the tops of the deer's scalps with bunches of antler gashes. That's when the screw worm flies move in, and they work fast! In as little as eight hours, the fleshly laid eggs can hatch and bore down almost an inch. Necrosis follows with equal alacrity, and if immediate care isn't sought, it's game over."

"Cool."

"But here's the freakiest part: Although the host animal is already hopelessly doomed, they're still alive and semi-functioning. That's what happened recently on Big Pine Key. Nobody knew there was an outbreak until they started seeing these zombie-like deer staggering around with parts of their heads gone. They had to euthanize around fifty of the poor fellas. It was the big news down here all season."

"Now I'm sad."

"Maybe this will cheer you up." Serge pulled a photo of a headstone from a manila folder.

Coleman blew another cloud out the window and leaned over. "Whatcha got there?"

"I've begun collecting tombstone rubbings." Fingers flipped through pages. "And the Keys are the best place to start! Whenever launching a new hobby, always pick a starting point that provides immediate success and encourages an obsessive-compulsive lifestyle of more and more hobbies until you retreat from all human contact, subsist on delivered pizza, and remain behind the closed curtains of a house crammed to the eyeballs with comic books, Civil War figures, postage stamp albums, ships in bottles, Coca-Cola signs, prison contraband, display cases of dead moths from across North America, jars of dirt from all fifty states, the world's largest ball of Scotch Tape, and a life-size model made entirely from matchsticks of the Lee Harvey Oswald shooting in the Dallas police basement."

"Never thought of it that way." Puff, puff, puff.

Serge nodded hard as he held up pages. "Take a gander. These are from the Key West Cemetery. The first one is obvious, from the verdigris bronze statue of a sailor overlooking twenty-seven graves of those killed in the 1898 explosion of the USS *Maine* in Havana Harbor ..." He raised another page. "From there, a severe mood swing to the tombstone of B. P. Robert: 'I told you I was sick,' and Alan Dale Willcox: 'If you're reading this, you desperately need a hobby.'" Serge turned and chuckled. "I fooled him ... You getting this?"

Coleman exhaled smoke and nodded. "Ball of Scotch Tape."

"The Key West Cemetery is my visual favorite, with aboveground crypts like New Orleans, fantastic statues of angels in various moods and severe tropical landscaping."

"All I know is you woke me up extra early."

"For my Maximum Key West Cemetery Morning Routine: Arise just before dawn and shuffle over to the tiny Five Brothers Cuban grocery on the corner of Southard Street, order pressed cheese toast and café con leche, stick coins in a metal box for a copy of the *Key West Citizen,* then stroll into the cemetery and stretch out on a slab with a great sunrise breakfast while reading an article about a homeless man with no pants arrested for knocking tourists off mopeds with coconuts."

"It doesn't get any better," said Coleman.

"But here's a fun fact to put the perfect coda on that first tour stop. About twenty-five thousand people live in Key West, but there are roughly seventy-five thousand in that cemetery." Serge raised a knowing eyebrow. "Makes you think."

Coleman pointed at the rubbings in Serge's lap. "What's that one?"

"From a cat grave on the grounds of the Hemingway House." He held up another. "And this is from where one of Hemingway's roosters is buried behind Blue Heaven restaurant in the island's Bahama Village section. And finally Mitzi the Dolphin, bringing us up-to-date."

"Was I there?"

"Yes, but pot gives you the short-term memory of a fungus." Serge stowed the file and pulled out fresh pages and wax.

Coleman followed his pal as they left the car behind. "Ever think about what you'd like on your own tombstone?"

Serge tapped his chin. "Maybe something like: 'This is bullshit.'"

"I can dig it." Coleman took another hit. "You know what I'd like?"

"You've stumped me."

"'Dave's not here.'" Giggles.

Serge slowly began nodding. "I like it. On a couple of levels. First, for its simple philosophical truth. Second, as an Easter egg for Cheech and Chong fans who lose their way going into a cemetery."

Serge entered a small, open park and snapped a few photos, then approached a monument and went to work with his wax.

"Wow," said Coleman. "That's the biggest tombstone I've ever seen!"

"Roughly the same shape, but not a tombstone." Rub, rub, rub. "It's the monument to those who lost their lives in the Labor Day hurricane of 1935. The cremated remains of nearly two hundred people are interred just under your feet."

"It looks kind of cool."

"Because it is." Rub, rub, rub. "A giant slab of coral with a bas-relief sculpture of blowing palms. Due to the era, the design is art deco. But it's so subtly placed and presented that most visitors just drive right by without noticing the massive history treasure . . . I don't think I'm going to have enough paper."

Coleman stared down and idly scraped the ground with the toe of a sneaker. "Whew, two hundred."

"Get ready," said Serge. "I have a feeling our next stop is going to be insane."

EIGHT YEARS EARLIER

Boys yelled from all directions.

"I got one!"

"I got one over here, too!"

Chris raced between rows, crashing through cane stalks. She had a bead on another jackrabbit. She began coughing in the thickening smoke, but there was never a thought of giving up. Her technique was to chase rabbits *toward* the fire and confuse them.

More slamming through the cane, scraping her arms up but good. Then she left her feet and stretched out in the air for her pounce.

"Got you!"

She was happily carrying the rabbit out of the field when something collided with her hard from the side, knocking her to the ground. A boy much older and bigger reached down. "Give me that fucking rabbit."

Chris was immediately back on her feet. "He's mine! Give him back!"

But she was just shoved again in the dirt.

This time Chris didn't get right back up. She felt she was about to cry, and she couldn't let that happen. She strained for composure, and dug her fists, clawing, into the rich soil. Then:

"What's this?"

Her left hand felt something strange. She pulled it from the soil and opened her palm. It was a coin. She rubbed the dirt off on her shirt and looked again. A *gold* coin. She read the date.

1907.

From collecting Lincoln pennies, Chris knew about other coins, too. And she still couldn't believe her eyes. It was a Saint-Gaudens twenty-dollar piece, one of the crown jewels of the numismatic world. She knew its value from her guidebooks and always figured she could only dream of having one. This was way better than a rabbit. She found a foot-long marking stake with an orange ribbon and drove it into the ground.

Chris was still studying her find as she came out of the stalks, so distracted she bumped into another of the big boys.

"What do you have in your hand?"

She clenched her fist shut and stuck it behind her back. "Nothing."

"Give it here!"

"No!"

He twisted her arm and pried her fingers open. "Thanks!" Then the final shove to the ground of the day.

Chris went home in a fuming funk and sat outside on a milk crate.

B ells jingled as a door opened in Pahokee.

The pawnshop owner set a jeweler's glass down and looked up. Pawnshops are universally the eyes of the community, and their eclectic brand of commerce tracks the town's secrets: who's gambling, on drugs, getting divorced, quitting the trombone.

Right now, these eyes gazed toward the person entering his shop and told him: *This isn't positive.* It was one of the junior high kids, nothing to buy, nothing to sell. But they were damn fast, and forget trying to catch them once they stole something and made it out the door.

"Stop right there, young man." The owner looked and sounded like James Earl Jones. But his name was Webber. "What's your business here?"

The boy reached in his pocket and held up a yellow circle between his thumb and index finger. "I found a coin."

This was different. A thousand-candlepower smile lit up the shop. "Come on over here, son! Let's see what you've got there."

But the pawnshop owner already knew. Such coins had been dribbling in over the years about one every six months. Always from kids he initially sized up as trouble. They claimed they found them in the cane fields while hunting rabbits, but who knew? Maybe someone's collection was getting poached. The fewer questions the better.

"I found it in a cane field," said an unusually tall fourteen-year-old named Ricky.

"You look like a football player." Webber examined the coin and poked the boy in the shoulder, buttering him up. "I'll bet you're going to win the Muck Bowl for us!"

Ricky bloomed with pride. "I still have a year to go, but Coach says I'm a natural tailback."

"I'm sure you are." Webber set the coin down on a cloth. "Did you take a look at this? Did you read what it says on the back?"

Eager nodding. "Twenty dollars! But it's old, and it's gold!"

"Except you realize that they don't use these coins anymore. They took them out of circulation."

"What does that mean?" asked the youth.

"It means I don't want to give you any bad news. What do you think is a fair price for this coin?"

Ricky pointed. "The back says twenty dollars."

Webber opened his register and pulled out bills to mollify negotiations. "How about fifteen? That's more than I should."

It had the desired effect as the boy stared at the cash and thought: *Shit, yeah. I just snatched it off that sissy girl anyway.*

"Deal."

Thus continued a daisy chain of underhandedness.

They shook hands.

The boy pocketed bills as he headed for the door.

"And bring me any others you find," Webber called out. "I'm good for fifteen dollars each, even though I'm probably losing money. But I can't help it; I'm just a nice guy."

Bells jingled again as the door closed.

Webber had just made his whole month. If melted for just the weight in gold, the coin was worth more than a grand. And a 1907 in this condition could fetch double.

An ebullient moment took a slight, sullen hit. Darn, he would have to notify the police as required under the law for anything of this value.

A beat cop arrived three hours later. Webber had sent the declaration fax of his purchase to police headquarters, and normally it would have stopped at that. But he knew the drill. Word of the coins was slowly getting out.

Bells jingled. The officer entered and twirled his nightstick. "So how many does that make now?"

"How many what?"

"Rare gold coins these kids are finding just laying on the ground."

"I don't know." The pawn owner wiped the lenses of his reading glasses. "A few."

"Seventeen by our count."

"That many?"

"Imagine the odds," said the officer. "Seventeen different kids just walking along and looking down."

"I understand some were under the dirt."

"Whatever you say." The officer walked along the glass display cases and resumed twirling his stick. He stopped and leaned over. "Is that the coin? May I see it?"

The owner sighed and handed him the small plastic protective holder.

"Real pretty," said the officer, turning it over in his hand. "It's just so unbelievable. If I didn't know you better, I'd say you might be fencing coins stolen from some collections."

"Really, they're just kids," said the owner. "You remember the million juke joints we had around here when the town was big? All those workers getting paid and drunk on a Friday night. I'm surprised they didn't drop more of these things stumbling around."

"Okay, I'll go along. And I'm sure you always pay these kids fairly." The officer held up the coin. "How much did this baby set you back?"

Webber stood mute.

"Did I stutter?" asked the officer.

"I-I don't remember."

"Now *you're* stuttering. Come on, it was only a few hours ago."

Webber was a very bad actor as he searched the top of a cluttered desk. "The paperwork's around here somewhere . . ."

"I'm sure it is," said the officer. "By the way, you know my boss's daughter?"

Webber welcomed the change of topic. "Great girl!"

"She's starting high school next fall and wow, is she fantastic in the band. Especially the trombone, except she—"

Webber sighed with renewed resignation as he turned to the shelf. "Just had one come in, real cheap. You probably heard the rumors . . ."

The officer nodded sadly. "Slide McCall. Who would have thought?"

"I just feel for his family," said Webber, handing the instrument across the counter as the daisy chain completed another link.

The officer whistled a merry tune as he headed toward the door with a long piece of brass over his shoulder. "Remember that fencing is a serious offense."

"They're kids. Really."

"Whatever."

Bells jingled.

Chapter 4

THE FLORIDA KEYS

S erge slapped his pal on the shoulder. "Look alive. Next stop."

"Okay." Coleman headed back to the car.

"Where are you going?" asked Serge.

Coleman grabbed a door handle. "Next stop, like you said."

"No, this way."

He led Coleman in the opposite direction, down local roads a couple hundred yards toward the ocean. They arrived in front of an ultra-luxury resort where the first President Bush often stayed during fly-fishing vacations.

"I get it," said Coleman. "We're going to crash another rich place and find a business conference reception with free food and booze. I'm down with that. Let me straighten myself up so we can get through security because this shit is worth it."

"Not necessary," said Serge. "Act however you want."

Coleman wiped his nose on his shirt. "What do you mean?"

"Just be yourself," said Serge. "It is indeed a world-class resort, but we're allowed to cut through the side of the property because the public has the right to access my next stop."

"Be myself? Okay." He pulled a pint of Southern Comfort from his pocket and lifted it to the sun as he guzzled.

"Once again, my words were not chosen with adequate care," said Serge. "Be like *other* people."

"That's different." Coleman stowed the bottle and stumbled after his friend.

They ended up on a sandy beach behind the hotel as waves from the Florida Straits lapped the shore.

"What the hell?" said Coleman.

"Told you it would be cool."

Before them stood a white picket fence surrounding a small cluster of graves and tombstones.

Coleman took a furtive swig from his flask and grabbed the fence for balance. "I never expected a cemetery in the middle of a beach."

"It's not just a cemetery but a *pioneer* cemetery." Serge snapped photos. "You've got three main family plots in there. The Pinders, Russells and Parkers, who settled here back in the 1800s and kicked off what this island is today."

"But how is it allowed on a beach?"

"Because of history lovers!" said Serge. "The die-hard locals knew this stuff here meant a lot, so despite the prevailing wisdom that tombstones are not your first choice for a tourist draw on the beach, they stood firm and dutifully tended the flame of heritage."

"*Whooooaaaaaa.*" Coleman hung on to the top of a picket with one hand, swinging off-balance and bouncing against the fence a few times like a screen door in the wind. "Getting a little funky here."

Serge was lost in the focus of the moment. "But I view the whole tourist-cemetery interface from an optimistic viewpoint that history is the future. A lovely family from Elk Rapids comes down here, and they're like: 'This is paradise. We've got a beautiful sun and sky, our blankets spread out, sodas and baloney sandwiches in the cooler, our kids laughing and splashing in the surf. How can it possibly get any better? . . . Wait, are people buried here?'"

"Where else can they get that?" asked Coleman.

"This is what I keep trying to tell people, but it's always the same closed-mindedness: 'Don't hurt me.'"

"I kind of dig that angel statue in the center."

"Remember the big hurricane monument by the highway? True story: When that storm blew through, it picked up that angel—I'm guessing by the wings—and sent it flying all the way back to the road. I mean, that's a pretty heavy chunk of rock. And it barely got scratched. The local history heroes returned it to its rightful place."

"Must have been a big storm to blow it that far."

"One of the biggest." Serge placed paper to headstone. "And Islamorada was particularly hard hit, with scores of victims. But of course all the people in this cemetery were already dead."

"So they survived?"

Serge stared at Coleman a moment and returned to his rubbing.

Soon they were strolling along the beach, Serge in a straight line, Coleman on a much looser course. His veering became more and more generous until he was offshore.

Serge sternly folded his arms and yelled at the ocean. "Can you please not do that?"

"Sorry." Coleman splashed back toward land. "Having a little trouble coloring inside the lines."

They continued on. Then they stopped and stared down.

"A dead seagull?" said Coleman.

Serge raised his eyes up the shore. "There's another one, and another . . ."

After walking twenty more yards, Serge paused again. "That's weird. Six dead birds, but no clues. No fishing lines or oil or trauma."

"Maybe it was the hurricane," said Coleman.

Serge shook his head. "The bodies are too fresh. Oh, well . . ."

They resumed strolling again and heard a chorus of rambunctious yelling. Three young boys charging down the beach to the water's edge.

"Now that's what I like to see," said Serge. "A footloose childhood like mine spent in the Florida outdoors instead of moving pieces of candy around on cell phones."

"What are they doing?"

"Looks like a bread sack. They're throwing pieces."

"Here come the seagulls." Coleman ducked as they swooped in. "How do they do that? Not a bird around, and then a million."

"Seagulls are the FBI surveillance teams of the animal world. You never know the FBI is there until the shit goes down, and then they're *everywhere*," said Serge. "Likewise, seagulls often don't make their presence known until someone tosses aside the last bite of a hot dog, turning the beach into a Hitchcock movie."

"What are those kids throwing now?" asked Coleman. "It doesn't look like bread anymore."

"What *are* they throwing?" asked Serge, heading off in a trot.

The trio of young boys giggled as they tossed stuff to the frenzy of birds.

"Excuse me," said Serge. "May I see what you're feeding them?"

One of the boys quickly hid something behind his back, and they all stopped laughing.

"Come *onnnnnn*," said Serge. "I just want in on the fun."

"Then okay," said one of kids. He produced a box of generic Alka-Seltzer.

Serge gasped and grabbed his heart.

From behind: "What the hell are you doing? Get away from those kids!"

It was a voice from someone Serge hadn't noticed on the beach before. He turned and saw a man running down from the palm trees around a resort swimming pool.

He arrived and got between Serge and the boys. "What are you, some kind of pervert?"

"No, but why do you have a video camera in your hand?"

"None of your business! And you're wrecking my shot!"

"I know what you were doing," said Serge. "You told these kids to feed Alka-Seltzer to the birds. And because birds can't burp, they would explode."

"No, I didn't."

"You're lying," said Serge. "And then you were going to film the whole shameful episode with your camera. That level of cruelty is a sickness."

"So what if I was?" He shoved Serge hard in the chest. "What are you going to do about it?" Another shove.

Serge stumbled backward a couple of steps. "Don't you know the whole tale about birds exploding is an urban myth?"

"What are you talking about?"

"They don't explode," said Serge. "They *can* burp, or whatever the avian equivalent is of dealing with the social awkwardness of unpleasant gas that gets looks from the rest of the flock."

"Then what's your problem?"

Serge pointed back up the beach at the half-dozen fallen seagulls that they'd just passed. "While the birds may not explode, you've given them an overdose of aspirin and anhydrous citric acid, the active ingredient in those tablets. A gull that weighs a pound or two can't handle what's meant for an adult human."

"I don't believe you."

"Believe this: The overdose symptoms include high fever, double vision, respiratory distress, cardiac distress, abdominal agony, brain-swelling, seizures. It's such a horrible way to go that those birds probably wished they *had* exploded."

"You—!" The man with the video camera noticed something out in the water and paused. "What's he doing?"

Coleman was up to his belly button in the surf with a strained look on his face.

Serge cupped hands around his mouth. "Coleman! No taking dumps in the ocean! We've talked about this." He turned back around to the man. "Sorry, where were we?"

"You were just about to leave!" Another shove.

"Jesus, there are kids here," said Serge. "What kind of example are you setting as a parent?"

"Ha! I'm not their father. I'm their uncle."

"Well then, by all means, ruin them, Uncle Jack Wagon."

"I've had enough of you!" A final shove, sending Serge down to the sand. "Fuck off!"

"Okay, now you're really being a bad example," said Serge. "Using profanity *and* ending a sentence with a preposition."

Coleman trudged his way back to shore. "What did I miss?" He received his own shove to the chest and toppled over. "Hey, what was that for?"

Serge got up and dusted himself off. "I've really tried to be nice, but now you're being mean to Coleman, which is a broad form of animal cruelty."

The man gritted his teeth in rage and lunged for another shove. This time, Serge quickly slipped aside, grabbed him by the wrist and locked up the man's arm under his armpit.

Now, in fights it's often the bigger combatant who prevails. But sometimes it's the little things. Like the little finger. Bend it back to the breaking point, and people bend to your will.

"Ow! My finger!"

"Tell the kids to go home."

"You mean to the motel room."

Serge rolled his eyes. "Whatever." He bent the finger harder. "Now."

"Boys! Go back to the room!"

"What about the birds?" asked a child.

"Get going!"

The young trio skedaddled.

"Alone at last," said Serge.

"Now will you let go of my finger?"

"Yes." Serge pulled a pistol from under his shirt and stuck it in the man's ribs. "I never got your name."

"Clyde."

"Clyde, start walking."

"Where are we going?"

"Oh, this is going to be a real blast, a regular humdinger," said Serge. "Have you seen the Pioneer Cemetery? . . ."

A little while later, Serge stared down into a car trunk. "Comfy?"

"W-w-what are you going to do—"

The lid slammed shut.

EIGHT YEARS EARLIER

Chris was a weird little kid.

In a good way. Other children take to education like they're being force-fed. But Chris was so naturally curious that she practically became another piece of furniture in the library, spending hours on the computer to look up more data than her course material had to offer.

Then the next day in science class, where they were discussing the basics of our sun, its age, distance. A hand shot up. "I found out that our sun bends time and space. The planets, too. It makes wormholes possible."

"What are you talking about?"

"Einstein. Others proved his theory with a telescope during an eclipse when a star appeared from behind the corona when it shouldn't have."

Then math class and a triangle with equal sides. A hand flew up again.

"The Romans killed Archimedes while he was working on a problem. 'Don't disturb my circles,' he said."

"What?"

Soon, other teachers were showing up out in the hall, pointing through the window of the classroom's door at the odd little kid in the front row with a hand enthusiastically in the air. Still more educators began joining Chris in the library to look up her tidbits, their own curiosity piqued. They glanced over at the young girl sitting a few desks away, leaning farther and farther forward, as if knowledge would pull her right through the computer screen.

Saturday meant no school, but Chris had her own curriculum. She grabbed a notebook, pens, an old compass, some tape and a lunch bag. Chris had grown up alone with her grandmother due to the broken-home epidemic that was going around. The old woman looked up as Chris wheeled her bicycle through the living room of their apartment.

"Where are you going, honey?"

"Treasure hunting."

"Have fun."

The ride was at least a mile, possibly closer to two, but when Chris put her mind to something, get out of the way or prepare to be run over.

Other kids probably didn't remember, but Chris could recall every word of the old schoolyard folklore stories about the evil sugar baron named Fakakta who was found shot to death after the 1928 hurricane. And of course the lost treasure. Kids are allowed to dream.

She was a cute little sight, tiny legs churning as she pedaled her pink bicycle up the side of Hooker Highway. She finally arrived at a cane field from one of her recent rabbit hunts, and turned down a dirt road. Chris had a good memory as she walked her bike through the rows of sugar stalks. She came to a marking stake with an orange ribbon. Then she got out her compass and triangulated her position with a pair of distant power lines. Numbers were jotted in her notebook. Then she commenced digging. It was a scientific sampling grid that only she would have thought of, moving out from the stake. The afternoon wore on under the unfiltered sun, her face filthy from wiping away sweat with dirty hands. She was quickly reaching the logical conclusion: probably just a one-time find. And she didn't have any proof that the bogeyman of the sugar field ever existed. That's when her fingers hit it.

The second coin.

Now Chris had two geometric points to work with. She stood up and aimed her compass, dutifully recording new figures in the notebook. She turned the page and drew a second diagram. The search field had become an elongated oval. Digging continued till she could barely see in the growing darkness, but no more finds. She stuck the coin, compass and notebook in the lunch bag she had brought along, and taped it flat to her stomach under her shirt. No way anyone was going to steal this stuff.

Two boys stopped her a block from the apartment building. "Hey, Milk Crate! What have you got there?"

She hated that nickname. "None of your business!"

"Empty your pockets."

"No!"

"I said empty!"

She turned them inside out. Empty.

"Okay, you can go."

As she put her feet back on the pedals, one of them punched her in the shoulder with an extended knuckle.

"Ow!"

She left laughter behind as she pedaled away . . .

Good thing the next day was a Sunday. Her power of will was locked in, and there was little chance she would have been able to focus in school. She rode her bike back to the cane field again. This time it only took her three hours to find the next coin. The compass and notebook came back out. Coordinates plotted, a new shape diagramed. She stopped and aimed her compass in the direction of Lake Okeechobee, squinting with one eye closed, the tip of her tongue sticking out the corner of her mouth in concentration. Math and science were just intuitive to Chris. Her mind's eye instinctively drew a line from the lake to where she stood, envisioning the shape of the debris field if some treasure chest burst open around here in a storm surge. She decided to load her search southeast of the last coin.

It was only an hour before grimy fingers pulled up the next gold piece. Excitement bubbled. There was a lot of time left before sunset. But that would be it for the day.

Chris pedaled home and ran inside.

"Where have you been?" asked her grandmother.

"Out." She dashed into her bedroom and closed the door. Chris ripped the tape off her stomach and lay on the floor next to her dresser. She stared up as she pulled out the bottom drawer. The two newest coins were taped underneath next to the previous one. She closed the drawer and jumped up just as her grandmother came in.

"Good gracious, child, you're filthy."

Chris dropped into the chair at her small desk and opened the notebook. "I'm fine." A pen clicked open.

"You go wash up right now before you make a mess of the whole place."

"Don't disturb my circles."

"Are you sassing me?"

"No, it's a math joke." She stood from the chair. "I'll go wash up. I love you!"

The next day in school, the teachers had a nagging feeling that something was different in class, but they couldn't quite put their fingers on it. By fourth period, the science teacher figured it out. Chris was unnaturally quiet. She hadn't asked a single question or added something arcane to the discussion, like, "Thomas Edison never slept more than four hours a night." And Chris kept glancing at the clock on the wall. Before this day, she always seemed as though she wanted class to go on forever. Maybe she had the flu.

The bell rang, and the teacher caught her at the door. "Chris, is everything okay?"

"Great! I just got a cool compass that I've been thinking about!" She ran off down the hall.

Weird little kid, the teacher thought. *But in a good way.*

Chris burst through the door of her grandmother's upstairs apartment, rolling in her bike. She ran right for her room. She rifled through papers and magazines and library books on her little desk. It became frantic. She ran out into the living room.

"Grandma, have you seen my green notebook? . . . *Grandma?*"

"In here."

Chris ran to the kitchen. "Grandma, what are you doing reading my notebook?"

"I wouldn't read it if it was your diary because that would be private." The old woman turned the page with sausage fingers. "But you left it open on your desk. All these numbers and complex diagrams, for a child your age no less. So this is how you always get straight A's?" She handed the book back. "I'm very proud of you. Just remember not to care what anyone thinks; you're going to do great things someday."

"Thanks, Grandma." A kiss on the cheek, and then she was off again with her bike.

Today would be a watershed, but it didn't look that way at first, taking two hours to find the next coin. But shortly after, her hands hit something else in the soil. She pulled out a piece of wood. A short thin plank with rusty rails on each end like it had been part of a packing crate. She tossed it aside and began excavating with vigor. The hole was wider than her others, exposing the surface of two more broken planks. She lifted them up and froze. Six more coins in a cluster. There was now no doubt that this wasn't just stray dropped money. The folklore was true. Chris wanted to tell the world, but "I can't tell anybody."

She made all the required documentation in her notebook, then taped everything to her stomach again, and pedaled her bike home like a maniac.

Now she had a problem. An embarrassment of riches, so to speak. If her hunch was correct, she would quickly run out of room under her dresser drawers. And the bag she taped beneath her shirt wasn't going to cut it much longer. She started taping coins inside her shoes, but that just made pedaling too hard. She had a stroke of brilliance.

The next day she raced home from the fields again. Boys stopped her bike at the corner of the apartments. There was a basket on her handlebars with daisies.

"Hey, Milk Crate! What have you got there?"

"None of your business."

The tallest boy looked in the basket. "Textbooks? *Ewww!*" A punch on the shoulder and they let her go.

Chris ran up to her room and removed the rubber strap holding the books together. She opened an old algebra text that she had found discarded behind the school. In the middle of the carved-out pages were her coins for the day.

Next order of business: Improve storage. This would be more difficult. She stared out the window. Then she got down on the floor and began removing tape from under dresser drawers . . .

And so it went. Days, weeks, then months, slowly building her haul. She had depleted all that apparently could be found from that first crate, and there had been a dispiriting lull. But it was followed by the wooden remnants of a second box. Then a hundred yards south, the discovery of the next planks.

A year passed. Then two years. At first it had been pure excitement. Nothing goes together better than kids and buried treasure. But now that she was getting older: "Am I doing something wrong?"

Chris sat at her usual computer in the library the next afternoon. She looked up site after site on salvage laws. She read about how if something sinks in a body of water, under certain circumstances, it's up for grabs. Then she went back to meteorology pages showing detailed computer models and maps of the tidal surge from the 1928 storm. The highest water levels rose twenty feet over the field she'd been working. She sat back and bit her lower lip in thought. "Technically, the treasure *did* sink. And I'm the finder."

Back to work.

More time passed, more trips to the cane fields. But all good things must come to an end. Chris's efforts dwindled in results as she depleted her find, until there was nothing. And she was sure about it, too, because she had dug her scientific sampling holes far and wide in the logical drift directions.

She was happy and sad at the same time. What an adventure it had been. On the other hand, Chris always felt unanchored when she didn't have an obsessive goal to focus her mental energy. She would just have to come up with something else.

It only took a few days. She rode her bike as fast as she could, hyper as hell, down to the high school. She knocked on a door . . .

Chapter 5

SOUTH FLORIDA

The Plymouth Satellite wound its way east on U.S. Highway 1 and crested the bridge out of Key Largo at mile 107. Then it entered what locals call "the Eighteen-Mile Stretch," a no-man's-land of mangroves and wild scrub from the bottom tip of the mainland to the first dribbles of civilization at Florida City. Do not break down, do not run out of gas.

Coleman sucked on his gator bottle and blew smoke out the window. "I never heard about trying to explode birds."

"A sad state of affairs," said Serge. "And not just Alka-Seltzer. Do any kind of Internet search on animal abuse, and it brings up a trail of tears. Pelicans get it especially bad for some reason, and now these ass-heads are filming the brutality and proudly posting it on the web. Rice is another one."

"Rice, like the San Francisco treat?"

Serge nodded. "People feed uncooked rice to birds, waiting for them to burst. It's another myth, and luckily, in that case, the birds aren't poisoned and can fly away. But the intent is still there. I can't get my head around that brand of cowardice."

"But, Serge, there must be another way."

"There is." Serge checked the clip in his pistol and stowed it under the seat. "That's one reason why a lot of people have stopped throwing rice at weddings. Instead they hand out bags of birdseed. Of course they don't realize that the rice is safe, but I'm heartened to see they care enough to err on the side of caution."

"You said it was one reason they stopped throwing rice?"

"The other reason is all the documented slips and falls on the tiny kernels," said Serge. "It dampens the mood when the lovebirds are driving away with tin cans bouncing behind the car and then Grandma Petunia takes a spectacular header in the driveway."

"You know, I admire the way you respect animals," said Coleman.

"Really?"

"Yeah, I like my little nature friends," said Coleman. "Squirrels dig my potato chips."

"You are noble in that way," said Serge. "Although the salt contributes to hypertension. Those tiny fellows are wound way too tight as it is. Especially the flying ones. What is their fucking hurry? I mean, damn, just slow your roll, man."

"What about jelly beans?"

"Diabetes," said Serge.

The Plymouth entered southern Miami on the Dixie Highway. Soon, they passed a church, and Serge craned his neck around as people entered. "Well, I'll be."

Coleman turned. "Someone's getting married?"

"We were just talking about weddings, and one's about to get started," said Serge. "This gives me a chance."

"For what?"

"To restore tradition," said Serge. "Whole generations know not of the rice joy."

"What about Grandma Petunia?"

"My solution is elegantly designed not to break any hips."

Serge drove on until he found what he was looking for. The Plymouth skidded into a parking lot.

An hour later, the pair waited alone in front of the church.

"So we're going to be wedding crashers?" asked Coleman.

"No, that would involve dishonesty," said Serge. "But there's nothing unethical about standing outside a church and rooting for strangers not to get divorced."

"The doors are opening," said Coleman.

"Here they come," said Serge. "Get ready."

Guests poured down the steps and formed crowds on each side of the walkway leading from the church. Finally, the happy newlyweds emerged. They headed down the walkway, showered with cheers and birdseed. They were halfway to their car at the curb when suddenly:

Plop . . . plop, plop, plop . . .

"What on earth?" said the bride.

Plop, plop, plop . . .

The groom looked up in rage. "Who's throwing rice? *Cooked* rice?"

"Me!" Serge raised his hand. "Because I care! There's no way those old geezers over there will crack their noggins."

The groom looked down at his chest. "It's brown! And greasy!"

Serge grinned sheepishly. "It's pork fried rice. Sorry, I got a little hungry and that's my favorite." *Plop, plop . . .*

"My dress!" screamed the bride. "It's ruined!"

"You bastards!"

Serge held out an innocent hand. "What? I'm so happy for you! This is your special day! Don't get divorced!"

"Special day?"

"Yeah," said Serge, "but keep up this kind of gloomy fixation on laundry and tonight you'll be wanking off into a honeymoon suite bathrobe."

"Fuckers!"

"Get 'em!"

"Coleman, time to run again."

Serge easily slipped out of grasp as usual, and just as usual, Coleman was captured. They had him squirming by the arms, and Serge was about to disperse them with a display of the Colt .45 pistol in his waistband. But Coleman was even more effective at the task by jackknifing over and rainbow-vomiting a bouillabaisse of Southern Comfort and Cool Ranch Doritos across the hems of black tuxedo pants.

"Son of a bitch!"

The Plymouth patched out and raced north on Dixie Highway. They heard a banging sound from the trunk.

"Jesus, can't I get any peace?" Serge slapped the steering wheel while fishing bullets from his pocket. "*I'm* being mellow, but everyone else is rowing against my harmony stream."

O n an overcast afternoon, a gold Satellite sat in the parking lot of a sub-budget motel on Highway A1A. Across the street, a nearly deserted beach in Fort Lauderdale. Purple clouds rolled in over the unstaffed vintage lifeguard stands. The sign above the motel office featured a smiling mermaid, in an attempt to make up for everything else.

Serge and Coleman crashed through the door of room 6.

"This is going to be the best party ever!" said Coleman, dumping a shopping bag on one of the beds and chugging from a bottle of Jack.

"Damn straight," said Serge, emptying his own bag. "We're going old school. And if you're going old school, then go all the way!"

"You don't mean—?"

"That's right!" said Serge. "Kindergarten!"

"Man," said Coleman. "That's off the hook."

"Those were the last of the truly great days," said Serge, pawing through his new stuff on the mattress. "All fun all the time, running around screaming on the playground, crayons and construction paper, those little milk cartons and nap time. No grade-point average yet, no pressure whatsoever except tying your shoes and trying not to spit up."

"But then the janitor could always come with the sawdust," said Coleman.

"It was like watching a miracle," said Serge. "The first time I saw it, I didn't give the sawdust a snowball's chance, but then *damn*! For a while, life was perfect. If there's ever a problem, just throw sawdust on it and everything will be lollipops and unicorns again. And one evening my mom was sitting at the kitchen table, crying over a pile of unpaid bills. She suddenly sits up straight and starts brushing all this stuff out of her hair: 'Serge, what the hell?' I say, 'Sawdust, Mom. Everything's okay now.' But instead I got a time-out in the corner. That was the death of innocence."

"Look at all this cool stuff on the bed!" said Coleman.

"And not a speck of digital." Serge stood. "That's how we lost our way."

"Where are you going?"

"To get the rest of our haul out of the car. I'll need your help."

It had been a whirlwind shopping spree, with stops at quite varied retail outlets until brimming bags filled the car. After several unloading trips, Serge and Coleman were safely ensconced back in the room, enthusiastically sorting their recent purchases on the bed. Paste, safety scissors, pipe cleaners, finger paints, glitter, tinfoil, clothespins, buttons, Play-Doh.

Coleman picked up a couple of the buttons. They were clear, with something round inside that rolled around. "What are these?"

"Eyes you glue on a drawing of a bear or something to make him look wacky."

Coleman held the buttons over his own eyes. "Serge, what do you think?"

"Overkill."

Coleman cast them aside and picked up the scissors. "Remember in kindergarten when you could make a costume out of just a pillowcase?"

"That was the best!" Serge grabbed a sixty-four-count box of Crayolas. "You cut holes for your head and arms and could color whatever your imagination dreamed up. You could be anyone you wanted."

"I was an Indian for Thanksgiving," said Coleman. "What about you?"

"Chief Justice Warren."

"Hey, let's make costumes!"

"Great idea!"

They dashed toward the head of a bed and stripped cases off pillows.

Coleman plopped down at a table and grabbed crayons. "Do you think the motel will mind?"

"We'll just slip them back on the pillows when we're done. They've seen worse."

Coleman leaned over the table, ready to go. "What do you think our costumes should be?"

Serge grabbed a blue crayon. "Superheroes. The pillowcases will imbue us with special powers."

"What hero are you going to be?"

"It's a secret." Serge began coloring furiously. "And don't tell me yours either until you're done."

"I love surprises." Coleman joined in the vigorous scribbling. "So where'd you get this idea for a kindergarten party, anyway?"

Serge intently colored on his own case. "You know how sometimes I like to leave my cell phone in the car and take off on foot?"

"I've been wondering why you do that."

"You take away someone's phone today, and it's like you've cut off their oxygen. They can't survive," said Serge. "But kids used to spend entire childhoods without phones and do just fine. That's why it's essential to leave my phone in the car every so often. My wallet, too. Because I have no money or credit cards, it recalibrates my senses back to grade school, forcing me to appreciate all the free stuff in life, like skipping or rolling around in the grass for no reason. It's about rekindling the lost art of being silly."

"I remember that one time you left your phone and wallet behind, and you were hanging upside down on the monkey bars, making farting sounds with your hands on your mouth."

"And the park officials made us leave just for that? I even explained it was part of my phone-and-wallet-free therapy, like EST, insulin shock or primal scream."

"I think you were freaking everyone out."

"They said it was inappropriate behavior for an adult, which I explained was the exact kind of thinking that now has everyone at each other's throats." Serge grabbed a different color crayon and scribbled. "Anyway, I realized I was severely limiting myself with those brief childlike excursions. I needed to invoke the Total Kindergarten Protocol. But of course society isn't ready, like the monkey-bar fiasco or how they laughed when the Beatles joined that ashram in India. So we need the privacy of a motel room."

"What do you do for this proto— . . . proto— . . ."

"Protocol," said Serge. "In order to cleanse ourselves of the toxicity from the growing-up process, we must revert and do nothing beyond the level of a five-year-old."

"Cool." Coleman grabbed a crayon in one hand and a bottle with the other. Chug, chug, chug.

"Ahem!"

Coleman looked up. "What?"

"I don't think Jack Daniel's is on the lunch menu next to the beanie weenies."

"Oh, judge me for a little snort?" Coleman pointed with a yellow crayon. "I don't remember *that* from childhood."

Serge looked over at a man tied to a motel room chair and gagged with duct tape. He slapped himself in the forehead. "I'd completely forgotten about Clyde."

Coleman scoffed sarcastically. "Did you tie people up in kindergarten?"

Serge walked over to the hostage. "Actually, there was this one incident. It's pretty funny now, but at the time: 'Where the hell did Little Serge get all that rope?'"

The hostage wiggled violently. "*Mmmmm! Mmmmm!*"

Coleman grabbed the bottle of whiskey and resumed coloring. "Sounds like he wants to tell you something." Chug, chug, chug.

Serge rapped knuckles on Clyde's forehead like it was a door. "Is that true?"

Vigorous nodding.

"Promise not to yell?"

More nodding.

Serge quickly ripped off the tape.

"Owwwwwwwww!"

"I thought you promised?"

"Please don't hurt me!"

"Hurt you?" said Serge, innocently pointing to his own chest. "Oh, *I'm* not going to hurt you."

"Then what are you going to do?"

Serge gestured toward the arts-and-crafts table. "First I need to continue my kindergarten reversion therapy, and then we'll have an after-school party. How about it? . . ." His gleeful expression became a frown. "What? You don't like parties? You're not in a festive mood? . . . Then you leave me no choice . . ."

Serge turned his back to Clyde and bent over a bed.

"No! Please! Whatever you're thinking . . ."

Serge spun back around. Two buttons were over his eyes. He shook his head back and forth, and the little objects in the buttons rattled around in circles. He removed the buttons. "Pretty wacky, eh?"

Clyde just whimpered.

"Jesus," said Serge. "I give and I give." He tore off another long strip of tape and forcefully wrapped it over Clyde's mouth again. Terrified eyes looked up at him.

"Hold that thought," said Serge. "I'll be back after I'm a superhero . . . But you can't tell anyone my true identity."

There were a number of stray crayon marks on the table, but Coleman was able to get most on the pillowcase.

Serge sat back down. "Wow, you're really going at it!"

"Yep, I dig kindergarten." Scribble, scribble, chug, chug. "And I'm just about done . . . There!" Coleman beamed proudly as he held his case up to Serge.

"It's wonderful! It's . . . It's . . ." Serge didn't want to discourage his buddy. "Absolutely fantastic! . . . Uh, what is it?"

"Can't you tell by the shield on the chest?"

"All I can make out are the letters *B* and *M,*" said Serge. "I hope that's not supposed to be bowel—"

"Of course not." Still smiling wide. "Don't you get it? I'm Bong Man!"

"I think it's safe to say that this particular superhero name isn't taken yet." Serge scratched his head. "But you don't have a superpower."

"Oh, I've got a superpower all right." Coleman grabbed the safety scissors. "It's a doozy!"

"What is it?"

"Just go back to your own pillowcase, and by the time you're done, I'll show you."

"If you say so." Serge resumed scribbling, skeptically watching Coleman out of the corner of his eye. *What's that idiot doing?*

Coleman had become a rare blur of industriousness. Construction paper, glue, tape and most of their other supplies came into play.

It was a race to the finish, and it was a tie.

Serge slapped down a crayon. "I'm done."

Coleman tossed an extra clothespin on the table. "Me too." Like poker players: "Show me what you got."

Serge held up a pillowcase with flamingos, rockets, sailfish, race cars, Cinderella's castle, Bok Tower and the lighthouse on Key Biscayne. In the middle, Serge had his own chest shield.

"What does the *CF* stand for?" asked Coleman.

"Captain Florida."

"What's your superpower?"

"I can name the state's sixty-seven counties in under a minute, sometimes." Serge pulled off his T-shirt and tried on the pillowcase. "Your turn. What are you hiding under the table?"

"Close your eyes and promise not to peek."

Serge did. He heard the unmistakable telltale sound of a Bic lighter coming to life. Then a familiar smell of smoke.

"Hey," said Coleman. "I didn't say you could open your eyes yet."

Serge's jaw came unhinged. "Your superpower is that you can make a bong out of ordinary kindergarten craft supplies?"

"Pretty super if you ask me." Puff, puff, puff.

Serge sat back and studied the contraption, held together solely with glue and tape, plus pipe cleaners and clothespins for extremities. Colorful construction paper was bent and rolled and folded like the work of an origami expert. "Coleman, your bong, is that a robot?"

"Robots rule! What do you think?"

"Danger, Will Robinson."

"And I used Play-Doh for the seals." Puff, puff, puff. "Your turn to put up."

Serge took a deep breath before spitting out words rapid-fire like an auctioneer. "Alachua, Baker, Bay, Bradford, Brevard, Broward..."

"Mmmmmm! Mmmmmm!"

Serge grabbed a tape dispenser and flung, ricocheting it off Clyde's soon-to-be-bloody nose. "We're trying to be five-year-olds, motherfucker!"

A pot cloud exhaled toward the captive. "Serge, could you hand me those two eye buttons? I want to glue them on my robot to make him wacky."

"Here you go."

"Thanks." Coleman squirted Elmer's Glue. "By the way, what are you planning to do with him?"

Serge reached into a shopping bag. "I've given this one a lot of careful thought." He pulled out a small blue box.

"Alka-Seltzer?" asked Coleman.

"No, a generic brand called Fizzing Circles because I wouldn't want to cast a pall on the good people at Alka-Seltzer."

"That's a weird name."

"Apparently, someone's tightening up trademark infringement laws, because generic names are getting pretty strange in order to keep their legal distance. You need look no further than the cereal aisle. I swear these are all real: Fruit Rings, Square Shaped Corn, Circus Balls, Crispy Hexagons, Pranks instead of Trix, and a knockoff of Life cereal called Live It Up. Children see right through those bowls of bullshit."

"So what's the plan with the tablets?"

"Stalled for now," said Serge. "The first hurdle was how do I get enough tablets in him without them activating before the Big Fizz? I finally found a solution, but the technique was so tediously long that I grew weary of the wit involved. So I went hard the other way..."

Serge grabbed a bottle of glue off the table and reached in his grocery sack again. Then he went over to the hostage with the safety scissors and began snipping off his clothes. "Sorry, I know this must be one of your favorite T-shirts because of the slogan on the front: 'I'm Not a Gynecologist, but I'll Take a Look.' Damn, that's funny."

Serge stopped snipping and began smearing glue across Clyde's bare chest. He opened a product from the supermarket and placed the pieces in a careful arrangement. "Now we just wait for the drying process."

Chapter 6

FOUR YEARS EARLIER

Tequesta, Florida.

The northeastern tip of Palm Beach County on the ocean. Named after the Native American tribe who lived, loved and built shell mounds here for two thousand years until ancestors of the current residents put a stop to that, clearing the way for golf.

It is a quiet, affluent bedroom community with many dockside homes and waterways, making it popular among sportsmen. Most prefer sailing out into the Atlantic under the bright sun for their recreation, but some are nocturnal. Night scuba diving is an exciting change of pace, with all the local reefs. So is night fishing.

On a Tuesday evening, just after eleven o'clock, a twenty-seven-foot Boston Whaler with twin Mercury engines cleared the jetties at Jupiter Inlet and began bouncing across the waves out to sea. The continental shelf off this coast is among the narrowest on the whole U.S. seaboard, sometimes barely a mile wide before precipitously dropping off hundreds of feet, where they call it deep-sea fishing.

The Whaler continued cresting small swells. Four heavy-duty spin-casting rods swayed in their holders like radio antennae. The boat's only occupant, a loner named Remy Skillet, also had two rifles and a shotgun. He was going *shark* fishing. He felt a slight pain in his mouth and thought of missed dental appointments.

A mile out, on the edge of the continental shelf, Remy cut the engine and drifted with the current. All lines went in the water, along with a dumped bucket of bloody chum that spread a grease apron off the stern. Seasoned anglers understand that the sport requires mental stamina, and Remy had the kind of patience of someone who brings guns with him to fish. He began blasting the water with an assault rifle before he realized he was shooting at his own chum slick, now glistening under the moon. He opened another beer. He was so far offshore that the lights of the oceanfront homes formed a single, horizontal thread of light, which was his only indication of where black sky left off and black water began. The ocean wind was more loud than stout, and carried a salty mist from the bow slapping the waves. The salt made Remy reach for another beer. That's when the shark hit the bait.

It was a seven-foot mako, gauging from dorsal to tail, and it began swimming back and forth under the boat, bending one of Remy's thickest rods to the breaking point. This required the shotgun. The water exploded off the port side, then the starboard, then port again. The next blast was decidedly louder than the others, and Remy took a step back and stilled his weapon. "That couldn't have been my gun. What was it?" Then he turned around and recoiled even more. "Holy shit!"

Remy's face glowed in the orange light as a fireball mushroomed into the sky a few hundred yards away. What remained after that was some kind of vessel, at least forty feet long, but it was difficult to determine much else because it had burned practically to the waterline. Remy started up his engine and headed in the direction of the explosion.

Minutes later, Remy idled his boat as it circled the smoldering wreckage. He felt his vessel bump something, and it wasn't the other boat. He looked over the side and couldn't see anything at first, because it was black. Not the water, but the scuba suit that the floating dead guy was wearing. Then he saw a second body in a wet suit, and a third, all bobbing in the waves. The toll ended at four, the last guy wearing jeans and a T-shirt with scorch marks.

Remy scratched his head. "What on God's green earth happened here?"

Then more confusion as one of the previously motionless bodies began to thrash. Remy fell into his captain's chair. "Jumpin' Jesus!"

In all the excitement and beer, Remy had completely forgotten about the shark on his fishing line that he'd dragged over to the scene and that was now devouring the bodies.

"Stop that! Stop that right now!" He racked his twelve-gauge. *Blam!... Blam! Blam! Blam!... Blam! Blam!...*

A steadier hand could have accomplished the objective with less ammunition, but Remy was still able to get the situation under control. The last shot sent the shark away from the bodies and diving under the boat . . .

In the days to follow, Remy would be arrested as the prime suspect, mainly because all the victims were presumed to have died from multiple shotgun blasts.

"No, really," Remy told them. "I was trying to preserve the evidence."

"How's that?"

"A shark was eating them."

"You do realize it's now impossible to determine how they died? And we wouldn't even have been able to identify two of them if it weren't for tattoos."

"Am I in trouble? . . ."

But right now, as the bodies were still bobbing around Remy's vessel, he had another question. "Where's that last Schlitz?"

A half mile away, night-vision binoculars watched a sinewy man crouching near the bait wells of a Boston Whaler, then standing up and appearing to drink from a can.

A whisper: "What's going on?"

"I think we just caught a big break."

"But what the hell was all that shooting?"

"That was the big break." The binoculars followed Remy as he headed toward the front of the boat, tripped over something and disappeared from view, then popped back up. "This clown just shot up the evidence."

"Why?"

"He was night-fishing. They use beer."

The three men continued hashing out their predicament in muted tones as they lay on their stomachs across the bow of a six-hundred-horsepower go-fast boat. The boat was as black as their jumpsuits, and all the running lights were off.

They waited silently. The reason was obvious. They were about to slip away from the crime scene, as they say, scot-free. All they had to do was remain dark and quiet until Remy departed without detecting their presence, and pray he didn't lose his navigational bearings and head toward them.

He headed toward them.

"Don't panic," said one of the jumpsuits. "He's still too far off to be on dead reckoning."

They waited.

"He's not veering."

"He'll veer."

Remy's bow light grew brighter.

"He's not veering."

"He'll— . . . Shit!"

The trio vaulted back behind the controls and gave it full

throttle. At the last second, the black void of a large powerboat with its lights off shot out from in front of Remy.

"Whoa!" Remy cut the steering wheel in a classic over-correction, careening for a slalom to port. And because all fishing boats are required to have way more engine than they'll ever need, the centrifugal force flung Remy over the side into the water.

Fortunately, the boat had a "kill switch" in the event the captain went overboard, and the fishing vessel quieted to a stop and settled into the water just a short swim away.

Remy sighed with relief as he floated. "What a night . . ."

Oh, and when the authorities would eventually question Remy, it would be in a hospital room. Because as Remy dog-paddled back to his boat, the shark still on his fishing line came over and bit him.

Chapter 7

Chug, chug, chug. "What are we waiting for?" asked Coleman. "It looks like that stuff on your prisoner is dry now."

Serge glanced out the window. "The weather's still really crappy."

"Is it going to rain?"

"You'd think it would cut loose any second," said Serge. "But it's holding up. Just a full canopy of black clouds. To this day, whenever the weather is crappy like this, I get a joyous sense of childhood déjà vu. Instead of becoming glum, we'd use our imaginations and play endless games indoors."

"You don't mean—"

"To the shopping bags! . . ."

A few minutes later, Serge chased Coleman around the room, running over the tops of beds. "I got you! I got you!"

"You did not!"

"Yes, I did!" Serge blasted his friend in the face.

"Hold on," said Coleman. "I need to refill my squirt gun . . ."

"Mmmmmm! Mmmmmm! . . ."

Minutes later. "Coleman, look! I'm walking the dog! Now I'm doing the cat's cradle. You try."

"Okay." *Zing, clack.* "Ow! My forehead!"

"It's bleeding," said Serge. "Apply pressure."

"I just remembered I hate yo-yos."

"Mmmmmm! Mmmmmm! . . ."

Moments after that: "Coleman, here comes the paper airplane."

"I've never played with paper airplanes like this before."

"It's no fun unless they're on fire . . . Oooh, shit, get it away from the curtains."

"Mmmmmm! Mmmmm! . . ."

More stuff came out of shopping bags. More games ensued. Until finally Serge had his eyes closed tightly as he walked around the room with outstretched arms. "Marco!"

"Polo!"

"Marco!"

"Polo!"

Serge grabbed a face and squeezed a nose. "Is that you, Coleman?"

"No," Coleman yelled from the bathroom doorway. "It's Clyde."

"Sorry."

"Mmmmmm! Mmmmm!"

Serge opened his eyes. "Fun's over."

Coleman took a slow sip of whiskey as he surveyed their room: Hopscotch chalk on the carpet, jump rope wrapped around a broken lamp, a burned smell from a cap-gun battle, a horseshoe sticking out of a wall, pencils stuck in ceiling tiles, scattered marbles, baseball cards, jacks, a pogo stick, a robot bong and a hostage. "This was the best party ever!"

Serge checked the window again. "Looks like the weather's

not going to clear. We'll just have to take our chances and pray there's no cloudburst."

"Cool," said Coleman. "I finally get to see what you have planned for him."

Serge ripped the tape off Clyde's mouth and grinned. "Bet you just can't wait to find out what's in store."

"Y-y-you, you're completely insane!"

"Me?" said Serge, tapping himself in the middle of his pillow-case costume. He reapplied mouth tape. "Coleman, look alive. It's time to get ready and head out."

"Are we going in our pillowcases?"

Serge shook his head and grabbed another shopping bag off the floor. "I've got a better idea." He dumped the sack on a bed. "Let's put these on."

"Where'd you get that stuff?"

"The Party Store has everything!"

Soon they were dressed again.

"Won't this attract extra attention?" asked Coleman.

"Just the opposite," said Serge. "This is like the concept of orange vests, clipboards and safety cones. If you're wearing these, the general public simply assumes that you're authorized."

Coleman looked in the mirror as he adjusted his red Afro wig and rubber-ball nose. "Are you sure about this?"

"When have you ever seen anyone question someone dressed like this?" Serge jauntily snapped his polka-dot suspenders. "People see clowns and they automatically think you know what you're doing."

Serge freed Clyde from the chair and walked him to the door. He peeked outside to make sure the coast was clear, then hustled Clyde into their car's trunk again and slammed the lid.

They began driving south, pulling up to a red light. Some teenagers in the next car began laughing and pointing. "Look! Clowns!"

Serge flashed a clown badge. "We're authorized."

The light turned green and they sped off.

Coleman sucked on a robot. "Where are we going?"

"To the far end of the beach, just before the port. It's a longer walk from the hotels and usually empty, especially with this kind of overcast weather."

They parked on a secluded corner of a public-access lot. "Coleman, grab that duffel bag at your feet."

A couple came off a walkway over the sea oats from the beach. Serge nodded seriously and respectfully.

"Who are those guys?" the wife asked her husband.

"Couple of clowns."

They drove away, leaving Serge and company alone with unfinished business. He popped the trunk. "Time to rock and roll!"

Serge led Clyde across the sand in the grim weather, poking a pistol in his ribs.

Coleman struggled to keep up alongside, continuously re-hitching the duffel's strap over his shoulder. "Serge, I still think the guy looks too weird with all the stuff glued on him. We're bound to get caught."

"And that's where you're wrong." Serge poked the barrel harder for motivation. "We're out in the open with a clear view of any approaching cops. If we do see any, I'll just slice off his wrist bindings and remove the mouth tape. What's he going to say? 'Help! Help! I've been held hostage by two guys who played kindergarten games all day while wearing pillowcases!' He'll come off like designer-drug fiend. Then if the cops question us we say that we just met him in the parking lot, and he must have relapsed after getting off the bus from rehab."

"But what about our clown suits?" asked Coleman. "Won't that make the police suspicious?"

"Again, just the opposite," said Serge. "I'll tell them: 'Look at us. We're professionals. Do we seem like pillowcase guys to you?' Of course the answer's obvious."

"Mmmmmm! Mmmmmm!"

"Where are we taking him?" asked Coleman, trudging through the sand in big, floppy shoes.

"Over there, behind that clutch of palm trees for a little privacy." Serge's own large shoes slapped the beach.

Moments later: "That's far enough." Serge poked a gun in a stomach. "Now sit down and don't give me any trouble or . . . or . . . well, there's really nothing left to hold over your head. Just do it out of politeness."

Clyde sat in the sand, and Serge began going through the bag Coleman had carried. First the rope, tent stakes and hammer. *Wham! Wham! Wham! Wham!* The captive's ankles were secured to the ground. Serge pulled out a bottle of drinking water, the tape and a baggie of pills.

Coleman puffed a robot. "What are those?"

Serge held the baggie to his face. "This was a real bitch to prepare, so I hope it works. Remember the Fizzing Circles I showed you before? And I mentioned a tedious process that caused a mood swing and change of heart? I've since come around on that kind of constipated thinking. I've decided to go for a two-pronged project."

"Dear God," said Coleman.

"That's right," said Serge. "All the most critical pieces of scientific apparatus have redundancy circuits, so why not me?" He tossed the baggie in the sand next to the captive and held up a video camera. "Those babies in that bag might not do the entire trick, but the added visuals will put it over the top. When you commit to a project, you can't just phone it in."

Chug, chug, chug. "I still don't know what those are."

Serge knelt next to Clyde. "It took three whole boxes of Contac. Except not Contac, but the generic called Colored Capsules, because the folks at Contac are good people, too. And since they come in capsules, I twisted them all apart and dumped out the original contents. Then I wiped a bowl down and hit it with a hair dryer to ensure a moisture-free receptacle. I mashed up a whole bunch of the Fizzing Circles until there was just powder in the bowl. Next I carefully spooned it into the empty halves of the previously disassembled capsules and twisted them back together. It took *forever,* but one of the strongest motivational forces in the universe is irony."

Serge reached into Coleman's bag again and pulled out thick plastic goggles. "Clyde, you're going to need these. Safety comes first." He fitted them over the hostage's head with a thick rubber strap.

"Mmmmmm! Mmmmmmm!"

"Man, hold your horses," said Serge. "The tape is just about to come off."

Rip.

"Ahhhhh!"

"Keep it down or . . . or . . . just keep it down." Serge uncapped the bottled water and wedged it in the sand. Then he opened the baggie and scooped out a handful. The other hand stuck the pistol in Clyde's cheek. "Are you going to play nice with others? A nod will do."

He nodded.

"Good. Now, as you heard me explain to Coleman, this isn't poison or any addictive prescription, because I just say no to drugs. The ingredients in these capsules are just for upset tummies, and yours must be doing backflips right about now. And in your self-crafted rationale that I observed on that other beach, it's totally moral for me to force you to take them. So open wide and don't chew; the water will be coming right up to wash it down."

The capsules were crammed in his mouth, then the water bottle. It was a struggle at first, but soon Clyde managed to get them swallowed.

"Good student," said Serge, reaching back in the bag. "Just a few more times and I won't bother you in this way again." He repeated the process as needed until the baggie was empty.

"Excellent!" Serge reached in the duffel for more tent stakes and rope. *Wham! Wham! Wham!* The hostage's arms were now stretched out over his head with wrists held fast to the ground.

Serge ripped off yet another strip of duct tape. As he pressed it in place: "You know, I did some Internet research on the subject of cruelty, and the stuff I read brought tears to my eyes. Someone actually crucified a pelican on a wooden light pole. I'll spare you the rest of the ghastly details, but the horrible deaths animals experience in the name of idle entertainment are nothing short of heartbreaking. Not to mention that the tormentors proudly post the videos. What's wrong with people like that?" Serge gestured skyward with the hand holding his own video camera. "I guess I just can't understand the concept of torture."

"Mmmmmm! Mmmmmm!"

Serge grabbed a pocketknife. The blade flipped open and stuck between the captive's lips. "Hold still," said Serge. "I'm going to cut a small slit to give you a little extra air, but I don't know why. I must be going soft or something." Slice. He inserted a drinking straw. "There! You still can't scream, but feel free to go 'toot, toot, toot' like a toy train . . . And now that I've thought about it, I require it. Go ahead."

The captive just stared up with horrified eyes.

"Come on!" said Serge. "Don't make me regret giving you that slit. 'Toot, toot, toot.'"

Clyde was tentative, and it came out more like a question. "Toot, toot, toot?"

The clowns doubled over with laughter. "I don't know why that's so funny," said Serge. "Maybe it's the goggles."

"Or maybe all the corn chips you glued on his chest and legs," said Coleman.

"You might have something there," said Serge. "I'll call him the Bandito."

Puff, puff, chug, chug. "What now?"

"We have to time this perfectly." Serge reached into the

shopping bag a final time. "The capsules in his stomach are just about dissolved."

"He's getting that look on his face like when I have gas," said Coleman.

"Here we go!" Serge reached into a bag of corn chips, and tossed a handful high into the air.

Coleman ducked. "Where'd they come from?"

"FBI surveillance team." Serge tossed another handful toward the sky. Seagulls swarmed and cawed and fought each other for crumbs.

Coleman held out his left arm. "Poop."

"We better back up." Serge looked skyward. "Today's forecast calls for a shitstorm."

"Damn!" Coleman felt the top of his head. "Another one got me. They're following us."

"Because they think we have all the chips." Serge stepped forward and dumped the rest of the bag liberally on the ground. And across Clyde.

"Look at 'em go!" said Coleman. "They're all over him. I think they're accidentally pecking him going for the chips, and he doesn't like it."

"What gives you that idea?"

"Just listen."

"Toot! Toot! Toot! Toot! Toot! . . ."

Serge doubled over again. "I don't know why that's so funny because it shouldn't be."

"I can barely see him anymore because of all the feathers," said Coleman.

Serge raised a video camera. "And for the record, I used nontoxic kindergarten glue. No animals were harmed during the production of this film."

"The tooting stopped," said Coleman.

"There's a good reason for that," said Serge. "Watch."

It began slowly at first, then a growing fountain of white fizz shot up from the tube in the mouth tape.

"You sure gave him a lot to think about," said Coleman.

"It's kind of pretty, like those dancing-water fountains."

"But, Serge, there's one thing I don't get." Coleman tightened the red ball on his nose. "How are birds eating chips off him supposed to teach any lessons?"

"Seagulls are widely misunderstood creatures." He zoomed in with the camera. "We think they're cute little guys nibbling popcorn and tacos. But that's just because they're creatures of opportunity. Did you know that gulls often grab clams, mussels, crabs and even small turtles, then fly to great heights and drop them in parking lots to crack them open for food? Amazingly, that's something they have to learn from scratch each generation because back thousands of years ago when genetic memory was forming their survival instincts, I don't think they had much pavement."

"That's trippy," said Coleman.

"But there's more. We really don't comprehend a seagull's primal nature because all we observe is their behavior around us: 'Let's see. I can bust my ass flying around with this tortoise or, fuck it, I'll just eat these onion rings.' But in the absence of human handouts, they're highly aggressive carnivores, often feasting on rodents, reptiles, amphibians, carrion. Even working in teams on severely injured larger prey that can't escape."

"By the way, what were the safety goggles for?"

"Gulls find the eyes tasty," said Serge. "I have a weak stomach. Another favor I did him, but do I get any thanks?"

"So which do you think will get him first?" asked Coleman. "The circles or the birds?"

"It's neck and neck," said Serge.

"The fizz is shooting higher."

"The circles have the edge."

"Hey, why is that one bird all pink?" asked Coleman.

"I think it nicked his femoral artery," said Serge. "The gulls have retaken the lead."

They stopped talking and watched the spectacle unfold a few more minutes.

Coleman stowed his flask and raised his smoking device. "I have to admit, this is one of your cooler projects."

"Society has become too fast-paced and jaded." Serge looked down at his clown suit, then the robot bong, then a corn-chip-covered hostage spewing fizz and blood through a blizzard of feathers. "But see all the fun you can have if you just leave your cell phone back in the room?"

Chapter 8

FOUR YEARS EARLIER

The office walls were concrete blocks painted with high-gloss institutional enamel. Framed photos, some decades old, hung sparsely. A couple of felt sports-team pennants. A bookshelf with trophies. The people in the photos wore football helmets.

The desk was standard fare for high school coaches. In other words, junk. Anything nicer, and they'd lose credibility. Behind it, almost overwhelming the desk, sat someone whom the whole town had known and talked about for years. This was the result of both the man's accomplishments and how small the town was.

Back in the day, Lamar Calhoun had been a star running back for the Pahokee Blue Devils, helping claim their first state championship in 1989. He had that rare combination at his age of college-level speed and size. Lamar could cut back in the open field at such mystifying angles that he made the fastest safeties and cornerbacks look foolish. But his specialty was leaping over the defensive line in short-yardage situations. And if one of the linebackers did meet Lamar at the peak of his jump, well, he was just along for the ride, falling backward with Calhoun into the end zone.

College scouts were all over him; cars practically lined up at the curb outside his house as a parade of famous coaches sat in the living room making offers, some quite generous, others NCAA violations. He left for an education in the Midwest. Everyone was certain they'd one day see him on television in an NFL uniform.

Then nothing. It was like he had just vanished. People talked for a while, and there were the typical rumors. But then more high school seasons came and went, more state titles, and even more stars, many of them reaching the pros.

Almost three decades later, when Lamar was all but forgotten, he was suddenly just *back*.

It was minutes before the final bell of the day when he simply strolled in the front entrance of Pahokee High School. Word swept the hallways. People peeked in the widows of the principal's office as faculty and the coaching staff surrounded the towering Lamar, showering praise and recounting glory on the nearby field.

"Appreciate you stopping by."

"Glad you haven't forgotten about us."

"So what brings you through town?"

They all just figured he was a big deal somewhere else and had taken a detour on a business trip to see the school where it all began.

"Actually, I'm not passing through," said Lamar. "I'd like a job."

It got quiet in a hurry. Then stammering from the principal. "Well, uh, sure, I, I mean yeah; it's just so out of the blue."

But it was Lamar after all. The principal said there was an assistant coach opening, running backs, no less, but . . . uh, they were a small-budget school. Would he mind also driving a school bus?

"That's great," said Lamar. "Thanks."

The former gridiron legend smiled and shook hands all around and walked out of the office.

Everyone stretched their necks to watch him leave, thinking: *Who comes back to Pahokee?*

L amar Calhoun sat in his coach's office going over report cards. Player eligibility. Tutoring.

There were some towel-snapping hijinks up the hall in the locker room. Calhoun shouted out the door to knock it off. It was quiet again. He looked back down at grades.

A timid knock at the door and an equally timid voice: "Coach C? Do you have a minute?"

"You again?" He was annoyed but also amused. He made himself smile.

A student walked in. "Have you thought any more about what we discussed?"

"I'm sorry, but it's just impossible," said Lamar.

"Why?" Chris took a seat on the other side of the desk. For the tenth time. Like a bad penny.

"Don't take this wrong, but you're a girl," said the coach. "Why don't you try soccer?"

"Because I want to play football," said Chris. "I've seen stuff in the news. A few girls have actually made boys' teams."

"And all of those were kickers," said the coach. "You want to be a running back."

Chris nodded. "I'm pretty fast."

"Why are you pestering me instead of the head coach?"

"Duh, because you're the running-back coach."

Lamar sighed. "What grade are you in anyway?"

"Junior high. Eighth."

"There you have it," said Lamar, relieved at the conversational escape route. "You've got another year before you should be bothering me again. End of conversation."

He resumed going through report cards.

Chris cleared her throat.

The coach looked up and raised his hands in frustration. "What do you want from me?"

"Make me a manager."

"What?"

"I'll carry water bottles, equipment, help with paperwork, anything. I just want to be around the team."

Lamar was actually smiling inside, but he'd learned that sometimes not being firm wasn't doing anyone favors. "Check back in a year. Now, if you'll excuse me, I have work to do . . ."

Violent grunting and shouts. Shoulder pads crashed. A running back slammed into the defensive line and purely willed himself for a two-yard gain before the punishment of a gang tackle.

A coach blew a whistle.

Water break.

The teenagers pulled off helmets and gathered round the coolers. Panting, dizzy, sweating, jerseys caked with dirt. They guzzled from paper cups, spitting most out and swallowing the rest. High school football practice was tough enough in the rest of the country, but rarely like out here in what they called The Muck, under the Florida sun in a withering soup of humidity from Lake Okeechobee and surrounding Everglades crop fields.

Another assistant coach sidled up to Lamar Calhoun. "What's going on over there?"

"Where?"

The other coach pointed. With all the players on the sidelines now, the view was clear to the far side of the field. Two rows of truck tires were lined up for high-stepping agility drills. A tiny person was running through them. Or trying to. There was a trip and fall every few tires. The person got right back up for the next several tires and promptly went down again.

"Oh geez," said Calhoun.

"You know who that is?"

Lamar nodded. "Can you take over for me a few minutes?" He headed across the field.

A whistle blew behind him, and the boys lined up again to scrimmage.

Lamar reached the tires. "What are you doing?"

Chris pushed herself up from the vulcanized obstacle course and managed a couple more steps. *Plop.* "I'm practicing, Coach."

Calhoun's voice was more perplexed than angry. "Okay, first, I'm not your coach, and second, you can't be out here."

"Why not?" Huffing and turning around at the end of the tires, then heading back.

Lamar watched as she ran by and fell again. "Because only players are allowed on the field."

"I'm going to be a player."

"Please don't make me throw you out," said Lamar. "It's . . . insurance. Yeah, insurance."

Chris stopped. A resigned "*Alllllll* right."

Calhoun watched with conflicted emotions as the young girl slunk off the field. He scratched his head and had no idea what to make of it . . .

Chapter 9

CENTRAL FLORIDA

A 1969 Plymouth Satellite sat quietly and alone in the shade of an oak tree. It was lunchtime.

Coleman finished chewing a bite and swallowed. "What are we doing here?"

Serge stuck a fork in his mouth. "Eating pie."

"No, I mean *here,*" said Coleman. "This place."

"It's our next stop." Serge chased the bite with more coffee. "The Antioch Cemetery, a few miles east of Micanopy and Cross Creek."

"I'm surprised you picked this one," said Coleman. "It's small and kind of dumpy. Just dirt with some brown grass and weeds."

"That part's a disappointment, but one Floridian buried here makes it more than worthwhile."

"So who is it?"

"Hold on," said Serge, digging in again with his fork. "I'm letting the moment build with pie. This is a celebration of astounding dimensions."

"If it's a celebration, I would have guessed you'd buy a cake."

"I'm done with cake!" said Serge. "Cakes are flashy and get way too much attention compared to pie. All that garish frosting. It's just gratuitous."

Munch, munch. "Why do you say that?"

"Because cakes are the pole dancers of the bakery world, but a pie is the girl you take home to Mom. If cakes had names, they'd be Jazmine, Sunshine, Cinnamon, Duplicity; pie would answer to 'Sarah' and 'Beth.'"

"Never thought of it that way."

"There are defining times in your life when you just have to speak up."

"I can dig it." Coleman took another bite. "And I have to say it's pretty damn good pie. But I've never tasted anything like it."

"It's sour orange pie." A fork scooped.

"Never heard of it." Munch.

"Almost nobody has." Serge chewed and slurped from his coffee mug. "But it's one of our state's most fantastic native dishes ever, made from centuries-old family recipes that are now virtually forgotten. Key lime pie gets all the headlines today. And Key lime's great, don't get me wrong. But sour orange is nirvana. And because it's so unknown, you have to work like the devil to get it. The main ingredient was brought here by the Spanish in the sixteenth century, and now grows wild across the peninsula, characterized by its extra-bumpy and thick skin, like a giant citrus golf ball. Just finding the fruit is a bitch, involving hiking boots and trespassing, or long drives to specialty grocery stores like Cuban bodegas in Miami, where they're sold to make mojo sauce—I like saying 'mojo.' Then boil to a syrup, add eggs and sugar, graham-cracker or saltine-crumb crust, whip more syrup into the meringue, and the crowd goes wild. I found several recipes online, including one in an article for *Gardens and Guns*."

"Is that a real magazine?" asked Coleman.

"I thought it was a joke, too, but it's quite real," said Serge. "I can just see the early organization board meeting to come up with a name: 'We need a concept that appeals to the broadest possible audience covering the entire spectrum, something no other magazine has ever dared! Let's shoot it around the table . . .' Second place was probably *Kittens and Whiskey*."

"I'd buy a subscription to that."

"This pie delivers more than a taste-bud party." Serge yanked the napkin from the neck of his shirt. "Symbolically harkening back to the glorious time and place of the legend laid to rest here. It was out in these sweltering pioneer badlands of Central Florida near Lochloosa Lake, where she had the fruit trees growing off her veranda, and it's a safe bet she baked sour orange pie. Today, a couple of local rustic restaurants in her area are among the few places left where you can still order the real deal."

"So that's why we made that long detour on the way here."

Serge opened the door. "We have rubbing a-callin'."

They strolled across the field until they came upon a slab with no tombstone, just statues of a family of deer, mom, dad, and baby.

"Marjorie Kinnan Rawlings." Serge got down on his knees with an oversize sheet of paper. "Most known for her classic novel *The Yearling*, hence the animals on her grave."

"They look cute."

Rub, rub, rub. "This tour stop is special, and not just for Rawlings. It marks a turning point in our odyssey, where we've picked up the beginning of a long strand of Florida connective tissue that will bring our trip to a fever pitch of heritage, lore and motel antics."

"So where to now?"

"It's amazing how you can jump across the shoulders of Florida giants." Serge stood with his finished page. "By no coincidence, our next stop involves one of Rawlings's writing students . . ."

They call it the Treasure Coast.

Why not?

Florida already had the Gold Coast and the Space Coast, and above that, the First Coast with St. Augustine and all its oldest-everything-in-the-United-States signs.

That left three counties in the middle—Indian River, St. Lucie and Martin—orphaned with no coast of their own. It was hurting business.

Then, in 1961, a group of treasure salvagers made international headlines by discovering wrecks from a silver-and-gold-laden Spanish fleet that disappeared in a hurricane in 1715. A total of eleven ships were lost after departing Havana and ultimately sinking off the Sebastian Inlet near Vero Beach. The local *Press-Journal* newspaper swung into action and coined the term *Treasure Coast*.

Today, there is an annual pirate festival commemorating the 1715 wreck, and souvenir maps are sold everywhere with the locations of the ill-fated ships. Divers still search the well-known and charted sites, occasionally finding an artifact. And after hurricanes, children digging holes in the beach—as they are known to do—are said to unearth a doubloon or two. There are even guidebooks telling metal-detector enthusiasts where to look when visiting the Treasure Coast. And even as late as 2015, a salvage team would rework one of the wrecks thought to be depleted, and recovered another $4 million in gold.

Of the eleven lost ships, three have never been found.

One of the people still looking for them was a crusty salvage operator named Cale Munson, but everybody knew him as

"Captain Crack Nasty." You don't want to know where the nickname came from. Cale tried to shake the moniker for years, then embraced it. He figured it was always good for a seafaring man to have a gritty air of reputation, even if it resulted from personal grooming.

On his business card, Crack wasn't a true treasure salvager, but the regular kind. He operated one of those boat-towing services for when engines blew at sea or a vessel began taking on water. His fees were steep, like all the others in his field, because it was a sellers' market. But the real money came when a boat went down, thanks to state and federal law. The government sought to provide high incentive to rescue unfortunates on the water, as well as mitigate ecological damage from a grounded ship. The statutes so heavily favored salvagers that it meant this: If a boat went down and was raised, the salvager now owned it and could sell it back to its original purchaser.

Captain Crack mulled these codicils as he became increasingly bitter about towing the ultra-wealthy back to shore. He wanted to be wealthy, too, like the owners of the mini-yachts he aided, and especially like the now-famous treasure hunters who pulled up millions in precious metals and gems. He already had scuba equipment from his current gig, which could easily reach a sunken galleon. All he needed was a break. Only one problem: He was lazy. The successful treasure finders did extensive homework, even flying to Spain and spending hours in special libraries poring over parchment ship manifests from the eighteenth century. Crack just put on his scuba suit and dove to scour a site that someone else had already put in the elbow grease to find, like being the second person to discover the *Titanic*. After years of diving, he had exactly one cannonball to show for his efforts.

On a sunny afternoon, Crack was motoring out to a fancy disabled boat that was sitting lower than usual in the waves. The emergency call over the radio said it wasn't a fast leak, but would eventually turn fatal without intervention. From a distance,

Crack could tell it was one of those boats where people didn't fish but sipped champagne. He began thinking about salvage laws again. He pulled back on his throttle. Another call over the radio. *What's the holdup?* Crack answered that everything was under control. He leisurely arrived at the boat to find a bunch of polo and tennis people standing in shin-deep water.

"No problem," said Captain Crack, climbing aboard with an assistant. "Have you out of here in no time." He explained the procedure with the water-pumping machine back on his vessel and the hoses he was sticking down in their bilge. Plus the temporary patch to help the pump outpace the leak.

A half hour later. "We have a problem." He said the patch wasn't holding and the leak was faster than his pump. He didn't tell them that he was running his pump at one-third steam. "Everyone grab your valuables and get on my boat! We don't have much time!"

The theatrics worked. They were actually grateful as they watched their pleasure craft disappear beneath the water. And after bringing the thankful party back to shore, the good captain went back out, strung inflatable bladders under the sunken hull and raised the boat. This time he used a real patch and quickly pumped her dry. Not a bad day's work for $200,000.

From there it was the rhythm of routine. Distress calls came in, and Crack waved off all the other salvagers, saying he was closest. Closest but not fastest. He built in delays and excuses and deliberately incompetent water pumping, until once again: "Everyone on my boat! Hurry!"

And so it went, scuttling vessel after vessel. Captain Crack suddenly had a lot of money. But to him, it wasn't real money. That required treasure. He sat in his dockside office one afternoon, windows open to the cross-breeze, staring at the cannonball on his desk. He got an idea. He wouldn't dive for Spanish wrecks that had already been salvaged. He would go after sites that were *still being worked*. Which was highly illegal because of the claims filed by the rightful discoverers. Which meant cover of night. Crack went down to a government auction and bought on the cheap a sleek black ultra-fast cigarette boat that had been seized from a cocaine cartel. He promptly put her back into criminal service.

The Treasure Coast officially stops at the Palm Beach County line, where the Gold Coast begins with Tequesta and the surrounding communities. But hurricanes don't take their orders from the chamber of commerce.

A highly professional salvage crew began faithfully showing up at the same spot offshore for two weeks. The descriptions in their claim were deliberately downplayed: just exploring for scant artifacts. But rumors began sweeping the treasure-hunting crowd. Could they have found one of the three missing ships from the 1715 fleet?

Captain Crack anchored a safe distance away and staked them out with a telescope. Divers were making too many trips up to the boat for simple historical excavation. Handing too many baskets of whatever up to a deckhand.

After three days of surveillance, Crack headed out at night with two trusted assistants he had handpicked because of their prison records. They anchored over the site and dove.

Jackpot.

The only pressure was time, and it wasn't how long it took to find the loot, but how fast they could fill their baskets. Gold, silver, rubies, sapphires. It all went up to the cigarette boat.

After the sixth dive, the baskets came aboard. Suddenly: "Uh-oh."

A bright search beam shone in the distance. It came at them fast from the deck of a speeding vessel. Then a megaphone. "What the fuck are you doing on our site?"

Soon they were side by side in the water. Because of the lawlessness of the seas, everyone out there has guns, and now they were all drawn in a standoff.

Captain Crack tried to chill it out with lies. "We had no idea the site was claimed."

"Bullshit! Give us everything you have on your boat!"

"We didn't find anything yet," said Crack.

"Then we're coming aboard!"

"Then we'll kill you," said Crack. "And we'll get away with it under federal piracy laws for illegal boarding at sea."

The professional crew fumed. They were hardened, but not tough enough to get in a gun battle over a fraction of their find. Their leader finally waved his rifle toward shore. "Get out of here and never come back! Or next time we *will* shoot!"

Chapter 10

CENTRAL FLORIDA

The back road ran through God's country.

Town after small town. Little Florida places with names like Weirsdale, Citra, Lochloosa, Waldo, Starke and several more that were so tiny they didn't appear on maps. Volunteer fire departments, hardware stores, barbershops, old movie theaters on Main Street playing only one film, always rated G. Signs at the city limits indicated the Kiwanis and Rotary Club were still at it. Other signs were handmade by Girl Scouts for a spaghetti dinner that Friday. There were antiques stores and ice cream stands, billboards for salvation and speed traps, water towers of all shapes, some celebrating high school championships.

And the churches.

Bright white wooden churches, red-brick churches, and churches in converted farm buildings. Some houses of worship sat crowded together in competition; others alone in cattle pastures.

There were short steeples, tall steeples, and open-sided steeples with big bells. Lutheran, Presbyterian, Pentecostal, and AME Zion. Baptist, Anabaptist, and Primitive Baptist. Some had lighted signs with attempts at humor: ETERNITY: SMOKING OR NONSMOKING? CHOOSE THE BREAD OF LIFE OR YOU ARE TOAST. Some unintentionally so: ACCEPTING APPLICATIONS FOR MISSIONARY POSITION.

The back road was actually several roads, stitched together on an old gas station map the night before by Serge. It would be a long drive to the next tour stop, and he shuddered at the thought of spending all that time on an interstate.

The '69 Plymouth entered Ocklawaha. Soon, a two-story country home with a sweeping front porch came into view. Serge's camera was out the window again. *Click, click, click.*

"It's just an old house," said Coleman.

"And one so historically important that when the land was sold from under it, they barged the whole thing across Lake Weir to this location."

"So what's its deal?"

"Back during the Depression, the infamous Ma Barker Gang terrorized the nation with a spree of bank robberies and kid-nappings. In 1935, the FBI finally traced the outfit to Florida and this house, where Ma Barker—also known as Machine Gun Kate—was hiding out under an assumed name with several as-sociates. A gun battle ensued, and the house was sprayed with more than four thousand bullets. Apparently the holes have been patched."

"That's a stone trip," said Coleman.

"It was a different era," said Serge. "They actually laid out the bullet-riddled bodies and sold the photos as postcards to mail back to loved ones: 'Having a great time in Florida, unlike these assholes.'"

Serge stowed the camera and sped north. They passed citrus stands and boiled-peanut stands and someone in overalls walking along the side of the road with a sewing machine in a wheelbarrow. They continued on over hill and dale. One of the countless churches was coming up. Threshing machines worked the field next door. It was a Sunday morning, and the last service had long since let out.

As Serge passed by, he noticed three people on the front steps. A pastor was comforting a distraught couple. The woman cried inconsolably.

"Uh-oh," said Serge. "That's my bat signal."

He made a fishtailing U-turn in the middle of the lonely road and sped back. He ran up to the steps in no time. "Pardon me, but I couldn't help but notice you're upset."

The pastor had an arm around the woman's shoulders. He looked up. "It'll be fine."

"No, it won't!" sobbed the woman.

"Why don't you tell me about it?" said Serge.

"Excuse me," said the preacher. "Who are you?"

"Who are *you*?" said Serge.

"Pastor Donovan, but I—"

"The name's Serge." He shook the preacher's hand. "I roam the countryside, enjoying fresh air, monitoring my hygiene, and helping the downtrodden. Favorite food: pizza. Turnoffs: the word *conflate* and women who think a small dog in a purse is a fashion accessory."

A voice arriving from behind. "I'm Coleman . . ." Trip, splat.

Serge looked down and shook his head, then raised his face again. "Now, how may I be of assistance?"

"I don't think you can," said Donovan.

"Then what have you got to lose?" He turned toward the couple. "And you are . . . ?"

"Buford and Agnes Whorley, of the Nantucket Whorleys," said the man. "We retired here ten years ago."

Agnes broke down again. "And now we have no place to go!"

Serge straightened up with an odd look. "Why not go to where you've been the last ten years?"

Her face was buried in her hands. "We can't! It was stolen from us!"

"This is sounding complicated." Serge turned to address Buford. "Can you back up and explain from the beginning?"

"The house was all bought and paid for, our life savings," said Buford. "But then we began running short on the monthly bills. Who knew we'd live this long, or stuff would get so expensive?"

"What did you do?" asked Serge.

"We thought it was a sign from God," said Agnes. "We began seeing all those ads on TV for reverse mortgages, and it sounded like the answer to our prayers . . ."

Buford nodded. "But then we mentioned it to Tyler from our congregation, and he told us that those reverse things were the biggest racket going. They'd gouge us on the interest rate, then compound it, not to mention hidden up-front costs."

"Let me guess," said Serge. "He offered to help you with a better deal?"

"Told us that a conventional equity loan from an upstanding local bank would accomplish the same goals but on much better terms. He even went and got the loan documents from the bank—"

Serge held up a hand. "I've seen this movie before. Then he asked you to sign some title documents that the bank needed for collateral. And the next thing you knew, the bank called to report a loan problem with the title, and the sheriff was at your door saying your home had been sold and you needed to leave."

"The deputies were so nice," said Agnes. "They told us they had investigated and knew exactly what was going on. But their hands were tied because, while it was totally immoral, it was also totally legal."

Buford nodded again. "And the people who bought the house were another retired couple who used *their* entire life savings. What can you do?"

Serge took a seat on the steps next to them. "This one really breaks my heart. The reverse mortgages on TV are generally legit—it's the lone wolves you have to watch out for. Scams in this department have gone so sky-high in Florida that it's an epidemic waiting to make the press. Worst of all, the predators come to town and weasel their way into positions of trust. The newest trend is joining churches to prey on your virtue and trust in a fellow worshiper. Let me guess: Was this Tyler character in the choir?"

"How'd you know?" asked the pastor.

"And he just joined your congregation?"

"Two months ago," said Donovan. "Seemed like the greatest guy. Explained he had just relocated for employment, and that his wife and children would join him as soon as the school year ended up north. He even showed me their photos."

"Probably came with the wallet," said Serge. "I've heard enough. I assume Tyler has made himself scarce."

"Nobody's seen him since the sheriff knocked," said Buford.

Serge shook his head again. "Anything at all I can go on to track him down?"

"Not really," said Agnes.

But Serge noticed the pastor making a furtive head tilt out of their view. "Serge, I'm sorry there's nothing you can do, but it was kind of you to stop by. Why don't I walk you back to your car?"

"How gracious." Serge looked down. Kick. "Coleman, time to get up."

They all met back at the Plymouth.

"Look, I don't know who you are," said the pastor. "Undercover law enforcement? Private investigator from Tyler's last victim? Bank auditor? But something tells me it's information you can't divulge for professional reasons."

"That would be accurate," said Serge.

"I may be a pastor, but I'm not naive about the world."

"Really?" Serge looked toward the edge of the street. "You had me fooled by your sign."

"What?" Donovan turned. "Whoa. 'Missionary Position.' Slipped right by me."

"Not everyone's an editor."

"What I'm getting at is that I did research on the Internet, and I found out about the angle you were describing," said the preacher. "How these predators are increasingly using churches as their hunting grounds. I rarely curse, but this was more than I could take."

"Understandable."

"I also read how they move on before the locals can figure out their dishonesty, but the land is too fertile in Florida, so they can only go so far."

Serge rested an elbow on the roof of the car. "What are you trying to say?"

"The pastors around these parts keep up with each other. Personally, we're not the Internet types, but our chat rooms have their purpose," said Donovan. "Usually it's positive, like how to pump up congregation attendance. But this time I put out a warning on this Tyler guy so it wouldn't happen to anyone else in the area. I also posted a photo that my secretary was able to grab from the last video of our choir performance."

"I think I see where this is going," said Serge. "Where is he?"

"Goes by 'Nicholas' now." Donovan pointed north up the empty road splitting wild meadows. "Pastor four towns up gave me the word. Joined his church two weeks ago. He's keeping an eye on him so he doesn't pull anything before we can explore our options."

"When is the next service with the choir?" asked Serge.

"Started at noon." The preacher checked his wristwatch. "That gives you forty minutes max to catch him before he leaves."

"How long a drive?"

"Hour."

FOUR YEARS EARLIER

A tiny cork ball rattled around the inside of a small metal enclosure. It had an extension that fit in a coach's mouth. A shrill whistle blew for the hundredth time that afternoon. But this time it was followed by the head coach storming onto the field.

"Dougan! Get over here!"

The player trotted up. "What?"

The coach grabbed a fistful of the wide receiver's jersey between the numbers. "You quit on that play! You were practically walking like my grandmother at the end of your route!"

"But it was a screen to the other side—"

"And now you're arguing with me?"

"No, sir."

"You never, ever quit on a play! You always run through the whistle!" The coach released his grip on the uniform. "Stadium steps! Now!"

The other players winced as Dougan removed his helmet and jogged toward the stacked rows of aluminum benches.

"Helmet on!" the coach yelled after him.

Another collective cringe.

Stadium steps were the worst. The punishment took place where the parents sat for all those Friday-night games under the lights. The punished player ran up the steps all the way to the top row of the viewing stands, then down, then up again, over and over as lactic acid built up in the legs and muscles cramped. But that was no excuse. You kept going without end in sight until the coach mercifully called you back to the field. Then, hopefully, lesson learned.

The exiled receiver's cleats began clanging off the steps. The rest of the players got the message. There would be no more letups before the whistle this day. Play resumed back on the field with noticeably renewed purpose. The blocking harder, pass routes fully run, tackles like car accidents.

It was now taking two or three whistles to stop each play.

Lamar Calhoun was on the sideline, bent forward with hands on his knees, studying the technique of his starting halfback taking a delayed handoff and waiting for the block to open daylight next to the noseguard.

Another assistant coach stepped up next to him, the same one as the day before. Receivers coach named Odom. "Lamar, isn't that you-know-who?"

"What do you mean?"

"Up there." Odom shielded his eyes against the sun. "Just below the press box."

Lamar squinted. "You've got to be kidding me."

Over in the viewing stands, there was now a second set of feet clanging up and down the aluminum steps.

"What's the deal with that kid?" said Odom. "Who the hell runs stadium steps because they *want* to?"

"Good grief," said Calhoun. "Can you take over for me again? . . ."

Lamar arrived at the bottom step just as Chris touched it— "Hey, Coach"—and pivoted to head back up."

"Stop," said Lamar. "What do you think you're doing?"

Heavy breathing. "Getting in condition, Coach."

"Didn't I tell you yesterday that only players were allowed on the field?"

"I'm not on the field, Coach. I'm in the stands."

"And stop calling me Coach."

"Sorry, Coach."

"Sit down." Lamar joined her on the bottom bench. "Maybe I wasn't perfectly clear yesterday, but when I said you couldn't be on the field, I meant the entire grounds, including the stands."

"You didn't say that."

"Now I am."

A pout. But not one of self-pity. Just a moment of frustration until Chris figured out her next move.

"And please don't pout," said Lamar. "Not that."

"Then make me a manager."

"I'll make you a *deal*," said the coach. "Just relax and stop all . . . this . . ."

"This what?"

"All of it. You're driving me nuts," said Lamar. "And when you're a freshman, I think you'd be a great manager."

Chris shook her head. "I'll lose a whole year."

"Of what?"

"Getting better. I want to learn."

She got up and began jogging away. "See you tomorrow, Coach."

"Stop calling me—"

"Sorry . . ."

H ut! Hut! *Hut!*"

The football was snapped. Players violently collided. The quarterback got leveled just after releasing a perfect fade route to the back corner of the end zone. Couldn't blame that one on the defender.

A whistle. The head coach clapped hard a single time. "Now that's what I'm talking about!"

Behind him, two assistant coaches stood next to each other, looking in a different direction.

Odom canted his head and said out the side of his mouth, "Technically she's not on the grounds."

"What do I have to do?"

They continued watching Chris run laps around the outside of the fence.

Odom shook his head, "I don't think she's going to quit."

"You don't have to smile about it."

Practice ended. Everyone headed for the locker room. Almost everyone.

Lamar strolled toward the student parking lot. Chris came dashing around the corner of the fence, head down.

"Sorry, Coach, didn't mean to run into you."

"You win," said Lamar.

"Win what?"

"You can be a manager."

Big grin. "Really?" Jumping up and down now.

"And no jumping when you're manager," said Lamar. "You need to take this seriously. You need to be a help, not a distraction. Meet me in my office before practice tomorrow. And bring your last report card."

"You got it, Coach." She began jumping again.

Lamar turned toward the locker room. "I'm already regretting this."

Chapter 11

CENTRAL FLORIDA

The Plymouth Satellite blazed north through that rural swath of the state where you were never more than five minutes away from the ability to purchase marmalade.

Coleman looked down and found a Cheeto stuck to his shirt. "Ooooh, my lucky day." He popped it in his mouth. *Crunch, crunch.* "Serge, don't take this wrong, but a cemetery tour is kind of dull. Nothing's moving."

"Visiting these final resting places is in large part a pretext." The speedometer needle climbed as the muscle car raced down the orange center line of the two-lane road like a 1970s B-movie starring Steve McQueen. "The graves of people who lived life to the fullest are highly inspirational. They're the perfect place to reflect and remind yourself to never stop chasing your dreams."

"I had a cool dream last night," said Coleman.

"It's not that kind of dream."

"Wait, I want to tell you," said Coleman. "I was sleeping."

"That's usually when you dream."

"No, I mean I was sleeping *in* the dream," said Coleman. "Nothing happened."

Serge turned and stared curiously. Coleman was nodding to himself. "Much better than my nightmares. A few days ago I dreamed that I had a job and had to work all night in the dream and then I woke up tired. I hate that. What about you?"

"Okay, here's the thing I love about dreams." Serge took his hands off the wheel and rubbed them together. "You get to meet famous people throughout history. I've gotten to know Genghis Khan, General Custer, Joan of Arc, Tolstoy—who by the way was really long-winded—Galileo, Gandhi, Gershwin, the Marx Brothers, Richard the Lionhearted. But the high expectations can also lead to major disappointment. For some reason I have this recurring dream that I'm on a passenger train with Jesus, and it begins with him showing me magic tricks, like pulling quarters out of my ear, and I'm like, 'We get it. You're Jesus. Give it a rest.' And every time, before it's over, we somehow end up in a fistfight. But here's the weird part: He's the one who always starts the shit, poking me in the chest with a finger, over and over: 'What are you going to do about it? Huh? Big man? What have you got to say now?' And I tell him, 'Christ, this isn't like you.' And then he sucker-punches me! Who would ever see *that* coming?"

The Satellite sped on down the winding road. Vultures were picking apart an armadillo and took flight. Coleman cracked a can of Pabst. "You're driving pretty fast, even for you."

"Nobody could ever write a better job description for me: Florida, no appointments and a tank of gas," said Serge. "Haven't I mentioned this to you before?"

"Only about a gazillion times."

"Unfortunately, today we have an appointment." He checked his wrist. "And it's going to be close."

Serge gave it more gas, and the red needle in the dashboard climbed higher. Twenty minutes later, they skidded onto the shoulder of the road, next to a barbed-wire fence and bales of hay. Across the street, bells rang in a steeple as congregants poured out the front doors.

"How do you know what he looks like?" asked Coleman.

"I don't." Serge climbed out. "I can narrow it down with choir robes, but then it's just my gut."

They walked against the stream toward the front of the church. Most of the choir people were still up at the altar, stretching out their fellowship time.

"I think I see him," said Serge. "That young guy on the end of the second row."

"How do you know?"

"Most of the others are a bit older. And he just has that entitled shit-grin. It's got to be him."

"What's the plan?"

"Pull the car around back, then wait outside by the entrance."

Ten minutes later, the first of the choir began dribbling out and strolling down the walkway, checking with each other about their next practice time. Serge stood in the grass next to the path. Then, like someone who steps off a curb in front of a bus, he just ambled into the flow.

Crash.

A taller man grabbed Serge by the shoulders for balance. "Are you okay? Sorry, I didn't see you."

Serge had his head down. "No, it was all my fault. I apologize. I just have a lot on my mind." He raised his face and wiped Oscar-winning tears from his eyes.

"Hey, hey, hey, what's the matter?" said the man, holding a folded choir robe.

"It's nothing I need to bother you about." Then Serge covered his face and resumed sobbing. He parted two of his fingers to peek.

"Take as much time as you need." The man placed a hand on Serge's shoulder. "If your life's troubled, you're at the right place. We're all family here. I insist you allow me to help, brother."

Serge finally dropped his hands and sniffled. "It's my mother."

Alarm: "Her health? Is she okay?"

Serge nodded. "It's about money. She might lose her house."

"What? She can't afford the mortgage?"

"No, the house is completely paid for," said Serge. "It's just that between the insurance and all the rising monthly bills, her Social Security doesn't make it anymore. If she can't pay next month's property taxes, the county will seize her house, and she's been there fifty years." He kicked the ground in anger. "I feel so guilty!"

"Why? What did you do?"

"I'm not a good son." Serge wiped his nose on the back of his hand. "I'd pay the taxes myself, but I got laid off, and my own family is behind on everything."

"Then you're in luck."

"Why are you smiling?" asked Serge.

"Because this is my field of expertise. I handle real estate matters all the time." He held out a hand to shake. "My name's Nicholas. Call me Nick."

"Serge."

"Well, Serge, your problems are already behind you," said Nick, extending an arm all the way around his new buddy's shoulders. "I can easily structure something to get more than enough equity out of her house to take care of those taxes. Heck, she'll have so much left over that this time next month, she'll probably be waving bon voyage from a cruise ship."

"But how is that possible?"

"Not only is it possible, it's easy." Nick interlaced his fingers. "But it involves knowledge of how banking and real estate knit together. I'm always amazed at how much needless grief people are going through these days."

"It must have been God who made me bump into you."

"He works in mysterious ways," said Nick.

"You have no idea." Serge's head swiveled as he watched the last of the other people at the church drive away. "How do we do this?"

A hearty laugh. "See? You're already bouncing back . . . The first thing I need to do is take a look at your mother's house to gauge how it will appraise, then check some of her documents to make sure the title isn't clouded. Tell her to get ready to limbo in Cancún." Another laugh.

"I don't know how I can ever repay you," said Serge.

"No need to repay," said Nick. "At this church, it's what we do for each other in His name."

"Okay, when can we start?"

"How about right now? Let's go."

"Fantastic," said Serge.

Nick pointed at the only car in the otherwise empty parking lot. A late-model BMW sports coupe. The vanity plate read: WINNING. "That's mine." He reached in his pocket for a blue-and-white key fob.

"Mine's around back," said Serge.

"I'll follow you out to her place."

"Actually, I'd like to show you something first."

"What is it?"

"When I was going through Mom's papers on the house, I found these other files with financial accounts and securities certificates that I didn't know she had. And I also don't know what they mean. They're in my car. I was hoping maybe you could make heads or tails out of them."

Nick thinking: *Can this get any better?* He stuck the Beemer's keys back in his pocket. "I'd be more than happy to look at those files."

They walked around the rear of the church to the glowing gold Plymouth. Serge stuck a key in the back and popped the lid. Nicholas leaned toward the trunk. "Hmm, I don't see any files."

"Because there aren't any," said Serge.

"Huh? What's going on?"

"I didn't want to embarrass you in front of the others, so I waited until we could have a private little chat back here." Serge held out his hand. "A hundred and fifty thousand dollars, please."

Sincere confusion. "What are you talking about?"

"That's how much you stole from the couple up the road. I'm sure you remember the Whorleys. The Nantucket Whorleys?"

"Oh, now I get it." A smirk. "Yeah, I heard about that. Terrible tragedy. I honestly tried to help them, but they made some bad financial moves. Retirees really have to watch out these days."

Serge's hand remained extended. "I'm still waiting."

"For what?"

"The only mistake they made was trusting you," said Serge.

"Now wait a second," said Nick. "I've tried to be nice, and now you're accusing me? This is all on them. Sorry, but those are the breaks."

"I've seen a lot in my years and didn't think the bar of human behavior could drop any lower, but joining church choirs to exploit people's faith?" said Serge. "There's a little chestnut out there about a special place in hell."

"I've grown weary of you," said Nick. "Okay, say I did it. So what? In fact, now that you've pissed me off, I'm *glad* I did it."

"Then I guess there's nothing more to say."

"Yes, there is," said Nick. "Go fuck yourself!"

"In that case . . ." Serge lunged. "In you go!"

"Ahhhhhh!"

The trunk slammed shut.

FOUR YEARS EARLIER

A bottle of Johnnie Walker sat on a desk next to a cannonball. Captain Crack sat behind the desk drinking Scotch and fingering gold doubloons. He had gotten the taste, and it put the fangs in him. The nerve of those guys! How dare they point guns at *him*?

After much tortured moral gymnastics, Crack decided that it was the guys who'd found the ship who were in the wrong. He made the decision. He looked up at his two associates, sitting in wicker chairs against a wall under an antique harpoon and a stuffed wahoo.

"Suit up," said the captain. "We're going back out tonight."

"But what if they're there?"

Crack stood and grabbed the bottle by the neck. "I'm actually hoping they are . . ."

T he night was moonless, and the wind howled.

A black cigarette boat with all the running lights off skipped across the waves at top speed. There was an element of stealth, but the prime strategy was a blitz attack. Come in dark and fast before they knew it.

From distance surveillance, Crack knew all the divers were in the water, leaving a single hand on deck. And from experience, Crack knew that the person would be monitoring the divers and sonar screens. The black boat circled for a downwind approach to cloak the sound of their engines until the last moment, which was now. The deckhand heard the distinct noise a hundred yards out and lunged for a shotgun.

Seconds later, another standoff.

"It's three to one," said Crack. "Give us your shit."

"Go to hell!"

"Then we're coming aboard!"

"I'll shoot!"

"No, you won't."

Bang!

Crack's eyes widened. He quickly looked down at his chest. No blood. He looked up at the salvage boat. Nobody standing.

Crack peered down into the deck at the still body of the deck-hand. Then he shot glances side to side at his henchmen. "Who fired?"

"It was an accident. My finger slipped."

"Fuck it," said Crack. "I'll deal with you later. Let's get aboard and off-load their haul before the divers surface."

The gang efficiently began passing expensive baskets over the gunwales.

Naturally, the divers surfaced. "What the hell's going on? Get off our boat!"

"You're not in a bargaining position," said Crack. "I suggest you just swim away."

"Fuck you!" The first diver started climbing up the swim ladder.

"Screw this!" A henchman dropped his basket and grabbed a rifle. "I'm not going back to prison!"

"What's that mean?" said Crack.

"One dead in a robbery gets you the same as four. No witnesses!"

Bang!

So the others got into the act.

Bang! Bang! Bang! Bang! . . .

When the proverbial smoke cleared, three lifeless wet suits floated and bumped against the hulls of both boats.

"What do we do now?" asked the second henchman.

"What the hell do you think? Finish loading!" Crack went to the inboard motor station of the divers' boat, lifted a hatch and pulled the gas line free, liberally splashing the stern and port.

When they were all back in the cigarette boat and drifting away, Captain Crack pulled out a Zippo and patiently lit an entire roll of toilet paper. It was hurled into the salvage craft. A yellowish fire flickered at first. Then blue flames violently shot out from any vulnerable aperture before a fireball billowed into the sky. Crack threw the cigarette boat in gear and took off.

After a couple hundred yards: "Stop the boat! Stop the boat!"

Crack pulled the throttle all the way back, and the boat settled. "What is it?"

A henchman stretched out an arm. "Someone's coming!"

Crack grabbed night-vision binoculars, and all three crawled out onto the bow on their stomachs.

"What's going on?"

"Shhhhh!" Captain Crack focused the binoculars on a wayward shark fisherman named Remy Skillet as he arrived at the burning boat and poked around, then inexplicably began firing a gun at the already dead. "Unbelievable."

It became even more unbelievable as Remy turned his boat and, instead of motoring off in any number of logical directions, decided to come straight at them.

"Shit!"

The black cigarette boat bolted out of its path at the last moment, and the henchmen turned around just in time to see the physics of the spinning vessel.

"He got thrown overboard . . ."

Crack decided to set a course south, parallel to land, putting distance between his boat and the natural vector out to the murder scene. A few miles later, he cut the engine again and admired the far-off ribbon of lights defining Singer Island.

"Why are we stopping?" asked a henchman.

"To celebrate," said Crack, reaching into a watertight compartment for three glasses and the bottle of Johnnie Walker he had dragged along. "I was planning to celebrate anyway, though I didn't think it would be under these exact circumstances. We had a few bumps, but all in all a successful run tonight."

He handed out the glasses and poured several fingers of the Black Label in each.

"We really appreciate the opportunity," said the first henchman.

"Definitely," said the second, sniffing his drink before sipping.

Crack clinked his glass with theirs. "Congratulations! We're all rich men now."

The first henchmen sipped. "I could seriously get used to this."

Crack turned his back. "Then be quick about it." He faced them again.

One of the henchmen's hands opened, and a glass of Scotch shattered on the deck. "W-w-what's the shotgun for?"

"Do the math," said Crack. "Six dead is the same as four. No witnesses."

"But—"

Blam! Blam!

The henchmen toppled backward into the water.

Captain Crack Nasty set the gun down and picked up a glass. He calmly finished his drink and headed back to shore.

Chapter 12

NORTHEAST FLORIDA

A Plymouth Satellite raced north along the shore of a formidable river.

"You know what really separates the United States from the rest of the world?" asked Serge.

"Cowbell?"

"Soccer."

"How so?"

"We're the only country that gives such a small shit about it that we deliberately call it by the wrong name."

"I don't know," said Coleman. "I've heard of some pretty scary soccer riots."

"How scary can it be when the rioters are called hooligans?" said Serge. "Visit Philadelphia after any championship game and watch tipped-over police cars burning. And that's when they *win*.

Soccer, on the other hand, has no upside, other than our women's team."

"What do you mean?"

"A little while ago I read where the U.S. national team narrowly defeated the island of Martinique three-to-two," said Serge. "That's like barely beating a Sandals Resort."

"It's just embarrassing." *Belch.* Coleman looked out the window as a swamp gave way to vegetation that thickened and seemed to crowd the road. Pines, oaks, palmettos. Moss hung from branches in a canopy. "Where the hell are we?"

"On the William Bartram Scenic and Historic Highway just southwest of Jacksonville," said Serge. "We're in St. Johns County, named after that big river off to our left. I'll save you the details on Bartram. Okay, I won't. Born in 1739, Bartram was a groundbreaking naturalist known for his colorful drawings of birds and plants. In 1774, he entered Florida and sailed down the river, encountering alligators and Indians and otherwise exploring in a fashion that makes people want to put your name on street signs."

"I see one of the signs now."

"But Bartram is just the aperitif. The main course is still coming up." Serge snapped photos out the window. *Click, click, click.* "Man, I love this highway. The flora is so much different from the southern part of the state, much denser." *Click, click, click.* "Do you realize what's happening again? We're in danger of too much linear thought. We must rage against the machine!"

"I thought soccer was our exit ramp."

"True, true," said Serge. "But now the whole country is into tangents, whether they realize it or not, so we amp up our game!"

"The nation is into tangents?" Coleman's construction-paper robot was starting to fall apart from saliva. He reapplied the wacky eyes and took another double-clutch hit. "How so?"

"Comment threads!" Serge handed Coleman his smartphone. "I've already dialed one up for you. Go to any news site that invites reader comments at the end of stories and start reading. Doesn't matter what the story is about: a new high-altitude diet from the Andes, debt restructuring for the mathematically deranged, royal wedding gaffes in pictures through the years, why Selena Gomez is mum about one sexy topic. The article I just gave you is about a seven-state egg recall for salmonella."

"What am I looking at?"

"Just scroll down. It's like the threads for all the other stories. This one starts with comments about food safety and the FDA and communicating with school cafeterias. But inevitably . . . wait, wait . . . Here it comes! . . . Here it comes! . . ."

Coleman squinted at the tiny screen. "'Food is regulated more than assault rifles! . . . During a robbery do you want to be holding an egg or a gun? . . . It's all the orange president's fault! . . . Lock her up! . . . Snowflakes! . . . Republic-tards!' . . ." Coleman handed the phone back. "I had no idea it was that bad. How did this happen?"

"Technology outpaced our evolution," said Serge. "All of humanity falls along a spectrum of love to hate, and the people bunched up on the shitty end are now defined by too much spare time and keyboards. It happened once before when some pricks got hold of a Gutenberg press—'Bullshit on the Renaissance'— until calmer heads prevailed."

Thud, thud, thud.

Coleman spun around in pot paranoia. "What the hell was that?"

"Relax," said Serge. "Just the guy in the trunk."

"I remember now," said Coleman. "Clyde, who's mean to birdies."

"No, you idiot. We got rid of Clyde back on the beach in Fort Lauderdale," said Serge. "This is the new guy."

"Sorry," said Coleman. "There's so much traffic through your trunk that it's hard for me to keep the players straight."

"Me too," said Serge, pointing up at names written on a row of Post-it notes stuck to the sun visor.

The Plymouth dramatically slowed down as Serge scanned the side of the road.

"What are you doing?" asked Coleman.

"We just passed Cricket Hollow, so it's coming up."

"What is?"

Serge eased off the right side of the road and pointed at an easily missed piece of crooked, weathered wood with carved lettering: BELUTHAHATCHEE.

Coleman sucked his robot. "I still don't know where we are."

"Beluthahatchee is the name of the historic four-acre compound of preeminent Florida folklorist Stetson Kennedy. It's from the Miccosukee tongue, meaning Dark Water. I love it when I find these compounds, like Graceland without amphetamines and sequins."

Serge turned down a dirt road covered with brown leaves. "Stetson is one of my all-time heroes, traveling the state writing books and recording oral histories. He studied writing under Marjorie Kinnan Rawlings, worked on the Federal Writers Project with Zora Neale Hurston, and Woody Guthrie often slept on his couch. Coincidence? You make the call!"

"I say nope."

"Our tour is like the Kevin Bacon game of Florida with lots of dot-connecting that will become more evident as our odyssey continues."

Coleman stared out his window, catching glimpses of water between the trees. "Is there a cemetery around here or something?"

"It's like Mitzi the Dolphin, just a single resting place." Serge slowed as the narrow road curved through an untamed southern jungle. "After Stetson passed away in 2011, they scattered his ashes on the pond next to us, and Woody's son Arlo gave a concert."

Serge finally parked behind the old cedar barn of a home perched on piers over the edge of the water. "I love how Stetson let most of the compound continue to grow wild. But what I love more is that back in the 1950s, he infiltrated the Ku Klux

Klan. He wasn't working with law enforcement or anything, just thought it up and did it all by himself on spec."

"What balls," said Coleman.

"Then he passed what he'd learned over to the authorities and journalists. It was a difficult time in America, and Woody Guthrie was roaming the countryside with an acoustic guitar that had a sticker on it: 'This machine kills fascists.' Woody became quite controversial, and when he needed breaks, he began spending a lot of time at Stetson's to retreat from it all. He was even staying here the night a fire started in the woods and threatened the house, but they put it out. Then they found a note on the front gate from the Klan threatening Kennedy. Mind you, this was after a previous incident when Stetson came home to discover the interior destroyed and all his writings thrown in the water. Anyway, Guthrie was crashing on the couch at Beluthahatchee so much that this is where he finished his memoir, *Seeds of Man,* and composed more than eighty songs, including 'Beluthahatchee Bill,' about Stetson. That resulted in this place being named not once, but twice, as a national literary landmark, for both Woody and Stetson. That's beyond exciting. Think of it, *two times*!"

"I remember when you got all excited after having two orgasms in a row and put that number two NASCAR racing sign on your driver's door."

"It's close, but I think this is bigger." Serge stared wistfully out across the water. "I'm on an urgent quest for the high-water marks of letters in this fine state."

"How come?"

"It's necessary," said Serge. "The state's literary laurels are a needed counterbalance to our recent cultural reputation."

"Which is?"

"Florida Man."

"Oh, yeah," said Coleman. "That maniac who's raising hell all over the place."

"Coleman, it's not just one dude. It's a whole army."

"Really? I thought he was just ambitious."

Serge shook his head. "The entire nation is into the embarrassing craze of Googling 'Florida Man' and seeing what pops up. Last year there was a spike in guys pooping in unpopular locations and contexts. This year they're getting naked."

"Naked?"

Serge pulled out his smartphone again, pressing buttons to enter search terms. "Check out these headlines: 'Naked Florida Man Eats Noodles and Plays Bongos at St. Petersburg Restaurant,' 'Naked Florida Man Rides Bicycle through Interstate 95 Traffic,' 'Naked Florida Man Chases Customers around Chick-Fil-A Parking Lot,' 'Naked Florida Man Continues Gardening Despite Pleas from Neighbors.'"

"But, Serge, how is it possible to fight that?"

"The answer is the written word," said Serge. "Let's just sit here quietly for a moment and take in the tranquillity as Stetson and Woody would have—"

Thud, thud, thud . . .

Serge closed his eyes for a long pause, then opened them. "Wait here."

Coleman turned around to see the trunk open.

Wham, wham, wham . . .

The lid closed and Serge got back in the driver's seat. "Where were we?"

"Tranquillity."

"Right," said Serge. "Here's my favorite impression of this place. When I was here for Stetson's memorial service—"

"Wait a second," said Coleman. "When you mentioned that before, I thought you read it somewhere."

"Nope, here in the flesh," said Serge. "How could anyone living in Florida at the time miss it? But I guess twenty million found some bogus excuse. Moving on: The best moment celebrating

Stetson's life came just before they went down to the pond to spread his ashes, when all those in attendance sang 'This Land Is Your Land.' Can you imagine the emotion?"

"Not me," said Coleman. "Are you about to cry?"

Serge wiped his eyes. "Just a little pollen." He pulled out a tissue and blew his nose. "Okay, I'm busted. It is getting to me a little . . . Mind if we sit until I compose myself—"

Thud, thud, thud . . .

Serge looked down to his lap, then over at Coleman without speaking.

"What?"

Thud, thud, thud . . .

Serge threw up his hands. "I can't live like this. I'm trying to have a private moment of reflection. But no . . ." He pointed back over his shoulder with his thumb. "Some people are so inconsiderate. Do *I* go around bothering people like that?"

"Not from where I'm sitting." Coleman looked down at two handfuls of soggy, falling-apart chunks of construction paper. "My robot's fucked up."

Serge twisted the key in the ignition and the Plymouth came to life.

"Where to now?" asked Coleman. He looked over his shoulder at the trunk. "I mean, I know we're going to have to stop at a motel first, but after that."

"The next visit really is a cemetery." Serge blew his nose a final time and stowed the Kleenex in an anti-litterbug bag hanging from his door. "It's the state's connective tissue I was telling you about. We just picked up the trail with Rawlings back near Cross Creek, now Stetson off Bartram Trail, and the rest of the stops will soon start falling like dominoes, as if actual planning was involved."

Thud, thud, thud . . .

"I forgot what that guy in the trunk did," said Coleman, picking paper off his tongue. "Not that I'm questioning your judgment."

"You were fading in and out back at the church," said Serge. "I'll refresh you on the way to the motel."

"Ready when you are." Coleman was about to toss damp kindergarten paper out the window.

"Stop! Hand it to me for the litter bag."

"Oops, my bad." Coleman passed the trash. "You're always thinking of others."

Thud, thud, thud . . .

"Sometimes even when I don't want to."

Chapter 13

Coaches led the team running out of the locker room for another day of torture in the Florida sun. The managers brought up the rear with sacks of balls and tees, ankle tape, first-aid kits. Everyone arrived on the field to find the newest manager already there, sitting quietly on the bench along the sideline, proudly wearing a new Pahokee Blue Devils T-shirt that Coach Calhoun had given her, now the nicest item in her wardrobe. In front of her, coolers of water and Gatorade were already in place. Paper cups arranged neatly in rows. She had kind of arrived early.

An afternoon of athletic violence and exhaustion wore on. Chris was Johnny-on-the-spot, dutifully keeping the paper cups filled, dashing on and off the field with water bottles and towels, and quickly volunteering for any errand. The reaction of the team was varied. Most didn't notice, others didn't care, the rest were amused.

Weeks went by. Chris kept her word. She didn't say a peep, didn't get in the way, just did her job. Players almost started taking it for granted that whenever they needed something from one of the managers, Chris was just right there in front of them, like a mind reader.

On a recent afternoon, the players didn't gather on the field for practice. It was a conditioning day, no pads or helmets. And it involved something else that made the kids from The Muck just that much tougher.

The Herbert Hoover Dike.

The dike was constructed in response to the hurricane of 1928, stretching 143 miles around Lake Okeechobee to contain the water in case of another deadly strike. From the outside, all that could be seen was an earthen berm rising thirty feet.

The players hated that damn dike.

At some forgotten point in the school's history, a coach was driving by the dike and got an idea. It was walking distance from Pahokee High. Make that running distance. And now, this afternoon, players grunted and cursed under their breath as they ran up it and down, fighting for footing, slipping, getting back up.

Chris kept her mouth zipped but kept glancing at Coach Calhoun. He could see her from the corner of his eye, knew what was in her head. Since it wasn't a contact practice, what the heck? He turned. "Go ahead."

"Thanks, Coach." She took off and headed up the dike.

The other players didn't have the luxury to react. They were too busy with the pain in their legs and lungs. But a few did wonder: *Who* wants *to run the dike?*

The receivers coach stepped up next to Calhoun. "She's faster than I thought. Practically keeping up with the boys."

"Told me she chases rabbits."

"Mm-hmm, one of those," said Odom.

Chris raced to the bottom of the dike, touched the ground and began sprinting back up.

The head coach blew a whistle. "Now backward!"

A chorus of quiet groans, then slow backpedaling and more suffering on the berm. A few repetitions of that and another whistle. "Now crab-walk . . ."

Chris got that burning in her calves but didn't quit.

Fifteen minutes later: "All right, bring it in!"

The players staggered down the hill like refugees, and Chris ran around with the water bottles.

The following day's practice was back in the friendly confines of the high school field.

Halfway through, one of the safeties came over to the coolers. Chris recognized him from the rabbit hunts. She held out a paper cup. He stumbled and bumped it, spilling the Gatorade on her T-shirt. *Accidentally.*

Coach Calhoun happened to notice, but it didn't register.

During the next break, the same player trotted off the field to the coolers. In a voice nobody else could hear: "Girls don't run the dike." Then he had another accident, bumping into her hard before running back onto the field. Chris crashed into the table with the paper cups.

This time Calhoun didn't dismiss it. He took a step forward. He felt a hand on his arm. It was Reggie, his first-string halfback. "I got this one, Coach." He put his helmet back on and ran out to the huddle.

Four plays later in the scrimmage, Reggie's number was called and a perfect block off-tackle broke him into the clear. Only one safety to beat. It was open field, which called for a cut, then easily outrunning him for the sideline.

Reggie cut, and the safety reacted. Then something happened that the safety never expected. Reggie cut again, this time the other way, straight *at* the safety.

Reggie caught him running sideways, trying to twist back, and plowed right through him—lifting him off the ground and dropping him on his ribs—before trotting into the end zone. On his way back to the sideline, Reggie bumped into the safety from behind. "Don't mess with Chris."

Practice eventually ended as they all did. Players wrung out beyond what they imagined they could endure. They headed for the locker room.

Chris ran after one of the boys. "Hey, Reggie, thanks!"

"For what?"

"You know, out there."

"I don't know what you're talking about."

"Can I ask you a question?"

"You just did."

"Can you teach me to cut?"

"To what?"

"Cut. You're the best! All-state first team from last year and sure to repeat!"

"Why do you want to learn to cut?"

"I'm going to be a running back."

A chuckle. "Okay, I'll play along. I'll teach you to cut."

"Great!" Chris stopped walking.

Reggie looked at her oddly. "You mean *now*?"

Eager nodding.

"Why not? . . ."

Coach Calhoun finished the day and locked up his office. He grabbed his briefcase and headed out of the locker room for the parking lot. The field was empty. Except for two people in the distance on the far sideline. He stopped and stared. Could it get any stranger?

"Okay, stand here," said Reggie. "You're a cornerback or safety."

"You got it."

"Now, here's the mistake most backs commit." He tucked a ball in the crook of an arm. "They have to make a defender miss an open-field tackle, so they juke or shake-and-bake"—Reggie shuffled his feet quickly in the same spot—"trying to fake him out. The problem is that the runner is waiting to react to how the *defender* will react. That's way too much time."

"So what do you do?"

"Totally commit. You plan your cut ahead of time and take it no matter what the defender does."

"What if he doesn't bite?" asked Chris.

"Then you're tackled."

"Doesn't seem like a good plan."

"It does if you're good at geometry."

"I like math."

"Then you'll understand this. We'll take it in slow motion." Reggie backed up twenty yards and shouted: "We're coming straight at each other." He took a single deliberate step. "So now I begin a slow turn to the right, toward the sideline. And you're going to follow." They each took two steps in unison. "The closer you get, the more I increase my angle until I'm almost running east–west."

"But that gives the defender the angle to run you out of bounds."

"And that's the whole key to selling your fake. You make it too good to be true. You run into their strength, which makes *them* commit." More slow, tandem steps. "Now you're just about on me, and I make my cut . . ." He sped back up and dashed by.

"Cool," said Chris.

"Unreal," said Coach Calhoun in the distance, and he walked to his car.

C oach Calhoun sat in his office going over the playbook for that Friday's game.

Knock knock.

He looked up. "Chris, come on in. Have a seat."

"Thanks, Coach."

"I have to admit, this is working out a lot better than I'd expected. And as for your report card . . ." He leaned back in a creaky chair. "I'll confess that part of the reason I did this was to hold the manager thing over your head to improve your grades, but they're already straight A's. I didn't know you were that smart."

Chris shrugged. "I like school."

"So what can I do for you today?"

"I need a favor. And I hate to ask, because of what you've already done for me . . ."

"Go ahead. You've earned it."

"I kind of need to borrow a football."

"Knowing you, I thought you'd have ten footballs."

"Not really."

"You can't afford a football?"

She looked at the floor. The answer was worse. Certain neighborhood boys always stole them.

The coach got up and went to a bookshelf and grabbed a ball off a stand. He returned and tossed it over his desk to Chris.

She caught it and noticed writing on the side in white letters: LAMAR CALHOUN, a date from the eighties and 216 YARDS. Chris looked up. "I can't accept this."

Lamar just smiled and looked down at his playbook. "Anything else?"

"Uh, actually there is one other thing . . ."

I t was a coaches-only meeting.

Calhoun and Odom arrived early.

The field was empty save for a tiny person at the far end. A ball was kicked. It landed pitifully short and left of the goalposts. The person ran after the ball, then ran back. The process was repeated with the same results.

"Where'd she get a kicking tee?" asked Odom.

"I gave her one."

"So now you're a kicking coach, too?"

"She wants to be a running back."

"How does this lead to that?"

"She said she read articles where a few girls in other parts of the country are now playing on boys' teams," said Calhoun. "I made the mistake of pointing out that those were kickers."

"So she's exploiting a loophole?"

They stared a few more minutes at sheer futile relentlessness. Then they went inside for the meeting. It was a marathon: rosters, films, discussion of college recruitment visits, and most importantly, the game plan for Friday. Their opponent was big on zone defense and double-teaming their best receivers, so they decided to rush between the tackles until it opened up the passing game. The agenda ran so long that it was night when they adjourned.

Calhoun and Odom were chatting about auto maintenance as they headed to the parking lot. They heard something near the far end zone. To them, the sound was unmistakable. A football being kicked.

"She still out there?" said Odom.

"I don't know," said Calhoun. "I can't see her."

"She's kicking in complete darkness."

"Maybe her eyes have adjusted."

They stopped and listened to a few more kicks.

"Something about kids like that," said Odom. "I've only known a few, but they're easy to spot."

"What do you mean?"

Odom faintly watched her tee up again, and miss again, and run after the stray ball again. "There's a big emptiness in there somewhere."

Chapter 14

COCOA BEACH

A gold Plymouth sat in a parking space. The sign on the motel roof was a rocket ship. A broken ice machine stood next to the dumpster.

Serge dragged a chair across the mauve carpet of room number 7.

A belch from the bathroom. Coleman emerged guzzling a bottle of Boone's Farm, then bites of jerky. "What are you doing?"

Serge was sitting with his face a few inches from the TV tube. "Ruining my eyes."

Coleman glanced at the screen. "Another protest march?"

"The new women's movement," said Serge. "I'm forcing it on myself."

"Why?"

"Because I'm embarrassed by my gender." Serge's eyes followed the sign-waving parade. "I'm in total solidarity with everything the protesters stand for. But something has become increasing clear to me: Because I'm a man, I'm not reminded fifty times a day of the shit women are expected to put up with. And I thought I was worldly-wise."

"You're not?"

"Until now, my experience has been limited to witnessing the cliché construction workers catcalling to the fairer sex. But I figured Darwin already had that one covered. I mean, when in the course of human history has that ever worked? Some woman in a business suit is hurrying down the sidewalk, and suddenly a guy in a hard hat starts whistling and making slurping sounds and yelling, 'Give me some of that *pussy*!' . . . And the woman stops in her tracks: 'Hold on a minute. I've got my priorities all screwed up. Forget that big board meeting I'm heading to. Why yes, I will give him pussy.'"

"That's pretty bad," said Coleman. "And you're saying it's even worse?"

"Way worse." Serge inched closer to the TV. "My mistake is that all these years, I've been projecting. In other words, if some notion can't remotely enter my head, I figured other guys were the same. And if it wasn't for newspapers, I never would have imagined that all across the country, men are just pulling out their dicks in unwelcome settings."

"Really?"

"And I'm not talking about Sterno bums or bowery flashers. I'm referring to wealthy, famous, powerful men who are supposedly educated. It's happening in hallways, elevators, during innocuous conversations in hospitality suites."

"It's just not right," said Coleman.

"You'd think this would go without saying, but as a general rule of thumb, if you're chatting with some woman you've just met, your best foot forward isn't to start spanking the monkey."

"That's obvious even to me," said Coleman. "I get embarrassed if there's a cat in the room."

"Speaking of cats in the room . . ."

Serge turned toward yet another motel room chair with a bound and gagged guest, wedged away in the far corner.

"He's been so quiet that I completely forgot about him," said Coleman. He covered his own face with a hand. "I'm so embarrassed."

"Why?"

"When you left me here and went to the store," said Coleman. "I think he saw me."

"Saw you? Doing what? . . . Wait, don't answer that. I think I'm getting the picture."

"I made some noises, too."

"For the love of God, please stop! It's going to be hard enough getting the image out of my head without audio as well." Serge walked over to the hostage. "I think you traumatized him. They may be naming a new syndrome after you."

He ripped duct tape off the mouth. "Sorry about my friend," said Serge. "That should be more than enough punishment for you, but I don't make the rules."

"Please let me go! I did everything you asked!" Whimpering. "I went to the bank with you and got a certified check for those people . . ."

Serge held up a driver's license. "What's wrong with Malcolm Reynolds Greely? Much better than Tyler or Nicholas."

"How many times do I have to say I'm sorry?"

"Yeah, but you don't mean it." Serge tossed the license in the trash and taped the captive's mouth shut again. He grabbed a shopping bag off the dresser.

Coleman came over. "Is that what you bought at the store while I was—"

"Shut up! The image was almost gone." Serge walked over and dumped the bag on the bed.

"What's that stuff?" asked Coleman.

"Everything I need for my next science project."

Coleman picked up each item in turn. "A barber's electric razor, cheese grater, box of small trash bags and . . . I don't recognize this thing."

"It's a time lock." Serge picked up the razor. "A lot like a regular padlock, but you can set the timer to open it at a preordained point in the future."

"This isn't much stuff," said Coleman. "Usually your projects are a lot more complicated."

"It'll be more than enough."

"So what's the timer for anyway?"

"I've fallen into a rut," said Serge. "Different day, same shit. Into the trunk, out of the trunk, into the chair, duct tape, blah, blah, blah . . . But even though this started out predictable, I'm throwing in a twist at the end so nobody can say I was snoozing at the wheel."

"You're just being responsible."

Serge walked over to Malcolm and held up the razor. "A little off the top? . . . Ha! Ha! Ha! . . . Just kidding. Actually a lot off the top."

"Mmmmmmm! Mmmmmmm!"

Serge flicked on the razor and placed it at the back of Malcolm's head just above the neck. He pushed the device upward and deep. Huge clumps of hair fell off the front of the razor as it continued over the top of the captive's scalp, right down the middle, until it reached the edge of his forehead.

Serge turned off the razor. "There you go. I hear reverse mohawks are coming into style." Next he grabbed the cheese grater. "I'd be lying if I said this won't hurt . . . Coleman, grab a towel and come here!" He placed the grater where he'd just shaved and began rubbing.

"Mmmmmm! Mmmmmm!"

"Pipe down," said Serge. "I'm only using the extra-fine side."

Coleman arrived with the towel. "Here you go . . . Jesus, he's bleeding."

"Just a few scrapes." He tossed the grater on one of the beds and applied the towel. "Coleman, hold this in place while I go out to the car."

Serge ran out the door.

Coleman bent down to the captive's face and whispered. "Malcolm, is it? Listen, what you saw earlier? I'd really appreciate it if we could keep that between you and me. If it ever got back to my mom—"

Serge returned. "What are you talking about?"

"Nothin'."

Serge placed a clear rectangle on the bed.

"Hey, I remember that," said Coleman. "It's the storage bin you were putting bacon strips in down on Big Pine Key."

"And it worked. You can let go of the towel."

Coleman joined Serge as they crouched down and peered through the side of the bin.

"It's a bunch of flies."

"*Cochliomyia hominivorax,*" said Serge. "Otherwise known as the dreaded screw worm flies that recently plagued the Florida Keys."

"Most of them are dead on the bottom."

"That was inevitable," said Serge. "But there are enough left to do the trick. They have a twenty-day life cycle under ideal conditions."

"How did you know that bacon would lure them into the bin?"

"Read it in a medical journal." Serge ripped open the box of plastic garbage bags. "As I said before, sometimes the best cure is to go low-tech. In the rare cases where screw worms attack humans, doctors use bacon, because the larvae are more attracted to that than human flesh, and the parasites unscrew themselves from their hosts. All completely true: Type 'bacon therapy' into any search engine."

Serge opened one of the trash bags, inflated it with air and fit it over the storage bin. "This is the tricky part. I'll hold the mouth of the bag in place, and you carefully pop the lid and slide it out from underneath."

It went off without a hitch, and Serge shook the bin until enough of the flies took flight into the bag. "Coleman, slide the lid back on."

Serge cinched the mouth of the sack and strolled over to Malcolm.

"Mmmmm?"

"You must be getting pretty confused about now." Serge carefully fit the bag's opening over the top of Malcolm's head. "Coleman! Duct tape!"

"Coming right up."

Several strips were wrapped around Malcolm's forehead, sealing the bag in place. "It's not your fault you don't know what's going on. You simply don't have the scientific background. So I'll tell you a little story . . ."

He did, explaining all about the gruesome infestation in the Keys, right up to: ". . . And I used a cheese grater to mimic lesions when those little deer have antler fights. That's pretty much it."

"Mmmmmmm! Mmmmmmm!"

"Why so glum?" said Serge. "I always give my contestants a bonus round and a chance to survive."

A tap on his shoulder.

"What is it, Coleman?"

"Uh, hate to mention this, but you didn't give the seagull guy a bonus round."

"Of course I did."

Coleman shook his head.

Serge pondered; then: "Damn! . . . I'll just have to make it up to Malcolm to balance my karma account . . . Malcolm, did you hear that? Another jerk's loss is your gain. I'm adjusting the time lock in your favor." He knelt behind the chair. "What you're feeling is me refitting your wrist restraints so the lock will free your hands in, say, three days?"

"Mmmmmm! Mmmmmm!"

"You're going to get pretty hungry, but the key is hydration, so I'll get you some sports bottles and stick the tubes through the tape. Just remember to conserve." Serge hopped and clapped. "And most important of all, when the time lock opens and the bonus round begins, what do you need to do?"

"Mmmmmm! Mmmmmm!"

"That's right!" Serge said with a widening grin. "Find bacon!"

Chapter 15

FOUR YEARS EARLIER

A stuffed wahoo stared down from the office wall with glassy eyes.

Captain Crack Nasty tilted his head to consider the fish. Then he considered his career position. That shootout on the high seas the previous night wasn't exactly tailored for the long game. He glanced at the bottle of Johnnie Walker on his desk and stuck it in a bottom drawer: *Last time I make business decisions on that stuff.*

Overall, though, Nasty viewed the evening a huge success, even if it was a one-timer. He'd recovered a serious amount of treasure, and he didn't have to split it with anyone. Then there was that ugly violence. Crack hadn't known this about himself before. But he liked it.

Now it was just a matter of tweaking his corporate model. Minimize risk. Captain Crack opened another drawer in his desk and pulled out an empty notebook. He turned on his computer. He had decided to do something quite unnatural to him: homework.

He found a number of wreck sites that weren't exactly inactive. The original salvagers still had valid claims. It was just that they had reached diminishing returns, and the locations were being worked more sporadically. Also, Crack began employing a spotter boat, on the off chance that the claim holders picked the wrong day to come back. He employed more care in selecting his associates, more stable, reliable, less trigger-happy. The bottom line: Take it slow and there could be a long future.

His new crew began doing quite well at five sites from Cape Canaveral to Port Salerno and Hobe Sound, never staying too long, never taking too much at once. Treasure would still be there when they came back, as they did, time after time, until there were only a few items in the bottom of a single dive basket. Then on to the next location.

But there were only so many sites off Florida—even dormant ones—that could produce any decent yield, especially if you had to dart in and out like thieves in the night. That meant even more homework for the good captain. And a funny thing happened. He began to find the research interesting, even enjoyable. The history of maritime trade routes back to the Old World, the life and times of sailors on the galleons, all the unnamed and forgotten hurricanes.

Captain Crack pored over notes he had recently scribbled. Of particular interest was a bit of treasure folklore that didn't have any foundation in the official records. Which meant virgin territory. He was intrigued at the prospect of his first legitimate find . . .

The sun had just gone down when he was interrupted by a knock on his office door. "You wanted to see me?"

"Yes, yes, come in."

It was one of his newest hires, a former marijuana bale loader released from Raiford. Went by Corky.

"What's up?"

"Follow me, Corky." He led him down the dock, making a mental note to hammer down some of the rusty nails that were popping up. They arrived at a black boat. "Climb in. We got work."

"Okay." Corky jumped aboard and looked around. "Where are the other guys?"

"Just us." Crack untied the bowline from a mooring cleat. "No diving. Only recon to GPS a potential wreck with sonar . . ."

Since there wouldn't be any violation of a claimed site, there was no need for speed. Crack motored unhurriedly out to sea, sipping coffee and Scotch. He became quite chatty. It was a new development ever since he'd gotten the research bug, and the crew was getting used to it, in a negative way. They rolled their eyes at all the boring knowledge that Crack now spouted. But only behind his back.

"Corky, you wouldn't believe what I've been researching. Potentially my first legitimate find. It's fascinating!"

"Really?" Corky concealed a sigh. "Tell me about it."

"Our work is inextricably entwined with hurricanes and their storm surges that sent doomed ships down off our coasts." The captain adjusted his course bearing. "Corky, did you know there was a hurricane in 1928 that had a storm surge unlike any other?"

"I can't say that I did."

Crack nodded earnestly. "The surge didn't come from the ocean, but from Lake Okeechobee, producing a tidal wave that wiped out entire neighborhoods of fieldworkers. Then I stumbled upon a wild coincidence. I began hearing about a folktale circulating to this day out at the lake. A treasure was lost in the hurricane! Some sugar baron supposedly squirreled away a fortune. When the storm hit, it took him, his house and whatever he was saving, and decades of farming have since covered up all traces. But to this day, it's said that children playing out in the sugarcane fields occasionally come across an old gold coin. Can you imagine it? An *inland* storm surge producing an *inland* wreck?"

"Wow," Corky said with feigned enthusiasm. "So you're going to go after it?"

Crack sagged slightly. "More homework first. I don't know anything about this sugar baron, which is the key to narrowing the search to a specific location." He cut the engine.

Corky looked over the side as the quiet boat rolled mildly in the swells. "We're here?"

"Yes, we are."

Corky climbed over gear on the deck. "I'll start checking the sonar."

"I've got something I want to show you first."

"What is it?"

"See this tube on the side of the shore radio?" asked Crack.

"Yeah, but I still don't know what I'm looking at."

"It's a pinhole video lens. Covers the whole boat from here on back, kind of like a nanny cam."

"I'm not following," said a bored Corky.

Crack reached down into bow storage and pulled something out. "Now do you follow?"

Corky was no longer bored. He'd had guns pointed at him before, but a twelve-gauge always dials it up to eleven.

"What's going on, Captain?"

"I'm sure you have a pretty damn good idea." Crack gestured with the end of the gun. "That tiny camera was filming every time you stuffed shit in your pockets when we came up from a site. Have I not treated you well? And then you steal from *me*? Don't even try to lie. I could show you the tapes, but I don't care about your opinion."

Corky silently reviewed options.

The captain racked the shotgun with the distinct sound that is a natural stool softener.

"Wait! Wait! Wait!" Corky began babbling. "I just took a little. I was going to give it back. I had car troubles. The electric bill. I was drunk. My girlfriend needed braces—"

Blam!

Corky hit the water and bobbed, well, like a cork.

"That was fun." Crack throttled back up toward land. "Now to do some homework on this sugar baron . . ."

MR. FAKAKTA

Sugarcane is actually a grass.

A grass that changed the march of history in the New World.

It can't entirely be attributed to rum, but that's a good start. During the colonial period, from the Caribbean to the South American coast surrounding French Guyana, farming took off due to the region's conducive blend of climate and rich soil. Bananas, coffee beans, nutmeg, rice, cocoa. But when they started using sugarcane to make molasses, which was shipped north to rum distilleries, sugar took the lead and never looked back.

Jamaica, Trinidad, Barbados, Belize, Cuba, Guadalupe. Plow that other stuff under, boys, and plant that cane. The cash flowed in, but at a price. Brutal conditions in a brutal business, cutthroat competition and politics.

On the island of Hispaniola, in the Dominican Republic, there was a particularly heated rivalry among the four chief growers in the early twentieth century. And it wasn't gentlemanly. Threats, vandalism, workers attacked and maimed. Alliances shifted back and forth like on one of those survival reality-TV shows, until one of the four growers was voted off the island.

Fulgencio Salvador Fakakta drew the short straw. But it was impossible to feel sorry for him. Fakakta was one of those rare comeuppance cases where the bad guy actually lost. He had bribed, cheated, stolen and even murdered his way to wealth and power. And now it had come full circle. In short, the other growers were just tired of this asshole.

Fakakta saw it coming, and it wasn't going to be a polite eviction notice. If he was lucky, they'd burn his plantation home, seize everything he had down to the last penny, and allow him to escape with the shirt on his back. If he was lucky. So Fakakta quietly and quickly liquidated everything into gold, which was all crated up one night and packed onto a chartered ship.

"What's in these crates? Rocks?"

"Shut up and keep loading!"

Fulgencio set sail. The other growers still burned his place to the ground, but at least he had enough for a new start.

Besides the Caribbean, there was one other place where sugarcane had just started to catch hold.

Florida.

It would be years before the crop asserted dominance, so for now, a fugitive sugar baron from the Dominican could affordably buy up bean fields around Lake Okeechobee to plant his stalks.

Fakakta had the experience and ruthlessness to make it work, and soon he was one of the wealthier farmers in the lake region. It wasn't enough. He began stealing from his workers. Docking pay for non-reasons, overcharging for rent on their ridiculous shanties and the food he required that they buy from him as a condition of employment. Then he realized there were far more people looking for work than there were jobs. Can't let that equation go to waste. So he took it up a notch and started not paying some workers entirely. Of course they'd yell and argue and quit. But what else were they going to do? He was white. He'd just hire more guys.

But one particular worker, named Jacob, wouldn't let it go. He kept demanding his money, day after day. Finally, Jacob went out to Fakakta's stately colonial plantation house on the edge of town and pounded on the front door. The next morning he was found hanging from a prominent cypress tree with signs of torture. It was meant to be obvious, unlike the other missing workers, who were never found. The white law didn't care, and everyone else got the message. Fakakta continued amassing his fortune, which he kept in gold. But nobody knew where.

Chapter 16

COCOA BEACH

Malcolm sat quietly in his chair.

Serge and Coleman sat quietly at a table.

Malcolm's eyes stared up at the plastic bag taped to his head. "Mmmmmmm! Mmmmmmm!"

Serge and Coleman wore plain white T-shirts. Open bottles of various colors were scattered across the table. Stains representing the same colors covered their shirts. Coleman leaned over and rubbed feverishly. "I'd completely forgotten about finger painting."

"Finger painting is the best!" Serge made a blue circle with his thumb. "I don't know why society cuts that off after kindergarten. I had dreams of becoming a world-class finger-paint artist. Huge gallery openings in SoHo, the toast of Paris. Then I found out it was just some bullshit to keep us busy until recess. It was the beginning of the counterculture, and that's when I started seeing through all the lies. Finger painting, Vietnam."

"This is excellent when you're high."

Serge looked across the table. "Not bad. You're painting a pumpkin."

"It's a bong," said Coleman. "What are you painting?"

"An egret." Serge chugged a mug of coffee, then stood up and grabbed the page. He taped it to a wall.

"Why are you doing that?"

"Because this motel room has no artwork. We got screwed." He straightened his egret and sat back down. "All motel rooms are supposed to have artwork. But sadly, most guests never notice. You ask ten people what the painting was in the room they stayed in last night, and dollars to doughnuts none will have a clue. Not me! It's the first thing I look for when I open the door!"

"Why?"

"Reminds me of baseball cards, because you never know what you'll get." Serge grabbed a fresh page and resumed work. "I'd buy a pack of cards at the five-and-dime and then sit on the curb out front, gently and affectionately removing each card to reveal surprise after surprise: 'Cool, Carl Yastrzemski. Cookie Rojas, not bad. Do I already have Rollie Fingers? It says on the back of Félix Millán's card that he led the National League in triples. Who the fuck is Buzz Capra?'... Same thing with motel paintings, especially budget motels. You go to a fancy *hotel* and get high-quality art that makes sense, following the room's color scheme and local milieu. But the economy joints are the best, especially the kind with old wood paneling. They don't give a shit anymore and buy stuff from art-clearance warehouses that sell paintings by the pound. You're always in for a treat, so when I first arrive at a room, I stop outside and let the anticipation build, like holding that shiny new pack of sports cards. Then I quickly open the door and pump a fist in the air. 'Yes! Sailboats!' I can still see them to this day."

"You remember the sailboats?"

"I remember all the paintings!" said Serge. "The sailboats, a beach scene of three children playing with pails on the sand and each pail was a different primary color, a vase with sunflowers, a cherry pie on a windowsill overlooking corn, magpies on a power line, a train station when they still had baggage porters, a bowl of fruit, a cowboy leaning against a post, a lighthouse in Maine, a terrier, President Coolidge . . ."

"How do you recall all that?"

"Because I care." Serge dipped a finger in the green bottle while swigging coffee with the other hand. "If people don't watch out, there can be a lot of needless tedium in motel rooms by squandering spare time. But I rarely encounter that problem because I want to squeeze every second out of life. Even if I don't have spare time in a room, I'll *make* time, sitting in a chair staring relentlessly at the wall and metaphysically contemplating all aspects of the painting. What were the headlines of the day when it was created? How many people have straightened it on the wall? Who painted it and why? What about the backstories of the people on the sailboats? I imagine the painting hanging steadily and all-knowing in here since the mid-twentieth century, during poker games, extramarital affairs, kids jumping on beds, someone repeatedly peeking out the window, salesmen with straw hats from a plumbing supply convention, a coroner wheeling out the victim of a heart attack that everyone saw coming. Then I envision a woman at an easel in 1953 who decided to broaden her background of dependable typing skills by taking a mail-order art class, only to have her husband leave her for a Pan Am stewardess, and now she paints just to forget but has never been to the beach. And the little people on one of the sailboats are a family of six from Knoxville who take the same vacation every year to Myrtle Beach, where they always line up the children for an annual photo to document their growth, which after three decades will become the subject of a feel-good magazine article. But what are their political beliefs? How would they view the woman who painted them? Do they even know they're in a painting? These are questions for the ages." He raised his mug. "I'm out of coffee."

Malcolm heard buzzing in the bag taped to his head.

"Mmmmmm! Mmmmmm!"

Serge walked over to the captive. The trash bag had all but deflated on his head, and Serge held it upright and shook, giving the flies renewed space to work. He pointed at a page on the wall. "If you're bored, you can look at my egret and ask metaphysical questions."

He returned to his table and paint.

Coleman leaned toward his friend's new page. "What's this one?"

"Great blue heron." Serge got up and placed it on the wall.

Coleman noticed there was now a long row of overlapping finger paintings along the side of the room. "Serge, what are you doing?"

"Making a mural to compensate for this motel room's lost time without art." Serge aimed a yellow finger at Malcolm. "This science project requires an extended duration of babysitting, so a mural is the only way to go. The room's next guests will seriously get their money's worth."

"Why so long?" asked Coleman. "Can't we just leave him like the others?"

Serge shook his head and drew cattails with a finger. "I'll need to remove the bag and dispose of the remaining flies or I could be responsible for some kind of outbreak from breaching the Keys quarantine. It's the right thing to do."

"What kind of mural?"

"In full disclosure, it's not original." He sat down with another page. "I'm inspired by one of Florida's finest and most enduring works of art. While the state has a wealth of fine galleries, my favorite native painting of all time adorns the lounge of a historic erstwhile grande dame of accommodations in a small town on the southern shore of Lake Okeechobee."

"Mmmmmm! Mmmmmm!"

Coleman packed his alligator honey bottle. Puff, puff. "Even our hostage is into this now. Please tell us more."

"Unlike other swank hotels of bygone eras such as the Breakers or Biltmore, this place is now a bargain. But not because it's hit the skids. Far from it. In another freak of *Freakonomics,* the glory days faded and revenue dropped. But then an interesting thing happened. The place remained just popular enough to create a Goldilocks effect, not overheating or cooling off. Instead, it remains strangely suspended in time as a freeze-frame snapshot of the past. It's so quiet and peaceful that you're often the only person in the opulent period lobby, like staying in a museum."

"But, Serge, what is this fabulous place?"

"The Clewiston Inn, built 1938 by U.S. Sugar in Classic Revival architecture with stately white columns out front, now in the National Register of Historic Sites. It's unexpected to find one of Florida's most impressive hotels in such a modest community, almost nothing but miles of agricultural fields in all directions. The Everglades Bar and Lounge itself remains essentially closed because of lack of traffic, but the management is hospitable enough to open it up upon request for guests to bring their own beverages and food and sit just to enjoy the mural. That gets my five-star rating for dedication to heritage."

"But what about this mural?"

"Commissioned in the early 1940s and painted by J. Clinton Shepherd, director of the Norton Gallery and School of Art over on the coast. I can't tell you how many field trips my classes took to the Norton when I was a kid. And there are countless exquisite features that make the mural stand out from all the pretenders. First, it's not a traditional mural that stretches out straight, but instead wraps three hundred and sixty degrees around the whole lounge.

Also, the mural itself is a panorama of the Everglades, depicting a full menu of its wild inhabitants, from alligators, raccoons, deer and turtles to ibis, ducks and storks. Shepherd prepared for the task by making frequent excursions to the Glades to sketch his wildlife subjects. Then he began painting—and this is the funky part—not on the walls of the bar, but back in his gallery in West Palm Beach. He set up a series of separate, massive canvas panels and, along with his students, went to work with his brushes. When it was complete, they transported it all through empty acres of sugarcane fields until reaching the inn, where they permanently assembled it. But wait! There's more! In the hallway leading to the lounge hangs a row of gold-framed black-and-white photos showing the mural in progress back on the coast. That bonus material alone is so overwhelming that it's easy for visitors to get dizzy and knock over chairs. Actually, that was just me."

"Plus it's a bar," said Coleman.

"Normally I'd smack you, but in this case you're right," said Serge. "No snooty gallery patrons standing back and rubbing their chins in a passive-aggressive jab that you're a Philistine. Just a bunch of regular folk who know what they love."

Coleman crumpled a beer can. "I dig art." A fat finger made a red line on paper.

"Then your big chance is at hand, because the inn's upcoming on our tour." Serge walked over and taped another page to the wall. "Meantime, I'm going to keep working until my paintings encircle this entire room in homage to Shepherd and the hotel."

"But do we have enough time?"

Serge strolled over behind Malcolm. "The time lock says definitely." He raised the drooping bag again over his contestant's head. Buzzing increased.

He rejoined Coleman again at the table. "But I do need to pick up the pace." His index finger mixed red and white paint for a roseate spoonbill. His other hand clicked the television's remote.

"Excellent! I love it when you turn on a motel TV and *Law & Order* is automatically rolling through a marathon! It's like a sign from God."

"Why are you so into that show?"

"Because it's a comedy. Or at least the chase scenes are."

"How's that?"

"The writers apparently spend so much time on the genius of the legal twists that they just backhand the action sequences into the script."

"For instance?"

"If I've seen it once, I've seen it a hundred times: Lenny goes to question a suspect at an automotive garage and flashes his badge at the boss. 'Is Frenchy here?' And the boss turns to some guy repairing a car up on a lift: 'Hey, Frenchy, the cops want to talk to you.' So the guy now has this data: The cops know his name, where he works, and most likely his home address. And what's the logical thing he does every time? Throws a wrench at them and runs out the back. Okay, first, that's a serious uphill explanation to your boss later. Although I don't know the auto repair culture. Maybe everyone's constantly throwing tools and running away, and after lunch they all have a big laugh. Anyway, they always catch Frenchy trying to climb a fence or cornering himself on a rooftop. To mix it up, sometimes it's a loading dock at a shipping company. 'Hey, Three-Fingers Louie, the police are here again.' And they catch Louie every time because he runs into a huge stack of empty cardboard boxes that are placed right where everyone walks."

"How do you know they're empty?"

"The way they fly like they're filled with helium," said Serge. "Let's watch."

They turned toward the TV.

"Hey, Bugsy, the police want to talk ..."

"There goes the wrench," said Coleman. "He's running ... damn, cardboard boxes *and* a fence."

"I called it."

Coleman pointed with a purple finger. "Where's the science project at?"

Serge swirled his own finger on a page. "The screws have definitely begun anchoring, just a matter of reaching their depth."

"Mmmmmm! Mmmmmm!"

Serge sat back and sighed. "Am I the only one he's annoying?"

"No. He's getting under my skin, too."

They leaned over the table again and continued painting in silence . . .

The next morning, Serge shook Coleman's shoulder. Bloodshot eyes cracked open as he sat up and bonked his head. "Ow! Where am I?"

"Between the toilet and sink again." Serge checked his watch. "Look alive, we have miles ahead."

They went back into the main room.

"Damn, you really did finish your mural," said Coleman. "There's even a wild turkey. I recognize it from the bottles."

"You had any doubts?"

"Don't take this the wrong way, but sometimes you get super excited and throw yourself into a really long project, and five minutes later you say fuck that and trash everything and take off in the car with your camera."

"You're thinking of the time I wanted to build an exquisitely detailed cardboard model from my own design of the old Orange Bowl during Super Bowl Three in Miami, complete with the Jets and Colts players and each person in the stands. I misjudged the seating capacity."

"What was the seating?"

"Eighty thousand."

"How many seats did you make before you quit?"

"Five. But let's not dwell on setbacks beyond our control." Serge stood behind Malcolm, carefully peeling the tape off his forehead and gathering up the edges of the plastic garbage bag.

At the first glimpse of the captive's head, Serge sprang backward. "Jesus!"

"Mmmmmm! Mmmmmm!"

"Can I see?" asked Coleman.

"It'll give you bad dreams."

Coleman looked anyway. "God-*daaaaaamn*! . . . Man, this is you at your sickest."

"Not my intention. I underestimated the gross-out factor." Serge tied off the plastic trash bag and threw it in a motel garbage can. "Oh, well. I'll just think about that retired couple he tried to swindle and it'll balance the scales . . . Get your luggage."

Coleman grabbed a handle. "He doesn't look like he feels so hot."

Serge opened the motel room door and turned to the hostage one last time. "Remember: Bacon, it's not just for breakfast anymore."

Chapter 17

Friday. Game day.

After school, Coach Calhoun was at his desk finishing up notes on the opponent's defensive line.

A light knock at the door. "You wanted to see me, Coach?"

"Yes, yes, come in."

Chris respectfully took a seat, and Calhoun walked around his desk, leaning casually against its front edge, just as he had during so many other player discussions. Like most of the coaches in The Muck, he knew that football was often the only anchor in these kids' lives. A whistle hanging from your neck meant serving double duty as a priest.

"Chris, other than your report cards, I realize I really don't know anything about you. What's your family like?"

"You mean my grandmother?"

"I mean your whole family."

"It's my grandmother."

"What about your dad?"

"I don't know."

"Mom?"

"I don't know."

"Brothers and sisters?"

She shook her head.

"How old is your grandmother?"

"Old."

"Friends?"

"A few. Mainly boys. All the girls where I live are much older."

"Where do you live?"

She told him. He knew the place. One of those long two-story apartment buildings that looked like a converted motel, because it was. Not a blade of landscaping, just hot dirt and litter. People coming and going at odd hours for wrong reasons.

Calhoun took stock. "You said you had a few friends?"

"Mainly at school. Actually all."

"So what do you do for fun when you're at home?"

"I like to read."

"Like what?"

That got her bubbly. "Oh, wow, I found this great book at the library." She unzipped the backpack in her lap and handed a volume to the coach.

He examined the front cover. "What's this?"

"Astrophysics."

"You're reading about the big bang?"

"It's the foundation for everything. You have to learn that if you're going to study anything else." Chris grew animated with excitement. "Most people don't realize that the bang wasn't an explosion but actually an expansion of space and time, like a balloon inflating, which allowed early matter to exceed the speed of light without violating Einstein's theory."

The coach blinked hard and flipped the book over to the back cover. "You actually understand this stuff?"

"Sure, the author breaks it all down and makes it real easy."

Calhoun handed the book back. "Chris, I know this might be sensitive, but . . . are you okay?"

"What do you mean?"

"Well, I mean, for example, have you ever been bullied?"

Excitement stopped. Chris folded in . . .

I f you've ever had a full handful of sand thrown directly in your eyes at point-blank range, it's something you'll never forget. It's not like you've *got* something in your eyes that you have to get out; you're totally shut down. Disabled in every way. Nose running. The insane pain from the first time you try to raise your eyelids. The only option is to stagger and grope blindly for a place with a water source to flush it out.

It helps if there's someone to guide you. It doesn't help if there's only cruel laughter as you stumble for safety that isn't available. Especially if the nearest water source is a canal full of alligators.

It was one of her earliest recollections. Followed by the sound of a rusty old pickup truck speeding away on a dirt road from another rabbit hunt. Then quiet. Chris felt along with her feet to locate the edge of the road, then down the embankment into the reeds. Fortunately there were no gators today. Chris splashed her face until she could manage to open two red slits and find her way back to town.

The public health clinic gave her prescription ointment for scratched corneas.

"Who did this to you?" asked the nurse.

"I did it to myself."

There were the other times. *All* the other times. It never involved sand again, but you get the picture. Some of the boys actually felt sorry for her and knew it would be the right thing to step in, but they lacked that certain gravitas in the pecking order, and so life went on as it does in the jungle of childhood.

One time that was different. A new mix of boys in the pickup truck. Before long she was facedown again between cane stalks, a large boy pinning her with knees in her back, twisting her right arm almost to the point of a radial fracture. Chris prayed for him to let go, but she never screamed.

Then, suddenly, her arm was free. And the weight was off her back.

"Dammit, Reggie! Why'd you punch me in the head?"

"What's wrong with you? She's half your size."

"Fuck off!" The tormentor ran away.

Chris rolled over in the dirt, and the boy named Reggie helped her up. "Maybe you shouldn't come out here with these guys."

"I want to play football."

That was the last day Reggie was with her group, and then it was back to old routines again. At least she did catch the occasional rabbit, which meant a buck or two toward her football fund. Chris had bought a number of footballs in her short life. Sometimes she was able to play with one for two or three days before it was gone. A football was too precious for Chris to forget and leave somewhere. It was just snatched from her hands. One ball was even stolen as she stepped out of the store where she bought it. She stopped buying footballs and started sitting.

Chris would sit on a milk crate on the balcony outside her grandmother's apartment. Elbows on her knees, chin resting on her fists. She stared out into the empty street with eyes that were lasers of rage. She was one of the happiest kids you'd ever meet, which meant other kids had to make her sad. An hour could easily go by with Chris not moving, eyes locked in that fierce gaze. But it wasn't a gaze of negativity that eats you alive from the inside. It was a look of ferocious, distilled determination. She began sitting out there so often and so long that many adults in the apartment building began subconsciously associating her with that milk crate.

She usually sat on the crate after being run off from whatever the neighborhood boys were having fun doing. The few girls who were around were much older, with their own social castes and more subtle ways of hurting. Chris just kept sitting and glaring with such intensity you'd think she was going to hemorrhage. What was she thinking about all that time?

When Chris wasn't sitting on that crate or getting run off, she spent time in her room, tending curiosity. That meant books from the school library. She loved the science ones. Volcanoes, the planets, how clouds form, photosynthesis. But her all-time favorite was a book about sea creatures. The only thing she knew from Pahokee was Lake Okeechobee and all the bass fishermen, because it was fresh water. But this book brimmed with gripping pictures that filled her imagination with the faraway world of the ocean. Urchins and rays and giant squid. She was particularly fascinated by every detail in the life cycle of the hermit crab. Then there was another book she had purchased, one with holes in it. A collector's book. She would press pennies into the holes according to year, and read voraciously about the mints in Denver and San Francisco, and the wartime pennies made of zinc because artillery shells needed the copper.

But a child like Chris was meant to be outdoors, which meant she was relentless at trying to join in and being run off and sitting on a crate. Here's what she was thinking on that crate: *I'll show them. Someday they'll want to be my friend. They all will . . .* Of course she was just a little kid and only had so much life experience to work with, so she thought: *Yes, something urgent will come up with the boys. Suddenly they'll all need really important information about hermit crabs or Lincoln pennies, and then where will they have to come? That's right, me . . .* She maintained her severe glare of tunnel vision, fantasizing about all the kids in the neighborhood coming up the street in a V formation, led by the biggest and most popular. They'd climb up to her apartment balcony and beg forgiveness, and she'd tell them about crustaceans or loose change or both.

Adults weren't the only ones who observed Chris's devotion to that milk crate. Some of the boys also began to notice. They pointed up at the balcony and laughed. Then it became a running joke. Whenever she tried to hang out and participate in whatever they were doing: "Why don't you go home to your milk crate?"

It began following her around, even when she wasn't trying to join in. She'd be walking down the sidewalk and then shouts from across the street, in a shitty, singsong taunting chant: "Milk *crate* . . . Milk *crate* . . ."

Then they took it further, and it became her nickname. "Where are you going, *Milk Crate*?"

It only made Chris stomp her feet harder on the way home. Ironically, her main source of solace and strength became sitting on that crate. So sit she did. *One day! . . . One day! . . .*

Then one day Chris came home from school and found that someone had stolen her milk crate.

C hris? Chris?" said Coach Calhoun. "Did you hear me? Have you ever been bullied?"

"Huh, what?" She raised her chin from her fists. "I'm sorry. I drifted there for a second."

"I was asking about bullies."

"Oh no. Not really."

"I've never seen a look like that in your eyes before," said Calhoun. "You almost scared me."

"Just tired."

"I heard they call you Milk Crate, not out of affection. And they stole yours."

"No big deal. I got another."

"Okay, if you say so . . . We need to start getting ready for the game."

"You got it, Coach." Chris went to a storage locker for the paper cups.

The game went pretty much as expected, a rout by Pahokee. Reggie was awarded the game ball.

An hour later, the last of the team dribbled out of the locker room in street clothes, laughing and recounting key plays that now loomed larger in their imaginations. Coach Calhoun emerged and headed for his car.

He stopped. The field and stands were empty now, just a single small person at the far end repeatedly trying to kick a football through the uprights.

One of the field maintenance people walked past the coach, opened the main power box and threw a large circuit breaker, turning off the stadium lights. Chris just teed up again and kicked one in the dark.

"Excuse me," Calhoun said to the maintenance guy. "Could you turn the lights back on?"

Chapter 18

THE ATLANTIC COAST

Florida has a lot of cities and towns with *fort* in the name. Given everything else, why not?

Fort Lauderdale, Fort Myers, Fort Meade, Fort Lonesome, Fort White, Fort Walton Beach. Tampa used to be Fort Brooke, and Ocala was Fort King. And there are more than a hundred other well-known actual forts, many still in existence, for which communities are not named. As late as the early twentieth century, the Sunshine State was still frontier country. While people in Manhattan attended operas and Yankee games, many Floridians were, well, Seminoles, the unconquered people, living down in the Glades.

A gold Plymouth Satellite revved south down coastal Highway A1A, through one of the last long, relatively empty and nonberserk stretches of Florida seaside where you can hear yourself think, and that voice is whispering not to take it for granted. Driving by Patrick Air Force Base, through Indialantic, Melbourne Beach, Sebastian Inlet, Wabasso Beach, past the Navy SEAL Museum before turning inland at the jetties.

Into Fort Pierce.

The city is located on the east coast of Florida about sixty miles north of West Palm Beach, named after the army fort built during the Second Seminole War in 1938, which in turn was named for Colonel Benjamin Pierce, brother of the fourteenth president of the United States, for what that's worth. Fort Pierce is the home of the A. E. Backus Gallery, in honor of the famous natural-landscape artist, and birthplace of the Florida Highwaymen painters movement. But in more recent years, as more and more people discover the past, it's developed a growing reputation for something else.

Zora Neale Hurston was a black woman traveling Florida in the 1930s. Not the best time for that combination in the Jim Crow South. Yet she carried it off with such class and dignity that you can only genuflect. She was a novelist, historian, anthropologist and a standout in the Harlem Renaissance scene. Or that's how one avid Floridian put it.

"Stetson Kennedy was often at the wheel of the car," said Serge, at the wheel of the gold Plymouth heading west on Avenue D. "The state's connective tissue I spoke of earlier. Rawlings to Stetson to Zora. She roamed the back roads with him, preserving local history and chronicling her times, kind of like us."

The Plymouth turned north as Serge chugged a travel mug of coffee. "Zora is often associated with Eatonville, one of the first self-governing African American communities, which used to be north of Orlando, and is now engulfed by it. They have a festival for her each year." The car continued a short distance until easing to a stop at 1734 Avenue I. "But Hurston spent her last years here." An arm pointed.

Coleman looked oddly out the window. "That tiny-ass house?"

"Realtors prefer to call it cozy." Serge got out of the car with his mug. "While Zora was well known and respected in literary circles, her body of work never really gained traction with the general public until well after her death in 1960. In fact, Zora lived out her last decade in destitute obscurity. She taught briefly at a local school, wrote a few articles for the local paper, even worked as a motel maid. But her undaunted pride and individual spirit never waned. Near the end she wrote: 'I have made phenomenal growth as a creative artist . . . If I die without money, somebody will bury me.'"

They walked across a tidy lawn toward a modest light blue stucco house with a flat roof. Couldn't be more than five hundred square feet.

"This was her last home." Serge stopped to absorb invisible rays coming off it. "Sometimes history puts the right person at the right place at the right time. Just after Hurston died, a sheriff's deputy named Pat Duval happened to be driving by here when he noticed someone burning trash in a big oil drum. He stopped to inquire, and the man said he was disposing of stuff from the house. Now, the deputy happened to be one of the few people at the time who had read Hurston and knew her worth. He quickly put out the fire, saving invaluable manuscripts and personal papers. Doesn't that spin your derby?"

Coleman was paying attention to something else. "What's with that big sign?"

"Official marker for the house, stop number three of eight on the Hurston Dust Tracks Heritage Trail," said Serge. "The city of Fort Pierce rightfully stepped up to honor Hurston and educate the masses, which I'm totally down with."

"Then why that look on your face?"

Serge finished his coffee in a long swig. "I like to dig up these off-the-path places on my own, and the sign makes it look like I cheated. But I knew about this place before the sign, I swear!" He grabbed Coleman by the front of his shirt. "After I'm gone, you're the only one who can set the record straight!"

"Sure thing," said Coleman. "My shirt . . ."

"Sorry." Serge released him. "Do you think I'm over-reacting?"

"Who am I to judge?"

"I've been thinking of getting a service animal," said Serge. "Or switching to decaf."

"Service animal?" said Coleman. "You're not disabled."

"Oh, how wrong you are," said Serge. "I'm crazy, whack job, nut-bar, basketcase, Looney Tunes, Froot Loops, cuckoo for Cocoa Puffs, screws loose, not playing with a full deck, batshit, bats in the belfry, off my rocker, off the deep end, out where the buses don't run. Stop me when I've made my point."

"No, I get it. I already knew but didn't want to say anything." Coleman whistled. "Wow, you're really admitting that to yourself?"

"Of course. What's the big deal?" Serge got out his camera. "Everyone's a little bit crazy, but my case is state-of-the-art. Usually it's a blessing, endowing me with supernatural powers of free-range thinking: Pavlov's dog, pinecones, softer bath tissue, covalent molecules, Pyrrhic victories, Lou Gehrig, nuance, the induction cooktop, the Yalta Conference, rationalization, pasteurization, Lou Gehrig's *disease,* Lemon Pledge, the number fifty-six, 'Jailhouse Rock,' opening products to void warranty, Hot Pockets, rainfall at the airport, Aztec beating hearts, osmosis, buy-one-get-one, frequent having to go, Netflix original series . . ."

Coleman crushed another beer can. "What about the rest of the time?"

". . . Hydraulic fluid, *Portnoy's Complaint,* the camel's nose under the tent, vote motherfucker! . . . What?"

"The rest of the time?" said Coleman. "When it's not a blessing?"

"Then there's screaming and pointing, and we have to run away again."

"I don't see how a service animal can fix that."

"When you say service animal, most people think of a guide dog leading the blind or performing other essential tasks for the handicapped." Serge handed his camera to Coleman. "But there's a whole other sub-category called 'emotional support animals,' who take the edge off mental conditions. Except that when you're dealing with crazy, you get the kind of animal selections you'd expect. And you wouldn't believe the growing list that is now confounding the transportation industry: from tiny pigs and iguanas to parrots and even boa constrictors, who are said to be able to detect certain seizures in advance and give a little warning squeeze. Other times the squeeze is a different warning—'Get this fucking snake off me!'—so there's an obvious downside. Even some *animals* have support animals. Thoroughbred horse breeders often place a donkey in a stall if one of their studs has a history of spazzing out."

"That's weird."

"I'm thinking of getting a meerkat."

"You mean those cute little guys on nature shows who stand up to look for trouble?"

Serge nodded. "A meerkat could level me out." He walked to the front of the house and smiled. "Take my picture at Zora's. Make sure not to get the sign . . ."

MEANWHILE . . .

In a Cocoa Beach motel room: a ticking sound, then a loud snap.

Malcolm frantically pulled his wrists free from the time lock. He felt the top of his head. *"Ahhhhhhhhh!"*

He ran out of the motel room and into the office.

The jaundiced manager jumped back from the counter. "Ahhhhhh! What happened to your head? . . ."

Ten minutes later, the motel parking lot swarmed with police vehicles. In the motel office, someone pulled a sheet over a body. The officer in charge looked up. "What the hell happened?"

The motel manager shrugged. "He came in here demanding bacon and then collapsed."

An officer stuck his head in the door. "Lieutenant, I think there's something you need to see."

They rushed up the walkway and entered room number 7. The officer nodded toward a wall.

"Finger paintings?" said the lieutenant.

"I recognize it," said the officer. "The Everglades mural from the Clewiston Inn. The lounge is closed now, but they're really nice about letting guests in. You should go."

The lieutenant glared. "I thought you had some key evidence." He pointed in the general direction of the office. "What's wrong with you? There's a body getting cold back there."

The officer told the lieutenant to take a closer look at one of the paintings.

He did.

It was signed by the artist.

Chapter 19

FOUR YEARS EARLIER

A faithful stuffed wahoo with glazed eyes stared down from an office wall at a man cradling the receiver of a desk phone between his shoulder and neck. That left his hands free to take vigorous notes.

"Thank you very much for your time." He hung up.

After that final international call to a Dominican Republic historical society, Captain Crack Nasty had everything he could possibly find on one Fulgencio Fakakta, right up until he fled the island in 1921. After that, the years in Florida were still a mystery that phone calls couldn't solve. From here, it was in-person homework.

Time for a road trip.

Crack climbed into the cab of his Dodge Dakota pickup and headed west on Southern Boulevard. He left the outskirts of coastal development, passing the vintage Lion Country Safari roadside attraction, subconsciously thinking, *How old are those animals?* Then onward through Twentymile Bend, all the way out to where the first fumes of development picked up again as he neared the big lake. The road's name changed to Hooker Highway. The schoolkids got a kick out of that.

The captain started at the Pahokee and Belle Glade libraries, looking through special collections of old newspaper microfilms. He drove past the hurricane monument on the way over to the courthouses for records of faded deeds. He cruised the back roads around the addresses he had jotted down. Then he widened his circles of driving out into the nearest sugarcane fields. He picked up a tail. Not law enforcement, but local young men in their twenties. He thought: *What has gone insane in this world when blacks are allowed to follow whites in the Deep South?* Except his surveillance wasn't threatening; it was concerned. The three youths were watching out for their neighbors because Crack's movements around town came off like he was planning some kind of crime. Which was accurate.

The salvager was more than relieved when he reached his next stop, the local police department. Crack asked to speak with their public-affairs spokesman, and was led into an office with a football in a display case on the desk. The captain said he was writing for one of those metal-detector hobby magazines, and he wanted to ask about some rumors he'd been hearing.

"Oh, so that's why you've been driving around here all suspicious like," said the sergeant.

"You know I've been driving around?" said Crack. "Then I need to tell you there were these dangerous characters following me."

"How do you think we found out you were driving around?" said the sergeant. "The guys following you called us on their cell phones. And they're not dangerous; they used to play on the football team. They just thought you were up to something. Are you?"

"Me? What? Huh?" Crack displayed upturned palms. "Just working on my article. I heard some folklore about a sugar king-pin who supposedly went missing in the 1928 hurricane, along with some artifacts of historical significance and maybe a couple coins."

"I've heard the same." The sergeant smiled. "And that's exactly what that is. Folklore."

"But I also heard that children playing out in the sugarcane fields have found a few of these coins over the decades since the storm."

"Another bit of fanciful folklore," said the sergeant. "In all the years, we haven't known a single actual child who found any-thing. And do you think little kids can keep something like that a secret? They'd bring it to school and show it all around in class, and by the end of the day it would be confiscated by a teacher for depriving others of their education."

"But I've learned so much about the history of this sugar guy from the Dominican that it seems more likely—"

The sergeant held up a hand. "My advice to you? And I mean this politely: Forget about your article. We've got a nice friendly town here, and we mean to keep it that way. Visitors are always welcome, especially all those college football scouts. But what we don't need is a bunch of people running around like headless chickens with metal detectors, trespassing and digging up the whole place. Do you see how it could get messy?"

"Well, it also won't do my magazine's reputation any good if we direct people here and nobody finds anything." Captain Crack stood and stretched. "Not all of these article ideas pan out. Guess I'll just be getting back to West Palm."

"You seem like a reasonable person," said the sergeant. He shook Crack's hand. "Stop in anytime."

Crack left the office, and the sergeant picked up the phone. "I need you to follow someone . . . Yeah, Dodge Dakota with a mag-netic sign on the door for a boat-towing service . . ."

Captain Crack tapped the steering wheel to a country music tune about only being able to trust his dog anymore. The pickup truck passed vacant concrete buildings of pink, green and blue. He checked his rearview. Just as he thought. A police tail. But it was a loose one, not meant for strict surveillance as much as making sure he kept his word to leave town.

A few minutes later, Highway 98 said goodbye to the last building, and Crack left the city limits. He looked up in the mirror again, and watched the police car make a lazy U-turn in the road and head the other way. The captain drove another half mile through nothing but cane fields, then made a sharp left onto a road usually used only by the sugar company. After a few zigzags, he navigated a wide route back into town. He deliberately parked out of sight behind a small business near Main Street.

Bells jingled.

A pawnshop owner named Webber looked up from a newspaper. *Finally,* he thought. Not a kid, not police, but a real customer. He folded the paper. "How can I help you?"

"Gold pieces."

"Only have a few." Webber opened the back of a glass display case. "But a real nice one came in a few years ago. Just haven't been able to sell it because, well, the economy around here. Saint-Gaudens double eagle, 1907. If you don't know, it's one of the—"

"I know the coin," said Crack. "How'd you come by it in these parts?"

"I'm sorry, but that information is confidential." Webber set the coin on the counter for Crack to examine. "We strictly protect the privacy of all our customers."

"It was a kid, wasn't it?"

The pawnshop owner's head jerked up straight on his neck. "How'd you know?"

"Been doing my research. I'll bet you've had a number of kids bring these in over the years. What can you tell me about them?"

The owner stepped back with hands on his hips. "Mister, what's really your business here? You didn't come to buy a coin."

Crack opened his wallet. "How much?"

"You're really going to buy it? You haven't even looked at—. . . I mean I usually have to work harder for a sale." He glanced at the gold circle still sitting on the counter. "In that condition it books for . . ."—Webber adjusted the number upward in his head mid-sentence—". . . seventeen hundred."

Crack pulled money from the billfold. "Would you settle for, say, two thousand? In cash."

Webber scratched the top of his head. "You sure have a funny way of negotiating."

"There's a catch."

"That, I assumed."

"I'll also need the name and address of the person who sold it to you."

Webber paused again. "So you really believe kids are bringing these coins in?"

"Sure, why not?"

"Because the police think I'm fencing stolen collections."

"That's because they haven't done their homework. Do you know anything about an early sugar baron around here named Fulgencio Fakakta?"

"Everyone's heard the stories," said Webber. "Especially the part about his hidden treasure lost in the Great Hurricane . . . Wait, you're not looking for . . ."

"I never said anything about treasure. You did." Crack leaned down to the counter. "Why? You don't believe that these kids found pieces of the baron's stash?"

"Not really," said Webber. "As I was telling the cops, from the dates on these coins, that's when there were all these juke joints—"

"I've read up on the local history," said Crack. "The name and the coin? Do we have a deal?"

Webber considered the stranger a moment, then began writing on a blank sheet of paper.

"On second thought," said Captain Crack, pulling out more bills. "Make it an even three thousand."

"Another catch?"

"I was never here."

Webber handed him the paper. "You're already a ghost."

"One more thing." Crack gave him a business card. "If any other kids come in here with more coins, call me and I'll buy them. Same price and terms."

"You got it."

Bells jingled.

Chapter 20

FORT PIERCE

The gold Plymouth Satellite rolled up to the corner of Avenue S and Seventeenth Street. Serge got out and looked at another sign.

GARDEN OF HEAVENLY REST.

For a cemetery, it was sparsely populated. No big monuments or even large headstones. The rows of modest markers and slabs were widely separated in an otherwise sunny grass field where kids would have room to play ball. Coleman looked side to side as they walked past graves. "I'm guessing you have a cool story to drag me out here."

"One of the best stories yet!" Serge continued on until they reached the middle of the field. A single grave sat in the grass, surrounded by a small brick walkway. The whitewashed slab was raised slightly higher than the others, although the headstone was still only knee-high. It was the only one where people had been by recently to leave flowers. There was a candle. Some had left rocks on the headstone in the Jewish tradition.

Serge got down on a knee and placed his page over the letter Z. He began rubbing. "Hurston's undeserved obscurity had become so complete that her grave was unmarked for years and nobody could precisely pay their respects. Then the story takes a hairpin turn, extending beyond the grave to Zora's proper place in the public's awareness."

"It was only right," said Coleman.

"The year? Nineteen seventy-three. The person? Alice Walker." Serge rubbed on. "Walker was still nearly a decade away from writing her Pulitzer Prize–winning novel, *The Color Purple*. But back in the early seventies, the budding writer, still only twenty-nine years old, stumbled across Zora's works and became intrigued, even obsessed to the point of visiting Florida to get the vibes of Zora's life. She started in Eatonville, where she learned Zora was buried anonymously somewhere in Fort Pierce. So she drove out here to the coast and—this part I love—she fibbed that she was Zora's niece to get locals to open up about her 'aunt.' To her surprise, most had never heard of her, even those now living near Zora's last home. Finally, with a history-researching tenacity to which I can only aspire, she located the lost grave and bought this headstone for it." Serge began rubbing the words on the next line: A GENIUS OF THE SOUTH. "Two years later, Walker wrote a watershed article for *Ms.* magazine, 'Looking for Zora,' using her grave search as a vehicle to showcase the forgotten literary lion. That first-person piece slowly but surely rekindled interest in Hurston's work until she now stands in the pantheon. Oh, and she's from Florida!"

The gold Plymouth left the cemetery and headed south on U.S. 1, down through Jensen Beach and Stuart.

"Where to now?" asked Coleman.

"Our next stop," said Serge. "But first I need to make a *stop* before our next stop."

He pulled into a strip mall and opened the door.

"I'll wait in the car," said Coleman.

"As a general rule, that's the best plan." Serge went inside . . .

Coleman was unconscious when Serge returned, head resting against the passenger window and trademark drool stringing down from his lower lip.

Onward, south. Hobe Sound, Tequesta, Jupiter.

Coleman stirred from his liquid-induced nap. "Hmm, huh, where am I?"

"Still in the car."

Coleman reached down between his legs and popped a Schlitz to restore chemical equilibrium. "Did you get your meerkat back at that pet store?"

"No," said Serge, racing south into Juno Beach. "I didn't have any clue that they're like a thousand bucks, and they'd have to order one. Plus the pet-store guy told me that meerkats may be social creatures among themselves, but they're a little confused by the whole pet concept. Some never conform to domesticity, constantly screeching and jumping on lamps, and the ones that do work out will keep peeing on your clothes to mark you as their owner."

"That's messed up," said Coleman.

"Not exactly the definition of a support animal," said Serge. "I want a pet to wind me *down*."

"You'll figure something out." Coleman took a long swig of beer. Suddenly: "Ahh! Shit! What the hell?" The can of Schlitz went up in the air, Coleman batting and bobbling to catch it, foam everywhere.

"Are you spraying beer all over my car again?"

"Not my fault." Coleman finally got a handle on the can and pulled his neck way back in alarm, looking down in his lap in terror. "What the fuck is that thing?"

Serge glanced over. "Say hello to Mr. Zippy, my new ferret."

"Ferret?"

"When a meerkat became a non-starter, the pet-store dude suggested a ferret because they're roughly the same size and cuteness factor, easier on the wallet, and they don't pee on you. Not much."

The ferret began chattering at Coleman. "Get him off me! Get him off!" Beer flew again.

"You're frightening Zippy!" said Serge. "You need to win him over. Give him that Cheeto."

"Where?"

"Where else."

"Oh." Coleman picked it off his shoulder and tentatively extended a hand. Mr. Zippy snatched it, munching away. Then he climbed over the shoulder of a wide-eyed Coleman. "Where'd he go?"

"To explore the back seat."

"You're just going to let him run loose in the car?"

"It's what I'd want if the roles were reversed," said Serge. "Now back to live action! Our next stop is some more Florida connective tissue, this time leading from Hurston. In her now-acclaimed 1937 classic, *Their Eyes Were Watching God,* Zora depicts the hard life of African Americans along the southern shore of Lake Okeechobee early last century, culminating with the Great Hurricane of 1928—"

The ferret jumped on the dashboard and ran along the windshield, then jumped down and disappeared again.

"Jesus, Serge, how can you drive with that going on?"

"It's actually quite comforting." A calm grin crept across his face. "After the storm, Zora described the formidable task of dealing with almost three thousand bodies, so many that it took at least four burial sites . . ."

The Plymouth entered West Palm Beach and navigated south on Tamarind Avenue, into an economically scuffling section of the city, or, among the whites, the other side of the tracks. They parked on the corner of Twenty-Fifth Street.

"Hurston's novel described the mass burial activity here, but the site became so forgotten that even those who knew about it didn't have the exact location, and a warehouse was almost built on top of it. Luckily, community leaders stepped in and hired a Miami firm that used ground-penetrating radar to discover a seventy-by-thirty-foot trench." Serge placed paper against stone. "This is the granite memorial they erected in 2003."

Coleman curiously watched Serge.

"What?"

He pointed. "Where'd you get that?"

"This?" Serge looked down at something new on his chest attached to shoulder straps. "From the pet store. It's like those things that moms wear to carry infants."

Mr. Zippy poked his head out the top of the canvas pouch and looked around.

"He's growing on me," said Coleman.

Back to the car. A couple miles south on Dixie Highway, another stop.

"There's the Norton Museum of Art. Remember? From the Everglades mural?"

"We're going there?"

"No, other side of the street."

"On one condition," said Coleman.

"Now you're setting conditions, are you?"

Coleman told him what it was. "... *Pleeeeeease!*"

The pair walked through a grand stone archway into Woodlawn Cemetery.

"Because of segregation at the time of the hurricane, the mass grave for the whites was here. Unlike the others, they got pine boxes ... How's it working out over there?"

Coleman smiled and looked down at the pouch on his chest.

"I think Mr. Zippy likes me." A burst of chattering and then a tiny head disappeared. "So you came to see another mass grave?"

"Not this time." Serge led the way through the ancient grounds until stopping at a stone with the name Charles William Pierce.

Coleman gently patted the pouch. "Who's that?"

"A bonus find unconnected to the hurricane, so how can I not stop?" Serge knelt to rub again. "In 1888, Charlie became one of the state's first legendary 'barefoot mailmen.' Because there was no land route back then between West Palm and Miami, mail carriers would make a six-day, hundred-and-thirty-mile trek, much of it traversed on foot along the beach, hence the name . . ." He turned and began running back to the car. "We're off!"

"Come on, Mr. Zippy!"

Chapter 21

FOUR YEARS EARLIER

A loud bell rang nonstop.

The local junior high was dismissed for the day. Kids poured out the doors like the Berlin Wall had fallen. Backpacks, skateboards, cell phones. Someone pushed someone else into the bushes.

A Dodge Dakota quietly eased up to the curb across the street.

A girl texted as she crossed the road.

"Excuse me?" Crack hung out the window. "Miss?"

She looked up. Uh-oh. Stranger Danger.

"Don't be scared," said Crack, checking the scrap of paper from the pawnshop. "I'm just looking for my nephew. Do you know a Ricky Aparicio?"

She pointed back at the school gates.

Captain Crack stretched his neck. "Which one?"

"I thought he was your nephew."

"Been a long time."

"Red shirt, blue shorts." She hurried along on her way.

The boy headed north on the opposite side of the street, along with a dozen other loud, laughing kids. Crack started up his truck and drove slowly. Parts of the gang peeled off as they reached the streets to their homes. It was down to just a few when Crack hung out the window again.

"Ricky! Ricky Aparicio!"

The boy looked over. "Who are you?"

Crack waved with his left hand. "Come over here. I need to ask you a question."

"Don't go," said one of the other boys.

"See what he wants," said another.

Ricky decided to split the difference and walked halfway across the empty street. "What do you want?"

"Come closer," said Crack. "I won't bite."

"I'm staying right here until you tell me what this is about."

"It concerns the gold coin you sold to the pawnshop."

"I didn't steal it!"

"Nobody says you did." The captain held out a piece of currency. "I just need some information. I'm writing an article for a hobby magazine."

"Ricky!" yelled one of the boys on the other curb. "Don't get any closer!"

"Ricky!" yelled another. "That's a hundred-dollar bill!"

Ricky got closer. "Exactly what kind of information?"

"I've been doing some research on your town, the hurricane and everything, and I think you might have stumbled onto something historic. I'll pay you a hundred dollars to show me where you found that coin."

Ricky stood like a statue. A beeping car drove around him.

Crack hung farther out the driver's window. "Listen, I know what you've been taught about strangers. But how would I know all this information about what you found? Besides, all those warnings are for little kids. You're practically a man now."

Ricky remained a stone.

"What do you say?" Crack waved the bill tauntingly. "Hundred bucks. Going once, going twice—"

"Okay, okay, but give me the money first."

"Once you're in the truck, or you'll just run away."

Ricky got in, and the Dodge drove off. The other boys dashed home to tell their parents . . .

It was ten minutes of dubious directions from the youth. "Take this left. Wait, the next left, that's it. No, that's not right. It's farther up."

"Are you sure you know where we're going?"

"Positive." Ricky clutched the hundred as if it was life itself. "Uh, could we go back to town and start again? I can figure it out better if we're coming from Main Street. From this other way, I'm not so good."

"Jesus," Crack said under his breath. But greed had gotten the better of him, and he was locked in for the ride, seeing nothing but piles of those coins.

T he Crossroads.

If the intersection had one of those signposts with wooden arrows pointing different directions with names of places and mileage, all the arrows on this post would have said NOWHERE.

Three of the corners were empty except for concrete-block ruins with collapsed roofs, and weeds now grew where there had been carpeting.

On the fourth corner sat a gas station that sold as much malt liquor as unleaded.

Signs said NO LOITERING, at least under the spray-paint graffiti.

Three young men lounged on a stoop. All high school graduates, all football players, all with onetime dreams of making the NFL. Now they spent their days here. This was not the NFL.

Wasn't their fault. Life had dealt them truly cruel hands of cards. If you take a hundred successful Wall Street types and have them born at the very bottom with no breaks, see how far they go. This particular trio all had jobs. The operative word was *had*. When the economy coughed, The Muck got pneumonia, and layoffs were a lifestyle. The three currently had a bunch of job applications submitted all over town, but where were the jobs? So they hung out here until something turned up.

"Remember that pass I caught in the fourth quarter? Right sideline?"

"You and that one freaking pass! All we ever hear: 'Remember? Right sideline?' Shit, I had three receptions that game."

"But all short yardage over the middle."

"Moved us into scoring position, didn't it?"

"Both of you are bullshit," said the third young man. "Just remember who *threw* all those passes."

They stopped talking and watched as a lone vehicle slowly rounded the corner at the station and accelerated east. Magnetic door sign for a boat-towing company. They all sprang to their feet.

"That son of a bitch!"

"He's back!"

"And he's got Ricky!"

They piled into a low-riding Datsun and took off.

"I knew that asshole was up to something, but I didn't know what. He's a pedophile!"

"He'll kill Ricky for sure if we don't stop him!"

"Shouldn't we call the police?"

"Screw that! We can take care of our own . . ."

A mile out of town, Ricky pointed. "Turn here. This time I'm sure."

"If you say so." The Dakota made a skidding left onto a dirt road.

Moments later, a tricked-out Datsun sailed by the turnoff. "I don't see his truck anymore."

"Drive faster. We'll catch up . . ."

Back in the cane field, Ricky hopped down from the pickup's cab and climbed through a couple rows of stalks. "It was right around here somewhere."

"You don't seem that sure."

Ricky stopped and stomped a foot into the black soil. "Right here."

"Exactly?" said Crack.

Ricky nodded vigorously. "Take me back now."

"Are you joking? I gave you a hundred. Show me!"

"How?"

"Dig!"

"What?"

"If you're so fucking sure, dig!"

Panic now. Ricky got on the ground and scooped dirt with shaking hands.

"Don't keep looking up at me!" yelled Crack. "Pay attention to what you're doing! Dig! . . ."

Up the road, parked on the right shoulder, more panic. "We just got Ricky killed!" said the wide receiver.

"Don't say that!" yelled the tight end.

"I knew we should have called the police," said the quarterback.

"What's done is done. We need to chill out and figure this thing out. What would a pedophile do?"

They looked all the way around the horizon. "Bring him out in a cane field," said the wide receiver. "For privacy and body disposal."

"Don't say that!" snapped the tight end.

"He must have taken a turnoff." The quarterback swung the car around. "Keep your eyes open . . ."

Somewhere out in the stalks, small hands flung dirt. A whimper.

Captain Crack had gotten back into the Johnnie Walker, swinging the bottle by his side. "What the hell are you crying about!"

"I want to go home."

"Shut up and dig!"

"I want my mommy."

Ricky never saw the open-handed slap coming. It cupped the side of his head over his ear and sent him sprawling.

Louder crying now. "I didn't find the coin. A girl did."

"You've been lying to me all along?" Slap. "Who is this girl?"

"I don't know! I swear!"

Slap.

"Kathy? Karen? I can't remember . . ."

Back on Highway 98, a Datsun was on a slow roll.

"Wait! Stop!"

"What is it?"

"Back up! I saw his truck!"

The quarterback threw the car in reverse, then barreled down the dirt road toward the parked Dakota. It skidded to a stop just as Ricky came bursting through the cane stalks, bloody nose, crying, ripped shirt.

The quarterback got down on a knee and hugged the boy tight.

Then another voice from an unseen source a few cane rows over. "Come back here, you little fucker!" The boat captain broke through the final row and stopped.

The quarterback stood up. Without looking down at Ricky, he placed a hand on the boy's shoulder. "Go wait in my car."

Crack Nasty pointed at them with the hand not holding the bottle. "Now you listen here! I gave him a hundred dollars and we had a deal!"

It was a short chase.

They gang-tackled the captain only a few steps from where he started. The ensuing beating was not for the squeamish. Savage kicks to the ribs and head as Crack desperately tried to crawl for sanctuary that wasn't there. More kicking and stomping in rage. It wasn't thug life. It was family life. One of them found a stick and smashed it over his neck. Another hit him with a rock. A few more kicks and Crack finally rolled onto his back, an unconscious, bloody mess. But the kicking continued.

The quarterback jumped in and grabbed the others. "Guys! Guys! Stop or you'll kill him!"

"So what?" Kick.

"I feel the same way, but if you think our lives are shit now . . ." He looked back at the Datsun. "Plus we need to get Ricky home. His mother must be worried sick."

They took turns spitting on Captain Crack.

Then the Datsun drove away.

Chapter 22

PORT MAYACA

The gold Plymouth picked up two-lane State Road 710, also known as the Bee Line Highway: an odd, almost perfectly diagonal shot northwest up through the unpopulated part of Palm Beach County, along the railroad tracks, through the Loxahatchee Slough, up past the old Pratt & Whitney aircraft-engine plant that brought thousands of transplants to the county in the early sixties. They reached Indiantown, and turned decidedly west on Route 76, into more and more nothingness.

Coleman petted the pouch on his chest and looked out the window at scraggly woods. "Are we actually heading anywhere?"

"Lake Okeechobee," said Serge. "Another of our crown jewels, so huge it dominates photos taken from the Space Shuttle. And to hell with it: I'm going on the record right now, and will take on all comers. At seven hundred and thirty square miles, Okeechobee is the largest freshwater lake in the country. Oh, sure, everyone else says it's the *second* biggest, behind Lake Michigan. But that one's open at the top, mixing with Canadian water. How is *that* the record? Where were the referees on that one?"

"It's just not fair."

"Canada, Christ." Serge shook his head. "*Our* lake is a damn force of nature. I like to think of it as Florida's moon."

"How is it a moon?"

"Give me some latitude on this, Judge Coleman, and I will show the relevance," said Serge. "Earth's moon is an oddity of our solar system, far closer and proportionately larger than any of the other planets' moons. So much so that it creates our ocean tides, affects the seasons and even stabilizes Earth's rotation, doing nothing less than making life possible at all. On a smaller scale, same thing with our freakishly large lake. Most Floridians have never seen it, and even fewer realize the overwhelming effect it has on the rest of the state. First, it collects much of the watershed in Central Florida, from the Kissimmee River and other sources. Then below it, the lake feeds the Everglades. And the extensive matrix of canals that were dug to channel its runoff created entire agricultural industries and—even more mind-blowing—the very dry land that allows much of South Florida, from Miami to Fort Lauderdale, to even exist. Otherwise, all the residents would be tits-deep in lily pads and gators instead of blissfully working skimming nets to scoop leaves from their swimming pools."

"I had no idea." Coleman held his beer away from the pouch and looked down at his chest. "You're not old enough."

"But here's the kicker, and it's a beauty . . ." Serge slowed and tracked their position on a GPS. "The Okeechobee hurricane of 1928 is still whipping up changes in the way we live, even to this day!"

"How can a storm that old still be messing with us?"

"I'll tell you!" The Plymouth slowed even further. "The three thousand souls that were lost made it the second-worst natural disaster in the nation's history, behind only the Galveston storm in 1900. Nobody saw it coming. Everyone was always preparing for storm surges from the ocean, but then that monster storm made a direct hit on the lake. And if you ever doubt how big that body of water is, imagine a tidal wave covering hundreds of square miles, much higher than virtually every house. First the storm's rotation flooded all the communities along the southern shore. Then the backside of the hurricane hit, pushing water north through the city of Okeechobee. After all the burials, the federal government stepped in to prevent such a tragedy. They built the enormous Herbert Hoover Dike, a thirty-foot-high, one-hundred-and-forty-three-mile-long earthen berm surrounding the lake. That's why so many people crisscrossing the state above and below the immense body of water never see it; they just dismiss it as a long grassy hill and have such screwed-up priorities that they aren't curious to take one of the access ramps to the top and marvel. That's why I've decided to carve out time and make the lake the culmination of our tour. Zora led us here."

"So we're almost at the end?" asked Coleman.

"Actually just beginning, but time folds in on itself." The gold Satellite pulled over on the side of an empty road without a sign of life. "I intend to drop anchor, explore the lake in every detail and get a bone-deep understanding of her people. It's an amazingly disparate culture: the old-cracker cattle ranchers up north with their rodeos, western-wear shops and steak houses; the impoverished farmworkers to the south; and all around, the visiting bass fishermen hoping to land that prized lunker."

Serge got out of the car with another large sheet of paper. He approached a green metal historic marker and began rubbing.

Coleman arrived with the ferret peeking around. "Where are we?"

Rub, rub. "Can't you read?"

"My eyes are having that focus problem again."

"We're at Port Mayaca, a ghost town with ghosts." Rub, rub.

"Out in that field somewhere lie the remains of sixteen hundred victims of the storm. As usual, people finally realized they needed to erect this sign decades later."

"Sixteen hundred?" Coleman blinked a few times.

"Right under our feet." Rub, rub. "It's important to remember."

"Shit! Dammit!"

"I know the storm was a heartbreak—"

"No, not that!" Coleman pointed.

"How'd you let Mr. Zippy get away?"

"He was too fast."

They began running around the field.

"Hold on," said Coleman. "I think I have some Doritos in my pocket."

"In your pocket?"

"Just in case." Coleman tossed one forward. "I think he's going for it."

"Here, let me have one." Serge crouched down and extended a hand. "It's working." The ferret stopped to nibble, and was gently picked up. "Give me that pouch!"

"No!" Coleman turned sideways and clutched it. "I want to carry him."

"You're obviously a bad influence," said Serge.

"I can change."

"Are we going to have a custody battle? The courts won't look fondly on your substance intake."

"What about you waxing dudes?"

Serge walked the legal proceedings through his head and saw them inevitably leading to foster care. "Okay, for *now*. Just keep on top of him."

The Plymouth drove a short distance farther west, over the train tracks, reaching Highway 98 and more emptiness. "Port Mayaca is another Florida settlement abandoned by time. Besides the cemetery, about the only other thing left, like a sore thumb out here, is that big white plantation-style house coming up on our left: the historic Cypress Inn, currently a private residence and on the National Register. Hard to imagine now that there was ever enough business to support the hotel, but once upon a time the constant, northbound winter railroad traffic of fresh vegetables made this a bustling corridor."

The Plymouth turned off the highway and drove up the incline of an access road. Serge got out with his camera, hitching a camping product to his belt.

Coleman petted Mr. Zippy. "What's that thing you put on your waist?"

"Canteen for my coffee." He uncapped it for a big chug, then re-capped it. "I just completed a blue-ribbon time-motion study on myself, and someone needs to get fired. The canteen was the number one recommendation in the report, because I'm so often reaching out a hand for coffee and coming up with a fistful of empty."

Coleman pointed in another direction. "Did we drive all the way to the ocean?"

"No." *Click, click, click.* "We're on top of the dike. That's the lake."

"*That's* the lake?" said Coleman. "I can't even see the other side. And we're way up honkin' high!"

"That's how it got its name." *Click, click, click.* "The Seminole word for *big water.*"

"There's like a row of weird clouds all spaced out," said Coleman. "Wait, each of them has a little thing stretching to the ground like a tornado. But they're black like smoke. Is something on fire?"

"That would be the sugarcane fields burning over the horizon on the opposite shore. The size of those clouds should give you some idea of the scale of those blazes. They need that to get rid of the leaves and weeds before the harvesting machines come through."

Coleman looked the other way, at something much closer. "What's that?"

"The Port Mayaca Lock and Dam." *Click, click, click.* "Something else people don't realize is that you can sail clear across the state of Florida, from Fort Myers to Stuart, along the Caloosahatchee and St. Lucie rivers. But there's a series of five locks in order to raise the vessels to get to the lake, then a clear shot across a bass fishermen's paradise before the rest of the locks lower the boats back down to sea level. Like the Panama Canal except bigger. Not as wide, but much longer. So I'm going on the record right now with that as well. Fuck 'em."

Coleman looked left and right. "If this is Port Mayaca, where's the port?"

"Pretty much just that lock," said Serge.

"What's the big gate-looking thing next to it? Part of the lock?"

"No, that's the spillway," said Serge. "Remember when I told you the 1928 hurricane was still surprising people in ways they never dreamed?"

"Not really, but go on."

"So remember when we were on the coast in Stuart last year? Remember the *smell*?"

"Oh, my God! That stink is still in my head again," said Coleman. "I've never smelled anything so nasty in all my life!"

"That's what everyone said." *Click, click, click.* "And at first, because they don't know how the state's ecosystem is interconnected, they couldn't figure it out. They just saw all this thick green sludge completely blanketing the coastal inlets, up through the Intracoastal Waterway to the boating canals behind homes, like an ice floe. The stench was so bad that it emptied beaches and restaurants, and residents were held prisoner in their homes with scented candles, praying the air-conditioning didn't give out."

"What was it?"

"It all started here, forty miles away," said Serge. "The Hoover Dike is getting old, and the Army Corps of Engineers has been sounding the alarm for years that it's in desperate need of repairs or the next hurricane could breach, just like the levees failed in

New Orleans during Katrina. So when the water levels get too high, as a precautionary step they open the spillways, releasing millions of gallons of water. Same thing simultaneously happened on the Gulf coast when they opened the gates at Moore Haven."

"But how did that cause the stinky green slime?"

"The Corps of Engineers caught a lot of flak, but it wasn't their fault. Their only responsibility is protecting life and property from a dike failure. The problem is that, over the years, the lake has become chock-full of nitrogen-rich fertilizer runoff. Some is back-pumped into the lake by Big Sugar, but probably just as much or more was carried down the Kissimmee River from the pasture and cattle land south of Orlando. The resulting algae bloom could easily be seen from space—I'm kind of hung up on the reference point right now. But oddly, it didn't get much national press, and if you weren't there, you couldn't imagine the extent of the environmental disaster. Beautiful, flowing waterways just choking to death, rotting fish, no-swimming signs. For the first time, thousands of people on both coasts became acutely aware of this faraway but dominant lake. Our moon."

Coleman used a single finger to scratch a furry head. "Mr. Zippy, you don't like algae blooms, do you?" He looked up at Serge. "He says he doesn't . . . Ow, damn!" He quickly yanked his finger back. "Mr. Zippy just bit me!"

"What kind of sickness did you inflict on him?"

"Nothing, I swear."

"Did it draw blood or was it just a little nip?"

"Just a nip." Shaking a finger. "Still hurts."

Serge nodded in understanding. "The guy at the pet store explained it to me. If they're scared or pissed off, they can really bite, but if it's only a nip, it's because they're so smart."

"How is biting me smart?"

"Their intelligence requires constant mental stimulation, and they let you know it. That's what is known as their *I'm-bored-as-shit-please-entertain-me* bite."

Coleman looked down at the pouch, wiggling silly fingers next to his ears and sticking out his tongue. Mr. Zippy squeaked. Coleman petted him.

"He bit me again."

"Here," said Serge, passing his smartphone across the front seat. "Let him watch some stuff on YouTube."

"Like what?"

"Zany ferret videos. There's like a thousand for every occasion. One thing YouTube has taught me is that other people are drilling deep into ways to waste their lives."

"Okay, let me try . . ." Coleman got a video going and held the phone to the pouch. "I think it's working. He's getting into it."

Serge glanced over. "What's it playing?"

"There's a ferret in a sweater, and now two more are losing their minds in a pile of packing peanuts, another one is rolling a watermelon across the kitchen, another is riding on the back of a house cat like a jockey, one just crawled completely inside an empty tube of Pringles . . . I had no idea they were so talented."

Serge got out of the car and stood gazing across a stunning vista. "Time to take in one last sunset look from the top of the dike before we proceed." He unhitched a camping canteen from his belt and slugged cold coffee.

A minivan came up the access ramp and parked nearby. The vehicle's sliding door opened, belching out children, who promptly began screaming as they ran in pointless circles. Exhausted parents climbed down from the front seat.

"A family!" Serge quickly chugged and capped the canteen. "People still care! I must congratulate and share the good news!"

The parents leaned against the minivan's bumper, soaking up the view and eating granola bars. Serge blustered over, jumping like he had a pogo stick. "Thank God you made it! You don't see anyone else up here. That means you're special for caring!" He bobbed on the balls of his feet. "You just *have* to visit the mass grave next, I insist. Your thoughts on the algae bloom? Seen it from space? That lake is our moon." Serge tapped the side of his head. "Let it set in. Did you know that the top of this dike is part of the thirteen-hundred-mile Florida National Scenic Trail? My faithful pal here is Coleman, and that's Mr. Zippy, my service animal. Mental condition, nothing you need to worry about. Others, maybe." He pointed at the kids, still running randomly and screaming. "Children have the best sense of hearing, and yet they're always shouting at the top of their lungs at each other, especially in motel pools. Could never figure that one out. On the other hand, kindergarten is my religion. The children will lead us . . . Coleman, you ready?"

"I'm in."

The pair began running aimlessly around the top of the dike, screaming shrill gibberish to mimic the children: *"Wa-wa-wa-wa-wa! . . . Yi-yi-yi-yi-yi! . . . Blobidy-blobidy-blobidy! . . .* Coleman! Tag! You're it! Can't catch me! . . . Can't catch me! . . . Try to catch me!—"

A panel door slammed shut. Serge stopped and watched the minivan race back to the highway. "Man, they must really want to see that cemetery . . ."

Chapter 23

I fell down some stairs."

The doctor glared at Captain Crack. "Only if the stairs then got up and fell on your head. Someone clearly beat the crap out of you. Probably more than one."

"How much longer?" snapped Crack, butterfly bandages across his eyebrows and cheeks. "I have to get back to work."

"Hold on, just need to finish taping up these ribs."

Crack didn't really have to lie. It was one of those off-the-books doctors, the kind you call for a GSW—that would be gunshot wound—when you want to avoid the mandatory reporting to police that the law requires. Every city's got a few, and all the shady types have them on speed dial.

The doctor finished treating the captain underneath a stuffed wahoo, and left Crack's office. Captain Nasty had some more people on speed dial who didn't advertise in the yellow pages. He punched buttons on his cell phone.

"Fallon, it's me, Crack," said the captain. "I know you probably don't remember, but we met a while back through a mutual friend. Vic Carver..."

The people the captain was contacting were consummate professionals, the kind he'd like working for him on his boats, but he couldn't afford their price tag for that sort of long-term employment. On the other hand, it might be for the better, because he wouldn't look forward to having any kind of business dispute with these cats.

"... The reason I'm calling is I have a job for you. . . . No, I'm calling from a burner phone. . . . Okay, check me out with Vic and then we'll meet ..."

The next day, Captain Crack stood on the side of the Flagler Bridge over the Intracoastal Waterway to Palm Beach. It was one of those old, low concrete drawbridges that the people who couldn't afford boats fished from. The fish were apparently biting because the bridge was unusually full. Mainly blacks and Latinos. Straw hats. Someone reeled in a flopping catfish and tossed it in a pail. There was talk, time and again, over on the wealthy island about passing some kind of law to get rid of the people on the bridge, but it never really worked out.

Captain Crack cast a lure out into the water and began reeling. The midday sun was a challenge, even with his ventilated fishing shirt, and patience wasn't among his virtues. He kept checking his watch. He looked one way toward the modest skyline of downtown West Palm Beach, and then the other toward the tony waterfront mansions with Spanish barrel tiles and royal palms. He heard someone next to him and turned.

Another fisherman set a bait bucket down on the cement next to Crack's bucket. Both pails were orange and white. The new arrival then cast a line in the water without speaking. He was a head taller than the captain, thinner, more muscular in a formfitting black T-shirt that matched his black hat and jet-black wraparound sunglasses. A formation of pelicans glided along the bridge's ancient railing. A cheap radio somewhere was playing Cuban salsa music.

"It's all in the bait bucket," said Crack. "Instructions, money, just like you told me on the phone."

The taller fisherman stared down at Crack with unseen eyes behind the sunglasses. It meant: *The instructions also were not to talk to me.* What did he not understand about standing next to a stranger on a bridge and simply switching identical bait buckets?

"Sorry," said Crack.

The man brusquely picked up the captain's bucket and left the bridge.

A white blop of pelican poop hit Crack's arm.

The sun had just gone down behind an emaciated gas station. The horizon was low and clear over the cane stalks from all four corners of the intersection. Someone walked out of the station scratching an instant lottery ticket with the edge of a dime. Someone else uncapped a bottle in a brown paper bag. The social circle on the stoop was more animated than usual.

"Jamal, if I have to hear about that stupid pass reception one more freaking time, I swear to God I'll slit my wrists."

"But it was an ESPN highlight moment!"

"In your dreams maybe."

A low-riding Datsun sat nearby with purple neon glowing underneath. All the doors were open for the listening pleasure of an over-powered stereo with the new Grenade sub-woofer. The song changed to Hendrix.

"*. . . I went down to the crossroads . . .*"

The traffic light changed, and a Dakota thumped to a stop in the intersection. Hank Williams blasted out the open windows.

"*. . . Kaw-Liga! . . .*"

The light turned green. Someone waved out the driver's window. A middle-finger salute. "Suck my dick, porch monkeys!"

One of the trio stood up from the stoop. "I don't believe my own lyin' eyes."

"What is it?"

"That son of a bitch is at it again!" said the tight end.

"You'd think he'd learned his lesson," said the wide receiver.

The quarterback angled his neck forward in the growing darkness. "And it looks like he's got another little kid with him!"

It was déjà vu all over again. The Datsun blasted out of the parking lot like before, except this time they took it careful not to overrun a detour down a cane road. For whatever reason, the driver of the Dakota made it hard to miss his vehicle. He drove the speed limit and left his high beams on, lighting everything up like a prison break. He turned into a cane field.

"There he is!"

"I ain't going to worry about killing him like last time!"

The Datsun raced down the dirt road following Crack's headlights. When they pulled up, they figured Captain Nasty would take off running and shitting his pants. Instead, they found him leaning against his driver's door, calmly smoking a cigarette. "What's up, boys?"

"You took another kid!" shouted the wide receiver.

"What kid?" Crack took a deep drag. "I don't see any children around here."

"In your pickup cab!" yelled the tight end. He ran up to the passenger window. "What the heck?"

"What is it?" asked the quarterback.

"A small mannequin."

"What?"

The young man pulled the straw-stuffed human figure from the car and walked back with it for all to see. "He tricked us!"

"But why?"

They were off-balance, staring back at the pickup truck with confused eyes.

Crack Nasty chuckled and snubbed out his cigarette. "Nice knowing you."

Suddenly a dark, windowless van crashed through the sugar-cane in front of them. The side panel flew open and four men in black jumpsuits leaped out. There was no Hollywood final banter. They simply opened up with ridiculous firepower from the latest battlefield mercenary weapons.

At least death was quick.

Helicopters and TV trucks converged on the field the next day. Police found a burst-open bag of cocaine in the Datsun, and more residue on the bodies. The three victims had no criminal records. But they were known to be young, black and hanging out with no employment. Everything pointed to a drug deal gone south. Locals weren't buying it. They brought in the larger outside law enforcement agencies, and a joint task force went in front of the TV cameras, swearing they would never rest until their investigation brought the killers to justice. But given the area and the evidence, not really.

Captain Crack Nasty was getting away with it again.

Chapter 24

COW COUNTRY

A gold Plymouth Satellite headed up U.S. Highway 98. A Styrofoam takeout dinner box sat on the back seat.

"One thing that should be mandatory on every Floridian's bucket list is to drive completely around Lake Okeechobee."

A ferret ran from one of Serge's shoulders to the other.

"I think Mr. Zippy wants to know why," said Coleman.

"Because it will recalibrate your sense of place. That's what we're doing now. One hundred and twenty miles of dynamically changing culture and landscape. And this empty section between Pahokee and the city of Okeechobee is one of the coolest!"

"He nipped me again," said Coleman. "He needs more stimulation."

"It's like channel-surfing inland Florida," said Serge. "We're on the east side, where the highway hugs the rim of the lake, through flats with sabal palms and heron swooping over the road. Moss-draped oaks, bogs and marsh, grassy straightaways with just that looming dike. Plus it continues following the thread, which I will recap for Mr. Zippy: Rawlings to Stetson to Zora to the West Palm Beach cemetery in her book to the Port Mayaca mass grave, and now circumnavigating the lake with more interrelated stops. And people think I'm just winging it . . ."

A deep horn blew.

Serge quickly checked his mirrors and skidded off the road.

"What are you doing?"

"Waiting for the train to catch up," said Serge.

"Huh?"

Another horn blast.

"Along the east side of the lake, the old train tracks that carried fresh produce up north almost a century ago still have traffic, and they lie in that short strip of easement between this road and the Hoover Dike. You haven't lived until you've raced a train up Lake Okeechobee . . . Here we go!"

Tires spun, black smoke, screeching. The Plymouth hit the road as if shot by a slingshot.

A yellow-and-black locomotive gained quickly from behind, and Serge pressed his right foot down all the way. He began honking and waving. One of the engineers glanced over. Serge leaned out the window, making a pumping gesture with his fist for the engineer to blow his horn.

A long blare followed, and the train pulled away.

Serge fell back in his seat with an afterglow. "It doesn't get any better!"

"Then why that frown?"

"Incoming thought," said Serge. "What's the deal with sales receipts these days?"

"Are we playing another round of tangent?" asked Coleman.

"I'll go in a darn CVS or Walgreens drugstore to buy a single toothbrush, and I get a receipt that reaches to the floor. You can't be doing that to people. It's a drugstore, so they have to know a certain wedge of their clientele have disorders. And now the pressure is on me to read the whole fucking thing because *you never know.* But it's always a bunch of coupons for back-to-school supplies or feminine products that make me blush. On the other hand, the receipts at gas pumps are these teensy-weensy little bastards you can barely read. We regulate the size of eggs, but where's the quality control on this one?"

Coleman nodded. "Half the long receipts seem to have a pink stripe somewhere."

"This is what I'm talking about!" said Serge. "And another thing: Society now has something called 'revenge porn.'"

"Is that where someone steals all your porn?"

"So you'd think," said Serge. "But I just heard through the grapevine that in the middle of a sixty-nine, people are pulling out their cell phones."

"This is really going on?"

Serge nodded. "You'd think a quaking orgasm would get a thank-you, but no, now it has to be in high def."

"What do they do with it?"

"Save it for the breakup," said Serge. "And it's never pretty: 'You know how you said I could trust you and ask the most embarrassing thing that you'd like me to do in bed? Well, I have a request . . .' And the next thing you know, a bunch of coworkers are in their cubicles glued to a text video involving handcuffs and a zucchini."

"Ouch."

Serge shrugged. "If those people are going to judge me on that . . . I mean, it was someone else."

The Plymouth began curling around the northwest shore of the lake. A roar came up from behind and whipped past in the opposite lane.

Coleman's head spun as he grabbed the dash. "There must be twenty motorcycles!"

"It's a popular touring route for them," said Serge. "Which means we're on the right track. Bikers are a noble breed, stripping away pretense to live in the *now*. You can always count on them to bird-dog the finest scenic byways."

More wetlands and vines and scrub brush went by. Drivers in other vehicles wearing camo baseball caps and pulling airboats.

"Now we're talking!" said Serge. "Florida's bayou country, the whole area like a Credence Clearwater album!"

He fumbled to start a boom box.

"... *Comin' up around the bend* ..."

The scraggly vegetation gave way to wild palms surrounding the first wisps of the mobile-home parks.

Serge nodded to himself in contentment. "Lake Okeechobee is Florida's heart, and its beat ripples a pulse far and wide."

"I thought the lake was the moon," said Coleman.

"Since when are you listening to me?"

The road wound past more evidence of population hugging the edge of the lake. RV dealerships and RV parks. Bass boats, a country store, a honky-tonk bar, a swamp buggy on tank treads. Signs for gravel and cremation. Then the trailer parks. Trailers on wheels, trailers on blocks, trailers on slabs. Trailers with screened porches, hot tubs and gazebos. There were flowerpots with no flowers, decorative stone turtles next to real ones, and a mailbox shaped like a lighthouse. Someone was casting a fishing line on his front lawn, and someone else walked by on the side of the road in shorts, sandals and a Santa Claus hat, indicating the breadth of the human condition.

Then the local economy. Big Lake Eye Care, Big Lake Bail Bonds, the Big "O" Flea Market.

American flags everywhere.

Another roar came up behind the Plymouth. Coleman turned around. "A bunch more bikers." They began streaming by the Plymouth. "Except these are all the three-wheel kind. Why are they riding separate from the others?"

"Probably unresolved tension between the groups that goes way back to an incident nobody can remember now," said Serge. "Most likely a few too many longnecks on a Sunday afternoon, and then one guy started some shit about the number of tires, threats were made, women disrespected. Best to let them sort it out among themselves."

The Plymouth reached the outskirts of the civilization. Signs for bait, fishing licenses and fried catfish.

"Where are we?" asked Coleman.

"The city of Okeechobee, also known as Cow Town." The Plymouth pulled into a parking lot. "We need to resupply before our excellent visit."

Twenty minutes later, they came out of the store. Coleman was pushing a shopping cart, and Serge was dragging a sales receipt across the pavement. He suddenly stopped and violently balled it up. Then into a garbage can—"Motherfucker!"—slamming the lid five times.

"What's the matter?"

"I don't want to talk about it."

Soon, they were checking into another economy motel. This one had a warning sign at the reception desk.

Coleman moved his lips as he read. "Serge, what are blind mosquitoes?"

"Tiny suckers that don't bite but sometimes swarm in biblical numbers off the lake after dark, and you have to keep your mouth closed unless you want extra protein. But they can still get in your eyes, ears and nose."

"Jesus."

"They're attracted to light, so that's why that sign asks guests to turn off all the lamps before leaving the room in the evening and close the door quickly. It's a whole different set of rules out here, and they're not in the humans' favor."

A young wrangler-Jane type stood behind the counter with a genuine smile. "I wouldn't worry too much. The mosquitoes are bad on the few nights they're out, but it's mostly quiet. What freaks newcomers most are the frogs."

"Frogs?" said Serge.

She nodded and held her hands apart a good half foot. "We have these giant ones that come out after a big rain, and people open their doors at night and see them all over the sidewalk and parking lot. They're harmless, but sometimes one or two will hop in a room. That's a lot of my night service calls."

"Service calls?"

Another nod. "I have to go in rooms and capture them because people say they can't sleep with those things under their bed making noise and just being creepy, and they're too squeamish to catch them on their own . . . So what are you fellas doing in town?"

"Historical research," said Serge. "Following connective tissue."

"History? Really?" She brightened further. "I love history!" She got out a paper and pen and began jotting feverishly. "Here are the area's high points . . ." She got to the bottom of the page. ". . . Finally, don't forget the Brighton Seminole reservation. There's a visitors' center with exhibits and souvenirs, plus they have a twenty-four-hour casino where you don't have to dress up. I usually go in my pajamas."

They retired to the room as the sun began to set.

Coleman stood in amazement. "This is like the best budget place we've ever stayed in. It's got a giant full kitchen and everything!"

"Scoped it out years ago, and now it's the only place I'll stay around here." Serge hung his toiletry bag on a mirror. "Where else can you rent a former condo unit at a bargain price? And there's always vacancy. That's why I'm keeping it a secret."

Rinnnng! Rinnnng!

Serge jumped. "What the fuck was that?"

"The phone," said Coleman.

"Of course it's the phone! But who could possibly know we're here?"

Rinnnnng! Rinnnnng!

Serge gingerly picked up the receiver. "Hello?"

"Hi! It's me, Cheyenne, from the front desk. I just thought of a couple more places that I forgot when I was making your list. Have a pen handy?"

Serge urgently lunged toward writing materials like he was taking a call for ransom demands. "Hit me!"

The call eventually ended, and the receiver went back in its cradle.

"Who was that?" asked Coleman.

"Our little history helper from the front desk. My love for country folk just keeps growing."

The pair commenced their respective chores. Coleman spread dope on the counter and swilled malt liquor. Serge unpacked notebooks, guidebooks, pamphlets, and recording devices. Coleman made a bong from a souvenir plastic cowboy-hat penny bank that he'd bought at the store.

"TV?" asked Coleman.

"Leave it off. I have other plans." Serge carefully arranged a configuration of needed materials on the nightstand: antiquarian novel, portable stereo, Styrofoam to-go dinner box. He took a deep breath in anticipation. Then he kicked off his shoes and lay on top of a bedspread in his stocking feet. "Here . . . we . . . go! . . ."

"What are you doing?"

"A lost art: constructing the perfect moment!" Serge bunched the pillow up under his head. "It requires the precisely engineered intersection of sensory, mental and emotional input: First, the motel room is in the ideal location: From the comfort of my bed, I have a fantastic view just outside the window of the Hoover Dike in the setting sun. Next"—he pressed a button on the portable stereo, and a growling voice came to life—"'Little Black Train' by Blind Joe Taggart, just the kind of blues song they would have been playing in the 1920s juke joints surrounding the lake's bustling packing houses . . ." He opened the Styrofoam box on his stomach ". . . And this is my soul-food takeout from that shack in Pahokee of smothered pork chops, pigeon peas and collards. Standard dinner fare in those old days . . ." Serge finally grabbed the book off the nightstand. "And last but not least, a collectible early copy of Zora Neale Hurston's masterpiece recounting the 1928 storm that struck right out there! . . ."

Serge became quiet. He turned up the tiny stereo, stuck a fork in a pork chop, opened the book and stared out the window. ". . . I'm starting to feel it. I'm getting tingly . . . Here it comes! . . . Here it comes! . . . It's almost here! . . . It's here!" Serge's eyelids fluttered uncontrollably as his pupils rolled up in his head like he was possessed. Then, a few seconds later, it was over. "Coleman, did you see it? The Moment! . . . It was just here . . . See? There it goes . . ." He closed the book and swallowed a bite of pork. ". . . Whew! Exhausting! . . . If everyone could experience motels like this, prostitution as we know it would end."

"They would have to get other jobs," said Coleman.

"Then one day you order a pizza and open the door: 'Hey, didn't you used to be a hooker?' 'Shut up.'"

Serge paused curiously and considered the closed book next to him. He opened it again and read down a page. "Wait . . . just . . . a minute!"

"What is it?"

He ran for the desk and opened another, thicker green book. "I need my bible."

"The *Bible* Bible?"

"No, the Florida bible. WPA Guide published in 1939, two years after Zora penned *Their Eyes Were Watching God* and around the time when she was crossing the state with Stetson Kennedy. The government commissioned the Depression-era guide series to put writers to work, and all these incredible people of letters contributed with flourishes never seen before in a travel guide. But nobody got a byline, and all the writing is uncredited . . ." Serge found the page he was looking for and thrust a fist in the air. "I knew it! I knew it!" He grabbed Coleman's arms and danced in a circle. "I rock tonight!"

"What did you find?"

Serge plopped down at the desk again, holding up one of the books. "I knew I recognized it from somewhere! Hurston's novel described the Seminoles evacuating ahead of the storm because of how the sawgrass bloomed." He set the book down and picked up another. "And in the guide, virtually the same description. I just discovered an anonymous Zora passage! Prostitution is history!"

"Woo-hoo."

Serge stopped and held the open books side by side, one in each hand. He looked out the window at the sunlit dike, then down at the books, up at the dike, books, dike, books, dike. His eyelids began fluttering again and his pupils rolled back up. Then it passed. "Whoa! . . . Two in a row!"

"Remember that time you had—"

"I know," said Serge. "But this is better than orgasms, give or take . . . There's nothing else in life to compare . . . unless I can figure a way . . ." He let his thought trail off.

"Figure a way what?"

"I don't want to jinx it." Serge reached in one of their shopping bags and pulled out a copy of the morning's *Okeechobee News*.

Coleman popped another can of malt liquor. "I think I'm going to use all the extra space in this room to run around again."

"Knock yourself out."

"Yi-yi-yi-yi-yi . . . Wa-wa-wa-wa-wa . . . Oops, that's enough."

"Why'd you stop so soon?" asked Serge.

"The key is to stop just before you spit up in your mouth."

"I think you've just nailed what to put on your tombstone."

Coleman strolled over to a spacious desk. "What's that? What are you doing now?"

"*Trying* to read the newspaper," said Serge. "I'm required to buy a local newspaper whenever I arrive somewhere, to get in rhythm with the residents. And these small-town papers are the best! No bullshit about celebrity Twitter feuds or a cabinet member spending ten grand on a wastebasket. Check out this front page . . ." He held it up to his pal. ". . . Big photo at the top, 'Veterans Honored,' and another photo of a teen holding up two fish that won a tournament. Over in a box on the side where the weather forecast would normally be: 'Lake level 15.51 feet.' And last but not least, a front-page story you would only find in a paper like this: 'Ball of Light Reported over Lake Okeechobee,' complete with a photo someone took with a cell phone."

Coleman leaned closer. "It's just a black square with a fuzzy circle in the middle. Looks like a streetlight."

"Good a guess as any." Serge grabbed something else. "I get the feeling a lot of people around the lake are often staring up at the sky: 'Sweet Jesus! The aliens are landing again!' 'You're looking at a streetlight like last time, Uncle Biff. Why don't you hand me that beer.' . . . And here's the free town flyer with announcements for lawn-mower races, taco night at the American Legion, and a dunk tank for charity." Serge flipped through the paper until he came to a full-page ad. He leaped up. "Coleman!"

"What?"

"There's a rodeo tonight!"

"What's that mean?"

Serge tossed a duffel bag on the bed. "It means we have to get our uniforms ready . . ."

Chapter 25

The twangs of a guitar floated down the dirt street in pre-dawn hours. A gusting wind picked up pieces of cardboard and newspaper. Men in grimy pants and overalls sat on the porch steps of one of the many juke joints in Belle Glade and Pahokee that stayed open around the clock: small cabins with patrons stumbling in and out, some sleeping in the grass by the back door. Cats and dogs foraged for scraps.

The front of this particular saloon was a random patchwork of corrugated sheet metal. There were signs for Nehi and Royal Crown Cola and Atlantic Ale. Inside the cramped room, loud conversation and thick smoke from filterless cigarettes. A poker game became heated. Under a window stood a wooden pinball machine with a racehorse theme. At the front of the bar, a sweaty, rotund gent sat on a stool that looked like it might collapse from physics. He was the only one wearing a suit, but the jacket had long since been removed, and perspiration pasted the white dress shirt to his chest. A kerosene lantern illuminated other beads of sweat generously cascading down his cheeks. He hunched over his Gibson Archtop guitar, strumming a three-chord Chicago progression and howling the lyrics to "Rope Stretchin'" by Blind Blake. They don't call it the blues for nothing.

In the back corner, beneath other signs for Ice Cold Jax Stout and Cobbs Creek Blended Whiskey, three men huddled over brown bottles.

"I am so sick of this shit," said Johnson.

"Me too," said Cabbage.

"How does he get away with it?" asked Mozelle.

"How? What color is his skin?" said Johnson. "I lost two weeks' pay."

"Then you had it good," said Cabbage. "I was the fool who worked a third week after he kept puttin' me off."

"Somebody needs to do something about that asshole!"

"And end up like Jacob? You weren't there."

"I also heard he got run out of the Dominican for pulling a bunch of the same bullshit."

"They say he doesn't trust the banks or anyone since," said Mozelle. "Keeps everything in gold, who knows where?"

"That's just a crazy rumor," said Johnson.

"Is it? I know a guy who saw him at the bank—"

"I thought he didn't trust banks."

"Not to deposit," said Mozelle. "To change his cash into twenty-dollar gold pieces. Had a big-ass sack of 'em."

Johnson lit a Lucky Strike, and they got another round of Blatz. They sat looking at each other.

"You thinking what I'm thinking?" said Cabbage.

"I'm in," said Mozelle.

"No time like now," said Johnson.

They quickly finished their beer and headed out into the wee hours . . .

After brief trips home, they crept through the night with Colt revolvers and a crowbar, across tomato and strawberry fields. Then they entered rows of tall stalks yielding in the whipping wind.

"You heard about this storm that's supposed to come?" asked Cabbage.

"We always get storms," said Johnson.

"But what about that hurricane two years ago?"

"Lightning doesn't strike twice. Like that's going to happen again so soon."

A gust came through, knocking them off-balance.

"I don't know," said Mozelle. "I heard the Seminoles already came through before sunset for higher ground. They tend to be right."

"They tend to be Indians," said Johnson. "We going to do this or not?"

They finally crouched on the edge of the cane field. Ahead, one of the nicest homes for miles. Columns and a second-floor wrap-around veranda. Johnson took off running, and the rest followed until they were crouched again by a side door. They all reached in their back pockets and pulled out canvas flour bags with holes cut in strategic spots. They pulled them over their heads.

Johnson stuck the crowbar in the frame and cracked the door open. They charged inside and up the stairs to the master bedroom. Fakakta was snoring.

"Where's his wife?"

"This other bedroom," said Johnson, quietly closing another door in the hall.

Mozelle stuck his gun to the baron's head and shook his shoulder. A whisper: "Wake up."

Fakakta finally roused, then sat up quickly. "What do you want?"

"Gold."

Then it all went south in an urgent hurry.

"I recognize your shirt from the fields," said Fakakta. "Blue stripes. What was your name? Mozelle something?"

"Fuck!" He yanked off his flower bag. "Where's the gold?"

"Mozelle, put your bag back on," said Cabbage.

"Why? If he wasn't sure about my name already, you just repeated it!" He swung his gun back to Fulgencio and pressed it between his eyes. "The gold!"

"What gold?" said the baron. "Go ahead and shoot. You're all dead men anyway."

Mozelle cocked the hammer. "You don't seem to be taking this seriously. You think you can just steal from everyone around here and get away with it? Not to mention lynching Jacob. You may not have known, but he was my cousin."

A loud crackle outside as lightning laced the sky. The wind was now up to a roar, whistling through the clapboards and eaves. The shutters began coming loose, banging with a violent rhythm against the side of the house. Other stuff in the yard became airborne and crashed into things. Then another crash, but this one was different. It was inside. The trio saw glass and water explode on the wall over the headboard. Mozelle spun with his pistol.

Bang.

A thud in the doorway.

"Jesus!" yelled Cabbage. "You just shot his wife!"

"She threw a vase at me!"

"We've got more trouble."

They heard footsteps pounding up the stairs. Fulgencio's adult son and chief enforcer, Pablo. With a rifle.

Johnson dashed to the door and fired his Colt, easily picking Pablo off before he reached the landing. The body slumped and tumbled backward down the stairs.

Cabbage grabbed his own head with both hands. "Shit! This was a bad idea! We never should have come!"

"We're way past that now." Johnson smacked the side of Fakakta's head with his pistol. Blood spattered. He smacked him again the other way, then a third time.

"Damn!" said Mozelle. "Aren't you going to ask him any questions?"

Another crack to the skull. "I don't like to repeat myself."

He raised the gun again, and Fakakta raised his hands. "Okay, enough. I'll take you to the gold."

Everyone marched out the back door and leaned forward in a driving rain. Fakakta led them out behind a falling-down old barn that came with the property. He placed his back against the wall, then counted out twenty measured paces. He stopped and pointed down.

Johnson shoved him out of the way and fell to his knees. "Keep him covered." His hands clawed at the dirt. About a foot down, his fingers found netting. He grabbed it and stood, pulling hard. Earth flew. They all froze. An open pit with crate after wooden crate stacked to an unknown depth. Johnson opened the first box. Gasps.

"Look at all that money!"

Then they were all on their knees, running their fingers through the coins. "How much do you think is here? . . ."

Fakakta knew the effect gold had on people. He'd been waiting for his chance. He slowly inched backward, then all at once took off for the house.

"He's running!"

Johnson stood and didn't hurry his shot. Careful aim.

Bang.

Fakakta fell forward into the mud.

"He's crawling," said Cabbage. "He's not dead."

Mozelle calmly crossed the thirty or so yards, until he had walked around in front of the slithering Fulgencio.

The sugar baron raised his face to see the barrel of a gun.

Mozelle cocked it again. "This is for Jacob."

Bang.

"We're definitely going to have to leave the state," said Cabbage. "I got some relatives in Natchez."

"First things first." Johnson grabbed the initial crate and heaved. "Let's get all this out of the ground."

The wind and rain became a brutal impediment, but they were motivated. Soon, crates were spread everywhere.

"He just left all this in a hole?" said Mozelle.

"It ain't going to spoil," said Johnson. "Gold doesn't even tarnish. We need to go back and get your brother's pickup truck. And it'll take more than one trip."

Cabbage wiped water from his eyes and looked up. "Shouldn't it already be getting light out?"

"We just lost track of time," said Mozelle, falling down in the wind and struggling to rise.

"I'll stay here and watch this," said Johnson. "You guys go get the truck—"

There was a sharp cracking sound. Louder than a rifle.

"What the hell was that?"

Then another loud report. More and more followed in quick succession.

"It sounds like trees snapping, but that can't be—"

"Shut up!"

They all stared silent at the woods a quarter mile north of the home. More savage cracking until it was a constant chorus. They strained with their eyes but couldn't make out anything. The noise became a roar of ground-level thunder.

Finally, the last rows of trees on the edge of the woods gave way and splintered and were gone. They looked up in the darkness.

"What the hell is that?" said Cabbage.

Whatever it was, it was traveling fast, at least sixty miles an hour.

When they finally figured out what they were looking at,

it was too much for their brains to process. A couple hundred yards away, they watched the plantation home explode and disappear.

Seconds later, it was right in front of them. Nothing to do but freeze and conjure one last thought: *That fucking lake.*

In surrender, they simply stared straight up into the black, twenty-foot-high tidal wave.

Part Two

Chapter 26

RODEO NIGHT

S erge drove north with a high-end tape recorder in his lap and a microphone in his hand.

CAPTAIN FLORIDA'S LOG, STAR DATE 376.693

The city of Okeechobee rests on the northern tip of the lake by the same name. You just have to love a town that runs off the cliff with its identity, and you never need to be reminded you're in cattle country: the Brahman Theater, Brahman Restaurant & Lounge, Okeechobee High School (Home of the Brahmans), Cowboy's Barbecue, the Cowtown Café, the Cattlemen's Association rodeo arena. The economic center of downtown is the bustling Eli's Western Wear. You can be driving down Main Street on a Tuesday morning and suddenly realize you desperately need a two-thousand-dollar saddle, lassos, spurs, rhinestone belt, and five-foot-long decorative steer horns to hang over the TV. You're in luck! Eli's has amassed a staggering supply. Then there are the cows themselves. Cattle dot the fields all over Central Florida, but nothing like here, where they vastly outnumber the humans, in herds not seen since buffalo covered the prairies in *Dances with Wolves*. Billboards everywhere along the pastures: BEEF, IT'S WHAT'S FOR DINNER, next to grazing livestock unaware of the advertisements for their impending execution.

Speaking of downtown, Main Street is actually called Park Street and there are two of them laid out parallel through the center of the city. Between the pair runs a wide, shaded green space like a series of football fields, starting with a military display of a Vietnam-era Huey helicopter, M60 Patton tank and a couple pieces of heavy ground artillery. From there, the public park has nowhere to go but mellow, with quiet benches, picnic tables, thatched-roof huts and vintage-style lampposts. But wait! There's more! Get ready to seriously crap yourselves! I've kind of been hung up on murals lately, and I'd completely forgotten my favorite part of Okeechobee! It's Mural City, USA! Remember the batshit town-identity thing? And just when you thought the insanity had reached critical mass. That's right: They found more mass! Most antique communities have lots of old brick buildings with empty brick sides, and the residents think nothing of it. Not the fine people here! Sometime back, they went on the mural version of a crack binge, and now you can't throw a cow pie in this place without it sticking to public art. There's a mural celebrating the arrival of the railroad in 1915 with scenes of ice delivery and catfish; another touts an important cattle drive with happy people waiting at the end; there's a car dealership that opened in 1933, and a pioneer hardware store. The side of the Big O drive-through liquor barn has marsh birds flying over the lake, and a country restaurant sports a mural within a mural: a painting of one of those old postcards, WELCOME TO OKEECHOBEE, with each of the giant letters in the city's name a separate homage. And you know how a lot of main streets have abandoned buildings that are simply boarded up with plywood, and jerks spray-paint gang symbols and FUCK THE SYSTEM and giant penises? I think we can all agree that's not going anywhere special. But at the historic and defunct 1923 tan-brick Okeechobee bank, instead of plywood, the town painted all the windows to look like a bunch of customers in period clothing are still inside conducting business! And finally the cherry on the sundae: There's even a mural depicting the history of local phone service ("First Operator, Byrd Sizemore"). I thought something like that would only reach an audience of one. Me. But these are my people! I must stop dictating this now and interact with them . . .

The convenience store had cedar slats. It was sparsely stocked and otherwise empty except for a retired couple at the counter. A wagon wheel leaned against the front of the building, intended to drum up business, but now there were doubts.

Serge and Coleman walked up behind the old people.

The couple was taking an extra-long time with the clerk. An involved conversation, and it wasn't about a transaction.

"Serge, are you going to do anything crazy like the other times?"

"No."

"But when people take forever in convenience stores, you always flip out."

"This is different. I want to listen to small-town talk." Serge blew across the top of a Styrofoam cup. "I already have my coffee, so I can drink it while waiting. Legally they can't touch me as long as I pay."

The old woman clutched a purse in front of her with both hands. "When does Charlie come on?"

"He doesn't work here anymore," said the clerk. "Actually, I'm his son."

"You're Billy?" asked the old man. "You've really grown. I remember when you were this high."

"Billy's my older brother."

"Then that makes you Donny," said the woman. "You've *really* grown."

"Where does your dad work now?" asked the old man.

"Retired," said the clerk. "Just smokes cigars on the porch with the dogs."

"We've always thought the world of Charlie. Your whole family," said the woman. "Can you give him our best?"

"Absolutely."

The couple thanked him and left, and Serge stepped up.

The clerk smiled cordially. "How's your day been going?"

"Magically!" Serge set a cup on the counter. "I already love your family, and we haven't even met!"

The clerk looked down. "It's an empty cup."

"I know the rules." Serge slapped down a couple of dollars. "Technically, I'm still in my lane, so there's no need for trouble."

"No, I mean, don't you want coffee in it?"

Serge patted his stomach. "Already in here."

The clerk leaned over the cup. "Oh, yeah. I see the drops." He smiled again and rang Serge up. "Will there be anything else?"

"Yes!" Serge tossed the cup in the trash. "A side order of country-fried conversation."

"Uh, what?"

"Like you were having with those old folks. I love small-town friendliness!"

"Then you've come to the right place," said the clerk. "If we got any friendlier, people would think we were trying to sell something."

"You are," said Serge. "You're a clerk in a store. Isn't that the program here? Just because the wagon wheel out front didn't fulfill the big dreams, the answer isn't Communism."

Coleman raised his hand. "You should get a mannequin of a hot chick and stick her by the road."

"Coleman! Shhhh!" said Serge. "I'm talking to the guy here. The mannequins draw the wrong crowd, who just want to use the restrooms and aren't too precise about it."

The clerk chuckled. "You guys are funny. What brings you to town?"

"The *town*!" said Serge. "I love everything about it. Right now I'm mentally rocking out to your murals."

"Oh, the murals," said Donny. "Aren't they fantastic? My personal favorite is the telephone one."

"Me too!" said Serge. "Byrdie Sizemore! I know her name is Byrd, but I like to refer to her as Byrdie because it's a free country. I'm always thinking about her. Was she musical? Petulant? Did she find her life's work fulfilling, or just start smashing telephones near the end? And exactly what switchboard call was she connecting in that mural? A family reunion at the old Forsythe place? Gossip about the preacher and the Widow Milsap? An emergency involving moonshine and a two-person tree saw?"

The clerk chuckled again. "Never quite thought about it."

Serge pointed at the duffel bag near his feet, then at the corner of the store. "Can we use your restroom? I actually made a purchase, so we're not from the mannequin crowd. But I will need a while because we have to get dressed for work. Really important gig."

"Take as long as you want," said Donny. "If there's a problem, I'll tell everyone to use the women's room."

"You're good people . . ."

Donny sat back on a stool and resumed flipping through a

magazine with blueprints for patio decks. After a couple minutes, he thought he heard something. He leaned over the counter, looking down the hall to the restrooms. There was a muffled banging sound, then a crash and arguing in hushed tones. *"Let go of me!"* *"Don't screw this up again!"* Another bang. A clanging noise. The door opened and Serge stuck his head out with a grin. "Almost done. There's nothing unusual." The door closed. Bang, bang, bang. *"Dammit!"* *"Shit, my bad."* Then a suspiciously long pause. The door finally opened again.

Serge and Coleman stepped out, and Donny stepped back, scratching his head. "What exactly is this job you do?"

Serge told him.

"Ohhhh." Donny nodded with understanding.

"Don't fib," said Serge. "At first you thought this was weird. Anyway, pleasure to meet, thanks for use of the restroom, and any damage in there was from the other guys."

They left the store, and a gold Plymouth sped off north through the fading light on U.S. Highway 441. Pot smoke wafted out the windows.

"I'm beginning to see why you like country folk so much," said Coleman. "First your little history helper at the motel desk, and now that cool guy in the convenience store."

"Country folk are the best!" said Serge. "That is, most of the time."

Puff, puff. "What do you mean?"

"Don't get me wrong: Everything is usually finger-lickin' fantastic," said Serge. "Until you get lost driving through deep fog in the woods at night with no cell service or GPS. Then you notice a tiny light on in the distance at an isolated farmhouse. So you knock on the door for directions, and the next thing you know, you're handcuffed to a radiator while a family in bib overalls giggles and rubs mice on your face, and one of them says, 'Go get the twins.' And someone else opens a cellar door, and these two little albinos with pointy teeth show up, and you're like, 'Where in the fuck is this going?' But you know that all the signs so far are not positive, and then somehow you free yourself and run outside. Your car is just feet away and the keys are still in your pocket, but for some reason you tell yourself, 'That's a stupid idea. I'll run for a barn way out in that dark field.' You dash inside the rickety structure to find all kinds of thick chains hanging from the rafters with hooks and rusty scything blades, and a mottled hand is reaching up from a fresh grave in the dirt floor. Then a chain saw roars to life outside and you dive behind bales of hay as flashlight beams pierce through slats in the barn wall. And that's if you're lucky. Sometimes the family is into Amway: 'No, I don't want to join!' 'It'll change your life!' And then they're chasing you to the barn with pamphlets and brochures."

"Amway," said Coleman, shaking with the willies.

The Plymouth pulled off the road. "Here we are."

Other cars were already parked, many more arriving. People streamed toward what looked like an old minor-league baseball stadium in Oshkosh. Erector-Set girders and rusty metal sheeting over the stands in case of rain.

Serge and Coleman made their way to the entrance of the rodeo arena. A cashier in the ticket booth gave their outfits a double take, then asked for the admission fee.

Serge shook his head. "We're clowns. We're authorized."

"You're in the show?" asked the cashier.

Serge adjusted the red ball on his nose. "Why else would we be dressed like this? Just because we decided to pretend like we work here?"

"But the clowns have already arrived."

"They called for backup." Serge flashed a clown badge. "There could be trouble tonight. I'd count on it."

She shrugged and let them pass.

Coleman slapped floppy shoes on the walkway. "What do we do now?"

"Act like we belong."

They arrived at a fence along the side of the dusty arena. A cowgal in scarlet-fringed riding chaps went by on a horse. Sandy-blond locks flowed out from under her black Stetson hat. She proudly raised a giant American flag as they played "The Star-Spangled Banner."

Coleman nudged his buddy. "Look who it is."

"I know," said Serge. "My little history helper. Imagine that."

Coleman nudged him again. "She's wearing a plaid shirt."

"Shut up."

After a few preliminary announcements over the PA system, a galvanized metal gate burst open. A cowboy swung a free arm in the air as a bronco fiercely fought to dislodge him. After eight seconds, he hit the dirt in a nasty spill. The crowd stood in silent concern. The cowboy jumped right up and waved to them with his hat.

The PA announcer: "Let's hear it for Sundance Cassidy."

Wild cheering.

Serge wound his way through spectators along the fence— "Excuse me, excuse me, coming through . . ."—until he came to an access gate and a security guard. "Thank you for your service. Could you please open that?"

"Who are you?"

Serge looked at Coleman. "Who are we?" Then back at the guard. "Who does it look like we are? Is this your first rodeo?"

"But the clowns are already out there."

"New liability insurance rule: more clowns."

"I'm going to have to check with a supervisor."

"Go ahead," Serge said as a bronco thundered by, throwing the rider into the fence. "Meanwhile, someone gets hurt, lawsuits fly, and then you're stuttering on the witness stand about why you withheld lifesaving clown procedures."

PA: "Let's hear it for Blueridge Grymes!"

"Well, okay, you seem authorized."

Serge and Coleman waved to the crowd as they strolled across the dirt. Coleman stopped and looked at something stuck to the bottom of one of his big floppy shoes.

"Seriously?" said Serge. "Already?"

"It's everywhere."

Serge pointed. "There's our command post."

They took up positions behind a pair of oak barrels, leaning with their elbows.

"This is it? This is a job?" Coleman whistled. "Clowns have it all figured out."

"The clowning life is extreme boredom punctuated by bursts of sheer terror."

"I remember those birthday parties."

PA: "Let's hear it for Omaha Kid Sloane!"

Gate after gate flew open, and cowboy after cowboy flew through the air. More names from the PA were announced and applauded: Boone Cartwright, Doc Hickock, Austin Buck, Deadwood Dixon, Medicine Hat McCoy.

"What are those big animals over there?" asked Coleman. "They look nasty."

"They are," said Serge, resting his chin on top of a barrel. "Brahma bulls. Unlike horses, they have vicious horns. Only the bravest ride them."

"People *ride* them?" said Coleman. "And we're going to be *out* here? What if they come after me and I get scared?"

"Just get inside one of these barrels. That's what they're for."

Coleman nodded. "You know what I'm thinking about now?"

"The panel is stumped."

"My taste buds."

"Still goose eggs. Please proceed."

"You know how you loved some foods as a kid, but unless you make it a point, you don't get the chance anymore?" said Coleman. "I miss SpaghettiOs."

"This is your news flash?" said Serge.

"Just sayin'."

"But I do feel your pain," said Serge. "Our taste buds have changed, despite all my efforts. It's no coincidence that Chef Boyardee has two different gustation formulas for kids and grown-ups, developed through rigorous kindergarten focus groups. Same thing with the little McDonald's hamburgers. They needed a gateway drug to get kids hooked, but adults were unreliable test subjects, so the winning formula had to be the result of random permutations screened by the preschool set. How else would you explain the counterintuitive final strokes of adding a dollop of mustard and diced pieces of sautéed onions? I remember when I was five taking one of my hamburgers apart: 'I must learn what kind of party is going on in this thing because Mom never comes close!' And the next time she made hamburgers at home: 'Mom, I'll get the mustard and you grab the little translucent squares.'"

"I still like peanut butter and jelly," said Coleman.

"Those sandwiches are critical to keeping your childhood taste buds in shape, or you end up an asshole in a restaurant mispronouncing *foie gras*— . . . Shit, terror time!"

"What is it?"

"That cowboy's starting to slide off the horse but it looks like his left foot is stuck in the stirrup! . . . We're on!"

Serge dashed out into the arena, just as the bronco rider hit the ground and began being dragged through the dirt. Other clowns ran in from the other direction, trying to distract the horse and slow it down. The rider was taking a beating.

Then something nobody had seen before. Serge kicked off his clown shoes, running alongside the slowed horse to get his timing right. Suddenly he leaped, grabbing the saddle knob, getting a foot in the right stirrup and pulling himself aboard. He had the advantage of being able to use both hands, while the horse was hampered by the weight of what he was dragging.

Serge leaned all the way forward, wrapping his arms around the horse's neck, stroking it and whispering in a big brown ear.

The horse began to calm until it stopped. They freed the rider's foot as Serge hopped down and walked around to the front of the horse. He said a few more words in private. The horse whinnied, nickered and snorted. Serge patted him above the nose.

Nearby, the fallen cowboy leaped to his feet.

"Let's hear it for Kyle Lovitt!"

Thunderous cheers.

An older man in a white Stetson ran out onto the dirt. "What have you done?"

"Official clown business," said Serge.

"You broke my bronco!"

Serge patted the side of the horse's head. Another whinny. "He doesn't look broken."

"I mean he won't buck anymore," said the ranch owner. "He's useless at rodeos now."

Serge held out upturned palms. "No good deed goes unpunished..."

Meantime, the thrown rider named Kyle had walked over to one of the officials at the fence, who relayed a message up to the PA booth.

"Ladies and gentlemen, this is quite unusual, but just before our intermission Kyle is going to ride again. Of course it won't count in the official standings, but it's the least we can do for one of our brave military veterans."

More wild cheering.

Kyle climbed onto another saddle, gripped tightly with one hand and nodded that he was ready...

Chapter 27

S enior year.
Coach Calhoun had finally resigned himself to wearing bifocals.

He was sitting behind his desk going over the tryout sheet for the upcoming season. Seemed everyone wanted to play for Pahokee. He ran a finger down the list of names. The finger stopped. A slight smile. No surprise there.

A knock at the door.

He removed the glasses. "Chris, come in."

"Thanks, Coach." She'd gone through a growth spurt over the last three years and was nearing five ten. The chair on the other side of the coach's desk was getting small.

"As usual, you want to talk about something?"

"I'm not asking for any favors . . ."

"I already know where this is going," said Calhoun. "You signed up again for tryouts."

"Four years in a row," said Chris. "This is my last chance."

The coach took a deep breath with paternal eyes. "Chris, I want you to listen carefully to me and take it to heart. I never saw this coming when we first met, but I can't tell you what a pleasure it's been. You make all this worthwhile. You're the kind of student that inspires teachers to teach, and coaches to coach. You've got the best attitude, been the best manager, but most important, you've kept your grades way up."

She sat silent and serious.

"Look," said Calhoun. "Yes, a lot of these boys are going to get athletic scholarships, but I'd be more than shocked if you didn't land an academic one. You're going to go on and make everyone at this school proud."

"Thank you. It means a lot." She looked down.

The coach sighed in frustration. "Chris, you're asking the unrealistic." He held up the tryout sheet. "Do you know how many students we're going to have to cut as it is?"

"Coach, I don't care if I have to ride the bench. I don't care if I never play. I would just be proud to wear the uniform." She placed a hand on her chest where the numbers would go. "As I said, no favors. If I don't earn it, so be it. But I've really been working on my kicking over the summer. Can you just come out to the field and take a look?"

Calhoun slowly began to nod. "Okay, you've more than earned a look. But promise me that this won't get your hopes up . . ."

The receivers coach, the one named Odom, had been promoted to the head position a couple seasons back. He heard a knock on his office door.

"Lamar, come in. What's up?"

The coach pulled out a chair. "I want you to keep an open mind."

"Uh-oh, I've heard that one before."

Calhoun explained what he had in mind. "What do you think?"

A long pause. "Lamar, I know how fond you are of Chris. And you know I am as well. But we already have two solid place kickers coming back from last year, and an even better punter."

"A lot of teams carry three place kickers," said Calhoun.

"I know, in case of injury or ineligibility," said Odom. "But often the third-stringer plays another position. We have a cornerback who can easily fill in."

"Would you send him out for a field goal in the final seconds?"

"Are you trying to tell me Chris will be our best kicker?"

"No, third best. But a solid third," said Calhoun. "Can you do me a favor? . . ."

Minutes later, both coaches stood with folded arms on the side of an empty field. Chris was waiting at the thirty-yard line with a big sack of footballs spilled onto the ground.

"Okay, Chris!" shouted Lamar. "Show him what you showed me."

She teed up a ball between the hash marks, took the requisite steps back and stopped. She let her arms dangle in concentration. Then she loped forward and let it fly.

It was a perfect end-over-end kick—that hooked left of the upright.

Calhoun looked sideways. "But it had plenty of distance." Odom didn't respond.

She teed up another. It split the uprights.

"See?" said Calhoun.

"That's just one-for-two," said Odom.

Chris proceeded through the rest of the balls on the grass. Except for one that bounced off the crossbar, they were all true down the middle.

"What do you think now?" asked Calhoun.

"It's different in helmet and pads," said Odom. "Even more so in game situations . . ."

The next day, all the returning players and would-bes covered the field. Whistles blew. Students were sorted according to position. And a handful collected around the coach in charge of kickers. They started at the fifteen-yard line. The coach made notes on a clipboard as each player took shots at the goalposts.

The field had been such chaos earlier, with so many more players than usual, that they didn't notice. But now they did, nudging each other and pointing downfield at a particular player with the number 00.

Chris kicked a modest-length field goal. Then the players didn't pay any more attention. They were too busy trying to make the team. They moved the kicking tees back ten yards and the hopefuls went at it again . . .

Tryouts continued pretty much as they all do. Triage. The ones who were definitely going to make the team, the ones who had no prayer, and the middle group clinging to a dream.

The day of reckoning came. Tryouts were over. Players filled a hallway, nervous silence, waiting. A door opened and they perked up. The head coach came out of the locker room and taped a sheet of paper on the wall. The final list. Students lined up single file, taking turns, one by one, looking for their name. Then either an under-the-breath "Yes!" or demure heartbreak.

Chris's nerves couldn't take it. She had deliberately placed herself at the very end of the line, because she didn't want anyone else around when she got the news. Finally there was only one boy left in front of her. He read down the list, twice, then hung his head and walked away. She watched until he was out of sight, and took a deep breath. "This is it."

She stepped up to the wall and read down the first column with no luck. Her eyes started down the second and she had to take a break from the tension. There weren't a lot of names left, and that would be it. Chris summoned courage and went back to the list. Almost exactly where she had left off, she immediately saw it. And her hand went over her mouth. "Oh, my God."

Her name.

She kept blinking and checking again because she didn't trust her eyes. But each time it was still there.

The empty hallway echoed with joy. *"Wooooo-hoooooooooo!"*

She jumped up and down and spun around, crashing into Coach Calhoun. He steadied her by the arms. "Easy, you don't want to hurt yourself before the season."

"I didn't know you were there. Where'd you come from?"

"I kind of wanted to be here."

"Oh, thank you! Thank you! Thank you!"

Now Calhoun grabbed her wrists and pulled them back. "Okay, new rule. You don't hug coaches."

"Sorry, it's just . . ."

"I know." He began walking away. "Get some sleep. Practice starts tomorrow."

Chapter 28

OKEECHOBEE RODEO

The gate burst open wide with an explosion of horse.

It was the encore performance everyone had been awaiting from the service veteran. This bronco bucked even meaner than the first, but Kyle Lovitt was more than up to it. This time, the ride went flawlessly through the required eight seconds, and Kyle jumped down like a dismounting gymnast to stick the landing.

The PA announcer needn't comment. The crowd was already on its feet.

A smaller gate opened, and a cowgal ran into the arena. She tearfully hugged Kyle. "You were magnificent!"

Serge strolled over. "Hope I'm not interrupting anything."

The woman turned, and suddenly Serge had tight arms around

his neck. "I saw what you did for Kyle! Thank you! Thank you! Thank you! . . ."

"Easy now." Serge grabbed her wrists to pull them down. "All in a clown's day, Cheyenne."

"Thank you . . . Wait, how do you know my name?"

The clown removed his red-ball nose and replaced it. "It's me, Serge, from the motel. You're my little history helper."

"Serge?" Cheyenne said in surprise. "I didn't know you were with the rodeo."

"Neither do they," said Serge. "So I guess Kyle's your boyfriend."

"No, silly. My brother."

Serge extended an earnest hand. "I always appreciate a chance to thank one of our heroes who protects the cornucopia of freedoms in this land."

Kyle shook the hand. "I'm not a hero."

"And that's exactly what every single hero says, or they wouldn't be heroes," added Serge. "If you walked around all day bragging about how great you are, I guess you'd be . . . I don't know, elected something?"

Cheyenne squeezed his hand. "Thanks again for helping him with that horse."

"And thanks again for his service," said Serge. "Kyle, where were you stationed?"

"Two tours Afghanistan, one Iraq."

The cowgal glanced around. "So is your friend with you?"

"Coleman?" Now it was Serge's turn to look around. "I completely forgot in all the excitement. Where is that idiot?"

They checked in every direction, until Serge's eyes stopped. Smoke was drifting out of one of the barrels. "Excuse me," he said. "This will only take a sec . . ."

The lid of a wooden barrel was raised, and Coleman looked up. "Hey, Serge."

"What the hell do you think you're doing?"

"Nuthin'."

"I never thought I would utter this sentence, but you can't smoke dope in a clown barrel."

"I got scared," said Coleman. "Just trying to take the edge off."

"Well, don't!" snapped Serge. "Now get out here. There's someone I want you to meet . . ."

Serge grinned with embarrassment as he led his pal back across the arena. "Coleman, I'd like you to meet Cheyenne's brother, Kyle, one of our nation's military heroes."

Coleman stared at an empty sleeve in Kyle's cowboy shirt. "You only have one arm."

"Coleman! For God's sake! You can't just go up to people and say they only have one arm. *Especially* when they only have one arm." Serge turned. "My deepest apologies."

"Don't worry about it," said Kyle.

"What happened to the arm?" asked Coleman.

"Jesus!" Serge smacked his forehead.

"That's all right," said Kyle. "IED went off outside Kandahar. We lost a good woman that day. She was my flank. Next to that, the arm's nothing."

Serge lowered his head. "Your breed never ceases to amaze me. Living by your own high moral code when the rest of us seem to be living by an anti-code. Just so you know, I also live by my own code, drawn from ancient Greeks, Renaissance thinkers, the Age of Reason, President Lincoln and Stones lyrics—'the better angels of our nature,' and 'you can't always get what you want'—if you catch my drift. A lot of my code still doesn't make sense, but that's the whole point, isn't it? Kant borrowed from the Roman poet Horace the Latin phrase *sapere aude,* which translates to 'dare to know,' or essentially, 'Challenge yourself to accept hard and inconvenient truths,' as opposed to the current prevailing wisdom: 'Fuck you and the facts you rode in on.' I don't know the Latin for that."

A pause. "What are you talking about?" asked Kyle.

"I'm not sure," said Serge.

"Uh, you don't know what you're talking about?"

"No, I mean that's the title of my life's philosophy. The only thing I'm absolutely certain of is that *I'm Not Sure,*" said Serge. "It's my catchphrase. Walk through the concrete human rain forest with that perspective, and ninety-nine times out of a hundred you'll be more correct than the people who *are* sure. Why? you ask. Okay, hold on to your hat, Kyle, because you've been out of the country for a while . . ." Serge leaned closer and dropped his voice ". . . believe it or not, it's now totally okay to make up every single thing that comes out of your mouth." He stopped and nodded hard. "I know, I know. It's hard to believe, but it's so widespread it's often the person standing right next to you."

"I agree," said Coleman, "because pot makes me smart."

"Excuse me." Cheyenne pointed to activity in the starting gates. "Intermission's ending. We need to be going before the Brahma bulls start."

"Good talk!" said Serge, glancing toward the far side of the arena. "Back to live action . . ."

Elbows rested atop the barrels again. A gate swung open. A bull bucked.

"Those were some good folk," said Serge. "Gives me hope."

"One arm, geez."

"Can you stop?"

"No, I'm just trying to remember what not to say. Anything else?"

"If someone has a mole on their face the size of a pepperoni," said Serge.

"How many times do I have to apologize for that?"

"But did you actually have to use the word 'pepperoni'?"

Yelling and gasps from the crowd.

"Uh-oh," said Serge. "We're needed again."

Serge took off across the dirt, and Coleman dove in a barrel.

A frenzy of clown activity swirled in the middle of the arena. The rider had been thrown clear, but the bull came back to stomp and gore, as they're prone to do. The clowns jumped and whooped to distract the ton of fury from the hapless cowhand . . . Across the arena, a curious head popped out of a barrel and peeked around, puffing a joint.

For some reason, this interested the bull. He turned and stared toward the barrel.

Coleman casually looked around the arena as he puffed. Until his eyes locked with the bull's. He shrieked in alarm. The joint went flying, and the bull came running.

"Crap!" Coleman pulled the lid back down on top of the barrel and squeezed his hands together in prayer. "Please, please, please . . ."

Thundering hooves approached. The point of a long white horn pierced the barrel, and the whole thing was suddenly on its side. Another horn attacked the wood as the container began to rotate across the dirt under the momentum of the raging steer. If it had been a car wreck, it would have been called a barrel roll. In this case, it literally was a barrel roll.

Coleman looped and spun and looped some more in an unending violent cascade down the length of the arena. He covered his mouth between bulging cheeks. "Starting to get a little sick in here . . ."

Meanwhile, everyone else was able to flee to safety either through hurriedly opened gates or by wildly scrambling over fences. After he helped vault the last person's butt up over the barrier into safety, only Serge was left.

He spun in highly emotional concern. "Coleman, my best pal! . . ."

Angry horns drove the barrel forward, rolling by in front of Serge.

"I don't like this anymore," Coleman yelled with an echo, as if he was shouting from the bottom of a well. "I'm too high."

"Hang tight! I'm so sorry for getting you into this! I'll never forgive myself!"

The rest of the clowns reemerged with the other rodeo staff, who were expert in handling this most dangerous aspect of the event. They surrounded the bull, speaking softly with calm movements. Then they lassoed its horns and brought the beast under control before guiding it into a secure chute.

The clowns righted the barrel, and Serge pulled off the lid. "Buddy! Are you okay?"

"What's happening?" Coleman had made himself into a ball. "Is it over?"

"You're safe now."

Coleman slowly stood up in the barrel. As soon as his curly red wig was visible, the crowd went wild.

One of the top rodeo officials trotted over in seriousness. "We saw everything that happened. We know what was going on."

"You do?" said Serge.

The official nodded. "And you guys aren't on our official list. What's your name?"

"Serge."

"No, him."

"Uh, Coleman."

"Coleman, come with me . . ." They pulled him out of the barrel, and the official took him by the arm. "This way."

Serge ran alongside. "I can explain."

"Save your breath." They reached the center of the arena, and someone handed the official a wireless microphone. He tapped it to make sure it was on, and the sound bounced off the metal roofs. "Ladies and gentlemen, we have just witnessed an amazing display of heroism. While Idaho Jack was in danger of serious injury, and the other clowns weren't having luck controlling the bull, Coleman here . . ." He turned. "It's Coleman, right? Coleman here took stock of the situation and swung into action without regard for his personal well-being, getting the bull's attention and bravely provoking it to attack his barrel, thus averting tragedy . . . Coleman, to what do you owe your quick thinking?"

Coleman leaned toward the microphone. "Pot makes me smart." He stood back up straight and grinned extra wide.

"Uh . . ." said the official. "Well, there you have it. Let's hear it for Coleman."

The standing ovation was deafening.

Serge stood next to Cheyenne and Kyle. "Unbelievable."

T he quartet of new friends grabbed nachos and sat at a picnic table on the side of the rodeo.

Serge scooped salsa and sour cream. *Crunch, crunch.* "Normally I never eat sporting-event nachos because they're covered with the kind of kiosk-vat molten cheese that you're forced to deal with later, so I'm baking that into my schedule ahead of time. Don't let it affect your appetite . . . Kyle, what's next for you?"

Kyle looked at his sister. "I have that thing tomorrow morning, so I need to come by and get the flags."

"What thing?" said Serge. "What flags?"

"A funeral," said Cheyenne. "North of here an hour."

Kyle wasn't eating. "Someone from my unit."

"Sorry for your loss," said Serge. "So the flags? You're in the color guard or something?"

"I wish it was like that." He pushed his cardboard container of chips toward the center of the table. "No matter how hard I try, I just can't understand it."

"Understand what?" asked Serge.

"Protesters," said Cheyenne. "They picket military funerals."

"Come again?" said Serge. "You're stringing words that don't go together."

"And they shouldn't," said Cheyenne. "But here we are."

"What on earth can they be protesting?" asked Serge.

"Our nation's growing tolerance for gays in general, and those serving in uniform in particular," said Cheyenne. "The protesters claim that *all* our fallen heroes—gay, straight, whatever—are

God's punishment for our wicked ways. I can't bear to repeat what's on the signs they wave."

"Wait," said Serge. "Is this that wacko church in Kansas?"

"They may have started it and gotten the headlines," said Kyle. "But the movement's spread. They also picket recruitment centers and pride parades and even other Christian churches that they consider too inclusive. But the worst are the funerals."

"Not to make any excuses," said Serge, "but relative to the size of the country, we're talking about an extremely tiny number."

"How few is an acceptable number when you know the person being laid to rest?"

"True, true."

"But you raise a good point," said Kyle. "The idiots yelling in the streets are a small fraction. The problem is the complicit silence of a large segment of the population. They may not care for that kind of cruelty at funerals, but they're plenty cruel the rest of the time."

"Please elaborate."

"The bellwether is political campaigns," said Kyle. "One thing politicians can be counted on is to follow the polls, regardless of what they personally believe or who gets hurt. A while back it was 'don't ask, don't tell.' Then society evolved, or at least fifty-one percent did, and that cynical ploy is no longer reliable. So now when some elected cretin needs a poll bump, they've moved on to attacking one of the last acceptable targets—transgender citizens—which is code for broader hate that's not exactly cool to articulate anymore. And these leaders wouldn't be doing it if the polls didn't tell them enough of the public was behind them. That's what really hurts . . ."

Serge didn't know what to say, so he did the right thing and didn't say anything.

"Those of us out in the field know these people. We *are* these people, whether it personally applies or not, because all we have out there is each other, and when you know you can trust someone with your life, you wouldn't notice or care if they're a Martian. When all is said and done, you realize these are some of the finest people you'll ever meet in life. That's why it's so hard to fathom our political leaders today. Can you imagine what it's like to be in a gun battle, and you're fighting shoulder to shoulder with a member of your unit who just heard on the news that morning that some idiot back home is trying to score votes by saying people of his faith aren't welcome in the very country that he's risking his life to protect? And people cheer this shit in large arenas. The funeral protesters are just the spearhead."

"So this cause of yours is a liberal thing?" asked Serge.

"Not remotely," said Kyle. "It runs the whole spectrum. We got artsy-fartsy types, bikers, pointy heads, guys with shotguns in the back windows of their pickups. Most of us are vets, and the one principle that unites us all is: Don't mess with our brothers- and sisters-in-arms."

Serge nodded. "Explain the business about the flags tomorrow."

"Courts have ruled that the protesters are protected by the First Amendment, which I agree with because that's part of what I fought for—"

Serge inadvertently glanced at an empty sleeve.

"—But they also ruled that the picketers must stay at least three hundred feet away from the funeral. Me and my friends, on the other hand, aren't protesting, so the buffer zone doesn't apply to us. We arrive early and line up twenty feet in front of the protest with our huge, overlapping American flags that completely block the view of those at the cemetery paying their respects."

"But I'm sure the protesters are shouting," said Serge.

"That's why we play inspirational music on boom boxes," said Kyle.

"Like what?"

"Like 'This Land Is Your Land.'"

"Where do I sign up?"

"Can you carry a flag? . . ."

The night eventually wound down, and the friends bade each other good night with plans to meet in the morning.

Serge went back in the motel room, heading for the fridge. "I'm already regretting the nachos." He uncapped a bottle of water and turned around. "Coleman!"

"What?"

"You left the door open! Here come the frogs!"

Coleman looked down at something huge leaping through the wickets of his legs.

"Dammit!" Serge dropped to the floor and crawled under the bed. Coleman screamed and ran out the door.

Serge snagged the jumbo amphibian and scooted backward out from under the box spring. As he did, two more frogs hopped under the bed. "The door's still open! Where's that fool?"

He headed for the sidewalk to release his captive and almost bumped into someone.

"Cheyenne! Sorry, didn't see you." He bent down to let the creature hop off into the dark parking lot. "What are you doing back here?" He checked out the cowgal outfit she was still wearing. "I thought this was your rodeo night."

"If you work at a motel, you accept the hours." She gestured back over her shoulder at a sheepish Coleman. "He said you needed a frog rescue."

"Not me, but Coleman definitely needs a rescue, and frogs are the least of it." Serge looked up at a small swirl of insects around one of the porch lights on the motel's walkway. "Are those the blind mosquitoes?"

"That's them."

"What's the big deal everyone's talking about?" said Serge. "I've seen worse swarms of butterflies."

"Oh, that's not remotely close to a swarm. Just a few stragglers out for a stroll. But it does mean they're coming."

"How long?"

"Could be a day, could be three." Cheyenne didn't even know

she was doing it, but she leaned against the doorway with subconscious body language. "You know, you were pretty good out there tonight. Most clowns just run around randomly to create confusion in the animals."

Serge noticed she was absentmindedly rubbing the tip of a cowboy boot on the ground. He cleared his throat: "Uh, you wouldn't happen to have any more vacant rooms tonight?"

"Sure, right next to yours. Why? Expecting anyone?"

"Something's come up. We'll take it."

"I'll go get the key . . ."

She returned in a moment, opening the second room herself. "There you go."

Serge grabbed Coleman by the arm, shoving him inside. "And there *you* go."

"Hey!" yelled Coleman. "What's the deal? . . . Ah, frogs came in! Help!"

"And there are plenty more where that came from if you open this door. Now stay put!" Serge slammed it shut.

"What's going on?" asked Cheyenne.

"Coleman's a crowd. Please, come in."

The second the door closed, Cheyenne's head slowly swiveled around the room with open eyes. "If you're a motel manager, you develop instincts, but I didn't peg you for the damage type. Did you invite a rock star you didn't tell me about?"

Serge threw his arms up in exasperation. Just about everything was knocked over. Broken lightbulbs, torn curtains, pillows disemboweled. "It's Mr. Zippy."

On cue, a ferret jumped up to the TV, standing on his hind legs and chattering demonically. Then he hopped down and scattered Coleman's empty beer bottles like bowling pins. "He's wrapped way too tight, and I'm afraid we're unfit parents. But I've been putting off the inevitable because I didn't want it to reflect poorly on the adoption rights of two dudes."

"No problem," said Cheyenne. "This is a family-run place, and we have a large cage in the back room for the day manager, who has an older cat that needs care. I can put the ferret in there, and I know lots of pet people around here who would be more than happy to take him."

"Thank God," said Serge. "He was getting on my last nerve."

"Be right back." Cheyenne lovingly grabbed the ferret and disappeared.

Then she returned. As soon as Serge opened the door, she slammed into him without warning, and they fell onto the still-made bed. Violent kissing and groping. Clothes flew in all directions. "Can you leave the boots on?" asked Serge. "You can make requests, too."

"Shut up!"

"Haven't had that one before."

They were soon going at it like—well, they deserve *some* privacy.

Shrieking and banging came from both sides of the wall connecting Coleman's room to theirs.

Serge raised a hand. "Can I talk now?"

"Sure, just don't stop."

"That's not really my call," said Serge. "If you haven't noticed, you're the one on top."

"*Oh, yes, yes, yes, yes!*..."—pounding the headboard—"*... Yes! Yes! Yes!* ... Before we go any further, I need to ask a question."

"Further?" asked Serge. "I don't see any more stop signs."

"It's about commitment. You're not one of those guys, I mean..."

Great, Serge thought. *Here we go again.*

Cheyenne continued thrusting. "Did you just roll your eyes at me?"

"No, that was a twitch. Please, ask your question."

"Every once in a while I'll find a guy where there's the perfect combination of a meeting of the minds and broiling animal attraction. But more often than not, they turn out to be clinging vines."

"Wait," said Serge. "*That's* your commitment question? You were worried I'd be the smothering one?"

She nodded and thrust. "I hope you understand. There's too many places I've got to see. I'm sure you've heard the song."

"In my sleep," said Serge. "Believe me, you have no worries. And I completely understand about the travelin' jones."

More screaming from Coleman's room. A crash against the wall. "*Frogs!*"

Thrust. "Is your friend okay?"

"Not even close. I just tune out the meltdowns."

Thrust, thrust. "The whole history thing is what first attracted me to you."

"Really?" said Serge. "Me too! Would you like to see my tombstone rubbings?"

"Now?" Cheyenne thrust harder as she whipped her hair side to side. "Isn't that part supposed to come before, when you're trying to *get* me in bed?"

"You're right," said Serge. "Life is all about timing."

"Man, you're weird," said Cheyenne. "For some reason, that just attracts me more."

"And this concludes the slow middle movement of our song. Now it's time for the triple-guitar crescendo." Serge quickly flipped her on the bed, and moans became shrieks, louder and louder. To the point where Coleman stopped shrieking himself and became more afraid of the sounds coming from the next room . . .

The lovers finally collapsed on their backs in pools of sweat.

Serge wiped stinging perspiration from his eyes. "My compliments to the chef."

"I'm still fluttering," said Cheyenne. "And speaking of fluttering, what was that deal with your eyelids and your pupils going up in your head?"

"I had a simultaneous."

"Don't you mean *we* had a simultaneous?"

Serge shook his head. "Just me. I came *and* had A Moment. Thinking about all the murals in town and early telephone service."

"You're shitting me."

"You'd rather me think about old girlfriends, or picture you wearing a walrus mask?"

"I'm not sure." She turned her head on the pillow. "Let's find out."

"Serious?"

She nodded eagerly.

"Where's your cowboy hat?"

"In the office." Cheyenne jumped out of bed. "I'll go get it."

She wiggled into her blue jeans and opened the door. A truck with a full rack of amber lights was pulling up. "What the hell is that?"

"Ordered a rental fishing boat," said Serge. "They attach a temporary hitch on your car and everything. I always figure if you're going in, go big!"

"If you say so."

"Just realized something," said Serge. "What if other guests are trying to call you at the front desk with an emergency?"

"Screw 'em. They're just frogs."

Chapter 29

PAHOKEE

The Blue Devils were an early-season favorite, and they lived up to the hype. Pahokee tore through their district schedule, undefeated after six games. And it wasn't even close. All double-digit victories. You could always pick out the loudest voice on the bench shouting encouragement. Guess who?

A few weeks earlier, before a game, Coach Calhoun was smiling behind his desk as Chris sat on the other side. He actually looked forward to her visits now, and felt something conspicuously missing on the days she didn't show up.

She was wearing her shoulder pads and game jersey: 00. He noticed she was unusually serious.

"Is something wrong?"

"Oh, no, no, no," said Chris. "It's just that I feel awkward asking you for something."

"Never stopped you before."

"But you've done so many favors for me in the last few years."

"What's one more? Fire away."

"But I promised you."

"Promised me what?"

"That I didn't care if I never got on the field," said Chris. "I just wanted to wear the uniform."

"And?"

"I learned that to earn a varsity letter, you have to be in at least one play during a regular-season game."

"Is that so?"

"Coach, in several of these games we've had big leads late in the fourth quarter."

"Some actually huge."

"What I'm asking is, if we're leading by several touchdowns near the end and we score, uh—"

"You'd like to kick off?"

She nodded.

"All right, you've asked," said Calhoun. "We'll just see how it goes. Now, if I could have the office, there's a few things that need dealing with before tonight."

That evening's game proceeded like the previous six Fridays. The Blue Devils built up an early lead, and the defense held their opponent to only three first downs. By the beginning of the fourth quarter, it was 35–0. It was raining.

Calhoun walked over to the head coach for a private talk. By the body language, it seemed that Lamar had to be persistent. Finally, and in no small part simply in order to get Calhoun off his back, the head coach said: "We'll just have to see."

Rain poured harder and the field began turning to mud. Runners lost their footing and passes were impossible to catch. Referees had towels on the field to wipe the ball down between each snap.

It was time to call running plays from here on out. Not to move the ball, but to burn the clock. It was also one of those unwritten rules of football decorum. Don't pass and run up the score at the end. That's why the entire team on the field was second and third string. And even then, Pahokee was unstoppable. They consistently moved the ball five to ten yards a play. They entered the red zone, which means the twenty. Three minutes left.

Lamar Calhoun finished another chat with the head coach and walked back over to the players' bench. "Chris?"

She was leaning forward, wrapped up in the game and still shouting encouragement. She raised her eyes. "Yes, Coach?"

"Start warming up."

It froze her.

"Did you hear me?"

An eager nod. She sprang off the bench and began running toward the practice kicking net.

"Aren't you forgetting something?" Calhoun pointed back under the bench. "You're going to need that."

Chris raced back and snatched her helmet.

Pahokee scored again even faster than expected. Chris barely had time to stretch, no practice kicks. She ran onto the field with ten boys as the rain whipped even harder. Some of her teammates raced past her, slapping her shoulder pads. "Show 'em what you got, Chris."

As she teed up the ball, shouting came from the opposite sidelines. The other coach frantically waved his clipboard at his receiving team. They had just realized a girl was kicking. "Move up! Move up!"

The visiting team advanced ten yards.

The clipboard kept waving. "More!"

The players positioned themselves fifteen yards ahead of where they normally fielded a kick.

Chris stared down at the ball and took a few steps back. Thunder boomed from the clouds over the stadium lights. She looked left and right down the Blue Devil line. Boys nodded back, helmets dripping. The referee blew a whistle for play to resume. Chris ran forward and put her shoe into the leather.

Now here's the thing about kickoffs: they're live balls. Which means that after it travels ten yards, either team can grab it for possession.

It was an exceptionally high kick, which, along with the rain, threw off the receiving team's depth perception. They began slowly backpedaling. Meanwhile, the Pahokee line was sprinting full speed. By the time the visiting team realized the ball was seriously over their heads, all the players were at roughly the same spot on the field.

The ball bounced at the two-yard line and rolled into the end zone. Now it was a full-out race to see who could get there first. A player in a blue jersey leaped horizontally and landed on the ball just before it rolled out of bounds. The referee raised two arms straight into the air.

Touchdown.

The home crowd exploded.

All eyes were on the end zone. They didn't notice it at first. But back toward the other end of the field, whistles were blowing and numerous yellow flags had flown.

Pahokee wasn't trying to run up the score. But the other team felt they had done something far more insulting to rub their opponent's noses in it. They'd sent in a girl.

So here's what happened when the play began. The forward players of the receiving team usually begin moving back to set up their blocks. This time, however, the two players in the middle ran forward as fast as they could. The game was so unwinnable that penalties didn't matter anymore.

Chris had stood alone, watching the ball sail. Two seconds later, she was clobbered by a pair of players coming in from both sides. They sent her flying onto her back. That drew the first whistle and flag. After a few more seconds, as Chris started to push herself up, they pounced again, making sure to push her helmet hard into the grass. "Stay down, girl!"

More whistles and flags. People in the stands began to notice and point, and the celebration in the end zone ceased. The Pahokee team watched two cocky players trotting away from where their kicker was faltering as she tried to get up, a big chunk of muddy turf stuck in her face mask. "Chris!"

The offending players never made it back to their sideline. The Pahokee bench emptied and they were swarmed, then the visiting team entered the fray. It took a while to untangle, but coaches and cops were ultimately able to pull everyone apart.

For a victory, it was unusually silent in the Pahokee locker room. Normally a fight, let alone a bench-clearing brawl, would receive a tongue-lashing from the coaching staff. The players were waiting for the rebuke that never came. Everyone knew what wasn't said aloud. Chris may have been viewed in the past as just a girl, but now she was a Blue Devil, and nobody but nobody does that to one of theirs.

Chapter 30

THE NEXT MORNING

The sun had just peeked over the eastern sky of Lake Okeechobee when a Dodge Ram pickup with all the chrome and jacked-up tires and everything else it stands for rolled into the parking lot. There was the full complement of bumper stickers and decals: black POW-MIA logo, the yellow-green-red bar for Vietnam, silver parachutes for airborne, silver dolphins for submarine service, Purple Heart, Rangers, et cetera, et cetera.

Another pickup rolled in behind, a black Chevy Colorado with more decals, flying flags, American, Marine Corps. The pair of vehicles stopped outside an off-brand motel on the northern shore of Lake Okeechobee. The cabs of the trucks were already full, and more people squatted in the beds of the pickups as if there had been a pre-dawn street-corner call for migrant workers: *"We need ten for six hours . . ."*

A motel room door opened, and Serge and Cheyenne stepped out. He walked to the next door and knocked.

"Just a minute."

"Coleman! Come on! People are waiting!" said Serge.

"It's okay," said Cheyenne. "They have to stop anyway for the others to catch up."

"Others?"

The door opened and Coleman appeared. "All set to go."

Serge stared at a lumpy spot below Coleman's collarbone. "You're wearing the chest pouch?"

"That's right."

Ribbit, ribbit . . .

"A frog's in there?"

Coleman nodded and patted the pouch. "We worked things out last night. We're friends now."

"You do realize they're not like ferrets," said Serge. "I don't think he has any idea what's going on."

"You couldn't be more wrong." Coleman stroked the canvas. *Ribbit.* "And you wouldn't know it to look at him, but he's a raging maniac."

"Don't tell me."

"I found out that it's almost impossible to get a frog to smoke a joint—"

"Another sentence I never thought I'd live to hear."

"—So I grabbed one of the empty plastic bags that come with the trash cans in the room, and put the frog in it. Then I took a mondo, triple-clutch hit and blew it into the bag."

"I realize that among your people such gestures are tokens of goodwill, but we're bordering on animal unkindness here."

"He didn't mind at all." Coleman peeked down through the opening. "He liked the beer, too."

Serge covered his eyes with a hand.

Coleman reached into the pouch. "I know you and Cheyenne had your own thing going on in your room last night, but you missed the real fun."

"Did we?"

Coleman scooped out the frog, stroking its head lightly with an index finger. "Isn't that right, Jeremiah?"

"You call your frog Jeremiah?"

"Because he is a bullfrog."

"Naturally," said Serge. "But back to giving him beer."

"Three Dog Night let their frog drink wine, so I don't see the big fuss."

"Technically their frog *brought* the wine," said Serge. "Didn't that tell you there was some artistic license going on?"

"I don't know what that means, but you should have seen him last night," said Coleman. "When this little sucker gets his swerve on, look out! He was jumping straight up, sideways, even a back-flip. We had a contest."

"You jumped with him?"

"Duh!" said Coleman. "Then I used the plastic ice bucket to make him a little boat in the tub. But what he really liked was the toilet. Don't worry: I taped up the flush handle in case I forgot. I was responsible. And some of those blind mosquitoes had gotten into the room, and I was able to capture a few, but only crushed them a little, and then I sat on the edge of the tub throwing bugs to Jeremiah in the toilet. I wish someone had a camera."

"I can't picture anything more precious."

"I know," said Coleman. "He really had the munchies."

"But don't you think you should be releasing him now?" said Serge. "He probably wants to get back to his own kind."

"I think he's happy," said Coleman. "Remember how they were jumping all over the parking lot last night? Look at him now, happy to sit in my hand."

"Coleman, his eyes are closed. He's still fucked up."

"Then the nice thing to do is let him sleep it off." Coleman opened the pouch. "Back in you go."

A roar erupted from an unseen point around the bend, growing louder and louder until it was vibrating stuff. The source came into view and pulled into the parking lot.

The bikers had arrived.

Harleys, helmets and star-spangled bandannas. Most had black leather vests, festooned with medals and patches from every branch of service.

"Time to saddle up," said Cheyenne, and the three climbed in the bed of the second truck. The caravan pulled out of the parking lot and headed north.

Serge sat against the back gate next to Coleman. "I think I might have a problem."

"I'll do anything I can."

"It's not that kind of problem. It's Cheyenne." Serge searched for words. "She doesn't want a commitment."

"I don't see the problem."

"*That's* the problem," said Serge. "Almost every woman I've ever met wants a commitment. Some act like they don't at first, but it eventually comes up, and I'm a ramblin' kind of guy."

"I get it," said Coleman. "You think she's acting?"

"No, I think she's on the level."

"Then you're home free."

Serge was quiet a moment. "I can't describe it, but it's having some kind of effect on me. I'm oddly attracted to this. She's a ramblin' kind of *gal,* and that makes *me* want to commit. And then I'll be trapped following her around a Pottery Barn with an armload of guest towels and that feeling that I can't breathe."

"Jesus!" said Coleman. "Get a grip. You can't let her split us up."

"Thanks for thinking of me."

"No, seriously," said Coleman. "I don't know how to survive."

"You'll do fine."

"Serge!" He grabbed his friend tightly by the arm. "Don't mess around. You know I'd end up in the woods behind a 7-Eleven living on an old mattress."

"I see your point."

"Maybe it's all a trick," said Coleman. *Ribbit.* "If you find out that she secretly wants to commit, then you won't be attracted anymore."

"For once you speak as a sage, my finely toasted friend. And I know just how to find out . . ."

The patriotic procession of trucks and hogs cruised up through Osceola County, wind flapping hair and scarves. Serge scooted across the bed of the pickup until he settled in next to Cheyenne.

She smiled coyly. "Well, look who it is."

"Hi, Cheyenne. Uh, uh, I mean, uh, what I'm trying to say is, uh . . ."

"Wow, I've never known you to be at a loss for words."

"Cheyenne, would you like to go steady?"

"Is this a joke?" She had a good laugh. "Are you in seventh grade?"

"I've given this a lot of thought." Serge nervously picked at his fingernails. "I'd like to give you an ID bracelet with our names engraved."

"Whoa! Stop!" said Cheyenne. "You *are* serious. I thought I could trust you when we talked about this last night."

"You *can* trust me. That was just a test, to make sure what you said wasn't a trick."

"You sure?"

"When was the last time you were in a Pottery Barn?"

"Like, never."

"Case closed. You passed with flying colors."

Serge's butt scooted back across the pickup's bed until he was at the gate again.

"Well?" asked Coleman.

"It's worse than I thought. She's never even stepped foot in a Pottery Barn."

"Good God!" said Coleman. "How can you not love a woman like that?"

"I know, I know," said Serge. "I must think of something. She's just got to have some kind of a big turnoff that's a deal breaker."

"Maybe when she laughs really hard, she sounds like a donkey."

"She has a great laugh."

"You're fucked."

Nearly an hour later, the ad hoc motorcade arrived and parked along a remote country road where the only building had a steeple. Across the street, tombstones in a neatly manicured field. Nobody had arrived at the cemetery yet. Funeral workers had already set up the rows of folding chairs under a white sun canopy. A brass contraption with heavy-gauge straps sat over a freshly dug hole.

Across the street was a different story. Bullhorns, tightly screwed faces, and some of the most vile signs that have ever been painted.

Over a distant hill on the straight highway, various vehicles headed toward them. Moments later, the pickup trucks emptied and motorcyclists dismounted.

The new arrivals were heckled as they carried their flags toward the protest line. The malcontents noticed the size and nature of the people coming toward them, particularly the bikers. The protesters took an intimidated step back. "You touch us and we'll sue! We taking video of all of this!"

Not a word was spoken among the flag people. They formed a precise line from rehearsal, turning their backs to the picketers and presenting fifteen huge renditions of Old Glory that formed an effective red, white and blue curtain.

"Hey, you can't block us like that! We have rights!"

No response.

Up the road came a solemn line of cars with headlights on at noon.

Someone reached down and pressed a button on a boom box.

". . . This land is your land . . ."

The funeral procession pulled though the cemetery gates, and the hearse parked near the sun canopy.

The protesters screamed louder. The boom box was turned up.

Men with white gloves slid the casket out the back of the hearse and ceremoniously placed it on the support straps over the grave. It had its own American flag. An honor guard gave a salute with guns. A trumpet played. Two of the people with white gloves removed the flag from the casket and, with measured cadence, folded it into a triangle. One of them bent down to present it to a widow with small children.

The protesters had so much anger baggage, you wouldn't have thought there was room for more. But the flags in front of them were just too much. Not only did they block their view of the service, but more importantly, they blocked the mourners' view of their signs. On top of that, the boom box. It just wasn't fair!

"I'll fix this!"

The leader of the protest, a pastor, ran around the end of the line and stood facing them, waving his sign and screaming into a bullhorn.

Kyle Lovitt and the others looked up and down their ranks. They had been over this before in their meetings. In case the picketers ignored the court order: No violence. Don't even move lest there be inadvertent physical contact that could become courtroom fodder. Just get out cell phones and document the violation of the buffer zone.

Serge hadn't gotten the memo.

He handed Coleman his flag and ran over to the protest leader. "Excuse me, but you're out of your comfort zone. I suggest you slither back behind the buffer line."

"Go to hell! You and your queer buddies are interfering with our First Amendment rights. You're forcing us to step forward."

"There's the little matter of the court order," said Serge.

"What about it?" said the leader. "I don't see anybody here to enforce it."

"Oh, but I do." Serge swiftly nailed him in the chest with a stun gun, and just as quickly stashed it away. The leader collapsed, and his followers came running.

Kyle glanced back and forth. "Turn off your phones! Erase those files! . . ."

Serge nonchalantly sauntered over to his group as the picketers dragged their leader back behind enemy lines.

Kyle grabbed him by the arm. "Why did you go and do that?"

"What are you talking about?"

"You're just lucky that our flags blocked their video cameras."

"If you say so." Serge opened a brown billfold and removed a driver's license. "Hmm, his name's Jebediah."

"What's that?"

"A wallet I just happened to find on the ground." Serge replaced the license.

"Why'd you take it from him?"

"You don't want to know."

"And you didn't tell me that."

Chapter 31

PAHOKEE

Coach Calhoun strolled down the corridor outside the locker room. He heard slapping footsteps on the wax floor. A student ran past him practically in tears.

"Chris! Come back here!"

She stopped, embarrassed, trying to hide emotion.

"What's wrong?"

"Nothing."

"Don't 'nothing' me. In my office, now."

Chris sat quietly in a familiar wooden chair. Calhoun kept trying to get her to open up, but it was like prying answers from a hostile witness. She was staring at the floor, lips trembling, so shaken that the coach's mind ran through the menu of worst cases that can befall teenagers. The list was long and ugly in these parts.

All she kept saying was that it was "her fault." That only made the list grow in Calhoun's head. Finally, the coach was able to drag out enough details to learn that the problem was academic, and he practically collapsed with relief. But then puzzlement. What kind of problem could Chris have in class? So many straight A's now that he barely glanced at her report cards.

"Chris, I can't help you if you won't talk."

It wasn't that Chris was resisting the coach. She was one of those people who can hold in crying as long as they don't talk, or it all erupts. She couldn't have that. So she silently reached in her backpack with a quivering hand and pulled out a term paper.

Calhoun took it and looked at the top of the first page. A big red *F*. Now he was really confused. Chris never got an F in anything. Plus, this was a science paper, her best subject.

"Okay, Chris, I know you're upset, so can you come back here tomorrow, same time?"

She nodded.

"And can you leave the term paper with me?"

Another nod. She left.

Coach Calhoun leaned back in his chair with the paper and didn't know what to make of it. But the game plan for that Friday night's gridiron contest had just been put on hold. He scooted his chair up and logged on to his computer. Surfing the net, checking her footnotes. To himself: "What the heck is dark energy?" More clattering of the keyboard. "Quarks? Photons? Planck time?"

The next afternoon, the final bell of the school day rang. Minutes later, Coach Calhoun entered a classroom. The only person still there was a teacher behind his desk, starting to grade quiz papers. He had been a midterm replacement for the previous science teacher, who had left to accept a higher-paying position at a private school on the east side of the county.

"Mr. Garns?"

"Yes?"

"Coach Calhoun." They shook hands.

"How can I help you?"

"It's about one of your students, Chris Maples."

"Oh." Garns turned serious and looked down, making a mark on a test paper. "I guess she went running to you about her last grade."

Calhoun hit pause in his brain. This was not how he expected the conversation to begin. He reassessed. "She didn't come running to me. But I did see her paper. I've known her for a while, and I'm trying to understand this F."

Garns, not looking up: "She used the Internet."

"What does that mean?"

"Students aren't supposed to rely on the Internet for sourcing. It's unverified," said the teacher. "I made that extremely clear when I came on board."

"I agree," said Calhoun. "But I went through her footnotes. These weren't bulletin boards or blogs. They were scientific research journals with articles from professors at Caltech, MIT, Carnegie Mellon. I asked other teachers, and those Internet sources are allowed."

"The footnotes weren't in the proper format."

Calhoun took another deep breath. "I looked at your strikethroughs on her paper, like where she cited dark energy as the reason why gravity isn't slowing down the expansion of the big bang."

"We haven't covered that in class. And I don't believe it exists."

"She noted it as a theory. It has support in the research journals."

"You're a science teacher now?" Garns stood. "Second-guessing me?"

"Not in the least. I'm just trying to sort all this out."

"She also has a big attitude problem."

Calhoun's head practically spun on his neck. "Are we talking about the same person?"

"She undermines my authority."

"She talks back? That would surprise me."

"No, just smug like she's too smart for my class, challenging me in front of the other students."

"Challenging?"

"Interrupting to ask cynical questions, like the dark energy thing."

"I think she's just trying to learn."

"I see where this is going," said Garns. "You *coaches*."

"What's that supposed to mean?"

"Pressuring teachers to keep players eligible."

Calhoun stopped again, this time to check his temper. He knew there was a widespread stereotype about coaches tampering with grades. But in reality, the vast majority take a holistic approach to developing a student, both as an athlete and a person, getting to know their parents, talking to their teachers.

"Can we dial this back a bit?" said Calhoun. "It's not about us. It's a student's welfare."

"So you coddle your players?"

"We don't need to continue in this direction."

"You sports guys think you have so much influence."

Calhoun took a final pause to choose words, because a bridge was about to catch fire. "I've seen you before. Not often, but enough to know."

"Seen me?"

"Some of the finest people in the world are teachers. They work tirelessly for little pay. But what really makes them so special is they're like parents to the whole community. They find no greater joy than helping students succeed to their utmost potential . . . Then there's some of the worst people in the world. Also teachers, the rare ones here and there. Bitter because their lives didn't work out the way they'd hoped. And when they see a great kid with a bright future, they don't take pride in helping them along. Instead, they're jealous and try to crush their spirit. That is unforgivable."

The coach walked around the desk and got face-to-face with

Garns. "But you're right about one thing. Coaches do have undue influence in our culture. I make it a rule not to use mine. I also make exceptions."

Calhoun stormed out of the classroom and slammed the door.

C oach Calhoun sat in the principal's office. He'd finished laying out his case, and now the ball was in the other court.

"I find all this hard to believe," said the principal. "But since it's coming from you . . ."

"So you'll look into it?"

"With due diligence. If it's true, this is very disturbing news. It has no place at my school."

The principal kept his word. He interviewed students and parents, and the feedback was uniform. Some teachers use a tough style of teaching, but only to push the students to do their best. This new science teacher just seemed to genuinely dislike the kids.

By the end of the week, Garns was packing up his belongings in a cardboard box. And swearing he'd find a way to get even.

Chapter 32

OSCEOLA COUNTY

Creeping was afoot.

Two suspicious figures on their hands and knees inched forward in the night. North of St. Cloud, Florida. North of sanity.

Coleman raised his right hand and sniffed the palm, then held it to Serge.

"Get that out of my face." Serge's back was like a leopard's. "You're just going to have to deal with it."

They crawled forward across the pasture like a sniper team. At least Serge did. Coleman's stealth was more like that of something in a playpen. Serge looked up: "Full moon. That's the worst for our mission, but we were in no position to pick our timing."

Ribbit.

"You brought Jeremiah?" asked Serge.

"He's good luck."

"He's loud," said Serge. "He'll give our position away."

"Not my Jeremiah!"

"Shhhh! Keep it down!" Serge lowered his chin in the tall weeds. "People are up . . ."

Moments earlier, the gold Satellite had left the highway for the concealment of a dirt road that ran through pine hardwoods. From there, Serge drove across the bumpy pasture as curious cattle watched the silhouette of the Plymouth in the moonlight. They continued on until reaching some new-growth woods and brush at the edge of a property. That's where they left the car and commenced their crawl. Now they were in the perfect position that Serge had scoped out in advance with Internet help. Ahead: the target.

A white farmhouse sat atop a small hill.

It was a large farmhouse, as they go, two stories with an addition on back. The owner's budget apparently favored size over condition. A tin roof sagged above the front porch. The wood siding had termite damage and missing paint from the sun. A pond sat off the driveway. And now two strangers lay in the woods just a stone's throw from the front door.

"What do we do?" asked Coleman.

"Wait and watch." Serge got out binoculars and scanned windows. "I picked the best spot to launch our operation, but that's where my plan ends. I knew this extraction would be tricky because I figured he didn't live alone. We must recon the social structure of this abode and find its soft underbelly."

"What's going on in there?"

"Remember the pastor from the funeral protest? He just went in the kitchen. I've picked up five other people inside, but they're all young women. Long dresses and bonnets. They're holding candles like it's some kind of ceremony."

"No guys?"

"Something weird's going on in there."

Coleman kissed his frog on the mouth. "Weird how?"

"Looks like one of those cults where the leader preaches strict obedience to the gospels in order for him to have sex with everyone."

"Is that what the gospels are about?"

"I hate to judge without all the facts, but I'm guessing he's taking liberties." Serge handed Coleman the binoculars. "Stay here."

"Where are you going?"

"To get more facts."

Serge darted ahead toward the farmhouse, sweeping around the west side, which was shielded from the moonlight. He plastered his back against the building, creeping sideways. Soon he was under a window. He slowly rose on tiptoes until his eyes were just above the sill.

Inside the living room, the women stood in a line with heads bowed over their candle holders. The pastor held an open Bible with one hand and gesticulated wildly with the other. Then he stepped forward. The women's chests heaved with anticipation. He looked up and down the row before blowing out one of the candles. He took that woman by the hand and led her into another room.

Serge resumed creeping along until he came to another window. This one was a bit higher. He found some loose bricks on the side of the house and fashioned a little stack. Two eyes again rose above a sill. It was a bedroom. Mirrors everywhere, including the ceiling. A video camera sat on a tripod in the corner. Serge watched the pastor taking off his shirt. The young woman took off her bonnet and reached for the top button under her neck.

"Holy mother," Serge said to himself. "There's no way she's even close to eighteen. I can't watch."

He crouched down below the sill, and when he did, a couple of the bricks at his feet toppled. "Shit." Serge hit the ground and rolled himself as tightly as possible against the lattice along the farmhouse's crawl space. He looked sharply up and saw the shadow of the pastor's face against the windowpane. Serge held his breath as the shadow moved from one side of the window to the other, clearly convinced something was out there.

After the longest of times, the shadow left the window, and voices could be heard inside.

"Whew!" Serge scurried in a big loop around the side of the house and dove back into the brush next to Coleman.

"What did you see?"

"It's worse than I thought," said Serge. "First, I don't see any way of extracting the pastor without raising general mayhem from the women. They've been brainwashed. So we must abort the mission and put him under surveillance until we can identify an interception point away from his flock. Second, I think the one he's about to have sex with is underage. I should burst in there under general principles to stop it. But what if I'm wrong or she's older than she looks, or some kind of common-law wife?"

"Maybe you could phone in an anonymous tip."

"That's a great idea." Serge pulled out a disposable burner phone with prepaid minutes. He looked up as clouds drifted across the moon, cutting the light. "And our luck might be turning. We're getting extra cover of darkness . . ." He began pressing buttons.

A tap on his shoulder.

"Not now, Coleman. I'm phoning in the important information."

Another tap. "Uh, Serge . . ."

"I told you I'm busy!"

Tap, tap, tap.

"Dammit, Coleman! What is it that can't wait?"

A crunching of leaves. *"Who's out there!"*

Serge looked up to see the pastor aiming a double-barrel twelve-gauge shotgun.

"Damn," Serge whispered. "Keep your head down and don't move."

"I said, who's out there!"

The pastor kept walking, straight toward them.

The gun cocked, now only feet away. Just a thin, single row of bushes between them and discovery. The clouds began thinning and drifting away. The moonlight grew brighter on the leaves.

"Come out with your hands up or I'll blast ya!"

Stone silence. Then:

Ribbit . . .

The shotgun's twin barrels bore down on an exact spot in the bushes.

Jeremiah slipped out of Coleman's pouch, and before the pair could react, the amphibian leaped from the brush. Another big jump, and it landed at the pastor's feet.

"For heaven's sake! I'm giving myself a heart attack over a stupid bullfrog!" The pastor propped the shotgun on his shoulder and turned back toward the farmhouse.

That was all the opportunity Serge needed. He sprang from the vegetation and caught the pastor in the small of his back with the stun gun. The victim fell inert.

Serge and Coleman grabbed him under the armpits and dragged the limp body from view as several curious people in bonnets appeared in the front window . . .

J ust after midnight, the gold Plymouth returned to the motel on the north shore of Lake Okeechobee. It backed up to their room.

Serge stood idly next to the car like he was bored.

"What are you waiting for?"

"Cheyenne."

"You're bringing her in on this?"

"Just the opposite." His eyes scanned every conceivable direction. "I have to make sure she doesn't get the slightest whiff of what we're up to. I'm taking a wild stab this is a touch worse than romantic commitment."

Serge began to whistle as he leaned against the back of the car, slowly rocking. "That's long enough. She's not around. Open the room and I'll get our guest from the trunk." He bent down and began inserting a key in the lid.

A woman's voice: "There you are!"

"Jesus Christ!" Serge leapt up and landed sitting on the lid of the trunk. "Where the hell did you come from?"

"Uh, just around the corner," said Cheyenne. "What's gotten into you? You're awfully jumpy."

"Nothing, nothing," said Serge. "Almost had an accident up the road. Heart's still pounding."

A wary eye. "Are you sure that's it?"

"Definitely!"

"If you say so." An off-hand smile. "I didn't know where you went, because I was kind of hoping . . . uh, you could show me your tombstone rubbings."

"Yes, yes, sure. How long are you on tonight? I just have a couple pressing business matters to tie up, and then it will be a freaking tombstone jamboree."

"Are you positive you're okay?"

"I'll ring you in the office when I'm free."

"I'll be waiting." She headed back to her office, glancing over her shoulder in suspicion. Serge had a toothy grin and waved to her with wiggling fingers. Then she was gone.

"Hurry, Coleman!"

The trunk popped, and soon a familiar scene.

Two people sat next to each other on the edge of a motel bed. Coleman smiled and petted a frog. Serge petted a roll of duct tape.

A brief scream as the pastor regained consciousness and looked down at all the tight rope and his uncomfortable chair.

Ribbit.

"Where are my manners?" said Serge. "Jebediah, meet Jeremiah. Sorry, but he didn't bring his wine."

"What do you want from me?"

"Damn, you're fast." Serge began cleaning under his fingernails with the tip of a large-bladed hunting knife. "My conditions are nonnegotiable. First, release all the young women at your farmhouse. We both know what's going on. Second, no more protests outside military funerals. Make that anywhere in the world while we're at it."

"You can't do this!" said the pastor. "You're abrogating my First Amendment rights!"

"Couldn't agree more," said Serge. "Few things are as important to me as our blessed Constitution."

"You agree?" said the pastor. "Then how can you do this?"

Serge shrugged. "I'm wrong. Sorry."

The pastor fumed with flared nostrils. "You're going to hell!"

"Meet you in the elevator."

The pastor threw a tantrum in his chair, making the legs tap-dance on the wooden floor. "Who do you think you are?"

"An angel," said Serge. "Avenging or merciful. You make the call!"

"You're no angel!"

"I was using poetic slack," said Serge. "'The better angels of our nature.' That was Lincoln. And I want you to embrace all your fellow citizens as children of God."

"I don't want to."

"'You can't always get what you want.' That was Jagger."

"You won't get away with this!"

"I don't have to get away with anything if you agree to my simple terms."

"Never, you pervert! Not in a million years."

"I was kind of hoping you'd say that, because I have so been wanting to try this." Duct tape quickly went over the mouth, and the chair began being dragged backward.

Minutes later, Serge sat at the steering wheel of the Plymouth. "Coast clear? No Cheyenne?"

"Right-o," said Coleman, leaning over a bong.

"You're not even looking."

"I'm high. I have extra powers."

The gold Plymouth slowly pulled around to the dark side of the motel and the special parking area for the bass boats favored by the sportsmen staying at the inn. Serge backed up to one, got out and fastened the trailer hitch.

"You're stealing a boat?" said Coleman.

"No, this is one I rented earlier and had waiting here on standby." Serge climbed back in the car to the sound of banging in the trunk. "It's actually a pretty good deal around here. I grabbed this baby on the wings of hope that I could employ it in my next science project." The Plymouth pulled out of the parking lot and turned east . . .

Lake Okeechobee has various access points for fishermen. There are a number of ramps over the Herbert Hoover Dike to public launches. If you have a really big boat already in the water, then you have to enter through one of three locks.

"It's not a very big boat," said Coleman.

"No lock, no problem."

Serge followed the road curling south toward Clewiston until he found one of the ramps, dark and deserted. The bass boat slid into the water, including the captive, tied up again to the chair. Serge got behind the wheel and pushed the throttle just above idle.

At this part of the lake, the open water is a few miles away. In between, marshland laced with canals, including a large one around the rim, logically called the Rim Canal. Serge rode it awhile before reaching an opening off the port side, and turned left into what's known as the Old Moore Haven Canal.

From there it was a straight shot through ferocious thriving nature. Birds and bugs and bogs.

"Listen to that racket," said Coleman.

"The swamp sizzles at night," said Serge. "Humans might be at the top of the food chain, but out here we're seriously outnumbered."

"What is this place?"

"They call it Dynamite Pass. But it's nothing like the cool name of the spot where we're heading. In fact, I chose it just for the name." Serge pushed the throttle forward again, and the boat began to plane. "Florida has some of the best place-names: Cork-screw, Spuds, Festus, Roach, Howey-in-the-Hills, Two Egg, but we're about to reach my favorite one of all."

Moments later, they dropped anchor at a crossroads of canals, sitting just a short distance from the lake proper.

"Okay," said Coleman. "I give. What's the name of this place?"

Serge stood with spread arms and yelled at the sky: "Monkey Box, Florida!"

"That is catchy."

"In this case, I'm also media savvy: If you're going to pull some newsworthy stunt like this, and aren't geographically constrained, always pick a place with a name that makes the TV people go belly up. They won't be able to resist!"

Coleman turned all the way around. "But there's nothing here."

"Florida doesn't care, so why should we? Now help me with our newest best friend."

They dragged the pastor, chair and all, into the shallow water and up onto spongy ground.

Coleman kept slapping his arms and swatting in front of his face.

"They're attracted to carbon dioxide," said Serge. "Remember me telling you down in Flamingo at the tip of the state?"

"No." Coleman spit something out of his mouth.

The captive struggled fiercely in the chair. "You won't get away with this! I'll yell!"

"*I'll* yell," said Serge. "Ahhhhhhhhhhhhhh! Damn, that feels good. You should try it."

"Ahhhhhhhhhhhhhh!" The hostage stopped and coughed and spit something out. "You're insane!"

"Thank you."

Coleman continued swatting and spitting. "What are these things?"

"The blind mosquitoes," said Serge. "Scientific name *Chironomidae,* also known as lake flies, and in Florida—you'll love this—chizzywinks. Guess what? The chizzywinks are back in season! I checked with the locals, and they expect them to be at maximum swarm strength tonight in the darkest hours just before sunrise. And that's just their activity level back on land away from the lake. Out here—hoo-wee! . . . Back in the 1800s, there were rampant cases of entire herds of cattle dying from insect asphyxiation in this region. Just read *A Land Remembered.*"

Serge put on a surgical mask and safety goggles, and handed an identical pair to the now-coughing Coleman. He turned to the captive. "Oops, I'm short on supplies. I guess that's where the power of prayer comes in."

The pastor was blinking rapidly and trying to breathe through his nose.

"What a nature show you're about to experience," said Serge. "Kind of like something out of the Bible."

Serge sloshed back out to the boat and helped Coleman aboard. They motored away in the direction of Dynamite Pass.

A buzzer rang on the night window of a budget motel on Lake Okeechobee.

Serge swatted away bugs. He cupped hands around his eyes and pressed his nose against the window, looking at the empty front desk.

Someone emerged from a back room. "There you are! I was wondering what kind of business took so long."

"Totally tedious," said Serge. "But I do need to report a missing chair from our room. It kind of got away from me. I'm good for it."

"You know, I still have that extra room available next to yours, if, uh, your friend would like some privacy. On the house."

"You've read my mind . . ."

A half hour later, Serge lay on his back in the bed, holding up a series of large pages like flash cards. "Here's another cool tombstone rubbing, and here's another, and this one has a little cherub on top. I'm a sucker for that. And this is Mitzi the Dolphin . . ."

Cheyenne continued massaging him below the belt. "Um, Serge? Am I doing something wrong?"

"I can accurately say no. I believe most of my gender would concur."

"But you're still looking at your rubbings."

"Precisely." Serge flipped to another page. "What you're doing down there makes me appreciate them in a whole new light."

"Serge . . ."

"O-*kayyyyyyyy*." Serge set the pages on the nightstand and picked up something else. "What about View-Masters? No? My elongated penny collection? I thought women were into sex toys."

"Is that what you call those?"

"Who doesn't?" Serge set the penny album down. "Don't tell anyone I have all this stuff. I'd be mortified if the public knew about my kinky trove."

"What about simple vibrators?"

"You mean those things in the ads that people are using to rub tense facial muscles?"

"Those ads are kind of in code."

Serge crinkled his nose. "That would explain so much."

"Stop talking."

"What?"

Cheyenne got on her hands and knees and slowly crawled up the bed toward him like a jungle cat. She growled.

"Yikes."

Chapter 33

PAHOKEE

Coach Calhoun stuck his head in the principal's office. "You wanted to see me?"

"Come in. And close the door."

Uh-oh, that's never good. Hopefully one of his players hadn't made a mistake that couldn't be reversed.

"Lamar, I can't tell you how happy I was when you first showed up back at the school."

"It was a special day for me, too."

"I know, I know."

"But . . . ?"

"Lamar, we all kind of wondered a little bit about your missing years," said the principal.

"That would be natural," said Calhoun. "I'm sort of a private person."

"We weren't being nosy, mind you. It's just that you were so gifted, we all expected to see you someday in the NFL draft. But after a while, we simply assumed football didn't work out for whatever reason, and the rest was your business. Until you finally decided to come back to your roots."

"Life takes its turns," said Calhoun. "I worked in an auto plant for a while, then a drydock . . . But by that look in your eyes, you already know that."

It pained the principal, and Calhoun saw it all play out again like it was yesterday instead of more than twenty years ago . . .

T he winters in the upper Midwest were far more freezing than Calhoun had ever imagined. It was his senior year at the university, and while he hadn't torn up the Big Ten, Lamar was expected to go in the top six or seven rounds of the draft. He stared out at the snow that was crusting over the campus and piling up on the windowsill of the athletic dorm. His roommate was named Ted, but everyone called him Bruiser.

It was kind of a joke. Ted was a kicker, and they tend to be the smallest players on a team, usually by such a degree that they seem not to be football players at all. It held true in Ted's case. Hence, Bruiser. Ted was from a small farm in an equally small dot on the map in Missouri, and he was lost on the big campus. He didn't know the current music, how to talk to girls or even basic slang. "You mean when something's 'bad,' it's actually 'good'? That doesn't make sense." They went to a club one night, and Ted tried to dance. Lamar almost lost a lung from laughing. The huge player from Pahokee, Florida, appointed himself Ted's big brother, and they became the inseparable odd couple. That's how Calhoun first developed an affinity for kickers.

There are many scandals in big-time college sports that make headlines, and many more that never leave the practice field or locker room. The head coach was in the mold of Ohio State's

Woody Hayes, who punched a player on national TV. Which meant he was a dinosaur. It was a new era, and the assistant coaches struggled to keep him in check. It came to a head halfway through the season. Ted had shanked a thirty-yarder, costing them the game against Michigan. For the next few days, the coach's rage had been tightening in a vicious cycle until he was spring-loaded. On a Wednesday, the practice field was extra busy, pockets of activity where various specialty players honed their specialties. But the coach's eyes were locked in on the kickers. They call it staring daggers, and all the assistants went on high alert, like a domestic abuse victim detecting the first signs of that telltale mood swing.

Ted was back in form, nailing it down the middle. But the coach was just waiting. After, who knows, fifteen perfect kicks, Ted dinged one off the left upright, and the coach was on the field. The assistants chased. Before they could get there, the coach had his hands around Ted's neck. A similar incident had already hit the news, when an Indiana basketball coach was videotaped choking a player. But that was brief compared to this. It was a two-handed throttle that wouldn't let go. Ted vainly fought for breath. He was trying to cough and turning red. The assistants raced up and grabbed the coach's arms—too gently, under the circumstances, because they didn't want to lose their jobs. "Coach! Coach!" One of them looked up to an overhead booth and made a slashing gesture to stop filming practice.

Thumbs pressed harder into Ted's windpipe. A red face was becoming blue. "Coach!" They grabbed him around the waist and arms to no avail. Then, out of nowhere, a fist came flying in. It caught the coach in the jaw and he went down. So did Ted, finally free, gasping frantically before throwing up.

The assistants had a crisis on their hands. They looked around. All the other players had stopped practicing, standing and holding their helmets at their sides by the face masks. Even if they could destroy the video, there were too many witnesses. And if the coach went down, so did their assistant coaching positions. A new head coach would wipe the slate clean and hire all his own people. Panic turned into a plan. They would get out ahead of this and deflect. The solution was handed to them on a platter.

The punch.

They were initially thankful that Lamar had jumped in to help his friend. But thanks didn't pay power bills. In an instant, he was under the bus.

Handcuffs clapped on Calhoun's wrists, followed by expulsion from the team. But it was handled hush-hush, because any digging into the running back's arrest could lead back to the coach. They promised he'd stay on scholarship until graduation, to buy his silence. There was a quick plea bargain with no testimony, followed by a misdemeanor conviction and a suspended sentence.

Although it never made the papers, there was always the grapevine. Nobody knew the details, just that Lamar had attacked a head coach. It was a de facto blackball. Despite his credentials, the entire NFL draft took a hard pass on Calhoun.

He went to look for a job. "Sorry, we just can't do it." Like many athletes', his academic major was physical education, and schools weren't allowed to hire anyone with an assault conviction. Lamar began welding fenders . . .

That was then; this was now.

"I wish you would have said something." The Pahokee High School principal shook his head. "On the surface, it didn't sound at all like you. So we looked into it and learned the real circumstances, and then it all made sense. If we had known earlier, we might have figured something out, some kind of exemption, or gotten it expunged."

"But now?"

The principal held up a sheet of paper. "You didn't disclose it. You filed a false job application."

"I used bad judgment," said Calhoun. "It was just so long ago.

I wanted to put it behind me, and I wanted to get back to the kids."

"Dammit!" said the principal.

"I know this is putting you through a lot. I'm sorry."

"No, not you," said the principal. "That asshole Garns."

"Who?"

"The science teacher I got rid of."

"Oh, I remember him now," said Calhoun. "But what's he got to do with any of this?"

"He couldn't simply go quietly and get on with his life," said the principal. "I wish he was still here just so I could fire him again."

"I'm not following."

"He must have spent weeks digging, and then I still don't know how he found out," said the principal. "He's the one who reported you."

Calhoun sat a moment in helpless thought as the pieces of realization fell into place. "Someone like that has no business being around our kids. It was still worth it."

"Not from where I'm sitting," said the principal. "I wish there was something I could do."

"You've done enough." Calhoun stood. "I'll go get my stuff."

Chapter 34

OKEECHOBEE

The next morning it was breakfast in bed. Then Serge and Cheyenne took a brisk five-mile stroll along the Florida Trail on top of the Hoover Dike.

By ten o'clock, they were back in the room, making plans for her day off. By eleven, a crash against the wall from Coleman's room. "He's up."

By noon, it was on the news.

Law enforcement needed airboats to reach the scene, and they now sat clustered near the northern bank of the Old Moore Haven Canal.

TV correspondents in even more airboats began broadcasting from behind police lines.

"This is Soledad Torres reporting live from a place few have heard of. I'm standing here in Monkey Box, Florida, where a trio of bass fishermen heading out to Lake Okeechobee made a grisly early-morning discovery of a body in this remote swampland. The sheriff's office is releasing few details, but confidential sources tell me the victim may have been the leader of a controversial church infamous for picketing military funerals around the state. Sources also describe the murder victim as being bound and tortured with what are known in these parts as blind mosquitoes, also known as chizzywinks, which occasionally swarm in ferocious numbers. The most probable cause of death was asphyxiation, but prior to the victim's demise, the insects likely also filled his ears, eyes and even the sinus cavity via the nose, where he could feel them moving around behind his eyes. Sorry for ruining your lunch. This is Soledad Torres in Monkey Box, Florida. Back to you, Chet and Angela."

The broadcast switched to a pair of anchorpeople behind a desk in the home studio, sharing light banter and a chuckle. "I think she just likes saying Monkey Box . . ." "I like saying it, too. Monkey Box." "We'll be right back after these commercial messages. Monkey Box."

Cheyenne stared. "What exactly was your business last night?"

"Fake news! Fake news!" Serge clicked the set off and clapped his hands a single sharp time. "I'm famished! What do you say we grab a bite to eat?"

"Actually, I'm supposed to have lunch with my brother," said Cheyenne.

"Kyle? Fantastic! We'll make it a family affair," said Serge. "My treat. I insist!"

A knock at the door. Serge jumped and spun. "Who the hell is that?"

"Probably my brother. I told him where I was." She cast a suspicious eye over her shoulder as she went to the door and opened up. "Hey, Kyle."

"Hi, sis." He stepped into the room and glared at Serge without speaking.

Serge spread his arms. "What?"

The glare lasted a moment longer. "I just watched the news."

"That? Ha, ha, ha!" Serge waved a dismissive hand that signaled silly talk. "Where do they dream up all the crazy stuff they're putting on the air these days? I mean, death by chizzy-winks? Is there even such a bug? Such a *word*?"

Cheyenne wanted the subject changed. "Serge has offered to take us to lunch."

"Damn straight!" said Serge. "It's the least I can do for your service to the nation. The only condition is I get to pick the place. I've been dying to try one of Okeechobee's famous steak houses."

A loud crash on the other side of the wall, followed by a scream and a thud.

Serge pointed. "I'll go get Coleman."

A gold Plymouth pulled into a parking lot.

Kyle looked up at the sign. "I thought you wanted to go to one of our famous steak houses."

"I do. This is it!" Serge slammed down an empty coffee mug. "No finer choice!"

"Golden Corral? But you can eat at these anywhere in the country."

"Accept no substitutes!" said Serge. "Golden Corral is the pulse of America, where the Forgotten Fly-Over-Country People dine, and I mean that as a compliment. Pundits mention the Forgotten People like they genuinely care, but there's an unmistakable subtext of condescension. This is why the elitists can never get their predictions right. Whether it's elections, consumer confidence, shifting social tectonics, just chuck your fancy algorithms and scientific polls. Golden Corral is the Rosetta stone, the Oracle of Menestheus and the Magic Eight Ball rolled into one. The reasons are myriad, but one rises above all others: They have a chocolate fountain. There can be no greater symbol of straight-shootin', salt-of-the-earth integrity. As the pinnacle of the Corral's ziggurat, the chocolate fountain cannot be surpassed or even questioned."

The Plymouth slowly crawled through the gridlocked parking lot. "Wow, is this place jammed! Their food must be extra popular in these parts."

"It's veteran appreciation day," said Kyle.

"What's that mean?" asked Serge.

"Across the country, all veterans eat free today."

"The chocolate fountain has just been eclipsed."

An old man in a USS *Iowa* baseball cap suddenly jumped in front of the Plymouth with hands urgently raised for them to stop. At several other nearby points, more vets halted other cars.

"World War Two vet pulling out!"

Others were positioned behind a Buick Regal, using hand signals to help the driver inch backward like a snail. Serge jumped from his car and joined the flag-less semaphore team directing the vehicle. "God, I love these people! . . ."

Inside the restaurant, a color guard and a small contingent from the high school band. Most of the people at the tables wore some kind of hat or vest commemorating their service.

Serge grabbed a plate. "I've inadvertently entered an overkill of positive vibes." He led his group along the salad bar. "Let me show you how to make a salad. Most people simply throw a salad together because it's just a salad. But it's actually a statement. Please stand back . . ." They gave him space as he became a windmill of motion. Ingredients filled his plate, first in meticulous layers, then quadrants. ". . . A true salad is about architecture and engineering. I'm borrowing from the Romans for my potato salad basilica, and now for the victory arch . . ."

The packed dining room was a southern aroma symphony. Catfish, barbecued chicken, roast beef, okra, hush puppies, popcorn shrimp, three kinds of gravy.

Kyle pointed with a fork. "Serge, aren't you hungry?"

Serge sat back in his chair with his head tilted sideways. "This salad is way too damn big." His fork hovered over the single cherry tomato on top. "How does one even approach eating this without an avalanche?"

Cheyenne took a bite of beef. "So, Serge, what are you up to next?"

"Communing with these fine folks and learning their ways." He leaned toward the next table, where four old guys in suspenders and U.S. Navy caps were cutting steak. "Excuse me! Yoo-hoo! You know my new motto? Remember the Forgotten People! I think it's got legs. Don't pay no mind to the New York–L.A. cultural axis. There's an untapped reservoir of values and enlightenment in this room."

"Are you okay?" asked one of the guys.

"Fantastic, except for this ridiculous salad. But I've learned to accept what I can't change." A grin. "So tell me, what does Golden Corral have that those pointy-headed ivory tower types don't understand?"

One of the old guys continued chewing. "A chocolate fountain."

"Bingo!" said Serge. "It *looks* like an ordinary chocolate fountain, but you and I know what it really means." Wink. "All across the country there's an economic Mendoza Line, below which the middle and lower classes are secretly viewed by our oligarchs as the *livestock* class. How else can it be explained? Our paycheck-to-paycheck toil created their staggering fortunes. In return, all our safety nets are under siege in the name of corporate greed that won't be quenched until our lives are reduced to perpetual white-knuckled freak-outs hurtling toward premature, pre-existing-condition death. Who could do that in good conscience to another human being? On the other hand, if they see us as livestock instead of people, then it all makes sense: A political consultant stands at the front of a conference room with a projector. 'Our research shows we can easily convince the beef cattle to vote for the owners of the slaughterhouse. First we get them pissed off at the *dairy* cows—'"

"Quick," Kyle told his sister. "Grab his coffee."

"Just talkin' 'bout the chocolate fountain," said Serge. "It's the secret symbol of recognition among our people, like that creepy eyeball atop the pyramid on the back of a one-dollar bill."

Cheyenne smiled. "When I asked what you were up to next, I meant where are you going?"

"Oh, that's different." Serge stuck his fork in the salad, triggering a rockslide of croutons. "You're all witnesses. Not my fault . . . Anyway, I'm continuing my Florida odyssey of sweeping ramifications, but aren't they all? This one involves connective tissue that is pulling us in a tractor beam toward the lost town of Ortona, then Clewiston, before whipping under the bottom of Lake Okeechobee and visiting Belle Glade and Pahokee, collectively known as The Muck, for its rich earth. The welcome sign to Belle Glade says 'Her Soil Is Her Fortune.' The sign to Pahokee just says 'Pahokee.' It's hard to figure people out."

"I know all those places," said Kyle.

"Me too," said Cheyenne.

"How so?" asked Serge. "You're from the north side of the lake."

"But I played football," said Kyle. "We had away games. My father was one of the coaches in Okeechobee, and around the lake, all the coaches pretty much knew each other. From the time I was a little kid, we were always having dinner at someone's house in another small town."

"I was a cheerleader," said Cheyenne. "It's hard to believe now with the way many of those towns are boarded up, but I heard that back in the 1930s the whole area was called the 'winter vegetable capital of America.' It was a twenty-four-hour operation with refrigerated warehouses and trains constantly coming and going to rush the produce north while still fresh, not to mention thousands of workers filling the juke joints and gambling houses at all hours near the shantytowns that sprang up."

"Look at the Florida knowledge on you," said Serge.

"I'm your little history helper, remember? I've heard lots of stories about the whole lake region, some not on the books."

"Such as?"

"Lost treasure," said Cheyenne. "That was a favorite on the school yard. Trunks of precious metals supposedly went missing during the hurricane of '28."

"I'm sure a lot of everything went missing in that one."

"Yeah, but this tale had other scary and mysterious details," said Cheyenne. "Like a vicious sugar baron whose body was discovered with bullet holes and buried before the authorities found out."

"Then how did you and your schoolmates hear about it?" asked Serge.

"The guys who did the burying allegedly told their families, and the story was passed down generation to generation by word of mouth. But it's probably just that, a story." Cheyenne's fork toyed with the food on her plate. "It must be fun to take road trips like you do."

"I'm sure you've taken a million."

"Not really."

"But what about you saying there's too many places you've got to see?"

"That's why."

"Okay, then come with us." Serge collapsed the other side of his salad. "Shit."

"Really?"

Kyle touched her wrist. "What about the motel?"

"I've piled up a ton of vacation."

The brother grabbed his cowboy hat from under the chair. "Then I guess I'll need to make it a foursome. When do we leave? ..."

Chapter 35

PAHOKEE

Senior year of high school arrived with all the fanfare of raging hormones.

Social calendars filled up. A few students now had cars. Others got new clothes for the merciless battlefield that is popularity. And of course there was football season, with the mandatory post-game gatherings at burger joints. Yes, they still do that.

Chris was blossoming with her own crowd. The varsity team, the cheerleading squad, the marching band and various hangers-on. She was welcome at their restaurant tables, where they laughed and relived big plays and threw french fries at each other.

But Chris was still different. She didn't have any money. Others always chipped in for her food and told her not to worry, but good luck with that.

She never stopped smiling, but it began eating at her stomach, figuratively and literally.

One Thursday afternoon that fall, Chris thought hard about a dilemma that she'd been twisting in her mind and rotating to inspect from all angles. She made her choice. After all, how much difference can *one* make?"

That night, she left her grandmother's apartment and quietly headed down the stairs. Chris glanced around one last time before running off into the darkness behind the building and disappearing like a ninja . . .

The next afternoon, community fever grew as hours counted down to another huge gridiron contest in The Muck. The Blue Devils were still undefeated, and it was the second-to-last game of the season; the last before the Big Game. Signs that normally advertised breakfast specials and free tire rotation now had their letters rearranged into some variation of Beat Cardinal Newman! The barbershop was full of experts and bullshit.

At a storefront on a downtown street, bells jingled.

The pawnshop owner's hand was shaking a Rolex that had stopped working. He looked up. He saw her letterman jacket. "We going to win tonight?"

"Bank on it," said Chris.

"Are you one of the cheerleaders?"

"No, a kicker."

"You're on the team?" He paused with a finger to his mouth. "Wait, I heard something about you . . . Well, that's great. So how can I help?"

"I need to sell something."

"Let's see what you've got."

Chris pulled a shiny coin from her pocket and placed it on the glass counter.

"Wow, that sure is pretty." He turned it over. "Says twenty dollars. But of course you realize that they don't use these anymore."

"I know. We effectively went off the gold standard under Roosevelt," said Chris. "Some technically argue Nixon. Now it's full faith and credit."

"What do you say I give you—"

Chris removed a book from her backpack and placed it on the counter. *The Red Book,* the bible of coin-collecting price guides. "With all due respect, I know exactly what it's worth."

It was the last thing the pawn man expected. "Okay, I'm sorry. I'm not exactly killing it here in this town business-wise. Straight up, I need to make a profit, and who knows how long till I sell it. How about half of what it books for?"

"How about the melt value of the gold?" asked Chris. "That way you can't lose, and you get the whole numismatic collecting up-charge."

The pawn man thought: *Where did this kid come from? Most adults don't negotiate this well.* He slowly began to nod. "I can live with that. You just need to fill out this form. I'll get money from the register." He began counting out hundreds . . .

The football game went pretty much as expected. The home crowd had everything to cheer about all night as Pahokee took an early lead and never looked back for the trounce. There was even a late kickoff return that went all the way for a touchdown, crowning the night.

Revving convertibles and trucks, stereos blaring, converged again on Max's Shake Spot. It was a nicely converted old gas station from the thirties in the period's art deco design. Max had used old photos to replicate the original green-and-orange neon that trimmed the building all the way around to the outside restroom doors. Team pennants and banners filled the walls, along with a couple of framed jerseys and photos of former players who had gone on to the pros. The school's fall schedule and results had been dutifully tallied on a chalkboard. All the chairs were filled in the dining room, and the crowd spilled outside to the picnic tables on the porch.

"I can't believe about Coach Calhoun!"

"What have you heard?"

"Just rumors, but they can't be true."

"We have to do something!"

"Chris, you were pretty close to him. What do you think?"

"I feel the same as you," said the kicker. "But I know what he told me: Don't worry about him. And don't let anything distract us. We have to win the Muck Bowl."

The Muck Bowl.

More than historic.

Pahokee versus Glades Central. David and Goliath. Except David always had his slingshot. Either team could go undefeated the rest of the year, even win state championships in their separate divisions, but it wouldn't mean anything if they didn't prevail in the end-of-the-regular-season rivalry.

"The Muck Bowl." Nodding around the table. "Coach Calhoun is right. We'll deal with it later . . ."

The waitress came over and they ordered. It was pay in advance, and Chris stood up with her wallet. "I've got this."

"Chris, since when do you have money?"

"Since I started doing some odd jobs."

"Put your money away," said a starting lineman. "We always got you."

Then they saw the hundred-dollar bill . . . "Please, pay away."

The jumbo basket of buffalo wings arrived first and they dove in. Some of the loyal crowd were ex-students who had graduated in the last couple of years and were still trying to get in gear. They had minimum-wage jobs, unable to figure a way out. But they all looked forward to Friday nights in the fall, the connection to their true family. They wore their old team jackets.

The kicker felt a slap on her back.

"Chris, how's it going?"

She turned around. A young man named Ricky, who used to push her down in the dirt.

"Don't you mean 'Milk Crate'?"

"Sorry about all that," said Ricky. "And I think I owe you a football or two. Anyway, great game."

"I didn't even play."

"Still, you made the team. That's something."

"Thanks." She scooted over to make room. "Have some wings."

ORTONA

Kyle Lovitt looked out the rear window of a gold Plymouth speeding down the western shore of Lake Okeechobee. "Nobody can accuse you of letting moss grow."

"Why noodle around? When it's time to ramble, it should just be a matter of packing your bags and throwing them in the trunk," said Serge. "Of course in my case, my bags are usually already packed in the trunk, unless there's no room because . . . Let's leave it at that."

Ribbit. Coleman petted his chest. "Easy, Jeremiah."

Serge looked across the front seat. "Been meaning to ask. Cheyenne is such a fetching name, yet all the parents today go for Brittany or Kirsten. How come?"

"Because I'm Native American."

He pushed her shoulder playfully. "Get out of town!"

"Supposedly full-blooded, but I think someone in my family was fucking around and lying about it."

Coleman reached over from the back seat and tapped his shoulder. "Serge, a chick who says 'fuck.' That is so hot."

Serge smacked his hand away. "Shut up, you . . ." He turned. "Sorry about that on multiple male levels. But full disclosure: It *is* hot. Don't let that affect your level of lurid lexicon, for more or less . . . Please continue."

"So that's why I'm Cheyenne." The Plymouth's A/C was broken, and the wind from the open windows made her grab a rubber band and fashion a ponytail. "Imagine me. A Native American raised in Okeechobee. Half Indian, half cowboy."

Kyle stared at Coleman a moment, sitting next to him in the back seat, trying to give beer to a frog with an eyedropper. "So what's this next stop of yours? Ortona? I've never heard of it, and I've lived my whole life around here."

"It's the best!" Serge chugged coffee with a single brown rivulet running from the corner of his mouth. "A tiny hamlet down a long, inspiring country drive through our unspoiled nature. I would say it's a forgotten place, if it was ever known in the first place. There's a modest collection of canal-front homes down by the Caloosahatchee River, and that's about it for population. Otherwise, just a wild stretch of Route Seventy-Eight between LaBelle and Moore Haven. With one major exception: an incredibly important historic site that is right-on-point relevant! Which can mean only one thing."

"What's that?" asked Kyle.

"We must balance out relevance with non sequitur or The Man imprisons us in his plastic cage of linear thought. And we all know where that leads. Except I don't know where it leads because I've escaped the cage. See how it works? . . . Coleman, ready for another round of tangent? Get the list."

"Cool." Coleman reached in the glove compartment. "Next topic: best cowbell songs."

"Right!" said Serge, reaching under his seat.

"You brought a cowbell?" asked Kyle.

"I always have a cowbell nearby for any circumstance. Why? Without warning in polite cocktail-party society, you might need to urgently change the subject: 'Serge, did your friend Coleman just scratch his butt and sniff his finger?' You can interrupt and yell 'Gas leak!' or, if a stampede isn't needed . . ." He began hitting the bell with a drumstick. ". . . Get where I'm going with this? . . . *'Honky-tonk womannnnnnnnn!' . . .*"

"Shouldn't you be paying more attention to the road?" asked Kyle.

"The other hemisphere of my brain is at the wheel." *Clang, clang, clang.* "*'Mississippi queen!'* . . ." *Clang, clang.* "*'Fool for the city!'* . . . Remember the Chambers Brothers? *'Time has come to-day!'* . . ." *Clang, clang.* He threw the cowbell back under the seat. "Enough of that shit. Coleman?"

Coleman checked the list. "Homeland security."

"This is an important one," said Serge. "They say that our main strategic weakness against the terrorists is failure of imagination. But I'm just the guy to fix that! Two words: toupee bomber. Are we on that one?"

"Serge—"

"Hold that thought," said Serge. "We're here."

The Plymouth pulled up to the edge of the Caloosahatchee, and everyone got out.

"Is this the historic place?" asked Cheyenne.

"Not the main one," said Serge. "We need to build up to that or we could lapse into history shock. This is the Ortona Lock and Dam, part of a system of such structures that raise and lower boats traveling across the state on the one-hundred-and-fifty-four-mile-long Okeechobee Waterway. As opposed to, say, only forty-eight miles. I'm looking in your direction, Panama Canal."

"We've got a lock like this back near the motel," said Cheyenne.

Serge walked closer to the edge, carrying a paper sack.

"What's in the bag?" asked Kyle.

"You'll find out." Serge drank in the vista. "I love locks for their engineering feats. And especially the whirlpools."

"Whirlpools?" asked Coleman.

Serge nodded and aimed an arm. "When a boat's coming over from the coast and enters the lock, valves are opened, and water from the high side flows into it, raising the vessel like a rubber duck in a bathtub. But so much fluid rushes inside that it creates a vast vortex just outside the lock's upstream doors. In fact, this lock was recently closed two weeks for repairs because, among other things, serious whirlpools were forming *inside* the lock when lowering boats. Not good for the canoe people."

"Here comes a boat now," said Cheyenne.

"Let's watch the whirlpool." Serge led them up a path to the lock's eastern doors. "I love watching whirlpools the way cats watch a toilet flush."

"The whirlpool's starting," said Coleman. "Wow, it's getting big."

"I had no idea," said Kyle. "Forget canoes. It's a monster."

"Videos of these physics spectacles are all over YouTube, and someone just posted incredible footage from the Demopolis Lock in Alabama." Serge pulled something from his paper bag. "Watch this!"

"You carry a rubber duck around?" asked Cheyenne.

"A close second behind the cowbell." He heaved the yellow toy far out into the water.

They all watched it splash, then rotate in a wide but tightening circle until it was violently sucked under.

"Ta-da!" said Serge.

"Uh, you do realize you just littered," said Cheyenne.

"What? Oh, shit! I usually play with it in the tub, so there's rarely difficulty retrieving it. I wasn't thinking." Serge covered his face with his hands. "This negates my whole moment. I must atone." He ran back along the bank and stared at the water and waited. Finally, a rubber duck popped to the surface inside the lock. He cupped hands around his mouth. "Hey, you in the boat! I need a big favor! I just accidentally littered because I was watching water like a house cat. See that rubber duck about to float by? If you could just snag the sucker, it would center my karma . . . Thanks." Serge wiped his forehead. "Whew! Another close one! . . . Back to the car!"

They drove a short distance until three people were standing beside a Plymouth, watching Serge standing proudly atop a small hill.

"And this is one of the fabulous Ortona mounds, believed to have been created seventeen hundred years ago by the Calusa, who were the busy bees of early Florida, also digging a network of navigable canals . . . Back to the car!"

Another short drive. Serge leaped from the Plymouth. "You've been properly warmed up, so here it is! But first look around and let the context sink in: nothing, deserted, not even cars on the road. The closest thing to *anything* is that remote and idle quarry we passed on the way in. And I can't get enough of it! Dig!" Serge walked fifty yards out into a roadside field that was blanketed in yellow. He called back to the gang: "Florida, literally the Land of Flowers, and all these beautiful babies around me are the state's official wildflower, coreopsis." He stretched out his arms and began spinning joyously amid the blooms. "*The hills are alive with the sound of—*' . . . whoa, getting a little dizzy again." He staggered back to the road. "And now for our feature presentation."

Serge opened the Plymouth's trunk for his gravestone-rubbing supplies. A brief hike followed. "This is the Ortona Cemetery. It's hard to imagine now with all the surrounding emptiness, but for a few days in 1928, this was one of the busiest spots in the state. That year's hurricane was so devastating that it required three mass graves, including this last one." He placed his oversize sheet of paper against a historical marker and began rubbing. "We're back in Zora country! Can you dig it?"

"Uh . . ." said Kyle. "This has been an . . . interesting day."

"This is nothing," said Serge. "I'm getting a familiar tingle in my bones. That means the biggest day of this entire tour is about to dawn and blow your hat off! Come on! . . ."

Chapter 36

WEST PALM BEACH

Captain Crack Nasty grabbed a stuffed wahoo by the tail and ripped it off the wall. He smashed it over and over against the edge of his desk until it was almost dust.

His treasure business was turning to shit. The losing streak had reached six wreck sites that he had been sure would pay off like slot machines. All he had to show for it was another cannonball. Some of his workers left in frustration, and the rest found a way back to prison.

He fell in his chair and grabbed a bottle and fumed. He began thinking of an older "can't miss" treasure site. The one that had slipped through his fingers.

Crack Nasty had indeed gotten away with that ugly business out at the lake with those three young men. Four years had quickly passed without a knock on his door from the cops.

But he had also screwed himself.

Pahokee was too small a town, and he had been too visible. If he wanted to keep getting away with the killings, he had to stay extremely clear of the area. Dammit! Why did he let emotions make business decisions? And after the homework he'd put in. He had been so close he could taste it. He grabbed a nautical map, out of habit, to look for another offshore site. "What's the point!" He threw it and grabbed the bottle instead.

The phone rang.

"Hello? . . . No, I don't know who this is. . . . Been a long time? You said to call and you'd pay? If you say so. . . . What do you mean, 'prepare for happiness'? . . . What! Seriously? I'll be there this afternoon . . ."

Captain Crack pulled the magnetic door sign off his pickup truck, kicked caution to the curb, and headed west into sugar country.

Bells jingled extra hard as Crack burst into the pawnshop. "When did it come in?"

The owner stuck a clarinet on a shelf. "A few weeks ago, but I couldn't find your business card until this morning." He reached into the display case for a coin dated 1911.

Crack held it to his face as waves of dormant greed resurfaced. "Who sold it?"

"Young girl from the local high school." The owner pulled out a ledger book. "Her name was Chris something . . . Yeah, here it is. For whatever reason I didn't get her address, but she plays for the football team." He scribbled on a sheet of paper.

Crack laid a stack of hundreds on the counter and snatched the coin. "Remember . . ."

"I know. You were never here."

Bells jingled.

The owner shook his head. "I will never understand white people."

The gold Plymouth swung down under the lake and passed a welcome sign: AMERICA'S SWEETEST TOWN.

"This is it," said Serge. "Clewiston. Epicenter of Florida's sugar industry. Here we begin our exploration of the southern lake culture, moving on to South Bay, then swinging northeast along the shore. See the plumes of smoke dotting the horizon, as well as these recently burned black fields we're passing?"

"We're familiar with the harvesting process," said Kyle. Still, it was always a sight, and he and Cheyenne leaned toward the window.

"Then I'll tell Coleman," said Serge. An elbow. "Coleman, you awake?"

"Just resting my eyelids. They've been going all day."

"Look alive. We're in a hallowed place." He startled everyone by swinging into a convenience store at the last second, and running for the far wall.

Coleman caught up. "Coffee. What a surprise."

Serge shook a small packet and ripped it open. "Know what I'm pouring in my coffee?"

"Sugar?"

"History!" He tore open a second packet. "And since I'm in Clewiston, I need a second helping of heritage. From the molasses and rum trade routes to modern-day Florida, the sugar industry has sparked economy and controversy. Back to the car!"

Moments later, the quartet stood quietly in the middle of a large, gleaming space.

"Have to hand it to you," said Cheyenne. "You sure can pick 'em. This is incredible."

"The Clewiston Inn? Easy call." Serge swept an arm through the air. "Now *this* is a lobby! Other lobbies today are sterile nightmares that disagree with my colon: a few chairs, artificial flowers, rack of tourist pamphlets, and the counter where they lay out the free breakfast, which has been reduced to a plastic bin of Froot Loops where you have to turn a crank like a gumball machine. And then strictly at ten A.M., they actually *lock up* the Froot Loops! Will the madness never end? But not here! I can't get enough of a lobby that is a virtual church of varnished dark-wood walls, with the original mail slots behind the vintage counter, antique sofas and bookshelves with more old stuff that makes you want to leave your room just to sit in the middle of bygone days. Check out the hotel's preserved switchboard next to the fireplace, with the old cables and everything. And this coffee table over here is a glass display case. See those shiny metal things in there that look like a baseball catcher's shin guards, except if they'd come off a medieval suit of armor? Those are the old sugar cutters' leg protectors, because back before mechanized harvesting they were working so fast and swinging such sharp machetes to slice down the stalks that they kept hitting their legs, which was no good for anybody. And next to the protector things is one of the ancient cane blades. Notice the size and width of that bastard. If I ever have to attend a machete fight, that's what I'm bringing." He marched back to the receptionist's desk, where they'd just checked in.

"Sorry to bother you," said Serge, "but could I trouble you to open up the lounge for me and my friends to see art?"

"Wait, I remember you." A smile from behind the counter. "You're the mural guy."

"In some circles."

"No problem." She grabbed keys. "Follow me."

The quartet soon stood in another fabulous space, turning slowly to take it in.

"What do you think?" asked Serge. "Snazzy, eh?"

"I had no idea," said Cheyenne, stepping toward a wall to inspect a spoonbill. "I've driven by this place a million times but never stopped in because who needs a hotel when you live so close?"

"The history we most often overlook is in our own backyard." Serge parted blinds to look out one of the lounge's windows. "It's the little things about a small town, and in Clewiston it's stuff like that bank-style sign by the road, where in any other place the lightbulbs would display time and temperature, but here it's the lake level, just over fifteen feet. Wow, that's getting pretty high."

Serge pulled out a chair for Cheyenne, and they all sat at a table in the middle of the bar.

"Ladies and gentlemen!" Serge zestfully rubbed his hands together. "Our timing here is no accident! I have a surprise! But first an essential background briefing, which is mainly for Coleman . . . *Coleman!*"

"Huh? What? Right here."

"Can you at least raise your forehead off the table when I'm talking to you?"

"Crap. Always more work. Just give me a minute . . . Okay, I'm looking at you."

"As our journey continues, we're about to enter a most amazing place." Serge raised his arms to the heavens. "Some of the hardest-working folk you'll ever meet, with an astounding sense of family and community. It's actually two separate small towns ten miles apart on the southeastern shore of Lake Okeechobee— Belle Glade and Pahokee—but they're collectively referred to as The Muck, from the rich, dark soil—"

"Wait, what's the date?" asked Kyle. He checked his cell phone and smiled. "Now I know why your bones were tingling for the biggest day of your tour. The Muck Bowl."

"Ding, ding, ding!" said Serge. "We have a winner!"

"The Muck Bowl?" said Cheyenne. "That's so cool! I've never seen one."

Coleman looked left and right at the table. "What's the Muck Bowl?"

"Just the biggest high school football game in all of Florida," said Kyle. "Forget state championships. The rivalry between those two towns is more electric than anything. I played against both teams when I was in school, and they're unbelievable."

Serge nodded. "Go to any Muck Bowl, and a few years later you're liable to see several players on TV in the NFL."

"So you have tickets?" asked Kyle.

"I was going to pick some up when we got into town."

"You can't just *pick up* tickets to the Muck Bowl, unless you want to wait in line forever."

"What do you suggest?" asked Serge.

"I know one of the coaches in Pahokee, Lamar Calhoun." Kyle got out his phone again. "He might be able to hook us up."

"Lamar Calhoun?" said Serge. "Why do I know his name?"

"Because he used to be one of the best blue-chip running backs in all the state."

Serge snapped his fingers. "That's right. He was incredible, one that I would have bet for sure would make the pros. But then nothing. What happened?"

"I don't know," said Kyle. "I wasn't even born when he graduated, but our fathers were both coaches at opposite ends of the lake, and they became great friends over the years from crossing paths on the circuit. I even met Lamar at his dad's house a few times when he visited for the holidays. I heard he moved back to coach himself a couple years ago, and I've been meaning to call, but you know how that goes."

"I remember us having dinner at their house several times when I was a little kid," said Cheyenne. "Wonderful family." She turned to her brother. "Did you read where Pahokee has a girl on the team this year?"

Kyle shook his head, listening to his cell phone before hanging up. "No answer. They must have all left school for the day."

"She's a kicker," said Cheyenne.

"Who?" asked Kyle.

"The girl on the Pahokee squad," said his sister. "I saw a small thing about it in the paper, so I started following the team this year. I always get a good feeling when I see a girl making those kinds of strides against the odds."

Serge nodded. "And I always get a bad feeling when I see Internet trolls babbling that some successful girl is just a token who only made it through favoritism. Give me a break! I've been witnessing the behavior of my gender for years. Do you have any idea what it's like to be a woman in a man's world?"

"Yes."

"Okay, well, I don't," said Serge. "But I know the burden of the kind of brains we guys have to work with . . ." He grabbed Coleman by the hair and lifted his head up off the table again. "Exhibit A." He lowered the head. "And I can't believe the crassness I observed directed at women on the street."

"And that's only the stuff that guys like you overhear," said Cheyenne. "For us, it's such a perpetual, day-in-day-out gauntlet of leering and vulgar remarks that you eventually become numb."

"Coleman and I were discussing the phenomenon the other day," said Serge. "And I want to offer my deepest proxy apology for the dudes making slurping sounds and calling out anatomy by non-medical names. Personally, it confounds me. Putting the rudeness factor aside for a moment, on the mating level this is also their intelligence audition. It's like if a guy goes to a supermarket cashier a hundred days in a row and says, 'I don't have any money,' and she says, 'Then you can't have any food,' and he says, 'Okay, same time tomorrow?'"

"Did I just start a tangent with you?" asked Cheyenne.

"Well played," said Serge.

"So we're going to the Muck Bowl," said Kyle. "I'll just need to keep trying to reach Coach Calhoun. What in the meantime?"

Serge flipped open a notepad. "There's something huge that's been looming on my Florida bucket list. And now is the perfect opportunity to strike it off."

"What is it?" asked Kyle.

"This one is best left to be revealed in real time . . ."

An hour later, two flatbed pickup trucks sat on the side of a road with nothing around but a setting sun over vast acreage. Behind the trucks was a gold Plymouth and two people leaning against the fender with folded arms.

"What do you think they're doing in there?" asked Cheyenne.

Kyle covered his mouth as he began to cough from the smoke. "I have a good idea."

Serge dashed as fast as he could down the black-dirt rows. He crashed through stalks and dove on the ground over and over. Then running full speed again, smashing through more cane and another dive.

Exhausted, he rolled over onto his back and lay in the dirt, looked up into a circle of a half-dozen children's faces. Some of the kids were grasping cottontails. They giggled at Serge and ran off.

A few rows over, Coleman also lay on his back. Eyes shut tight. *Ribbit.* A bullfrog crawled out of a chest pouch and hopped away.

Serge got up and raced about, obsessively not giving up. But then it became just too dark. "Coleman! We have to head back to the car! . . . Coleman! . . ."

Coleman roused from an anesthesia fog. "Wha—? What is it?" He raised his head. "Oh, hello. It's another of my little nature friends." While Coleman had been unconscious, something had crawled onto his chest and found his girth, warmth and breathing to be a soothing elixir. He began stroking its back. He sat up and snuggled it under his chin, gently slipping it down into his chest pouch. "I'm coming, Serge!"

Over at the road, kids began jumping back into the pickups that had brought them. Most had sacks and makeshift chicken-wire cages with rabbits. Serge collapsed empty-handed over the hood of the Satellite.

"Jesus!" said Cheyenne. "You look like you're about to have a heart attack!"

"There's no other way to do a job than to end up looking like you're nearly in cardiac arrest. But you're a witness: I gave it my all."

"And then some," said Cheyenne.

The truck beds were noisy with animated tall tales from the cane fields. Then they went silent, all looking in the same direction.

Coleman strolled ho-hum out of the cane field, petting his newest furry friend. He looked up to see all eyes upon him. "What?"

Kids jumped down from the trucks and gathered around the plump, stumbling stranger. *"What's your secret?" "How'd you catch a jackrabbit?" "You must be super fast!"*

There was a banging sound. Serge's forehead against the hood of his Plymouth. Accompanied by fists.

"Easy," said Cheyenne. "You'll catch one someday."

"You're right." Serge stood and collected himself. "Besides, the big game is tomorrow. We need to be heading for the hotel to get our rest."

The gang piled back into the Plymouth and turned south on Main Street.

"Serge, why are you pulling over?"

"Just one last stop of the day on the way to the inn."

The Plymouth pulled around behind a government building.

"What is this place?" asked Cheyenne.

"Used to be the library," said Serge. "Now a museum."

Three people headed for the doors. One went another direction.

"Serge," yelled Kyle. "The entrance is this way."

"We're not going in the museum," said Serge. "Follow me . . ."

The foursome soon stood on the lawn on the north side of the building. All staring up at the same thing.

"This is just like our hotel," said Cheyenne. "I've driven by a thousand times but never stopped to really take a look."

"One of the most emotional historic monuments in all the state," said Serge. "Statues of a family of four: father, young son, and mother cradling an infant, all running for their lives and looking back up at the sky in terror, the parents raising futile arms to shield their heads. And on the monument's base, a stone-relief sculpture of giant waves washing away homes and snapping palm trees. And if you look real close in the water, there's a bunch of tiny people drowning beneath a simple inscription: 'Belle Glade 1928.'"

"Whew," said Cheyenne. "What can you say?"

"You can't," said Serge.

The monument was too much to take in at once, so they didn't.

"Every now and then, being at a place pulls at me in a way I don't understand," said Serge. "I get an odd feeling."

"Who wouldn't at a monument like this?" said Cheyenne.

"It's not the monument," said Serge. "Another kind of feeling. My bones again, but different this time. Like something big is looming just around the corner."

They all became quiet again, respectfully taking in the sight as the sun departed.

Chapter 37

GAME DAY

There had been talk of rain, but it never came. Instead, the departing clouds over Lake Okeechobee left the night air cool and crisp under the stadium lights. The faint smell of smoke from the surrounding cane fields competed with sausage grills in the concession stands.

Spectators had started arriving at the gates when the sun was still high. You had to for this one if you wanted any kind of decent seat. Those who arrived late were still more than happy to stand or watch from outside the fence, fingers clinging to chain link.

Twenty-five thousand were expected tonight. Insane for a high school. But the Muck Bowl was no ordinary game. The number of college scouts in the stands confirmed that. They always came out for the annual battle of the rabbit chasers.

The hype had been building for weeks among the nearby

communities. Signs outside restaurants and dry cleaners and lube shops cheered on the Blue Devils and the Raiders. They talked about it in the post office and the supermarket lines. Tailgate parties were planned with the logistics of military campaigns. And now it was time.

School buses arrived after the ten-mile drive up the rim of the lake from Belle Glade, and the players streamed out. Bands played, police directed traffic. The Blue Devils were already on their home-field sideline. Their uniforms were slightly different from the usual. It was the players' idea. On the front of each of their jerseys, just above the numbers, a strip of tape with lettering in Magic Marker: CALHOUN. It was unauthorized, but all the coaches looked the other way.

The cheering from the stands was like a jet taking off. And this was only the warm-ups . . .

. . . A gold Plymouth Satellite rounded the bottom of the lake.

"You sure we got tickets?" asked Serge.

Kyle nodded. "Coach Calhoun said they'd be waiting for us at the booth, but it might be standing room."

The Plymouth continued north. Even if they hadn't known there was a big game, they would've been able to tell something was definitely up. Everyone in motion, piling in cars, honking, good-natured yelling in traffic, making last-moment dashes into stores, well-wishes painted on the windows of homes and offices.

"This is what I'm talking about," said Serge, gripping his fingers against the steering wheel. "Small-town pride. The fabric of the community coming together like a Kevlar vest."

They left Belle Glade behind and then it was just an empty stretch of cane fields that connected destinies. The sun finally set over Pahokee, draping the town in darkness, except for the strings of headlights pouring in from all directions.

"There it is," said Serge.

The brilliantly glowing football field stood out in the surroundings like Yankee Stadium.

"Looks like we have a bit of a walk," said Cheyenne.

They parked down the street from the overflow lots and hiked to the entrance booth.

"Coleman, you let the jackrabbit free," said Serge. "Why are you still wearing the chest pouch?"

Coleman reached inside and pulled something out to show his buddy. Then put it back inside.

"Why are you carrying a doughnut in your pouch?"

"Emergencies."

Tickets were waiting as promised. This time Kyle took charge, leading them along the fence in front of the home section until they reached the area behind the Pahokee bench.

"Coach Calhoun!"

Lamar turned. At first there was a lack of recognition.

"It's me, Kyle."

Then Calhoun brightened, and a reunion hug. "I heard about your dad. Sorry."

"Heard about yours, too," said Kyle. "They were good men."

"Coach!" A hand extended to shake.

"And you must be Cheyenne." Lamar lowered his right palm to the height of his waist. "Last time I saw you, you were this tall."

"The years fly by," she said. "So you're back home coaching now?"

Calhoun rested a forearm on the top of the fence. "That's a complicated story."

"Where's this kicker I've been reading about?"

"Chris? Right over there. She's quite something."

They all looked down the bench at a slender girl with a pony-tail, leaning forward with spring-wound intensity.

Then more coiled intensity from another direction. "Coach! I'm Serge! Huge fan!"—shaking hands vigorously—"Can't tell you how much all of this means to our nation! Connective tissue from Stetson to Zora! This is Coleman . . ."

Coleman waved. "I caught a bunny."

"Don't listen to him," said Serge. "So what's the big plan for tonight? Razzle-dazzle, Statue of Liberty, flea flicker, fumble-rooski, triple-reverse sting operation, bark at the moon to confuse the blitz?"

Calhoun glanced over at Kyle. "You know these people?"

"Actually, yes," said the young man. "But they're harmless. Maybe not to themselves . . ."

Cheyenne pointed at the color guard marching out onto the field. "Looks like we're starting."

After the national anthem, thunder from the stands as the Devils took the field to kick off. They formed a rigid line. A referee blew a whistle. A ball sailed high under the lights.

The Belle Glade receiver took it on the fifteen and charged straight up the field, waiting for his wall of blockers to form. Then he abruptly swung left, and used ridiculous speed to curl around the end and race up the sideline. The blocking wall held. One by one, the defenders were picked off. The path to the end zone now clear.

Well, almost clear. The kicker was left, outmatched by at least eighty pounds and staring in headlights. Normally a tackle would have been impossible. But the receiver was running down the sideline. It wasn't necessary to *tackle,* just knock him out of bounds. So the kicker, as they say, took one for the team. He ran as best he could toward the edge of the field, left his feet and laid out. Which meant just diving and sacrificing his body horizontally in front of the runner.

It was a wincing collision, but it did the trick. Out of bounds at the thirty. The kicker didn't get up. Coaches ran over. They held fingers in front of his face. They gave him a pop quiz.

The referee leaned in. "What's the story?"

They shook their heads. "Concussion. He's out."

A rare moment of silence in the stands as medics wheeled the stretcher toward the waiting ambulance that had backed up through the gates. Then an eruption of applause from both stands as the player, still prone on the stretcher, raised a fist with a thumbs-up.

That bit of drama was the first of many. Key fumbles and interceptions. Lead swings. Fourth-down pass completions. Safety blitzes and trick plays. Spectators held their stomachs and hearts, not sure how much more they could take . . .

. . . Police officers kept an eye on the darkened parking lots. Every space was taken. Even spaces that weren't spaces. Vehicles up on curbs, in no-parking zones, blocking fire hydrants. It was the unwritten fine print of a small town: no parking tickets during high school games.

Just after halftime, a pickup truck arrived and drove up and down packed rows until parking on the grass behind a dumpster. The driver bought a standing-room ticket and stood as Pahokee kicked off. But the new spectator wasn't watching the field. He was looking at the bench.

Chris wasn't hard to spot. The players on the bench had their helmets off. Just look for the only girl.

Captain Crack Nasty reached into his pocket and rubbed the gold coin he had just purchased at the pawnshop. He smiled to himself and decided to enjoy the rest of the game . . .

With five minutes to go, the Blue Devils were down 27–21 and driving inside the five. But play stalled on a third-down shot out the back of the end zone. They were too close to risk another touchdown attempt and give up the sure three points. They sent out the kicker, who made good: 27–24.

The kicker trotted off the field as teammates slapped his pads in congratulation. Then he suddenly began hopping on his left foot and dropped down on the bench. His helmet came off with a grimace. The trainer arrived, then other staff.

"What is it?" asked the head coach.

The trainer rotated the leg slightly, and the player almost screamed. "Looks like a pulled groin."

"So how's he going to be?"

"He's in no condition for even an onside kick."

"Are you kidding me?" said the coach. "Can't you do anything? Tape it up?"

A headshake. "He might even need surgery."

Teeth gritted; then: "I know, I know. Shouldn't have even asked. Their welfare comes first." A frustrated kick in the dirt. "But why in a three-point game? One field goal to tie and send it to over-time? What am I supposed to do?"

"I guess you're just going to have to try for the touchdown and the win."

They carefully took off the kicker's jersey.

Chris was leaning way forward, trying to make out the com-motion at the other end of the bench. She saw them removing the shoulder pads of the second-string kicker, who was in obvious agony. She leaned back. "Shit."

The Devils defense made a clutch stop on third down in enemy territory, and the Raiders had no choice but to punt. The Paho-kee offense took the field. Time was running short, so they had to manage the clock. Which meant passing. And Belle Glade knew it. They loaded up deep and played soft for the short, underneath stuff. Pahokee started with a sideline route that went out of bounds for a four-yard gain. Then another for five yards. Then a short pass over the middle for a first down that stopped the clock at just over a minute. It was working, but it was taking far too long.

Chris would have been biting her nails if she did that sort of thing. Instead, her right knee nervously bounced up and down. She glanced over her shoulder at the roaring overflow crowd. She did a double take. She jumped off the bench and ran to the fence. "Coach Calhoun!" She hugged him over the top of the chain link.

"Easy now."

Chris let him go. "What are you doing here?"

"You kidding? I wouldn't miss this for anything."

She hadn't noticed because of the excitement at seeing the

coach, but someone was standing with him. He was home for a break from college.

"Reggie!" Another hug.

"Chris," said Calhoun. "There's time for this later. You need to get your head back in the game."

"Did you see what happened to our kickers?"

Calhoun nodded.

"What should I do?"

"I suggest you start warming up."

Chris nodded and dashed off. She found a spot behind the bench away from the others and began stretching.

The Blue Devils continued a consistent march down the field. But it was all still more short stuff, eating up way too much time. Both sides knew what was coming. The quarterback took the next snap and dropped back farther than before to give the receivers time to extend their routes. He looked right and saw tight coverage. He ducked and stepped up in the pocket as a defender leaped and flew by. He reached back with everything he had and launched a perfect spiral with plenty of air. It couldn't have been more on target, arcing down toward the back corner of the end zone. But Glades Central had time to shift an extra defender, and now the Pahokee receiver was double-teamed. The ball was swatted away.

Fourth and long. At the outer edge of field-goal range. The clock stopped at ten seconds. The head coach glanced at Chris, warming up at the practice net. "Time out!"

The roar of the crowd was a rattling blare of sheer white noise. Nobody had taken a seat for the last fifteen minutes. Even the cops were cheering.

The teams went to their sidelines, panting, gargling water and spitting it out. Nobody could say they weren't leaving it all on the field. Both sides had nothing left, and that's when the boys at the lake always found more. The head coach called the play. The players ran back onto the field.

Chris stayed behind the bench at the practice net.

Pahokee lined up identical to the last play. Spectators grabbed their heads and pulled their hair. The ball was snapped. The fastest receivers streaked down both sidelines. The quarterback dropped back deep. He cocked his arm to launch another long one. Then he pulled the ball in. It was a delay play. The tight end threw a block on the right tackle, then slipped over the line five yards. The quarterback stepped forward and hit him running full speed. The defense was covering all the long routes and had left the middle open. Bedlam in the stands. The end raced up the clear middle of the field. Ten yards, fifteen, twenty. The defenders converged. The end tried to get around the left side, but one of the Raiders dove for a perfect ankle tackle. The runner went down right on the hash mark at the fifteen-yard line. A second later, a horn on top of the scoreboard blared. No time on the clock. Final score: Glades Central 27, Pahokee 24.

One side of the field jumped in ecstasy, the other in furious protest. The referees were already huddling. They already knew they had a serious mess on their hands. They realized the implications of what they had to do, and in the back of their minds were thinking how to get out of the parking lot as fast as possible when it was all over. The runner was down, but the scorekeeper up in the booth hadn't stopped the clock in time. The refs all nodded in agreement, and the head official broke their huddle and signaled to the booth to put a single second back on the clock.

Now emotions reversed in the opposing stands.

The Pahokee coach yelled at a ref and made a T with his hands. "Time out!"

Then he turned. "Chris!"

There wasn't need for any strategy discussion. It was a straight field goal. If she made it, then overtime. If not . . .

"You got this one, Chris," said a teammate, slapping her on the butt. "Oops, sorry."

"Don't worry about it."

The crowd was apoplectic. Spectators dug fingernails into each other's arms. Some gasped for air. Others grabbed their hearts. Coleman reached in his pouch for the doughnut.

The intermission ended, and the players trotted back out under the bright lights.

To this day, almost everyone involved remembers what happened next like the climax of a sports movie, drawn way out in extra-excruciating drama. Not that it needed any more.

Chris stepped up to the holder and addressed where the ball would be placed. Then she took measured steps backward and two more to the left. She shook her dangling arms at her sides to loosen nerves. She looked up at the home stands. Berserk people jumping and clapping. She saw their mouths shouting but she couldn't hear them. She couldn't hear any sound. Then a shrill ringing grew louder in her ears, and a pounding heartbeat. She looked toward the holder and nodded. The holder turned toward the blocking line and nodded at the center. People held breaths, prayed.

The ball was snapped.

It was ultra-slow motion. A tenth of a second ticked off the clock. Shoulder pads violently collided. Chris had done this a million times. She began running toward the holder, synchronizing her approach with the arrival of the ball. *Click*. Another tenth of a second. The ball seemed to hang in the air forever on the way to the holder. More shoulder pads crashed. She saw the linebackers take their first step forward for their leaps to attempt the block.

The ball reached the holder's hands. *Click*. She could see individual laces. The ball went toward the ground. Chris took another step and got ready to plant her left foot. There would be another step after that. Her kicking leg would swing.

The holder got the ball to the ground. *Click*. He spun the laces away.

Chris was suddenly hit in the chest with utter terror.

While spinning the ball, the holder had muffed it. The ball slipped out of his hands and it now lay sideways on the ground.

He tried to right it, but too late. Chris was already there. She had to pull up and abort the kick.

The team had a plan for such a misplay. They'd drilled it and drilled it in practice. But it was never conceivably meant with Chris in mind. Nonetheless, she had dutifully gone through all the practices with the other kickers, and now it was the mindless instinct of repetition.

Click. The horn sounded. The clock read zero.

Chris swung out of her kicking approach, running wide right. The holder pitched her the ball. She caught it in stride. The Belle Glade defense had loaded up for the block, and now most of their players were entangled in that snarl of limbs at scrimmage, allowing Chris to round the end. And damn if she wasn't faster than anyone would have guessed. Rabbits.

But all appeared to be for naught. The Raiders were anything but slow, and a pair of them bounced outside and swept toward her path. The farther one was toward the middle and had a ways to go, but the closer was almost straight ahead and in perfect position.

He'd placed himself to be able to beat her to the sideline. Unless she wanted to run out of bounds and end the game, her only option was to do what he wanted: to veer inside toward the middle of the field, where he'd have help from the other player, and maybe more. She'd easily be tackled.

Either way, checkmate.

She kept running full sprint. Then she did something the defenders didn't expect. She began curling *toward* the sideline. Those in the home stands who had been holding their own heads began slapping them. *"What's she doing?" "He'll run her out of bounds!"*

The closest player couldn't believe his luck. *Must be her lack of experience, probably thinks she can beat me to the corner and tight-rope it into the end zone.* He adjusted his course along with hers. Then Chris surprised him even more. She increased her angle toward the sideline. He thought: *Has Christmas come early?*

They were only yards away, a split second left. He leaned forward to shove her out of bounds.

Chris took a last stride with her right leg toward the sideline. But instead of continuing, she dug her foot into the turf, hitting the brakes. The player flew by in front of her. His feet went out from under him as he tried to reach back, but Chris had already hit the gas again.

She still couldn't hear the crowd, but now it was because they were almost silent, mouths open.

The last defender had expected to merge with his teammate and sandwich her just inside the five. That was off the table now, and the footrace was on. He had the edge in distance and speed, but nothing was settled yet.

Chris had no more "Reggie" cuts in her bag of tricks. No argument that she'd be tackled inside the two. It was just a question of geometry.

She reached full sprint speed and left her feet like a track star in the long jump. Except this time it was headfirst. The Raiders player had been expecting that, and dove to hit her at the waist, hoping to drive airborne Chris off the field.

As she was coming down, Chris stretched out an arm and reached as far left as she could, swiping the tip of the ball against the orange pylon in the front corner of the end zone.

The referee's arms went up. Touchdown. No need for that overtime.

Players and fans swarmed the field. The insane jumping in the home team's stands would have registered on seismic instruments.

Calhoun and Reggie stood on their toes at the fence. They couldn't have been happier as they watched the team carry Chris off the field on their shoulders.

Chapter 38

CELEBRATION

Car horns honked nonstop all over town. Screaming on Main Street. People whipped team towels in circles over their heads. The epicenter of the bedlam, of course, was Max's Shake Spot.

Chris was the talk and the toast. She was still carrying the game ball that the head coach had presented to her. No way she would be allowed to pay for anything tonight. And not just Chris. Max himself came out and made the announcement personally: All players eat free tonight.

"Hooray!"

The revelry continued into the night, players becoming bloated on free burgers, chocolate shakes and root beer floats.

"Pahokee! . . . Pahokee! . . . Pahokee! . . ."

Players took selfies and group photos with cell phones. The

students, especially the seniors, knew this was a night they would well remember into the decades to come.

And for the first night all season, there were an unusually large number of white people. It wasn't suspicious. It was the usual suspects from the scouting ranks across the southeast and all the way up to Ohio and Michigan. They knew the delicate line of what they could and couldn't say to avoid violating eligibility. All night long: "*Great game! Here's my card. Florida State . . .*" "*. . . Here's my card. Georgia Tech . . .*" "*. . . Auburn . . .*" "*. . . Ole Miss . . .*"

Former coach Calhoun arrived and headed toward a picnic table, smiling bigger than he had in years. Chris suddenly noticed him in the crowd. She jumped up and gave him a strangling hug. "Thank you! Thank you! Thank you!"

"Easy, you'll break my neck," said Calhoun. "And I should be the one thanking you. At my age, you don't think there's much more to learn in life, but you've taught me so much."

A Plymouth pulled up and emptied. Serge led the gang through the crowd.

"Uh-oh," said Calhoun. "I think you have some more fans."

"Chris!" said Serge, shaking her hand. "I've heard so much about you! Such an inspiration in our times of crisis!"

"Uh, do I know you?"

"No, but I'm a friend of a friend of Coach Calhoun."

"Then you're my friend."

More students arrived and crowded round the table. "*That was fantastic!*" "*You were great!*"

Cheyenne tugged Serge by the sleeve. "We should let her be with her friends. It's her big night."

"I was going to start a wave in her honor, but I'll defer to your female judgment," said Serge. "That's my new life motto: When in doubt, ask a woman. Because us guys are doing such a bang-up job, right?"

She tugged his sleeve harder. "There are some seats in back . . ."

Chris said she had to go to the bathroom.

"Too much information."

"Just hold my seat."

She walked around the dark side of the building for the restrooms.

"Chris!" someone yelled. "Great game!"

She turned around. "Thanks . . . Do I know you?"

"Doubt it," said the man in the cab of the pickup. "I'm a college scout. If only you were a boy . . . I didn't mean that like it sounded."

"I know what you meant." She grabbed the handle of the door to the women's room.

When she walked out moments later: "Could you come here a second?"

"Why?"

"We don't recruit girls for football in Division One, but you're a natural," said Crack. "There are a number of sports you could easily adapt to."

Chris walked halfway to the truck. "Like what?"

"Tell me what else you play," said the captain. "You're probably thinking we're just trying to comply with Title Nine, which we are. But this is no charity: You can definitely play. Full scholarships rarely come along for girls. Ever try volleyball? Lacrosse?"

A couple more steps. "I really haven't tried any other sports."

Captain Crack opened his door and stepped out. "Let me show you these brochures from the school I represent."

"What school did you say that was?"

"I didn't."

And before Chris knew it, Crack had her by the arm, twisting hard. She yelped as he tried pushing her into the pickup. She was putting up a lot more fight than he had expected from a girl, but a sock in the jaw ended that nonsense.

Two boys came around the side of the building, yucking it up. Chris screamed from the open window as the pickup patched out.

The boys raced back to the picnic table. "Some guy just snatched Chris!"

"What? Who?"

"I got a picture on my cell phone." He held it up.

Someone leaned over his shoulder. "I know that truck!" yelled Ricky. "I know that *guy*. I'll never forget him as long as I live!"

It took mere seconds for alarm to sweep the crowd. Serge burst through and saw the phone. "I overheard you say that you know where he took her?"

The boy nodded.

"What's your name?"

"Ricky."

Calhoun frantically pushed his way in. "What's going on? Where's Chris?"

"No time," said Serge. "Seconds are precious . . . Ricky! Coleman! Come with me! . . . Coach, take the others in your car and follow us!"

Soon the Plymouth was barreling out of town, out into the darkness of flowing cane stalks. The needle spiked at over a hundred, leaving Calhoun and the others in the dust. Ricky filled Serge in along the way: His own beating in the cane fields years earlier, sure he was going to die until his rescue. Then the murder of his rescuers in the exact same spot, which the authorities ruled to be a drug deal gone sour, but Ricky knew better.

"Slow down," said the boy. "The turnoff's coming up."

The Plymouth rolled to a crawl.

"There it is," said Ricky.

Serge couldn't see anything down the dirt road, but he did make out fresh tire tracks leading into the field. "Ricky, you need to trust me. Get out and wait here by the road for the others for your own good. This is my specialty and I work alone." He pulled something from under the seat and Ricky opened the door. "And you didn't see this."

"What gun?" Ricky closed the door.

Serge hit his high beams and sped off into the black desolation of the cane field . . .

Soon, other headlights came up the highway. They caught Ricky waving madly on the side of the road. Calhoun pulled alongside. "What's happening?"

Ricky stuck his head in the window. "He went in after him. And I'm not supposed to tell you, but he has a gun."

"Shit!" Lamar cut the wheel and raced his car down the dirt road . . .

Serge's lights eventually hit the back of Captain Crack's pickup. Dark and empty. Bad sign. "Coleman, wait in the car. I may need you to drive this out of here in a hurry."

Serge planted his feet in the soil and crouched to listen. A brief gust of wind carried a snippet of noise. He crept like a ghost in its direction, quietly parting cane stalks. The sound grew louder. Voices. Soon they weren't hard to follow. The captain had chucked all his business rules. He chugged Johnnie Walker straight from the bottle as Chris lay crying in the dirt at his feet. "Please don't hurt me."

"Shut up!" A swift kick to her ribs. "Just dig!"

"I'm trying!"

More weeping, more kicks, more Scotch. Chris trembling too much to make progress in the soil. It wasn't going anyplace good.

"What the fuck is wrong with you?"

She heard a click and looked up and saw the cocked pistol. "No!"

Then another sound, unexpected. The clack of metal on skull.

Captain Crack thudded to the dirt like an unhooked punching bag. In the space where he had been standing, another person now stood. Chris recognized him as someone she had just met back at the burger joint.

She ran crying into his arms.

He quickly held Chris out by the shoulders. "You have to pull yourself together. I know you can do it! Others are counting on you, okay?"

She nodded and stifled her sobs down to sniffles.

"Good," said Serge. "If I'm correct, Coach Calhoun should be arriving just about now. I need you to walk straight down this one row of cane and start calling out for him."

"What are you going to do?" asked Chris.

"You and Ricky and the other kids deserve to be happy. And safe. And that will never happen under the status quo." Serge nodded in the direction of the cane. "Now get going. And don't look back . . ."

C oach Calhoun! Coach Calhoun! . . ."
Lamar's headlights had just hit Serge's Plymouth parked behind a pickup truck. He slammed the brakes and got out.

"Coach Calhoun! Coach Calhoun! . . ."

Lamar looked at Kyle and Cheyenne. "Did you hear that?"

"It's coming from over there!"

They crashed through stalks. "Chris! We're over here! We're on the way!"

Moments later, they all burst through the last rows of cane, and everyone embraced in terrified relief.

"What happened?" asked Calhoun.

"I don't know," said Chris. "The guy was going to kill me for sure. I just know it. But then that friend of yours came out of nowhere."

"And where are they now?"

She shrugged. "He just told me to leave and not look back."

Kyle and Cheyenne glanced at each other. They heard sirens in the distance. A lot of them.

Calhoun took off his Pahokee football jacket and wrapped it around Chris's shoulders. "We need to get you to my car."

Back at the highway, Ricky was waving a long line of police cars down the dirt road. Blue and red lights flashed through the crops as the speeding vehicles kicked up a long plume of black dust.

The officers arrived at Calhoun's car just as the former coach and the others emerged safely with Chris.

But the '69 Plymouth and pickup truck were gone.

HIGHWAY 78 REVISITED

High beams pierced the black countryside.

Nothingness for miles. The pickup's windows were down, allowing a cool night breeze to accompany the peaceful, silent, green glow from the instrument panel.

It hadn't started that way. In the passenger seat, the captain had been quite chatty. *What do you want? I have money. I'll give you anything. Blah, blah, blah.*

Serge put a stop to the annoyance with another bloody skull crack from his Colt .45. Calmly as a librarian: "Shhhh . . . I'm enjoying the tranquil drive." He kept the pistol in his left hand, aiming across the pickup's cab as he steered with his right.

It was indeed a mellow ride. Dim fields of wildflowers under the economic light of a crescent moon. More miles of blood-pressure-reducing serenity through the wilderness.

Finally, Serge let off the gas, and the pickup truck from a marine-towing company uneventfully rolled to a stop with the sound of small crushed white rocks under the tires. He ordered the good captain out of the car at gunpoint.

A gold Plymouth arrived and parked behind. "Coleman, wait here until I get back."

A hike began. Crack Nasty looked around in the night landscape. Emptiness only led to even more emptiness. His thoughts pinballed as they can at a moment like this. Heaven, hell, God, the devil. *Anything you want! I'm begging!* Crack!

Another half hour.

Serge poked a gun barrel in ribs. "Walk down the bank and watch your step."

It was precarious, with loose soil and gravel collapsing and rolling down the incline under their feet, but they made it with only a couple of stumbles. They arrived at a modest shoreline.

"We're here," said Serge. "Sit down."

"What are you going to do?"

"Wait for someone."

"Who?"

"I don't know."

"I don't understand."

"That's your problem," said Serge. "Your least."

They sat, as they say in kindergarten, crisscross applesauce, amid sounds of insects and bullfrogs and rustling leaves.

Serge's ears perked, and he stood. "Here they come."

"Who?"

"Like I said, I don't know."

"You're insane, aren't you?"

"My gain is your loss."

Crack Nasty opened his mouth to scream, but Serge bashed him once more before he could get it out. "Try to yell again, and it's game over. Two taps to the head. But play nice and you might get away. Here's my offer: If you behave and wait until I release you, you're free to swim for it. But utter a peep, even in the water, and I can plug you way over here. Deal? Just nod."

He nodded.

"Great! A cooperator! Sit still . . ." Serge listened intently as the distant motorized sound grew louder. "That's the person I've been waiting for. Okay, Florida Man, take off all your clothes."

"You want me to get naked?"

"I'm doing you a favor." Serge stretched out his shooting arm. "Play your cards right, and you could become an Internet heartthrob."

"But—"

"You'd rather stay here with me? How sweet."

"No, no!" Crack quickly ripped off his shirt and pulled down his pants. "I'll skinny-dip . . ." He looked around. "But where is this person you were waiting for?"

"They're arriving by boat." Serge aimed his pistol. "You're free to go. Swim . . ."

Crack didn't need to be told twice. He dove in the water and swam like it was the Olympics. He neared the halfway mark across the river and found he was veering in the wrong direction. He lifted his head and corrected course. It happened two more times, but no matter how hard he tried, the captain always found himself swinging back to face Serge. What was going on?

Then it became clear. He didn't know the name of the place he was at, but he understood the concept. Captain Crack began spinning wildly, screaming with abandon as he stared up at the large metal wall at the Ortona Lock and Dam towering over him.

And the violent, twenty-foot-wide whirlpool flushed him down like a turd.

Epilogue

As football signing day approached, college scouts again descended on The Muck like a migration of birds. Or locusts.

One particular scout from a perennial midwestern contender was interested in the star running back. The principal pulled him aside and reminded the scout that, years earlier, his university had recruited another of their running backs.

"That's right," said the smiling scout. "I remember him."

Then the principal adopted a grave tone and explained how it would be.

Now, mere mortals cannot comprehend what the power and money of big-college football are able to accomplish, just short of interstellar travel. And even that's arguable. It's only a matter of motivation, and the college boosters really wanted this tailback. The principal's conversation was highly inappropriate and totally the right thing to do.

A few weeks later, a knock at the front door of a modest concrete-block ranch house on Pahokee's south side.

"Principal Jennings, what brings you around?"

"May I come in?"

"Be my guest," said a former running back named Calhoun.

"Lamar, funny thing. We took another look at your situation, and it turns out there are no records whatsoever of any incident between you and a coach." He opened a file with stamped pages. "We've received notarized statements from both the university and local police department that your name is squeaky-clean up there."

"What? But how—?"

"Lamar, listen to me . . ."—telegraphing the unspoken with his eyes—". . . there are no records."

"Uh, okay."

The principal headed for the door and turned around just before he left. "Why don't you swing by my office Monday morning. I'd like to hear your plans for the team this year."

The body of Captain Crack Nasty was discovered sticking halfway out of an underwater valve at the Ortona Lock and Dam. Due to his blood-alcohol content, nudity and other factors, it was officially ruled death by misadventure, as if someone had planned it that way. Some of the locals had other theories about an unusual stranger who'd breezed through town, but none felt the slightest inclination to come forward.

Cheyenne Lovitt actually cried after opening the letter that had been slipped under the motel office door in the middle of the night: "For reasons that are now all too obvious, I must go away for a while and not have any contact with you or your brother, for your own protection. I guess there are too many places we've *both* got to see. I can't say when, but I promise after things blow over, I'll find a way to get back in touch with my little history helper. Serge."

Kyle Lovitt's passion for the rodeo only grew, and he became a crowd favorite on the southern circuit. He was back home again a year later for the annual Okeechobee Rodeo. It immediately got dicey in the starting chute. An extra-ornery bronco named Diablo crashed and bucked against the railings. Until now, nobody had been able to complete a ride, and most no longer dared try. "Hold on!" yelled one of the rodeo hands trying to steady the horse. "No, I've got it," said Kyle. "Just get that gate open fast." He practically had to jump into the saddle, and the horse blasted off. It was a magnificent ride, and after the full eight seconds, Kyle jumped down to a standing ovation from the crowd.

Cheyenne had begun nursing school, but still always found the time to slip into her cowgal duds and proudly carry the American flag to open each rodeo. After Kyle dismounted Diablo, she ran out across the dirt to congratulate him with a hug. "You were fantastic! Listen to that applause!" As their eyes moved around the arena, taking in all the standing, cheering people, they happened to look at the far end of the dirt and a pair of barrels. Suddenly, two clowns popped up and waved. Then ran off into the night.

"Did I just really see that?" asked Cheyenne.

Kyle turned to his sister. "Is this good or bad?"

C hris never played organized sports again.

Instead, she received a full academic scholarship to Johns Hopkins University. She had the grades and aptitude to become a highly paid, top-notch specialist in any number of disciplines, but her personal calling required her to become a general practitioner.

After graduation, she hired a lawyer. He had never heard such a story, about a little kid who discovered treasure in a cane field and patiently carried a little bit home every day until, over the course of years, she had buried, well, a lot of it in the woods behind her grandmother's apartment. He researched applicable law, and sure enough, the hurricane had given her the same salvage rights as if it had been a Spanish galleon. The question of a proper lease and trespassing were another matter, but the land had since changed hands, wiping the slate clean. She was free and clear. He set up a trust and took care of taxes.

Chris used the trust and her degree to return to The Muck, where she opened a much-needed pediatric health clinic. She accepted all kinds of insurance and Medicaid. If you didn't have any of that, it was free. She couldn't have been happier, and neither could the town.

This is how much the community loved Chris for all she had given to them: Four decades later, in the wrinkled winter of her career, they unveiled a bronze statue of a young girl running with a football.

A few days after that, Chris and her staff finished a Friday afternoon of treating the latest crop of local kids who came through her door. The staff and patients had all gone home, and Chris stayed behind to deal with some government forms.

A number of professionals in various walks of life like to decorate their offices with mementos of success: diplomas, plaques, trophies, medals and ribbons. Chris had her own idea of decorating.

She finished the paperwork and grabbed her briefcase. Just before turning out the lights, Chris did what she always did at the end of each day. She looked around at the various walls, completely covered with overlapping photos of children and thank-you cards.

Finally, Chris's eyes went over to her favorite trophy, displayed on a bookshelf. And she smiled.

She was looking at a milk crate.

ABOUT THE AUTHOR

Tim Dorsey was a reporter and editor for the *Tampa Tribune* from 1987 to 1999, and is the author of twenty-two other novels: *Florida Roadkill, Hammerhead Ranch Motel, Orange Crush, Triggerfish Twist, The Stingray Shuffle, Cadillac Beach, Torpedo Juice, The Big Bamboo, Hurricane Punch, Atomic Lobster, Nuclear Jellyfish, Gator A-Go-Go, Electric Barracuda, When Elves Attack, Pineapple Grenade, The Riptide Ultra-Glide, Tiger Shrimp Tango, Shark Skin Suite, Coconut Cowboy, Clownfish Blues, The Pope of Palm Beach* and *No Sunscreen for the Dead*. He lives in Tampa, Florida.

MOS Study Guide for Microsoft Excel Expert Exam MO-201

Paul McFedries

Microsoft Office Specialist
Exam MO-201

MOS Study Guide for Microsoft Excel Expert Exam MO-201

Published with the authorization of Microsoft Corporation by:
Pearson Education, Inc.

ISBN-13: 978-0-13-662752-4
ISBN-10: 0-13-662752-8

Library of Congress Control Number: 2020931640

9 2022

Trademarks
Microsoft and the trademarks listed at http://www.microsoft.com on the
"Trademarks" webpage are trademarks of the Microsoft group of companies. All
other marks are property of their respective owners.

Warning and Disclaimer
Every effort has been made to make this book as complete and as accurate as
possible, but no warranty or fitness is implied. The information provided is on
an "as is" basis. The author, the publisher, and Microsoft Corporation shall have
neither liability nor responsibility to any person or entity with respect to any loss
or damages arising from the information contained in this book or from the use of
the programs accompanying it.

Special Sales
For information about buying this title in bulk quantities, or for special sales
opportunities (which may include electronic versions; custom cover designs;
and content particular to your business, training goals, marketing focus, or
branding interests), please contact our corporate sales department at
corpsales@pearsoned.com or (800) 382-3419.

For government sales inquiries, please contact governmentsales@pearsoned.com.

For questions about sales outside the U.S., please contact intlcs@pearson.com.

Editor-in-Chief
Brett Bartow

Executive Editor
Loretta Yates

Development Editor
Songlin Qiu

Sponsoring Editor
Charvi Arora

Managing Editor
Sandra Schroeder

Senior Project Editor
Tracey Croom

Copy Editor
Elizabeth Welch

Indexer
Cheryl Ann Lenser

Proofreader
Abigail Manheim

Technical Editor
Boyd Nolan

Editorial Assistant
Cindy Teeters

Cover Designer
Twist Creative, Seattle

Compositor
codeMantra

Contents

Introduction

The Microsoft Office Specialist (MOS) certification program has been designed to validate your knowledge of and ability to use programs in the Microsoft Office 365 and Office 2019 suite of programs. This book has been designed to guide you in studying the types of tasks you are likely to be required to demonstrate in Exam MO-201, Microsoft Excel Expert.

> **Exam Strategy** For information about the tasks you are likely to be required to demonstrate in the core Excel exam, Exam MO-200, Microsoft Excel 2019, see *MOS Study Guide for Microsoft Excel Exam MO-200* by Joan Lambert (Microsoft Press, 2020).

Who this book is for

MOS Study Guide for Microsoft Excel Expert Exam MO-201 is designed for experienced computer users seeking Microsoft Office Specialist Expert certification in Excel and Excel 2019.

MOS exams for individual programs are practical rather than theoretical. You must demonstrate that you can complete certain tasks or projects rather than simply answer questions about program features. The successful MOS certification candidate will have at least six months of experience using all aspects of the program on a regular basis; for example, protecting a worksheet, applying conditional formatting rules, filling a series, and building a PivotTable.

As a certification candidate, you probably have a lot of experience with the program you want to become certified in. Many of the procedures described in this book will be familiar to you; others might not be. Read through each study section and ensure that you are familiar with the procedures, concepts, and tools discussed. In some cases, images depict the tools you will use to perform procedures related to the skill set. Study the images and ensure that you are familiar with the options available for each tool.

How this book is organized

The exam coverage is divided into chapters representing broad skill sets that correlate to the functional groups covered by the exam. Each chapter is divided into sections addressing groups of related skills that correlate to the exam objectives. Each section includes review information, generic procedures, and practice tasks you can complete on your own while studying. You can use the provided practice files to work through the practice tasks, and the result files to check your work. You can practice the generic procedures in this book by using the practice files supplied or by using your own files.

Throughout this book, you will find Exam Strategy tips that present information about the scope of study that is necessary to ensure that you achieve mastery of a skill set and are successful in your certification effort.

Download the practice files

Before you can complete the practice tasks in this book, you need to copy the book's practice files and result files to your computer. Download the compressed (zipped) folder from the following page, and extract the files from it to a folder (such as your Documents folder) on your computer:

MicrosoftPressStore.com/MOSExcelExpert201/downloads

> **IMPORTANT** The Excel 2019 program is not available from this website. You should purchase and install that program before using this book.

You will save the completed versions of practice files that you modify while working through the practice tasks in this book. If you later want to repeat the practice tasks, you can download the original practice files again.

The following table lists the practice files provided for this book.

Folder and objective group	Practice files	Result files
MOSExcelExpert2019\Objective1 Manage workbook options and settings	Excel_1-1a.xlsx Excel_1-1b.xlsm Excel_1-2a.xlsx Excel_1-2b.xlsx Excel_1-2c.xlsx Excel_1-2d.xlsx Excel_1-3a.xlsx	Excel_1-1a_results.xlsx Excel_1-2a_results.xlsx Excel_1-2b_results.xlsx Excel_1-2c_results.xlsx
MOSExcelExpert2019\Objective2 Manage and format data	Excel_2-1.xlsx Excel_2-2.xlsx Excel_2-3a.xlsx Excel_2-3b.xlsx Excel_2-3c.xlsx	Excel_2-2_results.xlsx Excel_2-3a_results.xlsx Excel_2-3b_results.xlsx Excel_2-3c_results.xlsx
MOSExcelExpert2019\Objective3 Create advanced formulas and macros	Excel_3-1.xlsx Excel_3-2.xlsx Excel_3-3.xlsx Excel_3-4.xlsx Excel_3-4a.xlsx Excel_3-4b.xlsx Excel_3-4c.xlsx Excel_3-4d.xlsx Excel_3-4e.xlsx Excel_3-4f.xlsx Excel_3-5.xlsx Excel_3-6.xlsm	Excel_3-1_results.xlsx Excel_3-2_results.xlsx Excel_3-3_results.xlsx Excel_3-4_results.xlsx Excel_3-5_results.xlsx Excel_3-6_results.xlsm
MOSExcelExpert2019\Objective4 Manage advanced charts and tables	Excel_4-1.xlsx Excel_4-2.xlsx Excel_4-3.xlsx	Excel_4-1_results.xlsx Excel_4-2_results.xlsx Excel_4-3_results.xlsx

Ebook edition

If you're reading the ebook edition of this book, you can do the following:

- Search the full text
- Print
- Copy and paste

You can purchase and download the ebook edition from the Microsoft Press Store at

MicrosoftPressStore.com/MOSExcelExpert201/detail

Errata, updates, and book support

We've made every effort to ensure the accuracy of this book and its companion content. If you discover an error, please submit it to us through the link at

MicrosoftPressStore.com/MOSExcelExpert201/errata

If you discover an error that is not already listed, please submit it to us at the same page.

For additional book support and information, please visit

MicrosoftPressStore.com/Support

Please note that product support for Microsoft software and hardware is not offered through the previous addresses. For help with Microsoft software or hardware, go to

support.microsoft.com

Stay in touch

Let's keep the conversation going! We're on Twitter at

twitter.com/MicrosoftPress

Microsoft Office Specialist

Exam MO-201

Excel 2019 Expert

This book covers the skills you need to have for certification as a Microsoft Office Specialist Expert in Excel 2019. Specifically, you need to be able to complete tasks that demonstrate the following skill sets:

1. Manage workbook options and settings
2. Manage and format data
3. Create advanced formulas and macros
4. Create advanced charts and tables

With these skills, you can manage, format, populate, and enhance the types of workbooks most commonly used in a business environment.

Prerequisites

We assume that you have been working with Excel 2019 for at least six months and that you know how to carry out fundamental tasks that are not specifically mentioned in the objectives for this Microsoft Office Specialist exam. This level of proficiency includes familiarity with features and tasks such as the following:

- Creating workbooks
- Adding worksheets to existing workbooks
- Copying and moving worksheets
- Inserting and deleting cells, columns, and rows
- Customizing the Quick Access Toolbar and the ribbon
- Freezing panes and splitting the window
- Setting a print area and adding headers and footers
- Changing fonts and cell styles
- Wrapping text within cells
- Creating and editing tables
- Using relative, mixed, and absolute cell references
- Using functions
- Creating and editing charts, and adding data series
- Inserting text boxes, SmartArt, and other images
- Applying styles and effects to objects
- Positioning objects

Exam Strategy For information about the prerequisite tasks, see *MOS Study Guide for Microsoft Excel Exam MO-200* by Joan Lambert (Microsoft Press, 2020).

Objective group 1

Manage workbook options and settings

The skills tested in this section of the Microsoft Office Specialist Expert exam for Microsoft Excel 2019 relate to managing workbook options and settings. Specifically, the following objectives are associated with this set of skills:

1.1   Manage workbooks

1.2   Prepare workbooks for collaboration

1.3   Use and configure language options

Every Excel workbook exists within a larger ecosystem of objects, including macros, versions, and other workbooks. Mastering workbook management requires knowing not only how to connect workbooks with these other objects, but also how to share a workbook's data with other users.

This chapter guides you in studying methods for enabling macros and copying them between workbooks, managing workbook versions, restricting changes to workbook content and structure, configuring formula calculation options, managing comments, and using language options.

To complete the practice tasks in this chapter, you need the practice files contained in the **MOSExcelExpert2019\Objective1** practice file folder. For more information, see "Download the practice files" in this book's introduction.

Objective 1.1: Manage workbooks

Copy macros between workbooks

If you receive a workbook that contains one or more macros that you find useful, you can continue to run those macros from within that workbook. However, you might find it useful or necessary to copy those macros to one of your own workbooks. For example, if you have a workbook that you keep open all the time you might prefer to run the macros from that workbook rather than always having to keep the original workbook open. Similarly, many macros make use of an Excel object named ThisWorkbook, which refers to the workbook in which the macro is running. The only way to get such a macro to run successfully in another workbook is to copy it to that file.

You can make all your macros easily and conveniently available by storing them in a special file called the Personal Macro Workbook. However, before you can use this file you must create it by recording a macro and using the Personal Macro Workbook to store the resulting code. After you have created the Personal Macro Workbook, it appears in the Visual Basic Editor's Project Explorer pane. You can then follow the steps from the procedure for copying macros to copy macros to the Personal Macro Workbook.

Tip Although you will be able to see the Personal Macro Workbook in the Visual Basic Editor, the workbook does not appear within the regular Excel interface because it is hidden by default. To unhide it, on the View tab, in the Windows group, click Unhide, click PERSONAL (or PERSONAL.XLSB), and then click OK. To hide it again, switch to the Personal window, click View, and then click Hide.

To copy a macro module from one workbook to another

1. Open the workbook that contains the macros you want to copy.

2. Open or create a macro-enabled workbook to which you want to copy the macros.

   IMPORTANT If you create a new workbook to hold the macros, when you save the file, be sure to use the Save As Type list to select the Excel Macro-Enabled Workbook (*.xlsm) file format.
   ---

3. Do either of the following to open the Visual Basic Editor:

   ● On the **Developer** tab, in the **Code** group, click **Visual Basic**.

   ● Press **Alt+F11**.

   ◇◇

   Exam Strategy The Excel Expert exam requires you to work with macros in several places, so you need to know how to display the Developer tab, which is hidden by default. To display the Developer tab, right-click the ribbon and then click Customize The Ribbon to open the Excel Options dialog box with the Customize Ribbon tab displayed. In the Main Tabs list on the right, select the Developer check box, then click OK.

   ◇◇

4. In the **Project Explorer** pane, locate the workbook that contains the macros you want to copy, and then open that workbook's branches until you see the contents of the **Modules** folder.

   Tip If the Project Explorer pane isn't open, click View and then click Project Explorer, or press Ctrl+R.

   ---

5. Drag the module you want to copy to the **VBAProject** branch of your other workbook. Excel copies the module, creating the **Modules** branch in the other workbook if necessary.

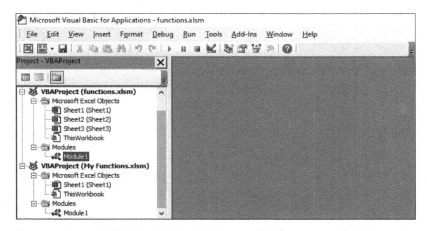

To copy macros, use the Project Explorer to drag a module from one workbook to another.

To create the Personal Macro Workbook

1. In any workbook, on the **View** tab, in the **Macros** group, click **Record Macro**. (Alternatively, on the **Developer** tab, in the **Code** group, click **Record Macro**.)

    See Also For more information about recording macros, see "Record simple macros" in "Objective 3.6: Create and modify simple macros."

2. In the **Record Macro** dialog box, in the **Store macro in** list, click **Personal Macro Workbook**, and then click **OK**.

To create the Personal Macro Workbook, select it as the storage location for a recorded macro.

3. Perform any task, such as selecting a cell or applying a format, and then click the **Stop Recording** icon in the status bar.

Enable macros in a workbook

Microsoft Visual Basic for Applications (VBA) macros are some of the most useful and most powerful features in the Office 2019 suite. You can use macros to automate repetitive tasks, run a lengthy series of commands with just a few mouse clicks or a keyboard shortcut, create custom Excel functions, and much more. However, this power also means that macros can be used for nefarious purposes, such as trashing files, stealing data, and installing malware. For this reason, when you open a workbook that contains macros, Excel disables those macros by default. You have three choices at this point:

- If the workbook came from a person or source you trust and you were expecting to receive the workbook, you can enable the macros.

- If the workbook came from a person or source you trust but you were *not* expecting to receive the workbook, leave the macros disabled until you can contact the workbook source and ask if they sent it. If they did, you can enable the macros; if they did not, leave the macros disabled.

- If the workbook did not come from a person or source you trust, leave the macros disabled.

When you open a file that uses the Excel Macro-Enabled Workbook (*.xlsm) format or the Excel Macro-Enabled Template (*.xlst) format, Excel displays the Security Warning information bar that tells you the workbook's macros have been disabled.

When you open a macro-enabled Excel workbook, click Enable Content only if you trust the document.

◇◇◇

Exam Strategy Passing the Excel Expert exam requires several different macro skills. Besides the skills you learn in this objective, be sure to also study "Objective 3.6: Create and modify simple macros" to ensure that you're proficient with macros in Excel.

◇◇◇

To enable macros in a workbook

➜ To enable macros in a workbook that displays the Security Warning information bar, if you trust the workbook, click **Enable Content** to enable the macros; otherwise, close the information bar to leave the macros disabled.

→ To enable macros in a workbook after you have already closed the Security Warning information bar, click the **File** tab, and on the **Info** page, click the **Enable Content** button, and then click **Enable All Content**.

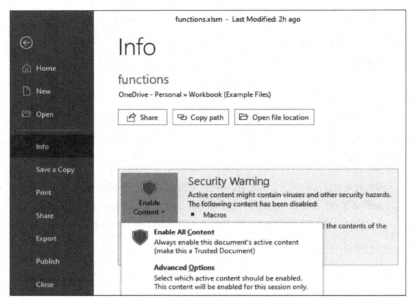

You can also enable macros in a trusted workbook by clicking Enable All Content on the Info page.

Reference data in another workbook

If you have data in one workbook that you want to use in another, you can set up a link between the two workbooks. This enables your formulas to use references to cells or ranges in the other workbook. When the other data changes, Excel automatically updates the link. You set up links by creating an external reference to a cell or range in the other workbook. The workbook that contains the external reference is called the *dependent workbook* (or the *client workbook*). The workbook that contains the original data is called the *source workbook* (or the *server workbook*).

If you're familiar with the structure of an external reference, you can also construct such references manually by using the following syntax:

'path[workbookname]sheetname'!reference

The following list describes the arguments:

- *path* The drive and directory in which the workbook is located, which can be a local path, a network path, or even an Internet address. You need to include the path only when the workbook is closed.

- *workbookname* The name of the workbook, including the file extension. Always enclose the workbook name in square brackets ([ ]).

- *sheetname* The name of the worksheet tab that contains the referenced cell.

- *reference* A cell or range reference, or a defined name.

Tip If the *path*, *workbookname*, or *sheetname* contains one or more spaces, or if the workbook is closed, you must enclose all three in a pair of single quotation marks.

The purpose of a link is to avoid duplicating formulas and data in multiple workbooks. If one workbook contains the information you need, you can use a link to reference the data without re-creating it in another workbook. To be useful, however, the data in the dependent workbook should always reflect what actually is in the source workbook. You can make sure of this by updating the link.

To create a link that references data in another workbook

1. Open the source workbook that contains the data you want to reference.

2. In the dependent workbook, start a formula and stop at the point where you want the external reference to appear.

3. On the **View** tab, in the **Window** group, click **Switch Windows**, and then click the source workbook.

4. In the source workbook, click the cell you want to reference in your formula. Excel inserts the external reference into your formula.

Start a formula (cell B3 in the back workbook), switch to the other workbook, and then click the cell you want to reference (cell N3 in the front workbook).

5. Complete your formula, and then press **Enter**.

To update a link

Tip If the source and dependent workbooks are both open, Excel automatically updates the link whenever the data in the source file changes.

→ Open the dependent workbook. If the source workbook is open when you do so, Excel automatically updates the link.

→ Open the dependent workbook. If the source workbook is closed when you do so, Excel displays a security warning in the information bar, which tells you that automatic updating of links has been disabled. Click **Enable Content**.

→ On the **Data** tab, in the **Queries & Connections** group, click **Edit Links**. In the **Edit Links** dialog box that opens, click the link, and then click **Update Values**.

Use the Edit Links dialog box to update the linked data in the source workbook.

Manage workbook versions

On occasion you might realize that you have improperly edited some workbook data or that you have accidentally overwritten an important worksheet range during a paste operation. If the improper edit or paste was the most recent action you performed, you can use Undo to reverse the action. Similarly, if the error was not the most recent action but you don't need to preserve any workbook changes you've made since then, you can repeatedly use Undo until the mistaken action is reversed.

The Undo command is a useful and important Excel tool, but Excel also offers a couple of methods to directly revert a workbook to an earlier state. The method you use depends on where the workbook is saved:

- If the workbook is saved locally (that is, on your computer or network), Excel's AutoRecover feature monitors your workbook for changes. Each time the Auto-Recover interval ends (which is, by default, every 10 minutes), if Excel sees that your workbook has unsaved changes it saves a copy of the workbook.

- If the workbook is saved in a OneDrive folder, Excel automatically activates the AutoSave feature, which saves the workbook every time you make a change. OneDrive also creates a copy of the workbook every few minutes.

Either way, you can restore a previous state of the workbook by reverting to an earlier autorecovered or autosaved version of the file.

To configure AutoRecover for local files

1. Click **File**, click **Options**, and then in the Excel Options dialog box, on the **Save** page, select the **Save AutoRecover information every *X* minutes** check box.

2. Use the arrows to set the AutoRecover interval in minutes.

Use the Save page of the Excel Options dialog box to configure Excel's AutoRecover settings.

3. To have Excel preserve the most recent autosaved version of any workbook that you close with unsaved changes, select the **Keep the last AutoRecovered version if I close without saving** check box.

4. In the **AutoRecover file location** box, you can optionally enter the path of a different folder in which Excel should store the autosaved versions.

5. Click **OK**.

To revert to an earlier autorecovered version of a local workbook

1. Click **File**, click **Info**, and then, under **Manage Workbook**, click the autorecovered version of the workbook to which you want to revert.

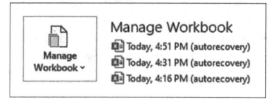

On the Info page, click one of the autorecovered versions that appear under the Manage Workbook heading.

2. If this is the version you want to recover, display the **Save As** page to save the workbook under a different file name or in a different folder; otherwise, you can return to the most recent version by clicking **Restore** in the information bar.

When you revert to an autorecovered version of the workbook, you can click the information bar's Restore button to return to the most recent version of the file.

To enable AutoSave for OneDrive files

When you open a workbook from a OneDrive folder, Excel enables the AutoSave feature automatically. To ensure that Excel is automatically saving your changes as you work, check that the AutoSave switch is On. Note that the AutoSave switch is part of the Quick Access Toolbar, which usually appears in the upper-left corner of the Excel window. If you don't see the AutoSave switch, click Customize Quick Access Toolbar and then click to select the Automatically Save command.

To ensure Excel is automatically saving your changes as you work on a OneDrive workbook, check that the AutoSave switch is On.

To revert to an earlier autosaved version of a OneDrive workbook

1. Click **File**, click **Info**, and then click **Version History** to open the Version History pane. (In some versions of Excel, you click **File** and then click **History**.)

   Tip You can also click the file name in the title bar and then click Version History.

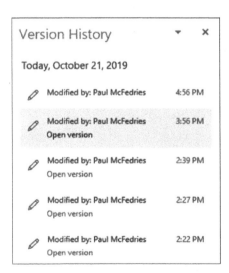

On the Info page, click Version History to open the Version History pane.

2. Click the version of the workbook to which you want to revert.

3. If this is the version you want to recover, click the **Restore** button in the information bar; otherwise, you can display the **Save As** page to save the workbook under a different file name or in a different folder.

PREVIOUS VERSION You can copy content from this version, or save this version as a separate file.	Restore

When you revert to a previous version of the workbook, you can click the information bar's Restore button to replace the current version of the file with the previous version.

Objective 1.1 practice tasks

The practice files for these tasks are located in the **MOSExcelExpert2019\ Objective1** practice file folder. The folder also contains a result file that you can use to check your work.

➤ Open the **ExcelExpert_1-1a** workbook and save the workbook as *MyMacros* in the macro-enabled format.

➤ Open the **ExcelExpert_1-1b** workbook and do the following:

❑ Enable macros in the workbook.

❑ Open the Visual Basic Editor and copy the macros from the **ExcelExpert_1-1b** workbook to the *MyMacros* workbook, and then close the Visual Basic Editor.

❑ Return to the *MyMacros* workbook and save it.

❑ Record a simple macro and store it in the Personal Macro Workbook.

❑ Return to the Visual Basic Editor, copy the macros from the *MyMacros* workbook to the Personal Macro Workbook, and then close the Visual Basic Editor.

❑ Unhide the Personal Macro Workbook, and then hide it again.

➤ Reopen the **ExcelExpert_1-1a** workbook and do the following:

❑ In cell A2, enter = to start a formula.

❑ Switch to the **ExcelExpert_1-1b** workbook and click cell A1 on Sheet1.

❑ Confirm your external reference formula.

➤ Save the **ExcelExpert_1-1a** workbook. Open the **ExcelExpert_1-1a_results** workbook. Compare the two workbooks to check your work.

➤ Switch to the **ExcelExpert_1-1c** workbook and do the following:

❑ Change the AutoRecover interval to one minute.

❑ Edit any cell in the range B2:B6, but don't save the workbook.

❑ Wait for at least one minute to give Excel time to autosave a version of the unsaved workbook.

❑ Edit another cell in the range B2:B6, but don't save the workbook.

❑ Wait for at least one minute to give Excel time to autosave another version of the unsaved workbook.

❑ Display the workbook versions, and then restore the workbook to the version prior to when you made the second edit.

Objective 1.2: Prepare workbooks for collaboration

Restrict editing

When you have labored long and hard to get your worksheet formulas or formatting just right, the last thing you need is to have a cell or range accidentally deleted or copied over. You can avoid this problem by using Excel's worksheet protection features, which you can use to prevent changes to anything from a single cell to an entire workbook.

For protecting cells, Excel offers two techniques:

- **Protection formatting** When you use this technique, you format those cells in which you want to allow editing as unlocked and you format all other cells as locked. You can also hide the formulas in one or more cells if you don't want users to see them. You can then turn on worksheet protection, which means that locked cells can't be changed, deleted, moved, or copied over and that hidden formulas are no longer visible.

- **Protect a range with a password** When you use this technique, you protect one or more ranges with a password, and then specify which users are allowed or denied editing privileges on that range.

By default, all worksheet cells are formatted as locked and their formulas are visible. Note, however, that "locked" in this context only means that the cells have the potential to be locked. That's because Excel doesn't perform the actual lock—that is, it doesn't prevent users from modifying the cells—until you turn on worksheet protection. With this in mind, here are the options you have when setting up your protection formatting:

- If you want to protect every cell, you can leave the formatting as it is and turn on worksheet protection.

- If you want only certain cells to be unlocked (for data entry, for example), you can select those cells and unlock them before turning on worksheet protection. Similarly, if you want certain formulas hidden, you can select the cells and hide their formulas.

- If you want only certain cells to be locked, first select all the cells and unlock them. Then select the cells you want protected and lock them. To keep only selected formulas visible, hide every formula and then make the formulas you want visible.

To unlock worksheet cells

1. Select the cells you want to unlock.
2. On the **Home** tab, in the **Cells** group, click **Format**, and then click to deactivate the Lock Cell command.

To lock only certain worksheet cells

1. Select all the cells in the worksheet.
2. On the **Home** tab, click **Format**, and then click to deactivate the Lock Cell command.
3. Select the cells you want to lock.
4. On the **Home** tab, click **Format**, and then click to activate the Lock Cell command.

To hide formulas in worksheet cells

1. Select the cells that contain the formulas you want to hide.
2. On the **Home** tab, click **Format**, and then click **Format Cells**.
3. In the **Format Cells** dialog box, on the **Protection** tab, select the **Hidden** check box, and then click **OK**.

To show only certain formulas in worksheet cells

1. Select all the cells in the worksheet.
2. On the **Home** tab, click **Format**, and then click **Format Cells**.
3. In the **Format Cells** dialog box, on the **Protection** tab, select the **Hidden** check box, and then click **OK**.
4. On the worksheet, select the cells that contain the formulas you want to show.
5. On the **Home** tab, click **Format**, and then click **Format Cells**.
6. In the **Format Cells** dialog box, on the **Protection** tab, clear the **Hidden** check box, and then click **OK**.

IMPORTANT Formatting protection doesn't go into effect until you activate worksheet protection.

Protect worksheets and cell ranges

If you don't want to protect the entire worksheet, you can restrict your protection to a more targeted area. That is, if you want to prevent unauthorized users from editing within a specific range, you can set up that range with a password. After you protect the sheet, only authorized users who know the password can edit the range.

When you set up protection formatting on one or more cells, or protect one or more ranges with a password, your restrictions don't go into effect until you activate worksheet protection.

To protect a range with a password

1. On the **Review** tab, in the **Protect** group, click **Allow Edit Ranges**.

2. In the **Allow Users to Edit Ranges** dialog box, click **New** to open the **New Range** dialog box.

3. In the **Title** box, enter a name for the range.

4. In the **Refers to cells** box, enter or select the range you want to protect.

5. In the **Range password** box, enter a password.

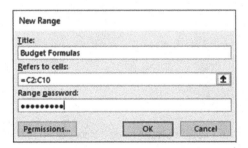

Use the New Range dialog box to name, specify, and password-protect a range.

6. If you want the password requirement to not apply to specific users or groups, click **Permissions**, and then in the **Permissions** dialog box, do the following:

    Click **Add**, enter the name of a user or group, and then click **OK** to add the user or group to the **Permissions** dialog box.

Click the user or group, and then for the **Edit range without a password** permission, make sure the **Allow** check box is selected.

Click **OK** to return to the **New Range** dialog box.

7. In the **New Range** dialog box, click **OK**, reenter the password to confirm it, and then click **OK**. Excel adds the range to the **Allow Users To Edit Ranges** dialog box.

Your protected ranges appear in the Allow Users To Edit Ranges dialog box.

8. Repeat steps 2 through 7 to protect other ranges, and then click **OK** to close the dialog box and save your changes.

IMPORTANT The range password doesn't go into effect until you activate worksheet protection.

To activate worksheet protection

1. Do either of the following to open the Protect Sheet dialog box:

    - On the **Review** tab, in the **Protect** group, click **Protect Sheet**.

    - If the **Allow Users To Edit Ranges** dialog box is open, click the **Protect Sheet** button in that dialog box.

2. In the **Protect Sheet** dialog box, do the following, and then click **OK**:

    Select the **Protect worksheet and contents of locked cells** check box.

    If you want, for added security, enter a password in the **Password to unprotect sheet** box. This means that no one can turn off the worksheet's protection without first entering the password.

In the **Allow all users of this worksheet to** list, select the check box beside each action you want unauthorized users to be allowed to perform.

Use the Protect Sheet dialog box to activate your protection formatting or range passwords.

3. If you entered a password, reenter the password, and then click **OK** to continue working in the worksheet.

Protect workbook structure

When you protect a workbook's structure, Excel takes the following actions:

- Disables most of the worksheet-related commands on the ribbon. For example, on the Home tab, on the Format menu, the Rename Sheet and Move Or Copy Sheet commands are unavailable.

- Disables most of the commands on the worksheet tab's shortcut menu, including Insert, Delete, Rename, and Move or Copy.

- Keeps the Scenario Manager from creating a summary report.

To protect the workbook structure

1. In the workbook you want to protect, on the **Review** tab, in the **Protect** group, click **Protect Workbook** to display the **Protect Structure and Windows** dialog box.

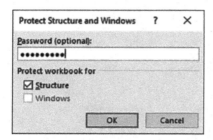

Use the Protect Structure and Windows dialog box to prevent changes to your workbook's formatting and worksheet structure.

2. Enter an optional password in the **Password** text box, and then click **OK**.

3. Select the **Structure** check box.

4. If you specified a password, reenter the password to confirm, and then click **OK**.

Configure formula calculation options

Excel always calculates a formula when you confirm its entry, and the program normally recalculates existing formulas automatically whenever their data changes. This behavior is fine for small worksheets, but it can slow you down if you have a complex model that takes several seconds or even several minutes to recalculate. To turn off this automatic recalculation, Excel gives you two ways to get started:

- You can use commands on the Calculation Options menu on the Formula tab.

- You can use settings on the Formulas page of the Excel Options dialog box.

Either way, you're presented with three calculation options:

- **Automatic** This is the default calculation mode; it means that Excel recalculates formulas as soon as you enter them and as soon as the data for a formula changes.

- **Automatic except for data tables** In this calculation mode, Excel recalculates all formulas automatically, except for those associated with data tables. This is a good choice if your worksheet includes one or more massive data tables that are slowing down the recalculation.

- **Manual** Select this mode to force Excel not to recalculate any formulas until you either manually recalculate or save the workbook.

With manual calculation turned on, *Calculate* appears in the status bar whenever your worksheet data changes and your formula results need to be updated.

See Also For more information about manually calculating parts of formulas, see "Evaluate formulas" in "Objective 3.5: Troubleshoot formulas."

When you manually recalculate a workbook, note that Excel doesn't necessarily recalculate every formula in the workbook. To minimize workbook recalculation, Excel builds a *dependency tree* that details not only the operands in each workbook formula (such as the functions it calls), but also any formulas used in cells referenced by each formula. A formula that relies on the results of calculations in another cell is said to be *dependent* on that cell. The dependency tree follows a formula's chain of references until there are no more references left to check.

See Also For more information about formula dependencies, see "Trace precedence and dependence" in "Objective 3.5: Troubleshoot formulas."

Using the dependency tree, when you recalculate a workbook, Excel only updates formulas in this order:

- Formulas that have changed or that have changed range names.

- Formulas that include volatile functions. (A *volatile* function is one where its value changes each time you recalculate or reopen the worksheet or edit any cell on the worksheet; the RAND worksheet function is an example.)

- Formulas that are dependent on other formulas that have changed, use range names that have changed, or use volatile functions.

When you manually recalculate a workbook, Excel updates every formula in the dependency tree. However, Excel might not update a particular formula if the dependency tree is incorrect or out of date (for whatever reason). Excel offers a manual workbook recalculation method that you can invoke to force Excel to rebuild its dependency tree.

You can also control various options for iterative calculations. These are calculations where you begin with a guess at the solution, plug that guess into the formula to get a new solution, plug that solution into the formula, and then keep repeating this procedure. Each time you plug a new solution into the formula it is called an *iteration*, so the entire process is called an *iterative calculation*. This type of calculation creates a circular reference, which is normally an error in Excel, so that's why iterative calculations are turned off by default.

How does an iterative calculation know when to stop? If during the iterative process the change from one solution to the next becomes smaller than some predetermined value, the formula is said to have *converged* on the solution. Because the formula might not ever converge—or it might only converge after an unacceptably large number of iterations—you can also tell Excel to stop after a predetermined number of iterations.

To enable the management of iterative calculations, the Formulas tab in the Excel Options dialog box offers two controls:

- **Maximum Iterations** This value is the number of iterations after which Excel must stop the calculation if it hasn't yet converged to a solution. The default value is 100.
- **Maximum Change** This value is the threshold that Excel uses to determine whether the iterative calculation has converged on a solution. If the change in the formula result from one iteration is less than this value, Excel considers the formula solved and stops the iteration. The default value is 0.001, but you can reduce this (for example, to 0.0001 or 0.00001) if you require a solution with more precision.

When performing an iterative calculation, Excel stops the calculation as soon as it hits the Maximum Iterations value or the Maximum Change value (whichever comes first).

To configure the formula calculation options

➜ On the **Formulas** tab, in the **Calculation** group, click **Calculation Options**, and then click **Automatic**, **Automatic Except for Data Tables**, or **Manual**.

On the Formulas tab, click Calculation Options to choose how you want Excel to calculate workbook formulas.

Or

1. Click **File**, then click **Options**.

2. In the **Excel Options** dialog box, on the **Formulas** page, in the **Calculation Options** section, under **Workbook Calculation,** select the option you want.

3. If you select the **Manual** option and want to run the calculation automatically when you save the file, select the **Recalculate workbook before saving** check box.

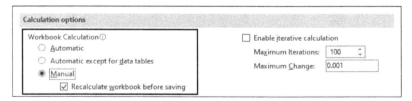

On the Formulas page of the Excel Options dialog box, select a Workbook Calculation option to tell Excel how to calculate workbook formulas.

4. Click **OK**.

To manually recalculate a single formula

1. Select the cell containing the formula.

2. Click in the formula bar, and then press **Enter** or click the **Enter** button.

To manually recalculate formulas in a selected cell range

1. Display the **Replace** tab of the **Find and Replace** dialog box.

2. Enter an equal sign (=) in both the **Find What** and **Replace With** boxes.

3. Click **Replace All**.

Tip This procedure doesn't actually change any formulas, but it forces Excel to recalculate each formula.

To manually recalculate formulas in only the active worksheet

→ On the **Formulas** tab, click **Calculate Sheet**.

Or

→ Press **Shift+F9**.

To manually recalculate changed formulas in every open workbook

→ On the **Formulas** tab, in the **Calculation** group, click **Calculate Now**.

Or

→ Press **F9**.

To manually recalculate every formula (changed or unchanged) in every open workbook

→ Press **Ctrl+Alt+F9**.

To manually recalculate every formula (changed or unchanged) in every open workbook and rebuild the dependency tree

→ Press **Ctrl+Alt+Shift+F9**.

Tip Excel supports multithreaded calculation on computers with either multiple processors or processors with multiple cores. For each processor (or core), Excel sets up a thread (a separate process of execution). Excel can then use each available thread to process multiple calculations concurrently. For a worksheet with multiple, independent formulas, multithreaded calculation can dramatically speed up calculations. To verify that multithreaded calculation is turned on, display the Advanced page of the Excel Options dialog box and, in the Formulas section, ensure that the Enable Multi-Threaded Calculation check box is selected.

To enable and configure iterative calculations

1. Click **File**, click **Options**.

2. In the **Excel Options** dialog box, on the **Formulas** page, in the **Calculation options** section, select the **Enable iterative calculation** check box.

3. In the **Maximum Iterations** box, enter or select the number of iterations Excel can try before it must stop the calculation.

4. In the **Maximum Change** box, enter the numeric value that you want Excel to use as a threshold to determine whether the calculation has converged on a solution.

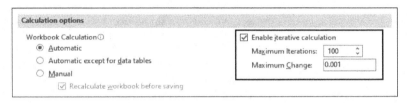

Use the Formulas page of the Excel Options dialog box to enable and configure iterative calculations.

5. Click **OK**.

Manage comments

When building a spreadsheet model, it is often useful to get feedback from other people. Feedback might include verification of some content, confirmation that a formula works as it should, suggestions for improving the layout, a critique of the overall model, or just general notes about the worksheet. If someone sends you a workbook and requests your feedback, you can place that feedback in a separate document such as an email message or a Word document. However, this means your feedback will lack context. You can work around this by specifying the cell or range you're talking about, but it still means the owner of the workbook has to go back and forth between the documents.

A better way to provide worksheet feedback is to add that feedback directly to the worksheet itself. However, rather than typing text into a worksheet cell, you can instead add a *comment*, which is text that Excel associates with an individual cell but keeps separate from the worksheet itself. A comment is a review feature that starts a conversation about the cell's contents because it enables other reviewers to read and respond to existing comments. A collection of one or more comments about a cell is called a *thread*. To close a particular comment thread and prevent further replies, you can *resolve* the thread. If you find that a comment thread is no longer required, you can delete it.

IMPORTANT Comment threads are a relatively new review feature in Excel. If you're a long-time Excel user, do not confuse a comment thread that enables interaction between multiple users, with the original Excel style of comment, which was a single-user text annotation associ-ated with a cell. The latter feature still exists in Excel but is now known as a *note*.

To start a new comment thread

1. Click the cell to which you want to add the comment thread.

2. On the **Review** tab, in the **Comments** group, click **New Comment**. Excel creates the comment and displays a pop-up window for typing the comment text.

3. Type your comment in the text box provided; then click **Post** or press **Ctrl+Enter**. Excel adds the comment and displays the comment marker in the top-right corner of the cell.

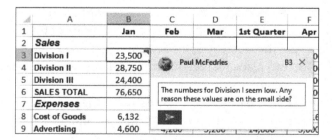

After you click New Comment, type your comment in the text box provided.

To navigate worksheet comments

→ On the **Review** tab, in the **Comments** group, click **Next Comment** to display the next comment that appears in the worksheet.

➜ On the **Review** tab, in the **Comments** group, click **Previous Comment** to display the previous comment that appears in the worksheet.

➜ On the **Review** tab, in the **Comments** group, click **Show Comments** to open the **Comments** pane, which displays all the comments that appear in the worksheet. You can also click the **Comments** button that appears near the right edge of the ribbon.

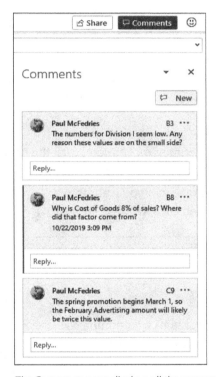

The Comments pane displays all the comments added to the worksheet.

To edit a comment

➜ Move the mouse pointer over a cell that contains a comment (that is, a cell that displays a comment marker in the top-right corner), move the mouse pointer into the comment box, and then click **Edit**.

Or

➜ Display the **Comments** pane, click the comment you want to edit, and then click **Edit**.

To read a comment

→ Move the mouse pointer over a cell that contains a comment (that is, a cell that displays a comment marker in the top-right corner).

→ Display the **Comments** pane and view the comment in the list.

To respond to a comment

→ Move the mouse pointer over a cell that contains a comment, click inside the **Reply** text box, type the response, and then click **Post** or press **Ctrl+Enter**.

→ Display the **Comments** pane, locate the comment to which you want to reply, click inside the **Reply** text box, type the response, then click **Post** or press **Ctrl+Enter**.

To resolve a comment thread

→ Move the mouse pointer over a cell that contains a comment, click the **More Thread Options** (...) button, and then click **Resolve Thread**.

→ Display the **Comments** pane, locate the comment you want to resolve, click the **More Thread Options** (...) button, and then click **Resolve Thread**.

Tip To reopen a cell's comment thread for more replies and for editing, move the mouse pointer over the cell and then click Reopen Thread.

To delete a comment thread

→ Move the mouse pointer over a cell that contains a comment, click the **More Thread Options** (...) button, and then click **Delete Thread**.

→ Display the **Comments** pane, locate the comment you want to resolve, click the **More Thread Options** (...) button, and then click **Delete Thread**.

Tip To delete a single comment reply rather than the entire comment thread, move the mouse pointer over a cell that contains a comment, move the mouse pointer over the reply you want to remove, and then click Delete.

Objective 1.2 practice tasks

The practice files for these tasks are located in the **MOSExcelExpert2019\
Objective1** practice file folder. The folder also contains result files that you
can use to check your work.

➤ Open the **ExcelExpert_1-2a** workbook and do the following:

❑ Unlock the cells in the range C3:C7.

❑ Activate worksheet protection. Do not enter a password. Do not
allow users to select locked cells or to format cells.

❑ Ensure that users can modify the loan parameters in the range C3:C7
but cannot change anything else on the worksheet.

❑ Save the **ExcelExpert_1-2a** workbook.

❑ Open the **ExcelExpert_1-2a_results** workbook. Compare the two
workbooks to check your work. Then close the open workbooks.

➤ Open the **ExcelExpert_1-2b** workbook and do the following:

❑ Unlock the cells in the range B2:B6.

❑ Protect the cells in the range B7:B8 with the password MOS123.

❑ Protect the worksheet with the same password.

❑ Save the **ExcelExpert_1-2b** workbook.

❑ Open the **ExcelExpert_1-2b_results** workbook. To unlock the range
and sheet, use the password mos. Compare the two workbooks to
check your work. Then close the open workbooks.

➤ In Excel, verify that formula calculations are set to automatic and
iterative calculations are turned off.

➤ Open the **ExcelExpert_1-2c** workbook, dismiss the circular reference warning, and do the following:

❑ Change the formula calculation method to Manual and turn on iterative calculations.

❑ Select cell C6, which contains the circular reference formula, and manually calculate the formula result.

❑ Open the **ExcelExpert_1-2c_results** workbook. Compare the two workbooks to check your work.

❑ To preserve the initial circular reference, close the **ExcelExpert_1-2c** workbook without saving it.

➤ Open the **ExcelExpert_1-2d** workbook and do the following:

❑ Add a comment to any cell that does not already display a comment marker.

❑ Use the Next Comment and Previous Comment commands to navigate the worksheet comments.

❑ Navigate to the comment you added and then edit that comment.

❑ Add a reply to the comment in cell B3.

❑ Resolve the comment thread you added.

❑ Delete the comment thread you added.

❑ Close the **ExcelExpert_1-2d** workbook without saving it.

Objective 1.3: Use and configure language options

1

Configure authoring and display languages

You can change the language that Excel uses for authoring and for the display (the ribbon, buttons, tabs, and other interface features). You are free to apply a different language for authoring and display, depending on the languages available in the version of Windows or Office that you are using and the Windows language packs that you have installed. You can install additional languages from the Language page of the Excel Options dialog box. If you have multiple languages installed, you can tell Excel which language you prefer to use. You can also set a language priority order, which tells Excel which languages to use, in order, if the display language is not available in your default language.

To add an authoring language

1. Click **File**, then click **Options**.

2. In the **Excel Options** dialog box, on the **Language** page, click **Add a Language**.

3. Use the **Add an authoring language** list to select the language you want to install.

4. Click **Add**. Excel adds the language to the **Office Authoring Languages and Proofing** list.

Tip For your new language, if you see Proofing Available, then you need to install the associated language pack from the Office.com website. Click the Proofing Available link to display the language pack page, click Download, and then run the downloaded file to install the language pack.

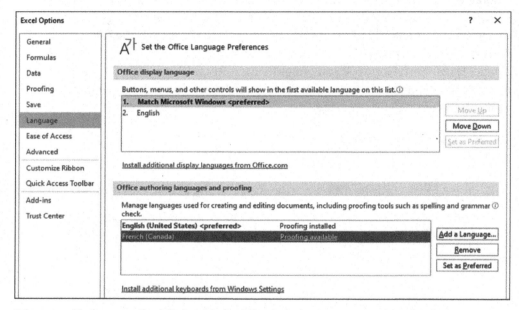

When you add a language, Excel displays it in the Office Authoring Languages and Proofing list.

To change the display language priority order

→ In the **Excel Options** dialog box, on the **Language** page, click a language in the **Office Display Language** list, and then use the **Move Up** (higher priority) and **Move Down** (lower priority) buttons to position the language in the list.

Tip To add more display languages, click the Install Additional Display Languages from Office.com link, which opens a page that enables you to download a language pack accessory for Office.

Use the Move Up and Move Down buttons to set a language's priority.

To set the preferred languages

→ In the **Excel Options** dialog box, on the **Language** page, click a language in the **Office Authoring Languages and Proofing** list, and then click the **Set Preferred** button that appears to the right of the list.

→ In the **Excel Options** dialog box, on the **Language** page, click a language in the **Office Display Language** list, and then click the **Set Preferred** button that appears to the right of the list.

To remove an authoring language

→ In the **Excel Options** dialog box, on the **Language** page, click a language in the **Office Authoring Languages and Proofing** list, click **Remove**, and then restart Excel to put the change into effect.

Use language-specific features

With your languages configured, you can now switch from one language to another within Excel. For example, you can switch to another language to add or edit Excel data and you can set another language as Excel's default proofing dictionary.

Another language tool that comes in handy when you are working with other languages is the Translate command on the Review tab. This command opens the Translator task pane, which includes From and To boxes, where From shows the original text and To shows the language to which you want the original text translated. Translator attempts to recognize the original language, but if it gets the language wrong, you can select the correct language from a list. You can also select the language to which you want the original text translated.

To add and edit text in another language

→ In the **Excel Options** dialog box, on the **Language** page, click a language in the **Office Authoring Languages and Proofing** list, and then click the **Set Preferred** button that appears to the right of the list.

To proof in another language

1. Click **File**, then click **Options**.

2. In the **Excel Options** dialog box, on the **Proofing** page, use the **Dictionary language** list to select the language you want to use.

Use the Dictionary Language list to select a proofing language.

To translate cell text

1. Select the cell that contains the text you want to translate.

2. On the **Review** tab, click the **Translate** button. The **Translator** pane appears.

Use the Translator pane to translate text form one language to another.

3. If Translator did not select the correct original language, use the **From** list to select the language.

4. Use the **To** list to select the language to which you want the original text translated.

Objective 1.3 practice tasks

The practice files for these tasks are located in the **MOSExcelExpert2019\ Objective1** practice file folder.

➤ Open the **ExcelExpert_1-3a** workbook and do the following:

❑ Add the authoring language French (Canada).

❑ Add the language French as a display language.

❑ In the Office Display Language list, select French, and move its priority up and then down.

❑ In the Office Authoring Languages and Proofing list, select French (Canada), set it as the preferred language, and then return the preferred to your original language.

❑ In the Office Authoring Languages and Proofing list, select French (Canada), remove it, restart Excel, and then reopen the **ExcelExpert_1-3a** workbook.

❑ Select cell A1 and then run the Translate command to translate the French text into English.

❑ Close the **ExcelExpert_1-3a** workbook.

Objective group 2

Manage and format data

The skills tested in this section of the Microsoft Office Specialist Expert exam for Microsoft Excel 2019 relate to filling cells with data, creating custom number formats, performing data validation, grouping data, inserting subtotals, removing duplicate records, and applying and managing conditional formatting rules. Specifically, the following objectives are associated with this set of skills:

2.1 Fill cells based on existing data

2.2 Format and validate data

2.3 Apply advanced conditional formatting and filtering

Many worksheets are drab, lifeless conglomerations of numbers, formulas, and text. If you'll be sharing your worksheets with other people, your numbers will have much more impact and will be more easily understood if they're pleasingly formatted and presented in a way that aids comprehension.

This chapter guides you in studying methods for using Flash Fill and advanced Fill Series options; creating custom number formats; configuring data validation; grouping and ungrouping data; inserting totals and subtotals; removing duplicate records from a table; and creating and managing conditional formatting rules.

> To complete the practice tasks in this chapter, you need the practice files contained in the **MOSExcelExpert2019\Objective2** practice file folder. For more information, see "Download the practice files" in this book's introduction.

Objective 2.1: Fill cells based on existing data

Fill cells by using Flash Fill

If you have inherited workbooks from someone else or if you have imported data from external data sources, you have probably come across data that was either structured or formatted (or both) in such a way that it was either difficult to read or difficult to work with. It could be mainframe data that arrives as all-uppercase letters, dates that appear in non-date formats, phone numbers that don't have dashes or parentheses, or fields that combine multiple pieces of data (such as first names and last names).

One way to tackle such data is to reenter it by hand in the structure or format you prefer or require. That works for a few records, but it gets tedious and time-consuming for dozens of records, and it becomes unworkable for hundreds or thousands of records.

Fortunately, creating your preferred data from existing data can often be done with only minimal work thanks to an Excel feature called Flash Fill. Given a column of original data, if you use the first cell in the next column to enter the corrected data (which could be data extracted from the original cell or the same data formatted in a different way), select the second cell, then run the Flash Fill command, Excel "recognizes" what you're doing and *automatically* fills in the rest of the column with the corrected data.

Let's look at a few examples:

- Column A contains a list of all-uppercase company names. In column B, I use cell B2 to type the title-case version of the text in cell A2 and then select cell B3. After I run the Flash Fill command, Excel recognizes the pattern and fills in the rest of the column with title-case versions of all the other cells in column A.

Company (Upper)	Company		Company (Upper)	Company
B'S BEVERAGES	B's Beverages		B'S BEVERAGES	B's Beverages
ISLAND TRADING			ISLAND TRADING	Island Trading
SPLIT RAIL BEER & ALE			SPLIT RAIL BEER & ALE	Split Rail Beer & Ale
CONSOLIDATED HOLDINGS			CONSOLIDATED HOLDINGS	Consolidated Holdings
EASTERN CONNECTION			EASTERN CONNECTION	Eastern Connection
AROUND THE HORN			AROUND THE HORN	Around The Horn
WHITE CLOVER MARKETS			WHITE CLOVER MARKETS	White Clover Markets
QUICK-STOP			QUICK-STOP	Quick-Stop
SEVEN SEAS IMPORTS			SEVEN SEAS IMPORTS	Seven Seas Imports
HUNGRY COYOTE IMPORT STORE			HUNGRY COYOTE IMPORT STORE	Hungry Coyote Import Store
BOTTOM-DOLLAR MARKETS			BOTTOM-DOLLAR MARKETS	Bottom-Dollar Markets
HUNGRY OWL ALL-NIGHT GROCERS			HUNGRY OWL ALL-NIGHT GROCERS	Hungry Owl All-Night Grocers
TRAIL'S HEAD GOURMET PROVISIONERS			TRAIL'S HEAD GOURMET PROVISIONERS	Trail's Head Gourmet Provisioners
THE BIG CHEESE			THE BIG CHEESE	The Big Cheese
SAVE-A-LOT MARKETS			SAVE-A-LOT MARKETS	Save-A-Lot Markets
OLD WORLD DELICATESSEN			OLD WORLD DELICATESSEN	Old World Delicatessen
GREAT LAKES FOOD MARKET			GREAT LAKES FOOD MARKET	Great Lakes Food Market
LAZY K KOUNTRY STORE			LAZY K KOUNTRY STORE	Lazy K Kountry Store
LAUGHING BACCHUS WINE CELLARS			LAUGHING BACCHUS WINE CELLARS	Laughing Bacchus Wine Cellars
CHOP-SUEY CHINESE			CHOP-SUEY CHINESE	Chop-Suey Chinese
LONESOME PINE RESTAURANT			LONESOME PINE RESTAURANT	Lonesome Pine Restaurant
RATTLESNAKE CANYON GROCERY			RATTLESNAKE CANYON GROCERY	Rattlesnake Canyon Grocery
THE CRACKER BOX			THE CRACKER BOX	The Cracker Box

You can use Flash Fill to convert all-uppercase text (far left) to title case (far right).

- Column A contains a list of full names, where each cell contains the first name, middle initial, and last name. In cells B2, C2, and D2, I typed the first name, middle initial, and last name, respectively, from cell A2. When I select cell B3 and run Flash Fill, Excel recognizes the pattern and fills in the rest of the first names; similarly, selecting C3 and running Flash Fill adds the middle initials, and selecting D3 and running Flash Fill adds the last names.

Full Name	First Name	Initial	Last Name	Full Name	First Name	Initial	Last Name
Maria Z. Anders	Maria	Z.	Anders	Maria Z. Anders	Maria	Z.	Anders
Victoria T. Ashworth				Victoria T. Ashworth	Victoria	T.	Ashworth
Helen K. Bennett				Helen K. Bennett	Helen	K.	Bennett
Christina C. Berglund				Christina C. Berglund	Christina	C.	Berglund
Marie X. Bertrand				Marie X. Bertrand	Marie	X.	Bertrand
Elizabeth G. Brown				Elizabeth G. Brown	Elizabeth	G.	Brown
Philip Z. Cramer				Philip Z. Cramer	Philip	Z.	Cramer
Simon W. Crowther				Simon W. Crowther	Simon	W.	Crowther
Ann G. Devon				Ann G. Devon	Ann	G.	Devon
Catherine Q. Dewey				Catherine Q. Dewey	Catherine	Q.	Dewey
Peter Y. Franken				Peter Y. Franken	Peter	Y.	Franken
Thomas V. Hardy				Thomas V. Hardy	Thomas	V.	Hardy
Paul M. Henriot				Paul M. Henriot	Paul	M.	Henriot
Michael C. Holz				Michael C. Holz	Michael	C.	Holz
Janine S. Labrune				Janine S. Labrune	Janine	S.	Labrune
Maria A. Larsson				Maria A. Larsson	Maria	A.	Larsson
Yoshi N. Latimer				Yoshi N. Latimer	Yoshi	N.	Latimer
Elizabeth J. Lincoln				Elizabeth J. Lincoln	Elizabeth	J.	Lincoln
Patricia D. McKenna				Patricia D. McKenna	Patricia	D.	McKenna
Roland U. Mendel				Roland U. Mendel	Roland	U.	Mendel
Liz W. Nixon				Liz W. Nixon	Liz	W.	Nixon
Rene M. Phillips				Rene M. Phillips	Rene	M.	Phillips
John V. Steel				John V. Steel	John	V.	Steel

You can use Flash Fill to extract substrings (right) from longer strings (left).

- Column A contains a list of phone numbers without any parentheses or dashes. In cell B2, I typed the phone number from cell A2 and added the parentheses and dash. When I select cell B3 and run Flash Fill, Excel recognizes the pattern and fills the rest of the column with the formatted phone numbers.

	A	B	A	B
1	Phone 1	Phone 2	Phone 1	Phone 2
2	3175557605	(317) 555-7605	3175557605	(317) 555-7605
3	3175559281		3175559281	(317) 555-9281
4	3175551452		3175551452	(317) 555-1452
5	3175555016		3175555016	(317) 555-5016
6	3175556433		3175556433	(317) 555-6433
7	3175559709		3175559709	(317) 555-9709
8	3175551890		3175551890	(317) 555-1890
9	3175559392		3175559392	(317) 555-9392
10	3175555877		3175555877	(317) 555-5877
11	3175554733		3175554733	(317) 555-4733
12	3175555123		3175555123	(317) 555-5123
13	3175551166		3175551166	(317) 555-1166
14	3175559826		3175559826	(317) 555-9826
15	3175555420		3175555420	(317) 555-5420
16	3175552765		3175552765	(317) 555-2765
17	3175557767		3175557767	(317) 555-7767
18	3175553038		3175553038	(317) 555-3038
19	3175555745		3175555745	(317) 555-5745
20	3175554453		3175554453	(317) 555-4453
21	3175558220		3175558220	(317) 555-8220
22	3175551191		3175551191	(317) 555-1191
23	3175559642		3175559642	(317) 555-9642
24	3175559113		3175559113	(317) 555-9113

You can use Flash Fill to add characters (right) to plain phone numbers (left).

To fill cells by using Flash Fill

➔ Type the first value you want in the first cell of the new column, select the second cell in the new column, and then on the **Data** tab, in the **Data Tools** group, click **Flash Fill**. Alternatively, on the **Home** tab, in the **Editing** group, click **Fill**, then click **Flash Fill**.

Tip You can also run the Flash Fill command by pressing Ctrl+E.

Or,

➔ Type the first value you want in the first cell of the new column. Starting in the second cell of the new column, drag the Fill handle through all the cells in the new column that you want to fill, click **Auto Fill Options**, and then click **Flash Fill**.

Fill cells by using advanced Fill Series options

Worksheets often use text series (such as *January, February, March*; or *Sunday, Monday, Tuesday*) and numeric series (such as *1, 3, 5*; or *2021, 2020, 2019*). Instead of entering these series manually, you can create them automatically by using the Auto Fill feature. That is, you enter and select the first couple of values in the series, drag the fill handle over the range you want to fill, and then click Fill Series in the AutoFill Options list.

You can use the fill handle and the Fill Series option to extend an existing series.

Instead of using the fill handle to create a series, you can use the Series command to gain more control over the process. By using the Series command, you can specify a direction for the fill (rows or columns); a step value (the value by which each item in the series is changed to produce the next item); a stop value (the value at which Excel should terminate the series); whether you want the series to extend the trend of the initial values; the date units (such as day or month) for a date series; and the series type, which can be one of the following four values:

- **Linear** This option finds the next series value by adding the step value to (or subtracting the step value from) the preceding value in the series.

- **Growth** This option finds the next series value by multiplying the preceding value by the step value.

- **Date** This option creates a series of dates based on the option you select in the Date Unit group (Day, Weekday, Month, or Year).

- **AutoFill** This option works much like the fill handle. You can use it to extend a numeric pattern or a text series (for example, Qtr1, Qtr2, Qtr3).

To fill cells by using the Fill Series command

1. Enter the starting value in the first cell you want to use for the series. If you want to create a series out of a particular pattern (such as 2, 4, 6, and so on), fill in enough cells to define the pattern.

2. Select the entire range you want to fill.

3. On the **Home** tab, in the **Editing** group, click **Fill**, then click **Series** to open the **Series** dialog box.

In the Series dialog box, specify the type of series you want to use to fill the cells.

4. Do either of the following to create the series, starting from the active cell:

   - Click **Rows** to create the series in rows.

   - Click **Columns** to create the series in columns.

5. In the **Type** group, click the type of series you want.

6. Do any of the following:

   - If you selected the Date type, click an option in the **Date unit** group.

   - If you selected the Linear or Growth type and want to extend a series trend, select the **Trend** check box.

   - If you selected a Linear, Growth, or Date series type, enter a number in the **Step value** box. This number is what Excel uses to generate the next value in the series.

   - To place a limit on the series, enter a number in the **Stop value** box.

7. Click **OK** to fill in the series and return to the worksheet.

Objective 2.1 practice tasks

The practice file for these tasks is located in the **MOSExcelExpert2019\ Objective2** practice file folder. The folder also contains a result file that you can use to check your work.

➤ Open the **ExcelExpert_2-1** workbook, display the **Flash Fill** worksheet, and do the following:

❑ In cell B2, type the company name from cell A2 using title case, select cell B3, and then run the Flash Fill command from the Home tab.

❑ In cell D2, type the first name from the full name shown in cell C2, select cell D3, and then run the Flash Fill command from the Data tab.

❑ In cell E2, type the initial from the full name shown in cell C2, select cell E3, and then run the Flash Fill command from the Data tab.

❑ In cell F2, type the last name from the full name shown in cell C2, select cell F3, and then run the Flash Fill command from the Data tab.

❑ In cell H2, type the phone number shown in cell G2, but include parentheses around the area code, a space after the closing parenthesis, and a dash between the sixth and seventh digits. Drag the Fill handle from cell H2 down to cell H24, click Auto Fill Options, and then click Flash Fill.

➤ Display the **Fill Series** worksheet and do the following:

❑ In column A, below the *Linear* label, create a linear series that begins at *0*, has a step value of *5*, and has a stop value of *50*.

❑ In column B, below the *Growth* label, create a growth series that begins at *1*, has a step value of *2*, and has a stop value of *250*.

❑ Fill the range C2:C11 with a Date series that uses a day unit and a step value of *2*.

❏ Fill the range D2:D11 with a Date series that uses a weekday unit and a step value of *1*.

❏ Fill the range E2:E11 with a Date series that uses a month unit and a step value of *6*.

❏ Save the workbook.

❏ Open the **ExcelExpert_2-1_results** workbook. Compare the two workbooks to check your work. Then close the open workbooks.

Objective 2.2: Format and validate data

Create custom number formats

One of the best ways to improve the readability of your worksheets is to display your data in a format that is logical, consistent, and straightforward. Formatting currency amounts with leading dollar signs, percentages with trailing percent signs, and large numbers with commas are a few of the ways you can improve your spreadsheet style. However, you can use Excel to go beyond these built-in formats to create custom number and date formats with which you can display your worksheet values exactly as you want them to be seen.

Excel's built-in numeric formats give you a great deal of control over how your numbers are displayed, but they have their limitations. For example, there is no built-in format you can use to display a different currency symbol, such as the Euro symbol (€), or to display temperatures using, say, the degree symbol (°).

To overcome these limitations, you need to create your own custom numeric formats. You can do this either by editing an existing format or by entering your own format from scratch. The formatting syntax and symbols are explained in detail later in this section.

Every Excel numeric format, whether built-in or customized, has the following syntax:

positive format;negative format;zero format;text format

The four parts, separated by semicolons, determine how various numbers are pre-sented. The first part defines how a positive number is displayed, the second part defines how a negative number is displayed, the third part defines how zero is dis-played, and the fourth part defines how text is displayed. If you leave out one or more of these parts, numbers are controlled as shown in the following table.

Number of parts used	Format syntax
Three	*positive format;negative format;zero format*
Two	*positive and zero format;negative format*
One	*positive, negative, and zero format*

The following table lists the special symbols you use to define each of these parts.

Symbol	Description
#	Holds a place for a digit and displays the digit exactly as typed. Displays nothing if no number is entered. For example, if a cell's custom format is ### and you enter 25 in the cell, Excel displays 25.
0	Holds a place for a digit and displays the digit exactly as typed. Displays zero if no number is entered. For example, if a cell's custom format is 000 and you enter 25 in the cell, Excel displays 025.
?	Holds a place for a digit and displays the digit exactly as typed. Displays a space if no number is entered. For example, if a cell's custom format is 0??? and you enter 25 in the cell, Excel displays 0 25.
. (period)	Sets the location of the decimal point. For example, if a cell's custom format is #.#0 and you enter 34.5 in the cell, Excel displays 34.50.
, (comma)	Sets the location of the thousands separator. Marks only the location of the first thousand. For example, if a cell's custom format is #,### and you enter 12345 in the cell, Excel displays 12,345.
%	Multiplies the number by 100 (for display only) and adds the percent (%) character. For example, if a cell's custom format is #% and you enter .75 in the cell, Excel displays 75%.
E+ e+ E- e-	Displays the number in scientific format. E- and e- place a minus sign in the exponent; E+ and e+ place a plus sign in the exponent. For example, if a cell's custom format is 0.00E+00 and you enter 123456789 in the cell, Excel displays 1.23E+08. Similarly, if a cell's custom format is 0.0E-00 and you enter 0.0000012 in the cell, Excel displays 1.2E-06.
/ (slash)	Sets the location of the fraction separator. For example, if a cell's custom format is 0/0 and you enter .75 in the cell, Excel displays 3/4.
$ ( ) : - + <space>	Displays the character. For example, if a cell's custom format is $##0.00 and you enter 123.5 in the cell, Excel displays $123.50.

Symbol	Description
*	Repeats whatever character immediately follows the asterisk until the cell is full. Doesn't replace other symbols or numbers. For example, you can create a dot trailer in a cell by adding *. to the format. So if the custom format is #*. and you enter *123* in the cell, Excel displays *123............* (where the dots continue until the cell is filled).
_ (underscore)	Inserts a blank space the width of whatever character follows the underscore, which can often help you to align your numbers. For example, the custom format _(#.00 inserts a blank space the width of the opening parenthesis at the beginning of the displayed value.
\ (backslash)	Inserts the character that follows the backslash. See the next item for an example. In general, you need to use the backslash only for reserved characters (such as # or @) or for the following letters: B, D, E, G, H, M, N, S, and Y. (For all other letters, if you just enter a single character by itself, Excel will display that character.) For example, if a cell's custom format is #.##\M and you enter *1.23* in the cell, Excel displays *1.23M*.
"text"	Inserts the text that appears within the quotation marks. For example, if a cell's custom format is "Part "\#00-0000 and you enter *123456* in the cell, Excel displays *Part #12-3456*.
@	Displays the cell's text. For example, if a cell's custom format is @" entry" and you enter *credit* in the cell, Excel displays *credit entry*.
[color]	Displays the cell contents in the specified color. For example, if the cell's custom format is *[green]0.00; [red]0.00*, Excel displays positive cell values in green and negative cell values in red. The predefined color values you can use are *black, white, red, green, blue, yellow, magenta,* and *cyan*, and the color codes *color1* through *color565*.

Although the built-in date and time formats of Excel are fine for most purposes, you might need to create your own custom formats. For example, you might want to display the day of the week (for example, "Friday"). Custom date and time formats generally are simpler to create than custom numeric formats. There are fewer formatting symbols, and you usually don't need to specify different formats for different conditions. The following table lists the date and time formatting symbols.

Symbol	Description
Date Formats	
d	Day number without a leading zero (*1* to *31*)
dd	Day number with a leading zero (*01* to *31*)
ddd	Three-letter day abbreviation (*Mon*, for example)
dddd	Full day name (*Monday*, for example)
m	Month number without a leading zero (*1* to *12*)
mm	Month number with a leading zero (*01* to *12*)
mmm	Three-letter month abbreviation (*Aug*, for example)
mmmm	Full month name (*August*, for example)
yy	Two-digit year (*00* to *99*)
yyyy	Full year (*1900* to *2078*)
h	Hour without a leading zero (*0* to *24*)
hh	Hour with a leading zero (*00* to *24*)
m	Minute without a leading zero (*0* to *59*)
mm	Minute with a leading zero (*00* to *59*)
s	Second without a leading zero (*0* to *59*)
ss	Second with a leading zero (*00* to *59*)
AM/PM, am/pm, A/P	Displays the time using a 12-hour clock
/ : . —	Symbols used to separate parts of dates or times
[color]	Displays the date or time in the color specified

The best way to become familiar with custom formats is to try your own experiments. Excel stores each format that you try. If you find that your list of custom formats is getting a bit unwieldy or that it's cluttered with unused formats, you can delete those formats.

To open the Format Cells dialog box, do one of the following:

➜ On the **Home** tab, in the **Cells** group, click **Format**, then click **Format Cells**.

➜ Right-click the cell or range, then click **Format Cells**.

➜ Press **Ctrl+1**.

To create and apply a custom number format

1. Select the cell or range of cells you want the new format to apply to.

2. Open the **Format Cells** dialog box.

3. On the **Number** tab, in the **Category** list, click **Custom**.

4. To base the custom number format on an existing format, click the base format in the **Type** list.

5. Edit or enter the symbols that define the number format.

Define custom number formats in the Type box.

6. When you are done, click **OK** to return to the worksheet.

To delete custom number formats

1. Display the **Number** tab of the **Format Cells** dialog box.

2. In the **Category** list, click **Custom**.

3. In the **Type** list, click the format you want to remove.

Tip You can delete only custom formats; you can't delete built-in formats.

---

4. Click **Delete** to remove the format from the list.

5. Click **OK** to close the **Format Cells** dialog box and return to the worksheet.

Configure data validation

Formulas are only as good as the data they're given. For basic data entry errors (for example, entering the wrong date or transposing a number's digits), there's not much you can do other than exhort yourself or the people who use your worksheets to enter data carefully. Fortunately, you have a bit more control when it comes to preventing the entry of improper data such as data that is the wrong type (for example, entering text in a cell that requires a number) or data that falls outside of an allowable range (for example, entering 200 in a cell that requires a number between 1 and 100).

You can prevent these kinds of improper entries, to a certain extent, by adding comments that describe what is allowable inside a particular cell. However, this requires other people to both read and act on the comment text. You can also use custom numeric formatting to "format" a cell with an error message if the wrong type of data is entered. This is useful, but it works only for certain kinds of input errors.

Exam Strategy The Excel Expert exam emphasizes collaboration between users, so be sure to also study the information related to setting up workbooks for other people to view and edit in "Objective 1.2: Prepare workbooks for collaboration."

The best solution for preventing data entry errors is to use the data-validation feature of Excel. With data validation, you create rules that specify exactly what kind of data can be entered and in what range that data can fall. You can also specify pop-up input messages that appear when a cell is selected and error messages that appear when data is entered improperly.

You configure data-validation rules on the Settings tab of the Data Validation dialog box. The following validation types are available:

- **Any Value** Allows any value in the range (that is, it removes any previously applied validation rule). If you're removing an existing rule, be sure to also clear the input message, if any.

- **Whole Number** Allows only whole numbers (integers). You use the Data list to select a comparison operator (such as Between, Equal To, or Less Than) and then enter the specific criteria. For example, if you click the Between option, you must enter Minimum and Maximum values.

- **Decimal** Allows decimal numbers or whole numbers. You use the Data list to select a comparison operator and then enter the specific numeric criteria.

- **List** Allows only values specified in a list. You specify the allowable values in the Source box on the Settings tab of the Data Validation dialog box, either by specifying a range on the same sheet or a range name on any sheet that contains the list of allowable values (preceding the range or range name with an equal sign) or by entering the allowable values directly into the Source box (separated by commas). You have the option of allowing the user to select from the allowable values by using a list.

- **Date** Allows only dates. (If the user includes a time value, the entry is invalid.) You use the Data list to select a comparison operator and then enter the specific date criteria (such as a Start date and an End date).

- **Time** Allows only times. (If the user includes a date value, the entry is invalid.) You use the Data list to select a comparison operator and then enter the specific time criteria (such as a Start time and an End time).

- **Text Length** Allows only alphanumeric strings of a specified length. You use the Data list to select a comparison operator and then enter the specific length criteria (such as Minimum and Maximum lengths).

- **Custom** You can use this option to enter a formula that specifies the validation criteria. You can either enter the formula directly in the Formula box on the Settings tab of the Data Validation dialog box (again preceding the formula with an equal sign) or enter a reference to a cell that contains the formula. For example, if you're restricting cell A2 and you want to be sure the entered value is not the same as what's in cell A1, you would enter the formula **=A2<>A1**.

On the Settings tab of the Data Validation dialog box, set up the criteria for your validation rule.

To configure data validation for a cell or range

1. Select the cell or range to which you want to apply the data-validation rule.

2. On the **Data** tab, in the **Data Tools** group, click **Data Validation** to open the **Data Validation** dialog box.

3. On the **Settings** tab, in the **Allow** list, click one of the validation types.

4. Enter the validation criteria you require.

5. To allow blank entries, either in the cell itself or in other cells specified as part of the validation settings, leave the **Ignore blank** check box selected. If you clear this check box, Excel treats blank entries as zero and applies the validation rule accordingly.

6. If the range had an existing validation rule that also applied to other cells, you can apply the new rule to those other cells by selecting the **Apply these changes to all other cells with the same settings** check box.

7. If you want a message to appear when the user selects the restricted cell or any cell within the restricted range, on the **Input Message** tab, do the following:

    Verify that the **Show input message when cell is selected** check box is selected.

    In the **Title** box, enter a title for the message.

    In the **Input message** box, enter the message that you want Excel to display. For example, you could use the message to give the user information about the type and range of allowable values.

You can configure an input message to appear when a workbook user selects the cell.

8. If you want a dialog box to appear when the user enters invalid data, click the **Error Alert** tab, then do the following:

Select the **Show error alert after invalid data is entered** check box.

In the **Style** list, click the error style you want: **Stop, Warning, or Information**.

In the **Title** box, enter a title for the message.

In the **Error message** box, enter the message that you want Excel to display.

IMPORTANT Only the Stop style prevents users from entering invalid data.

You can configure an error alert to appear when a workbook user enters an invalid entry.

9. Click **OK** to apply the data-validation rule.

Group and ungroup data

You can control a worksheet range display by grouping the data based on the worksheet formulas and data. Grouping the data creates a worksheet outline, which you can use to "collapse" sections of the sheet to display only summary cells, or to "expand" hidden sections to show the underlying detail.

Not all worksheets can be grouped, so you need to make sure your worksheet is a candidate for outlining. First, the worksheet must contain formulas that reference cells or ranges directly adjacent to the formula cell. Worksheets with SUM functions that subtotal cells above or to the left are particularly good candidates for outlining.

Second, there must be a consistent pattern to the direction of the formula references. For example, a worksheet with formulas that always reference cells above or to the left can be outlined. Excel will not outline a worksheet with, say, SUM functions that reference ranges above and below a formula cell.

If your worksheet meets these criteria, then you can use Excel's Auto Outline command to automatically group the worksheet data. Otherwise, you can group data manually.

When Excel creates an outline, it divides your worksheet into a hierarchy of levels. These levels range from the worksheet detail (the lowest level) to the grand totals (the highest level). Excel outlines can handle up to eight levels of data. In the Budget worksheet shown below, for example, Excel created three levels for both the column and the row data:

- In the columns, the monthly figures are the details, so they're the lowest level (level 3). The quarterly totals are the first summary data, so they're the next level (level 2). Finally, the grand totals (not shown) are the highest level (level 1).

- In the rows, the individual sales and expense items are the details (level 3). The sales and expenses subtotals are the next level (level 2). The Gross Profit row is the highest level (level 1).

	A	B	C	D	E	F	G	H	I	J	K	
		Jan	Feb	Mar	1st Quarter	Apr	May	Jun	2nd Quarter	Jul	Aug	
2	*Sales*											
3	Division I	23,500	23,000	24,000	70,500	25,100	25,000	25,400	75,500	26,000	24,000	24
4	Division II	28,750	27,800	29,500	86,050	31,000	30,500	30,000	91,500	31,000	29,500	29
5	Division III	24,400	24,000	25,250	73,650	26,600	27,000	26,750	80,350	27,000	25,250	25
6	SALES TOTAL	76,650	74,800	78,750	230,200	82,700	82,500	82,150	247,350	84,000	78,750	78
7	*Expenses*											
8	Cost of Goods	6,132	5,984	6,300	18,416	6,616	6,600	6,572	19,788	6,720	6,300	6
9	Advertising	4,600	4,200	5,200	14,000	5,000	5,500	5,250	15,750	5,500	5,200	5
10	Rent	2,100	2,100	2,100	6,300	2,100	2,100	2,100	6,300	2,100	2,100	2
11	Supplies	1,300	1,200	1,400	3,900	1,300	1,250	1,400	3,950	1,300	1,400	1
12	Salaries	16,000	16,000	16,500	48,500	16,500	16,500	17,000	50,000	17,000	17,000	17
13	Shipping	14,250	13,750	14,500	42,500	15,000	14,500	14,750	44,250	15,000	14,500	14
14	Utilities	500	600	600	1,700	550	600	650	1,800	650	600	
15	EXPENSES TOTAL	44,882	43,834	46,600	135,316	47,066	47,050	47,722	141,838	48,270	47,100	47
16	GROSS PROFIT	31,768	30,966	32,150	94,884	35,634	35,450	34,428	105,512	35,730	31,650	31

When you create an outline, Excel adds outline tools to the worksheet.

To help you work with your outlines, Excel adds the following tools to your worksheet:

- **Level bars**—These bars indicate the data included in the current level. Click a bar to hide the rows or columns marked by a bar.

- **Collapse symbol**—Click this symbol to hide (or collapse) the rows or columns marked by the attached level bar.

- **Expand symbol**—When you collapse a level, the collapse symbol changes to an expand symbol (+). Click this symbol to display (or expand) the hidden rows or columns.

- **Level symbols**—These symbols tell you which level each level bar is on. Click a level symbol to display all the detail data for that level.

Tip To toggle the outline symbols on and off, press Ctrl+8.

To group a worksheet using Auto Outline

→ On the **Data** tab, in the **Outline** group, click **Group**, then click **Auto Outline**.

To group data manually

→ Select the rows or columns you want to group, then on the **Data** tab, in the **Outline** group, click **Group**, then click **Group**.

Or,

1. Select a cell in each row or column you want to group.

2. On the **Data** tab, in the **Outline** group, click **Group**, then click **Group**. Excel asks whether you want to group rows or columns.

3. Select either **Rows** or **Columns**, as appropriate for your data, then click **OK**.

When you group data manually, Excel needs to know whether you're grouping rows or columns.

To remove an outline from a worksheet

→ On the **Data** tab, in the **Outline** group, click **Ungroup**, then click **Clear Outline**.

To ungroup data

→ Select the rows or columns you want to ungroup, then on the **Data** tab, in the **Outline** group, click **Ungroup**, then click **Ungroup**.

Or,

1. Select a cell in each row or column you want to ungroup.

2. On the **Data** tab, in the **Outline** group, click **Ungroup**, then click **Ungroup**. Excel asks whether you want to ungroup rows or columns.

3. Select either **Rows** or **Columns**, as appropriate for your data, then click **OK**.

Calculate data by inserting subtotals and totals

Although you can use formulas and worksheet functions to summarize your data in various ways—including sums, averages, counts, maximums, and minimums—if you're in a hurry, or if you just need a quick summary of your data, you can get Excel to do the work for you. The secret here is a feature called *automatic subtotals,* which are formulas that Excel adds to a worksheet automatically.

Excel sets up automatic subtotals based on data groupings in a selected field. For example, if you ask for subtotals based on the Customer field, Excel runs down the Customer column and creates a new subtotal each time the name changes. To get useful summaries, you should sort the range on the field containing the data groupings you're interested in.

	A	B	C	E	F	G	H
1	Customer	Country	Region	Unit Price	Quantity	Discount	Total
2	Cactus Comidas para llevar	Argentina		$ 46.00	7	0%	$ 322.00
3	Cactus Comidas para llevar	Argentina		$ 7.75	20	0%	$ 155.00
4	Cactus Comidas para llevar	Argentina		$ 15.00	10	0%	$ 150.00
5	Cactus Comidas para llevar	Argentina		$ 45.60	8	0%	$ 364.80
6	Cactus Comidas para llevar	Argentina		$ 14.00	20	0%	$ 280.00
7	**Cactus Comidas para llevar Total**						$ 1,271.80
8	Océano Atlántico Ltda.	Argentina		$ 6.00	5	0%	$ 30.00
9	Océano Atlántico Ltda.	Argentina		$ 21.35	20	0%	$ 427.00
10	Océano Atlántico Ltda.	Argentina		$ 30.00	6	0%	$ 180.00
11	Océano Atlántico Ltda.	Argentina		$ 34.80	5	0%	$ 174.00
12	Océano Atlántico Ltda.	Argentina		$ 21.00	30	0%	$ 630.00
13	Océano Atlántico Ltda.	Argentina		$ 81.00	15	0%	$ 1,215.00
14	Océano Atlántico Ltda.	Argentina		$ 18.00	10	0%	$ 180.00
15	Océano Atlántico Ltda.	Argentina		$ 13.00	15	0%	$ 195.00
16	**Océano Atlántico Ltda. Total**						$ 3,031.00
17	Rancho grande	Argentina		$ 81.00	5	0%	$ 405.00
18	Rancho grande	Argentina		$ 263.50	2	0%	$ 527.00
19	Rancho grande	Argentina		$ 17.45	6	0%	$ 104.70
20	Rancho grande	Argentina		$ 32.00	6	0%	$ 192.00
21	Rancho grande	Argentina		$ 19.50	20	0%	$ 390.00
22	**Rancho grande Total**						$ 1,618.70

Invoice data showing subtotals for each customer based on the values in the Total column.

See Also For more information on the outline tools that Excel adds to the worksheet when you insert subtotals, see "Group and ungroup data," earlier in this topic.

Note that in the phrase *automatic subtotals,* the word *subtotals* is misleading because it implies that you can only summarize your data with totals. However, you can also count the values (all the values or just the numeric values), calculate the average of the values, determine the maximum or minimum value, and calculate the product of the values. For statistical analysis, you can also calculate the standard deviation and variance, both of a sample and of a population.

To insert subtotals and totals

1. Select a cell within the range you want to subtotal.

2. On the **Data** tab, in the **Outline** group, click **Subtotal** to open the **Subtotal** dialog box.

3. Use the **At each change in** list to select the column you want to use to group the subtotals.

4. In the **Use function** list, select **Sum**.

5. In the **Add subtotal to** list, select the check box for the column you want to summarize.

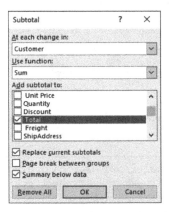

Use the Subtotal dialog box to apply subtotals to a range.

6. Click **OK**. Excel calculates the subtotals and adds them to the range and also adds a **Grand Total** row to the bottom of the range. Excel also adds outline symbols to the range.

To change the summary calculation

→ In step 4 from the previous section, in the **Use function** list, select the function you want to use, such as **Count**, **Average**, **Max**, or **Min**.

Remove duplicate records

You can make your Excel data more accurate for analysis by removing duplicate records. Duplicate records throw off calculations by including the same data two or more times. To prevent this, you should delete duplicate records. Rather than looking for duplicates manually, you can use the Remove Duplicates command, which quickly finds and removes duplicates in even the largest ranges or tables.

Before you use the Remove Duplicates command, you must decide what defines a duplicate record in your data. You have two choices:

- Two records are duplicates if, for every column in the range or table, the records contain identical values.

- Two records are duplicates if, for only certain columns in the range or table, the records contain identical values.

To remove duplicate records

1. Click a cell inside the range or table.

2. On the **Data** tab, in the **Data Tools** group, click **Remove Duplicates** to open the **Remove Duplicates** dialog box.

3. If your range doesn't have column headers, clear the **My data has headers** check box.

4. Select the check box beside each field that you want Excel to check for duplicate values.

Tip If your range or table has many fields, you may want Excel to use only one or two of those fields to look for duplicate records. Rather than clearing all the other check boxes manually, first click Unselect All in the Remove Duplicates dialog box to clear all the check boxes. You can then click to select just the check boxes you want Excel to use.

Use the Remove Duplicates dialog box to specify which columns must contain identical data for the records to be considered duplicates.

IMPORTANT Excel does not give you a chance to confirm the deletion of the duplicate records, so be sure you want to do this before proceeding.

5. Click **OK**. Excel deletes any duplicate records that it finds and then displays a dialog box telling you the number of duplicate records that it deleted.

Excel tells you how many duplicate records it deleted and how many unique records remain in the range or table.

6. Click **OK**.

Objective 2.2 practice tasks

The practice file for these tasks is located in the **MOSExcelExpert2019\ Objective2** practice file folder. The folder also contains a result file that you can use to check your work.

➤ Open the **ExcelExpert_2-2** workbook, display the **Custom Data Formatting** worksheet, and do the following:

❑ Select cells A1:A4. Create and apply a custom number format that displays the thousands separator, always displays at least one number, displays a leading minus sign and red text if a negative number is entered, displays 0 if 0 is entered, and displays the message *Enter a number* if a non-numeric value is entered.

❑ Select cell B1. Create and apply a custom number format that displays the thousands separator and the decimal point, always displays at least one digit before and after the decimal point, and displays *°C* (the degree symbol and the letter C, for *degrees Celsius*) at the end.

❑ Select cells C1:C2. Create and apply a custom number format that displays a six-digit entry with a dash after the first two digits, the text *Acct #* before the digits, and the text *Enter numbers only* if the user includes any non-numeric characters in the entry.

❑ Select cell D1. Create and apply a custom date format that displays the two-digit month, day, and year, separated by periods.

❑ Select cell E1. Create and apply a custom time format that displays the two-digit hour and minute with nothing in between them, followed by a space and the text *hours*.

➤ Display the **Data Validation** worksheet and do the following:

❑ Select cell B2. Create and apply a data-validation rule that restricts data entry to values between 0 and 1 (that is, between 0% and 100%).

❑ Include an input message titled *Interest Rate* with the following text: **Please enter a value between 0 and 1.**

- ❏ Then enter a stop-style error message titled *Invalid Interest Rate* with the following text: **The interest rate value you entered is invalid. Please enter a value between 0 and 1.**

- ❏ Select cell B3. Create and apply a data-validation rule that restricts data entry to positive values with a minimum of 1 and a maximum of 30.

- ❏ Include an input message titled *Loan Period* with the following text: **Please enter a value between 1 and 30 years.**

- ❏ Then enter a stop-style error message titled *Invalid Loan Period* with the following text: **The loan period value you entered is invalid. Please enter a value between 1 and 30 years.**

- ❏ Select cell B4. Create and apply a data-validation rule that restricts data entry to positive values.

- ❏ Include an input message titled *Loan Principal* with the following text: **Please enter a value greater than 0.**

- ❏ Enter a stop-style error message titled *Invalid Loan Principal* with the following text: **The loan principal value you entered is invalid. Please enter a value greater than 0.**

➤ Display the **Grouping** worksheet and do the following:

- ❏ Run the Auto Outline command to group the worksheet data.

- ❏ Create a manual grouping of the Advertising, Rent, and Supplies expense items.

➤ Display the **Subtotals** worksheet and create Sum subtotals for each customer based on the values in the Total field.

➤ Display the **Remove Duplicates** worksheet and remove the six duplicate records in the range.

➤ Save the workbook.

➤ Open the **ExcelExpert_2-2_results** workbook. Compare the two workbooks to check your work. Then close the open workbooks.

Objective 2.3: Apply advanced conditional formatting and filtering

Create custom conditional formatting rules

Many Excel worksheets contain hundreds of data values. You can make sense of large sets of data by creating formulas, applying functions, and performing data analysis. However, there are times when you don't want to analyze a worksheet per se. Instead, all you want are answers to simple questions such as the following:

- Which cell values are less than 0?
- What are the top 10 values?
- Which cell values are above average, and which are below average?

Exam Strategy Data analysis is a crucial component of the Excel Expert exam. This means that besides studying the conditional formatting techniques in this topic, be sure to also study the data analysis material in "Objective 3.4: Perform data analysis" and the PivotTable material in "Objective 4.2: Create and modify PivotTables."

These simple questions aren't easy to answer just by glancing at the worksheet, and the more numbers you're dealing with, the harder it gets. To help you "eyeball" your worksheets and answer these and similar questions, Excel lets you apply *conditional formatting* to the cells. This is a special format that Excel applies only to cells that satisfy some condition, which Excel calls a *rule*. For example, you could apply formatting to show all the negative values in a red font, or you could apply formatting to highlight the top 10 values.

You can apply five types of conditional formatting rules:

- **Highlight cells rules** A *highlight cell* rule applies a format to cells that meet specified criteria. You have seven choices: Greater Than, Less Than, Between, Equal To, Text That Contains, A Date Occurring, and Duplicate Values. In each case, you use a dialog box to specify the condition and the formatting that you want applied to cells that match the condition.

	A	B	C	D	E	F	G	H	I	J	K
1	Sales Rep	2019	2020	% +/-							
2	Nancy Freehafer	$ 996,336	$ 960,492	-4%	Less Than					?	×
3	Andrew Cencini	$ 606,731	$ 577,983	-5%	Format cells that are LESS THAN:						
4	Jan Kotas	$ 622,781	$ 967,580	55%							
5	Mariya Sergienko	$ 765,327	$ 771,399	1%	0			⬆ with	Light Red Fill with Dark Red Text	∨	
6	Steven Thorpe	$ 863,589	$ 827,213	-4%							
7	Michael Neipper	$ 795,518	$ 669,394	-16%				OK		Cancel	

For a Less Than conditional formatting rule, the specified formatting is applied to all cells that have a value that is less than the value specified in the dialog box.

- **Top/bottom rules** A top/bottom rule applies a format to cells that rank in the top or bottom (for numerical items, the highest or lowest) values in a range. You can select the top or bottom either as an absolute value (for example, the top 10 items) or as a percentage (for example, the bottom 25%). You can also format cells that are above or below the average. In each case, you use a dialog box to set up the specifics of the rule. For the Top 10 Items, Top 10%, Bottom 10 Items, and Bottom 10% rules, you use the dialog box to specify the condition and the formatting you want applied to cells that match the condition. For the Above Average and Below Average rules, you use the dialog box to specify the formatting only.

	A	B	C	D	E	F	G	H
1	Product Name	Units	$ Total					
2	Northwind Traders Almonds	20	$ 200	Top 10 Items			?	×
3	Northwind Traders Beer	487	$ 6,818					
4	Northwind Traders Boysenberry Spread	100	$ 2,500	Format cells that rank in the TOP:				
5	Northwind Traders Cajun Seasoning	40	$ 3,880	5 ⬍ with	Green Fill with Dark Green Text	∨		
6	Northwind Traders Chai	40	$ 720					
7	Northwind Traders Chocolate	200	$ 3,550		OK		Cancel	
8	Northwind Traders Chocolate Biscuits Mix	85	$ 782					
9	Northwind Traders Clam Chowder	290	$ 4,799					
10	Northwind Traders Coffee	650	$ 29,900					
11	Northwind Traders Crab Meat	120	$ 2,208					

An example of a Top 10 conditional formatting rule.

- **Data bars** If you're interested in the *relationship* between similar values in a worksheet, you need some way to visualize the relative values in a range, and that's where data bars are useful. *Data bars* are colored, horizontal bars that appear "behind" the values in a range. (They're like a bar chart.) Their key feature is that the length of the data bar that appears in each cell is related to the value in that cell: the larger the value, the longer the data bar. The cell with the highest value has the longest data bar, and the data bars that appear in the other cells have lengths that reflect their values. Excel configures its default data bars with the longest data bar based on the highest value in the range and the shortest data bar based on the lowest value in the range. You can also set up data bars based on a specific range of values (for example, the values *0* and *100* for test scores) or as a percentage of the largest value.

	A	B	C			
1	**Product Name**	**Units**	**$ Total**	Data Bars	>	Gradient Fill
2	Northwind Traders Almonds	20	$ 200	Color Scales	>	
3	Northwind Traders Beer	487	$ 6,818			
4	Northwind Traders Boysenberry Spread	100	$ 2,500	Icon Sets	>	
5	Northwind Traders Cajun Seasoning	40	$ 880			Solid Fill
6	Northwind Traders Chai	40	$ 720	New Rule...		
7	Northwind Traders Chocolate	200	$ 2,550	Clear Rules	>	
8	Northwind Traders Chocolate Biscuits Mix	85	$ 782	Manage Rules...		
9	Northwind Traders Clam Chowder	290	$ 2,799			
10	Northwind Traders Coffee	650	$ 29,900			
11	Northwind Traders Crab Meat	120	$ 2,208			More Rules...

You can apply data bars by using either a gradient fill or a solid fill.

- **Color scales** The color scales in Excel are useful if you want to get a "big picture" view of your data that shows, for example, the overall distribution of the values and whether there are any *outliers* (values that are much higher or lower than all or most of the other values). The color scales are also helpful if you want to make value judgments about your data. For example, high sales and low numbers of product defects are "good," whereas low margins and high employee turnover rates are "bad." A *color scale* is similar to a data bar in that it compares the relative values of cells in a range. Instead of bars in each cell, though, you see cell shading, where the shading color reflects the cell's value. For example, the lowest values might be shaded red; higher values might be shaded light red, then orange, yellow, and lime green; and finally the highest values could be shaded deep green.

1	**GDP — % Annual Growth Rates (Source:**				Color Scales	>				
2		**2002**	**2003**	**2004**	**2005**					
3	World	2.0	2.7	4.0	3.5	Icon Sets	>			
4	Albania	2.9	5.7	5.9	5.5					
5	Algeria	4.7	6.9	5.2	5.1					
6	Angola	14.5	3.3	11.2	18.3	New Rule...				
7	Antigua and Barbud	2.5	5.1	7.0	4.2	Clear Rules	>			
8	Argentina	-10.9	8.8	9.0	9.2	Manage Rules...				
9	Armenia	13.2	14.0	10.5	13.9			More Rules...		
10	Australia	3.9	3.3	4.2	3.0	3.1	3.6	3.8	1.4	2.3
11	Austria	1.7	0.9	2.6	2.4	3.7	3.7	1.4	-3.8	2.3
12	Azerbaijan	10.6	11.2	10.2	26.4	34.5	25.0	10.8	9.3	5.0

A Green - Yellow - Red color scale shows the lowest values in the deepest shade of red and the highest values in the deepest shade of green.

- **Icon sets** You use *icon sets* to visualize the relative values of cells in a range. Excel adds an icon to each cell in the range, and that icon tells you something about the cell's value relative to the rest of the range. For example, the highest values might get an up arrow, the lowest values a down arrow, and the values in between a horizontal arrow. Icon sets take advantage of symbols that people have strong associations with.

  For example, a check mark means something is good or finished or acceptable, whereas an X means something is bad or unfinished or unacceptable. A green circle is positive, whereas a red circle is negative (similar to traffic lights).

A 3 Arrows icon set indicates low, middle, and high values in a data set by using arrows of different colors and directions.

To create a custom conditional formatting rule

1. Select the range to which you want the custom conditional formatting applied.

2. On the **Conditional Formatting** menu, click **New Rule** to open the **New Formatting Rule** dialog box.

3. In the **Select a Rule Type** group, click the type of rule you want to apply.

The controls in the Edit The Rule Description area vary depending on the rule type you select.

4. Select the rule type's conditions and formatting.

5. Click **OK** to close the dialog box and return to the workbook.

Create conditional formatting rules that use formulas

Excel comes with another conditional formatting component that makes this feature even more powerful: you can apply conditional formatting based on the results of a formula. In particular, you can set up a logical formula as the conditional formatting criterion. If that formula returns TRUE, Excel applies the formatting to the cells; if the formula returns FALSE, instead, Excel doesn't apply the formatting.

When comparing worksheet values in a conditional formatting rule's logical formula, you generally set up the expression to compare the value you seek with a specific value from the range, and then use a mixed-reference format for that specific value so that Excel can compare all the values in the range to the target value. For example, suppose you have a list of percentage increases in the range D5:D13 and a "target" percentage in cell D2. You want to apply a format only on those entries where the percentage increase is greater than or equal to the target value. Here's the logical formula to use:

=$D5 >= D2

The mixed-reference format $D5 tells Excel to keep the column (D) fixed while varying the row number (in this example, 5 through 13), and in each case compare the resulting cell value with the value in D2.

To create a custom conditional formatting rule based on a formula

1. Select the range to which you want the custom conditional formatting applied.

2. In the **New Formatting Rule** dialog box, in the **Select a Rule Type** list, click **Use a formula to determine which cells to format**.

3. In the **Format values where this formula is true** box, enter your logical formula.

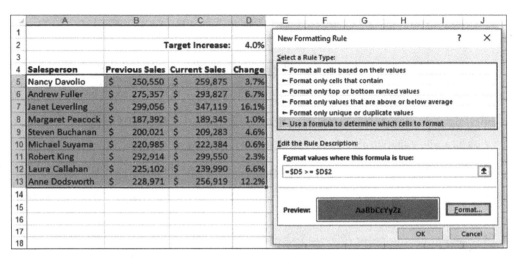

You can create custom conditional formatting rules based on logical formulas.

4. Click **Format** to open the **Format Cells** dialog box.

5. On the **Number**, **Font**, **Border**, and **Fill** tabs, specify the formatting you want Excel to apply when the formula evaluates to TRUE, then click **OK**.

6. In the **New Formatting Rule** dialog box, click **OK**.

Manage conditional formatting rules

Conditional formatting rules are extremely useful and powerful tools, so you might find that you use them frequently. As you use them, however, your need to manage those rules will increase. For example, you'll often need to edit existing rules to update the conditions or change the formatting. Similarly, if you've applied two or more rules to the same range, you should know how to change the order that Excel uses to apply those rules. Finally, you also need to know how to delete existing rules that you no longer require.

To edit a conditional formatting rule

1. Click any cell in the range that has the conditional formatting applied.

2. On the **Conditional Formatting** menu, click **Manage Rules** to open the **Conditional Formatting Rules Manager** dialog box.

3. Click the rule you want to modify, then click **Edit Rule** to open the **Edit Formatting Rule** dialog box.

4. Make your changes to the rule type, rule conditions, or rule formatting, then click **OK**.

5. In the **Edit Formatting Rule** dialog box, click **OK**.

6. In the **Conditional Formatting Rules Manager** dialog box, click **OK**.

To change the order in which conditional formatting rules are applied

1. Click any cell in the range that has the conditional formatting applied.

2. Open the **Conditional Formatting Rules Manager** dialog box.

3. Click a rule, then click either the up arrow or the down arrow until the rule is in the position you prefer.

4. Repeat for the other rules you want to move, then click **OK**.

To delete a conditional formatting rule

1. Click any cell in the range that has the conditional formatting applied.

2. Open the **Conditional Formatting Rules Manager** dialog box.

3. Click the rule you want to remove, then click **Delete Rule**. Excel removes the rule.

4. Click **OK** to close the dialog box and return to the worksheet.

Tip If you want to delete multiple rules, a quicker method is to click any cell in the range that has the rules applied, click the Home tab, click Conditional Formatting in the Styles group, click Clear Rules, and then click Clear Rules From Selected Cells. If you want to delete every rule in the current worksheet, click Clear Rules From Entire Sheet.

Objective 2.3 practice tasks

The practice files for these tasks are located in the **MOSExcelExpert2019\ Objective2** practice file folder. The folder also contains result files that you can use to check your work.

➤ Open the **ExcelExpert_2-3a** workbook and do the following:

❑ On the **Student Grades** worksheet, for the cells in the Grade column, create and apply a custom conditional formatting rule that applies the 4 Traffic Lights Icon Set formatting based on the cell values. Display the black icon for values less than 50; the red icon for values from 50 to 59; the yellow icon for values from 60 to 79; and the green icon for values of 80 and greater.

❑ On the **Projects** worksheet, for the cells in the Percent column, create and apply a custom conditional formatting rule that applies the Data Bar format with a green gradient fill based on the cell values. Set the minimum value to 0 and the maximum value to 1.

❑ On the **Product Inventory** worksheet, for the Product Name column, create and apply a custom conditional formatting rule that applies an Orange fill color to cells that contain duplicate product names.

❑ Save the workbook.

❑ Open the **ExcelExpert_2-3a_results** workbook. Compare the two workbooks to check your work, and then close the open workbooks.

➤ Open the **ExcelExpert_2-3b** workbook and do the following:

❑ On the **Customers** worksheet, for the cell range A4:K94, create and apply a formula-based conditional formatting rule that evaluates cell B1 and applies a Yellow fill color to all the cells of each row that has the same country/region in column I. Test the conditional formatting rule by changing the country/region in cell B1.

❑ On the **Accounts Receivable Data** worksheet, for the cell range A4:G55, use the MOD function (refer to Excel Help if you are not familiar with this function) to create and apply a formula-based conditional formatting rule that applies a light gray fill color to every other row. Test the conditional formatting rule by deleting a row.

❑ On the **Products** worksheet, for the cell range A2:B78, create and apply a formula-based conditional formatting rule that applies a Red fill color and Bold font to the cells in the rows that contain the highest and lowest values in the Change In Units Sold column. Test the conditional formatting rule by entering new high and low values.

❑ Save the workbook.

❑ Open the **ExcelExpert_2-3b_results** workbook. Compare the two workbooks to check your work, and then close the open workbooks.

➤ Open the **ExcelExpert_2-3c** workbook, display the **Accounts Receivable Data** worksheet, and do the following for the cell range A4:G55:

❑ Create and apply a conditional formatting rule that applies a Light Green fill color to the cells in each row that has an Invoice Amount value greater than $2,000.

❑ Create and apply a conditional formatting rule that applies an Orange fill color to the cells in each row that has a Days Overdue value greater than or equal to 30.

❑ Edit the first rule so that it applies the formatting to rows that have an Invoice Amount value that is greater than $1,500.

❑ Change the order of the conditional formatting rules so that Excel applies the Invoice Amount rule before it applies the Days Overdue rule.

❑ Save the workbook.

❑ Open the **ExcelExpert_2-3c_results** workbook. Compare the two workbooks to check your work, and then close the open workbooks.

Objective group 3

Create advanced formulas and macros

The skills tested in this section of the Microsoft Office Specialist Expert exam for Microsoft Excel 2019 relate to the advanced use of formulas and data analysis. Specifically, the following objectives are associated with this set of skills:

3.1 Perform logical operations in formulas

3.2 Look up data by using functions

3.3 Apply advanced date and time functions

3.4 Perform data analysis

3.5 Troubleshoot formulas

3.6 Create and modify simple macros

Although Excel works well as a simple database, in most of your worksheets you'll want to do more than just store data. You'll also want to summarize your data, apply statistical methods, perform data analysis, automate tasks with macros, and perform other techniques that you can use to interrogate your worksheet data and draw conclusions that are relevant to your business requirements. This level of dynamism requires creating worksheet models that use formulas, functions, and macros.

This chapter guides you in studying methods for performing logical operations by using functions, nesting functions, performing statistical operations with functions, looking up data with functions, applying advanced date and time functions, analyzing and consolidating data, creating financial formulas, troubleshooting formula errors, and recording and editing simple macros.

To complete the practice tasks in this chapter, you need the practice files contained in the **MOSExcelExpert2019\Objective3** practice file folder. For more information, see "Download the practice files" in this book's introduction.

Objective 3.1: Perform logical operations in formulas

Insert functions into a formula

Formulas that combine operators with basic operands such as numeric and string values are the mainstay of any Excel spreadsheet. But to get the most benefit from the spreadsheet model, you need to expand your formula repertoire to include worksheet functions. Excel includes dozens of these functions, and they're essential to making your worksheet easier to work with and more powerful.

To insert a function into a formula

1. Enter your formula up to the point where you want to insert the function.

2. On the **Formulas** tab, in the **Function Library** group, click the category that contains the function you want to use. Then on the category menu, click the function.

3. In the **Function Arguments** dialog box, enter the function arguments, then click **OK**.

Perform logical operations by using the IF, AND, OR, and NOT functions

In the computer world, we *very* loosely define something as *intelligent* if it can perform tests on its environment and act in accordance with the results of those tests. However, a computer is a binary machine, so "acting in accordance with the results of a test" means that it can do only one of two things. Even with this limited range of options, you can still bring a great deal of intelligence to your worksheets. Your formulas will be able to test the values in cells and ranges and then return results based on those tests. This is all done with the logical functions in Excel, which are designed to create decision-making formulas.

The following table describes the most common logical functions.

Function	Description
IF(*logical_test*, *value_if_true*[, *value_if_false*])	Performs a logical test and returns a value based on the result
AND(*logical1*[, *logical2*,...])	Returns TRUE if all the arguments are true
OR(*logical1*[, *logical2*,...])	Returns TRUE if any argument is true
NOT(*logical*)	Reverses the logical value of the argument

You use the IF function to test some condition and then return a value based on the result of that test. This is the simplest version of the IF function:

   IF(logical_test, value_if_true)

The *logical_test* argument is a logical expression—that is, an expression that returns TRUE or FALSE (or their equivalent numeric values: 0 for FALSE and any other number for TRUE); the *value_if_true* argument is the value returned by the function if *logical_test* evaluates to TRUE.

A *logical expression* compares two or more numbers, text strings, cell contents, or function results. If the expression is true, it's given the logical value TRUE (which is equivalent to any nonzero value); if the expression is false, it's given the logical value FALSE (which is equivalent to zero). The following table summarizes the comparison operators you can use in logical expressions.

Operator	Name	Example	Result
=	Equal to	=10=5	FALSE
>	Greater than	=10>5	TRUE
<	Less than	=10<5	FALSE
>=	Greater than or equal to	="a">="b"	FALSE
<=	Less than or equal to	="a"<="b"	TRUE
<>	Not equal to	="a"<>"b"	TRUE

3

For example, suppose cell B2 contains a sales rep's total sales and you want to give the rep a 10-percent bonus if those sales are greater than $100,000. Here's a formula that does that:

=IF(B2 > 100000, B2 * 0.1)

The logical expression B1 > 100000 is used as the test. Assume that you add this formula to cell C2. If the logical expression proves to be true (that is, if the value in cell B2 is greater than 100,000), the function returns the value B2 * 0.1—that is, 10 percent of the number in B2—and that's the value you see in cell C2.

C2		:	×	✓	fx	=IF(B2 > 100000, B2 * 0.1)	
⊿	A		B	C		D	
1	Sales Rep		Total Sales	Bonus			
2	Nancy Freehafer		$135,936	$13,594			
3	Andrew Cencini		$92,544	FALSE			
4	Jan Kotas		$89,803	FALSE			
5	Mariya Sergienko		$112,658	$11,266			

A formula that uses the IF function to return a bonus for reps with sales greater than 100,000.

When the IF function test returns FALSE (that is, the value in column B is less than or equal to 100,000), the function returns FALSE as its result. That's not inherently bad, but the worksheet would look tidier (and, hence, be more useful) if the formula returned, for instance, the value 0 instead.

To do this, you need to use the full IF function syntax:

IF(logical_test, value_if_true, value_if_false)

The extra value_if_false argument is the value returned by the function if logical_test evaluates to FALSE. Here's a modification of the sales rep bonus calculation that takes a FALSE result into account:

=IF(B2 > 100000, B2 * 0.1, 0)

It's often necessary to perform an action if and only if two conditions are true. For example, you might want to pay a salesperson a bonus if and only if dollar sales exceed a certain amount and unit sales also exceed some minimum value. If the dollar sales, the unit sales, or both fall below the minimum, no bonus is paid. In Boolean logic, this is called an And condition because one expression and another must be true for a positive result.

In Excel, And conditions are handled by the AND logical function:

AND(logical1[, logical2,...])

Here, *logical1* and *logical2* arguments are the logical conditions to test. (The ellipsis means that you can enter as many conditions as you need.) The AND result is calculated as follows:

- If *all* the arguments return TRUE (or any nonzero number), AND returns TRUE.
- If one or more of the arguments return FALSE (or 0), AND returns FALSE.

Consider a formula that uses AND to check whether a sales rep's sales total is greater than $100,000 and units total is greater than 10,000. That formula could look like this:

=AND(B2 > 100000, C2 > 10000)

	A	B	C	D	E
				=AND(B2 > 100000, C2 > 10000)	
1	Sales Rep	Total Sales	Total Units	Bonus	
2	Nancy Freehafer	$135,936	$13,966	TRUE	
3	Andrew Cencini	$92,544	$6,533	FALSE	
4	Jan Kotas	$89,803	$10,031	FALSE	
5	Mariya Sergienko	$112,658	$10,549	TRUE	

A formula that uses the AND function to test whether the values in columns B and C exceed a specified minimum.

In many worksheet models, you need to take an action if one thing *or* another is true. For example, you might want to pay a salesperson a bonus if she exceeds the dollar sales budget *or* if she exceeds the unit sales budget. In Boolean logic, this is called an *Or* condition.

In Excel, Or conditions are handled by the OR function:

OR(logical1[, logical2,...])

Here, *logical1* and *logical2* arguments are the logical conditions to test. (The ellipsis means that you can enter as many conditions as you need.) The OR result is calculated as follows:

- If one or more of the arguments return TRUE (or any nonzero number), OR returns TRUE.
- If *all* of the arguments return FALSE (or 0), OR returns FALSE.

Consider the following formula, which uses OR to check whether a sales rep's sales total is greater than $100,000 or the units total is greater than 10,000:

=OR(B2 > 100000, C2 > 10000)

D2	▼	⋮	✕	✓	fx	=OR(B2 > 100000, C2 > 10000)	

	A	B	C	D	E
1	Sales Rep	Total Sales	Total Units	Bonus	
2	Nancy Freehafer	$135,936	13,966	TRUE	
3	Andrew Cencini	$92,544	6,533	FALSE	
4	Jan Kotas	$89,803	10,031	TRUE	
5	Mariya Sergienko	$112,658	10,549	TRUE	

A formula that uses the OR function to test whether the values in columns B or C exceed a specified minimum.

You sometimes need to return the opposite of a logical expression. For example, you might want to set up a worksheet that looks for the sales reps who did not make their sales quota and then flag those reps for further training. If you have a worksheet that already returns a TRUE or FALSE value based on whether a sales rep meets his quota, flagging whether the sales rep needs more training is a matter of returning the opposite value: if a sales rep meets her quota (TRUE), she doesn't need training (FALSE); if a sales rep doesn't meet his quota (FALSE), he does need training (TRUE).

In Excel, you return the opposite of a logical expression by using the NOT function:

NOT(logical)

Here, the *logical* argument is the logical condition to test. The NOT result is calculated as follows:

- If *logical* is TRUE (or any nonzero number), NOT returns FALSE.
- If *logical* is FALSE (or 0), NOT returns TRUE.

The following formula uses NOT in the Training Required? column (E) to return the opposite of the logical value in the Bonus column (D):

=NOT(D2)

	A	B	C	D	E
E2	▼ : × ✓ fx		=NOT(D2)		

	A	B	C	D	E
1	Sales Rep	Total Sales	Total Units	Bonus	Training Required?
2	Nancy Freehafer	$135,936	13,966	TRUE	FALSE
3	Andrew Cencini	$92,544	6,533	FALSE	TRUE
4	Jan Kotas	$89,803	10,031	TRUE	FALSE
5	Mariya Sergienko	$112,658	10,549	TRUE	FALSE

A formula that uses the NOT function to return the opposite of the logical values in column D.

To insert a logical function into a formula

→ On the **Formulas** tab, in the **Function Library** group, click **Logical**, click one of the functions in the list (such as IF, AND, OR, or NOT), and then enter the arguments, if any, as described earlier in this topic.

Perform logical operations by using nested functions

You can create sophisticated logical tests by combining one or more logical functions within a single expression. In particular, you can create complex expressions by including one logical function within another. This is called *nesting*, and the inner function is called a *nested function*.

A good time to use nested IF functions arises when you need to calculate a tiered payment or charge. That is, if a certain value is X, you want one result; if the value is Y, you want a second result; and if the value is Z, you want a third result. For example, suppose you want to calculate tiered bonuses for a sales team as follows:

- If the salesperson did not meet the sales target, no bonus is given.
- If the salesperson exceeded the sales target by less than 10 percent, a bonus of $1,000 is awarded.
- If the salesperson exceeded the sales target by 10 percent or more, a bonus of $5,000 is awarded.

Assuming that cell D2 contains the percentage that each salesperson's actual sales were above or below her target sales, here's a formula that handles these rules:

=IF(D2 < 0, "", IF(D2 < 0.1, 1000, 5000))

E2	▼	⋮	×	✓	f_x	=IF(D2 < 0, "", IF(D2 < 0.1, 1000, 5000))	

◢	A	B	C	D	E
1	Sales Rep	Total Sales	Sales Target	Pct of Target	Bonus
2	Nancy Freehafer	$135,936	$119,000	14.2%	$5,000
3	Andrew Cencini	$92,544	$86,000	7.6%	$1,000
4	Jan Kotas	$89,803	$95,000	-5.5%	
5	Mariya Sergienko	$112,658	$113,000	-0.3%	

A formula that uses nested IF functions to calculate a tiered bonus.

To nest logical functions

1. Insert the first logical function into your formula.

2. Enter the function arguments as described earlier in this topic, including the logical function you want to nest as one of the arguments.

Perform multiple logical tests with the IFS function

Nesting one IF function inside another is a handy way to perform a couple of logical tests, but the method quickly becomes unwieldly and difficult to decipher when the nesting goes three or more IF functions deep. If your data analysis requires more than two logical tests, you can make your worksheet model easier to read by turning to the IFS function:

> IFS(logical_test1, value_if_true1, [logical_test2, value_if_true2,...])

The IFS function consists of a series of logical tests, each of which has an associated return value. IFS performs each logical test in turn, and when it comes across the first logical test to return TRUE, it returns that logical test's associated value.

For example, here's how you'd use IFS to calculate the tiered bonuses that I introduced in the previous section:

> =IFS(D2 < 0, 0, D2 < 0.1, 1000, D2 >= 0.1, 5000)

E2	▼	⋮	×	✓	f_x	=IFS(D2 < 0, "", D2 < 0.1, 1000, D2 >= 0.1, 5000)	

◢	A	B	C	D	E	F
1	Sales Rep	Total Sales	Sales Target	Pct of Target	Bonus	
2	Nancy Freehafer	$135,936	$119,000	14.2%	$5,000	
3	Andrew Cencini	$92,544	$86,000	7.6%	$1,000	
4	Jan Kotas	$89,803	$95,000	-5.5%		
5	Mariya Sergienko	$112,658	$113,000	-0.3%		

A formula that uses the IFS function to calculate a tiered bonus.

Perform logical operations with criteria

You use the SUM, AVERAGE, and COUNT functions in Excel to return the total value, the mean value, and the number of values, respectively, within a specified range. These functions operate over the entire range, but it's often the case that you want the sum, the average, or the count of only those cells that meet some criterion. For example, you might want the total sales for just the customers from the United States. Even more sophisticated calculations are possible when you use multiple criteria. For example, you might want the total sales for those customers who are from the United States and who are based in Oregon.

These seem like they would require complex combinations of the IF, AND, and OR functions nested within the SUM, AVERAGE, or COUNT function. Fortunately, Excel includes three summary functions that you can use to specify multiple criteria without complex nesting: SUMIF, AVERAGEIF, and COUNTIF. In each case, the "IF" part of the function name implies that an IF function is built into each function, without being explicitly invoked.

The SUMIF function is similar to SUM, except that it sums only those cells in a range that meet a specified condition:

SUMIF(range, criteria[, sum_range])

Here, the *range* argument is the range of cells to use for the criteria; the *criteria* argument is the criteria, entered as text, that Excel applies to *range* to determine which cells to sum; *sum_range* is an optional argument that specifies the range from which the sum values are taken. Excel sums only those cells in *sum_range* that correspond to the cells in *range* and meet the *criteria*. If you omit *sum_range*, Excel uses *range* for the sum.

For the *criteria* argument, you generally use the following format:

"*operator value*"

Here, you replace *operator* with a comparison operator such as equal to (=) or greater than (>), and you replace *value* with a comparison value. Many Excel functions also support text-only *criteria* arguments that optionally use one or more wildcard characters: * to match any number of characters and ? to match any single character.

For example, the following formula sums only those values in the range B3:B21 that are greater than 100000:

=SUMIF(B3:B21, "> 100000")

E1	▼	:	×	✓	*fx*	=SUMIF(B3:B21, ">100000")	

◢	A	B	C	D	E
1					$1,553,835
2	Sales Rep	Total Sales	Total Units	Return Rate	Bonus
3	Nancy Freehafer	$135,936	13,966	11%	$0
4	Andrew Cencini	$101,234	10,023	9%	$10,123
5	Jan Kotas	$89,803	10,031	8%	$0
6	Mariya Sergienko	$112,658	10,549	7%	$11,266
7	Steven Thorpe	$92,021	8,818	10%	$0
8	Michael Neipper	$99,021	5,545	9%	$0
9	Robert Zare	$121,454	14,685	15%	$0
10	Laura Giussani	$117,387	8,032	8%	$0
11	Anne Hellung-Larsen	$136,349	8,955	11%	$0
12	Maria Anders	$125,386	14,694	9%	$12,539
13	Thomas Hardy	$120,297	12,865	8%	$12,030
14	Hanna Moos	$137,914	7,293	10%	$0
15	Victoria Ashworth	$98,923	10,179	11%	$0
16	Patricio Simpson	$115,869	9,604	10%	$0
17	Elizabeth Brown	$108,428	6,059	14%	$0
18	Ann Devon	$93,914	13,082	15%	$0
19	Paolo Accorti	$102,601	7,846	12%	$0
20	Carlos Hernández	$118,322	7,429	10%	$0
21	Yoshi Latimer	$91,553	5,849	13%	$0

A formula that uses the SUMIF function.

The COUNTIF function counts the number of cells in a range that meet a single condition:

COUNTIF(range, criteria)

Here, replace *range* with the range of cells to use for the count; replace *criteria* with the criteria, entered as text, that Excel applies to *range* to determine which cells to count.

For example, you can use the following formula to count the number of cells in the range D3:D21 that are greater than or equal to 0.1:

=COUNTIF(D3:D21, ">= 0.1")

| E1 | ▼ | : | × | ✓ | *fx* | =COUNTIF(D3:D21, ">= 0.1") |

	A	B	C	D	E
1					12
2	Sales Rep	Total Sales	Total Units	Return Rate	Bonus
3	Nancy Freehafer	$135,936	13,966	11%	$0
4	Andrew Cencini	$101,234	10,023	9%	$10,123
5	Jan Kotas	$89,803	10,031	8%	$0
6	Mariya Sergienko	$112,658	10,549	7%	$11,266
7	Steven Thorpe	$92,021	8,818	10%	$0
8	Michael Neipper	$99,021	5,545	9%	$0
9	Robert Zare	$121,454	14,685	15%	$0
10	Laura Giussani	$117,387	8,032	8%	$0
11	Anne Hellung-Larsen	$136,349	8,955	11%	$0
12	Maria Anders	$125,386	14,694	9%	$12,539
13	Thomas Hardy	$120,297	12,865	8%	$12,030
14	Hanna Moos	$137,914	7,293	10%	$0
15	Victoria Ashworth	$98,923	10,179	11%	$0
16	Patricio Simpson	$115,869	9,604	10%	$0
17	Elizabeth Brown	$108,428	6,059	14%	$0
18	Ann Devon	$93,914	13,082	15%	$0
19	Paolo Accorti	$102,601	7,846	12%	$0
20	Carlos Hernández	$118,322	7,429	10%	$0
21	Yoshi Latimer	$91,553	5,849	13%	$0

A formula that uses the COUNTIF function.

The AVERAGEIF function calculates the average of a range set for those items that meet a specified condition:

AVERAGEIF(range, criteria[, average_range])

Here, the *range* argument is the range of cells to use for the criteria; the *criteria* argument is the criteria, entered as text, that Excel applies to *range* to determine which cells to average; *average_range* is an optional argument that specifies the range from which the average values are taken. Excel averages only those cells in *average_range* that correspond to the cells in *range* and meet the *criteria*. If you omit *average_range*, Excel uses *range* for the average.

For example, the following formula averages only those values in the range D3:D21 that correspond to those values in the range C3:C21 that are greater than or equal to 10,000:

=AVERAGEIF(C2:C21, "> 10000", D3:21)

3

| E1 | ▼ | : | × | ✓ | fx | =AVERAGEIF(C3:C21, ">= 10000", D3:D21) |

◢	A	B	C	D	E
1					10.3%
2	Sales Rep	Total Sales	Total Units	Return Rate	Bonus
3	Nancy Freehafer	$135,936	13,966	11%	$0
4	Andrew Cencini	$101,234	10,023	9%	$10,123
5	Jan Kotas	$89,803	10,031	8%	$0
6	Mariya Sergienko	$112,658	10,549	7%	$11,266
7	Steven Thorpe	$92,021	8,818	10%	$0
8	Michael Neipper	$99,021	5,545	9%	$0
9	Robert Zare	$121,454	14,685	15%	$0
10	Laura Giussani	$117,387	8,032	8%	$0
11	Anne Hellung-Larsen	$136,349	8,955	11%	$0
12	Maria Anders	$125,386	14,694	9%	$12,539
13	Thomas Hardy	$120,297	12,865	8%	$12,030
14	Hanna Moos	$137,914	7,293	10%	$0
15	Victoria Ashworth	$98,923	10,179	11%	$0
16	Patricio Simpson	$115,869	9,604	10%	$0
17	Elizabeth Brown	$108,428	6,059	14%	$0
18	Ann Devon	$93,914	13,082	15%	$0
19	Paolo Accorti	$102,601	7,846	12%	$0
20	Carlos Hernández	$118,322	7,429	10%	$0
21	Yoshi Latimer	$91,553	5,849	13%	$0

A formula that uses the AVERAGEIF function.

To insert a SUMIF function into a formula

→ On the **Formulas** tab, in the **Function Library** group, click **Math & Trig**, click **SUMIF**, and then enter the arguments, as described earlier in this topic.

To insert an AVERAGEIF or COUNTIF function into a formula

→ On the **Formulas** tab, in the **Function Library** group, click **More Functions**, click **Statistical**, click **AVERAGEIF** or **COUNTIF**, and then enter the arguments, as described earlier in this topic.

Perform logical operations with multiple ranges and criteria

The SUMIF, COUNTIF, and AVERAGEIF functions that I describe in the previous section replace simple nested functions with a single condition. However, there are many situations in which your logical formula requires multiple criteria applied to multiple ranges. To handle these situations, Excel includes five summary functions that you can use to specify multiple criteria: SUMIFS, AVERAGEIFS, COUNTIFS, MAXIFS, and MINIFS. In each case, the "IFS" part of the function name implies that multiple IF functions are built into each function, without being explicitly invoked.

The SUMIFS function sums cells in a range that correspond to those cells in one or more ranges that meet one or more criteria:

SUMIFS(sum_range, range1, criteria1[, range2, criteria2, ...])

The *sum_range* argument is the range from which the sum values are taken. Excel sums only those cells in *sum_range* that correspond to the cells that meet the criteria. The *range1* argument is the first range of cells to use for the sum criteria, and the *criteria1* argument is the first criterion, entered as text, that determines which cells to sum. Excel applies the criterion to *range1*. You can enter up to 127 range/criterion pairs.

Consider the following SUMIFS function example. In this model, SUMIFS is used to calculate the total bonuses (range E3:E21) just for those sales reps whose total units (range C3:C21) are greater than 10,000:

=SUMIFS(E3:E21, C3:C21, " > 10000")

E1	▼ : × ✓ *fx*	=SUMIFS(E3:E21, C3:C21, ">10000")			
	A	B	C	D	E
1					$45,958
2	Sales Rep	Total Sales	Total Units	Return Rate	Bonus
3	Nancy Freehafer	$135,936	13,966	11%	$0
4	Andrew Cencini	$101,234	10,023	9%	$10,123
5	Jan Kotas	$89,803	10,031	8%	$0
6	Mariya Sergienko	$112,658	10,549	7%	$11,266
7	Steven Thorpe	$92,021	8,818	10%	$0
8	Michael Neipper	$99,021	5,545	9%	$0
9	Robert Zare	$121,454	14,685	15%	$0
10	Laura Giussani	$117,387	8,032	8%	$11,739
11	Anne Hellung-Larsen	$136,349	8,955	11%	$0
12	Maria Anders	$125,386	14,694	9%	$12,539
13	Thomas Hardy	$120,297	12,865	8%	$12,030
14	Hanna Moos	$137,914	7,293	10%	$0
15	Victoria Ashworth	$98,923	10,179	11%	$0
16	Patricio Simpson	$115,869	9,604	7%	$11,587
17	Elizabeth Brown	$108,428	6,059	14%	$0
18	Ann Devon	$93,914	13,082	15%	$0
19	Paolo Accorti	$102,601	7,846	8%	$10,260
20	Carlos Hernández	$118,322	7,429	10%	$0
21	Yoshi Latimer	$91,553	5,849	13%	$0

A formula that uses SUMIFS to apply a criterion to a sum.

The AVERAGEIFS function averages cells in a range that correspond to those cells in one or more ranges that meet one or more criteria:

AVERAGEIFS(average_range, range1, criteria1[, range2, criteria2, ...])

The *average_range* argument is the range from which the average values are taken. Excel averages only those cells in *average_range* that correspond to the cells that meet the criteria. The *range1* argument is the first range of cells to use for the average criteria, and the *criteria1* argument is the first criterion, entered as text, that determines which cells to average. Excel applies the criterion to *range1*. You can enter up to 127 range/criterion pairs.

In the following example, AVERAGEIFS is used to calculate the average sales (range B3:B21) just for those sales reps whose total units (C3:C21) are greater than 10,000 and whose return rate (D3:D21) is less than 10 percent:

   =AVERAGEIFS(B3:B21, C3:C21, " > 10000", D3:D21, " < 0.1")

E1		▾	⋮	✕	✓	*fx*	=AVERAGEIFS(B3:B21, C3:C21, ">10000", D3:D21, "<0.1")

	A	B	C	D	E	F
1					$109,876	
2	Sales Rep	Total Sales	Total Units	Return Rate	Bonus	
3	Nancy Freehafer	$135,936	13,966	11%	$0	
4	Andrew Cencini	$101,234	10,023	9%	$10,123	
5	Jan Kotas	$89,803	10,031	8%	$0	
6	Mariya Sergienko	$112,658	10,549	7%	$11,266	
7	Steven Thorpe	$92,021	8,818	10%	$0	
8	Michael Neipper	$99,021	5,545	9%	$0	
9	Robert Zare	$121,454	14,685	15%	$0	
10	Laura Giussani	$117,387	8,032	8%	$11,739	
11	Anne Hellung-Larsen	$136,349	8,955	11%	$0	
12	Maria Anders	$125,386	14,694	9%	$12,539	
13	Thomas Hardy	$120,297	12,865	8%	$12,030	
14	Hanna Moos	$137,914	7,293	10%	$0	
15	Victoria Ashworth	$98,923	10,179	11%	$0	
16	Patricio Simpson	$115,869	9,604	7%	$11,587	
17	Elizabeth Brown	$108,428	6,059	14%	$0	
18	Ann Devon	$93,914	13,082	15%	$0	
19	Paolo Accorti	$102,601	7,846	8%	$10,260	
20	Carlos Hernández	$118,322	7,429	10%	$0	
21	Yoshi Latimer	$91,553	5,849	13%	$0	

A formula that uses AVERAGEIFS to apply multiple criteria to an average.

The COUNTIFS function counts the number of cells in one or more ranges that meet one or more criteria:

   COUNTIFS(range1, criteria1[, range2, criteria2, ...])

The *range1* argument is the first range of cells to use for the count, and the *criteria1* argument is the first criterion, entered as text, that determines which cells to count. Excel applies the criterion to *range1*. You can enter up to 127 range/criterion pairs.

In the following example, COUNTIFS is used to count the number of sales reps whose dollar sales (range B3:B21) are greater than $100,000, whose unit sales (C3:C21) are greater than 10,000, and whose return rate (D3:D21) is less than 10 percent:

=COUNTIFS(B3:B21, " > 100000", C3:C21, " > 10000", D3:D21, " < 0.1")

	A	B	C	D	E	F	G
E1		fx		=COUNTIFS(B3:B21, ">100000", C3:C21, ">10000", D3:D21, "<0.1")			
1					4		
2	Sales Rep	Total Sales	Total Units	Return Rate	Bonus		
3	Nancy Freehafer	$135,936	13,966	11%	$0		
4	Andrew Cencini	$101,234	10,023	9%	$10,123		
5	Jan Kotas	$89,803	10,031	8%	$0		
6	Mariya Sergienko	$112,658	10,549	7%	$11,266		
7	Steven Thorpe	$92,021	8,818	10%	$0		
8	Michael Neipper	$99,021	5,545	9%	$0		
9	Robert Zare	$121,454	14,685	15%	$0		
10	Laura Giussani	$117,387	8,032	8%	$11,739		
11	Anne Hellung-Larsen	$136,349	8,955	11%	$0		
12	Maria Anders	$125,386	14,694	9%	$12,539		
13	Thomas Hardy	$120,297	12,865	8%	$12,030		
14	Hanna Moos	$137,914	7,293	10%	$0		
15	Victoria Ashworth	$98,923	10,179	11%	$0		
16	Patricio Simpson	$115,869	9,604	7%	$11,587		
17	Elizabeth Brown	$108,428	6,059	14%	$0		
18	Ann Devon	$93,914	13,082	15%	$0		
19	Paolo Accorti	$102,601	7,846	8%	$10,260		
20	Carlos Hernández	$118,322	7,429	10%	$0		
21	Yoshi Latimer	$91,553	5,849	13%	$0		

A formula that uses COUNTIFS to apply multiple criteria to a count.

The MAXIFS function returns the maximum value from a range that corresponds to those cells in one or more ranges that meet one or more criteria:

MAXIFS(max_range, range1, criteria1[, range2, criteria2, ...])

The *max_range* argument is the range from which the maximum value is taken. Excel looks for the maximum only in those cells in *max_range* that correspond to the cells that meet the criteria. The *range1* argument is the first range of cells to use for the maximum criteria, and the *criteria1* argument is the first criterion, entered as text, that determines which cells to include. Excel applies the criterion to *range1*. You can enter up to 127 range/criterion pairs.

Consider the following MAXIFS function example. In this model, MAXIFS is used to calculate the maximum return rate (from the range D3:D21) just for those sales reps whose total sales (range B3:B21) are greater than $100,000 and whose total units (range C3:C21) are greater than 10,000:

=MAXIFS(D3:D21, B3:B21, "> 100000", C3:C21, " > 10000")

E1	▾ :	× ✓	f_x	=MAXIFS(D3:D21, B3:B21, ">100000", C3:C21, ">10000")	
⊿	A	B	C	D	E	F
1					15%	
2	Sales Rep	Total Sales	Total Units	Return Rate	Bonus	
3	Nancy Freehafer	$135,936	13,966	11%	$0	
4	Andrew Cencini	$101,234	10,023	9%	$10,123	
5	Jan Kotas	$89,803	10,031	8%	$0	
6	Mariya Sergienko	$112,658	10,549	7%	$11,266	
7	Steven Thorpe	$92,021	8,818	10%	$0	
8	Michael Neipper	$99,021	5,545	9%	$0	
9	Robert Zare	$121,454	14,685	15%	$0	
10	Laura Giussani	$117,387	8,032	8%	$11,739	
11	Anne Hellung-Larsen	$136,349	8,955	11%	$0	
12	Maria Anders	$125,386	14,694	9%	$12,539	
13	Thomas Hardy	$120,297	12,865	8%	$12,030	
14	Hanna Moos	$137,914	7,293	10%	$0	
15	Victoria Ashworth	$98,923	10,179	11%	$0	
16	Patricio Simpson	$115,869	9,604	7%	$11,587	
17	Elizabeth Brown	$108,428	6,059	14%	$0	
18	Ann Devon	$93,914	13,082	15%	$0	
19	Paolo Accorti	$102,601	7,846	8%	$10,260	
20	Carlos Hernández	$118,322	7,429	10%	$0	
21	Yoshi Latimer	$91,553	5,849	13%	$0	

A formula that uses MAXIFS to apply a criterion to a maximum.

The MINIFS function returns the minimum value from a range that corresponds to those cells in one or more ranges that meet one or more criteria:

MINIFS(min_range, range1, criteria1[, range2, criteria2, ...])

The *min_range* argument is the range from which the minimum value is taken. Excel looks for the minimum only in those cells in *min_range* that correspond to the cells that meet the criteria. The *range1* argument is the first range of cells to use for the minimum criteria, and the *criteria1* argument is the first criterion, entered as text, that determines which cells to include. Excel applies the criterion to *range1*. You can enter up to 127 range/criterion pairs.

Consider the following MINIFS function example. In this model, MINIFS is used to calculate the minimum units (from the range C3:C21) just for those sales reps whose total sales (range B3:B21) are greater than $100,000 and whose return rate (range D3:D21) are less than 10 percent:

=MINIFS(C3:C21, B3:B21, " > 100000", D3:D21, "< 0.1")

	A	B	C	D	E	F
E1		▾ : ✕ ✓ *fx*		=MINIFS(C3:C21, B3:B21, ">100000", D3:D21, "<0.1")		
1					7,846	
2	Sales Rep	Total Sales	Total Units	Return Rate	Bonus	
3	Nancy Freehafer	$135,936	13,966	11%	$0	
4	Andrew Cencini	$101,234	10,023	9%	$10,123	
5	Jan Kotas	$89,803	10,031	8%	$0	
6	Mariya Sergienko	$112,658	10,549	7%	$11,266	
7	Steven Thorpe	$92,021	8,818	10%	$0	
8	Michael Neipper	$99,021	5,545	9%	$0	
9	Robert Zare	$121,454	14,685	15%	$0	
10	Laura Giussani	$117,387	8,032	8%	$11,739	
11	Anne Hellung-Larsen	$136,349	8,955	11%	$0	
12	Maria Anders	$125,386	14,694	9%	$12,539	
13	Thomas Hardy	$120,297	12,865	8%	$12,030	
14	Hanna Moos	$137,914	7,293	10%	$0	
15	Victoria Ashworth	$98,923	10,179	11%	$0	
16	Patricio Simpson	$115,869	9,604	7%	$11,587	
17	Elizabeth Brown	$108,428	6,059	14%	$0	
18	Ann Devon	$93,914	13,082	15%	$0	
19	Paolo Accorti	$102,601	7,846	8%	$10,260	
20	Carlos Hernández	$118,322	7,429	10%	$0	
21	Yoshi Latimer	$91,553	5,849	13%	$0	

A formula that uses MINIFS to apply a criterion to a minimum.

To insert a SUMIFS function into a formula

→ On the **Formulas** tab, in the **Function Library** group, click **Math & Trig**, click **SUMIFS**, and then enter the arguments, as described earlier in this topic.

To insert an AVERAGEIFS, COUNTIFS, MAXIFS, or MINIFS function into a formula

→ On the **Formulas** tab, in the **Function Library** group, click **More Functions**, click **Statistical**, click the function—**AVERAGEIFS**, **COUNTIFS**, **MAXIFS**, or **MINIFS**,—and then enter the arguments, as described earlier in this topic.

Apply multiple exact-match criteria to a value

The IFS function that I describe earlier in this objective enables you to create sophisticated criteria using comparison operators such as less than (<) and greater than or equal to (>=). However, it's often the case that your comparisons require only exact matches using the equal operator (=). In such cases, it is often easier to use the SWITCH function rather than IFS.

The SWITCH function evaluates an expression, compares the result to a list of values that you supply, and then returns a value that corresponds to the first match that Excel finds:

SWITCH(expression, value_to_match1, value_to_return1[, value_to_match2, value_to_return2, ..., value_if_no_match])

SWITCH first evaluates *expression*. SWITCH then compares that result to each *value_to_match* argument; when SWITCH comes across the first match, it returns the corresponding *value_to_return*; if no match is found, SWITCH returns the *value_if_no_match* argument. You can enter up to 126 match/return value pairs.

For example, given a date, the MONTH function returns a number between 1 (for January) and 12 (for December). For a date in cell A2, you can use the following SWITCH formula to return the date's month name based on the results of the MONTH(A2) expression:

==SWITCH(MONTH(A2), 1, "January", 2, "February", 3, "March", 4, "April", 5, "May", 6, "June", 7, "July", 8, "August", 9, "September", 10, "October", 11, "November", 12, "December", "No matching month!")

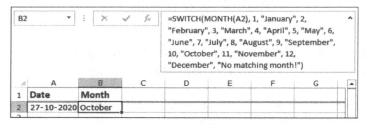

A formula that uses SWITCH to apply multiple exact-match criteria to an expression.

To insert a SWITCH function into a formula

→ On the **Formulas** tab, in the **Function Library** group, click **Logical**, click **SWITCH**, and then enter the arguments, as described earlier in this topic.

Objective 3.1 practice tasks

The practice file for these tasks is located in the **MOSExcelExpert2019 \Objective3** practice file folder. The folder also contains a result file that you can use to check your work.

➤ Open the **ExcelExpert_3-1** workbook and do the following:

❑ On the **Gross Margin** worksheet, add formulas to the Gross Margin field (H7:H14) that calculate the gross margin by subtracting Cost from Retail and then dividing by Cost. To avoid #DIV/0! (division by 0) errors, wrap the calculation inside an IF function that returns the gross margin if Cost is not 0, or the message **Cost is 0!** otherwise.

❑ On the **Inventory** worksheet, populate the Reorder Now? column with formulas that use nested logical functions to determine whether a product should be reordered based on two conditions: The Qty Available is less than or equal to the Reorder Level, and the Qty on Order is 0. Each function should return "Yes" if a reorder is required, and nothing otherwise.

❑ On the **Inventory** worksheet, create a formula in cell K1 that uses the SUMIF function to sum the Value range for products with a non-zero Qty Available value.

❑ On the **Inventory** worksheet, create a formula in cell K2 that uses the SUMIFS function to sum the Qty On Hand range for products with a Product Name value that includes *Soup* and a Qty On Hold value of zero. (Hint: To match cells that include some text, surround that text with the * wildcard character.)

❑ On the **Parts** worksheet, create a formula in cell F16 that uses the AVERAGEIF function to calculate the average of the Gross Margin values for the parts that cost less than $10. Use structured table references in your formula (the table name is *Parts*).

□ On the **Customers** worksheet, create a formula in cell L1 that uses the COUNTIFS function to return the number of customers with the Country value *United States* and the Region value *OR* (the abbreviation for *Oregon*, not the OR function).

□ On the **Orders** worksheet, populate the Weekday column with formulas that use the SWITCH function to return the weekday of each date in the Date column.

➤ Save the workbook.

➤ Open the **ExcelExpert_3-1_results** workbook. Compare the two workbooks to check your work, and then close the open workbooks.

Objective 3.2: Look up data by using functions

The table—more properly referred to as a *lookup table*—is the key to performing lookup operations in Excel. The most straightforward lookup table structure is one that consists of two columns (or two rows):

- **Lookup column** This column contains the values that you look up. For example, if you were constructing a lookup table for a dictionary, this column would contain the words.

- **Data column** This column contains the data associated with each lookup value. In the dictionary example, this column would contain the definitions.

In most lookup operations, you supply a value that the function locates in the designated lookup column. It then retrieves the corresponding value in the data column.

The lookup table theme has many variations. The lookup table can be one of these:

- **A single column or row** In this case, the lookup operation consists of finding the *n*th value in the column.

- **A range with multiple data columns** For instance, in the dictionary example, you might have a second column for each word's part of speech (noun or verb, for example), and perhaps a third column for its pronunciation. In this case, the lookup operation must also specify which of the data columns contains the value required.

- **An array** In this case, the table doesn't exist on a worksheet but is either an array of literal values or the result of a function that returns an array. The lookup operation finds a particular position within the array and returns the data value at that position.

The VLOOKUP function works by looking in the first column of a table for the value you specify. (The *V* in VLOOKUP stands for *vertical*.) It then looks across to the column that you specify and returns whatever value it finds there.

Here's the full syntax for VLOOKUP:

VLOOKUP(lookup_value, table_array, col_index_num[, range_lookup])

The following table describes the VLOOKUP function arguments.

Argument	Description
lookup_value	The value you want to find in the first column of *table_array*. You can enter a number, string, or reference.
table_array	The cell range or named table to use for the lookup.
col_index_num	The column number in *table_array* that contains the data you want the formula to return (the first column—that is, the lookup column—is 1, the second column is 2, and so on).
range_lookup	A Boolean value that determines how Excel searches for *lookup_value* in the first column. If FALSE, VLOOKUP returns the first exact match for *lookup_value*. If TRUE (the default), if no exact match is found, the function returns the largest value that is less than *lookup_value*.

Here are some notes to keep in mind when you work with VLOOKUP:

- If *range_lookup* is TRUE or omitted, you must sort the values in the first column in ascending order.

- If the first column of the table is text, you can use the standard wildcard characters in the *lookup_value* argument (use ? to substitute for individual characters; use * to substitute for multiple characters).

- If *lookup_value* is less than any value in the lookup column, VLOOKUP returns the #N/A error value.

- If VLOOKUP doesn't find a match in the lookup column, it returns #N/A.

- If *col_index_num* is less than 1, VLOOKUP returns #VALUE!; if *col_index_num* is greater than the number of columns in *table_array*, VLOOKUP returns #REF!.

As an example, assume that a worksheet uses a VLOOKUP formula in cell B4 to take the account number entered in cell B2, locate the exact match in the first column of the range D3:E15, and return the account name from the second column in that range. The formula would look like this:

=VLOOKUP(B2, D3:E15, 2, FALSE)

The HLOOKUP function is similar to VLOOKUP except that it searches for the lookup value in the first row of a table. (The *H* in HLOOKUP stands for *horizontal*.) If successful, this function then looks down to the specified row and returns the value it finds there. Here's the syntax for HLOOKUP:

HLOOKUP(lookup_value, table_array, row_index_num[, range_lookup])

A formula that uses VLOOKUP to look up an account name given an account number.

The following table describes the HLOOKUP function arguments.

Argument	Description
lookup_value	The value you want to find in the first row of *table_array*. You can enter a number, string, or reference.
table_array	The cell range or named table to use for the lookup.
row_index_num	The row number in the table that contains the data you want the formula to return (the first row—that is, the lookup row—is 1, the second row is 2, and so on).
range_lookup	A Boolean value that determines how Excel searches for *lookup_value* in the first row. If FALSE, HLOOKUP returns the first exact match for *lookup_value*. If TRUE (the default), if no exact match is found, the function returns the largest value that is less than *lookup_value*.

As an example, assume that a worksheet uses an HLOOKUP formula in cell C10 to take the month entered in cell C9, locate the exact match in the first row of the range C1:N7, and return the value from the TOTAL row (the seventh row in that range).

The formula would look like this:

=HLOOKUP(C9, C1:N7, 7, FALSE)

	A	B	C	D	E	F	G	H	I	J	K
C10			fx	=HLOOKUP(C9, C1:N7, 7, FALSE)							
1		**EXPENSES**	**January**	**February**	**March**	**April**	**May**	**June**	**July**	**August**	**September**
2		**Advertising**	$4,600	$4,200	$5,200	$4,600	$4,200	$5,200	$4,600	$4,200	$5,200
3		**Rent**	$2,100	$2,100	$2,100	$2,100	$2,100	$2,100	$2,100	$2,100	$2,100
4		**Supplies**	$1,300	$1,200	$1,400	$1,300	$1,200	$1,400	$1,300	$1,200	$1,400
5		**Salaries**	$16,000	$16,000	$16,500	$16,000	$16,000	$16,500	$16,000	$16,000	$16,500
6		**Utilities**	$500	$600	$600	$500	$600	$600	$500	$600	$600
7		**TOTAL**	$24,500	$24,100	$25,800	$24,500	$24,100	$25,800	$24,500	$24,100	$25,800
8											
9		**Month**	May								
10		**Total**	$24,100								
11											

A formula that uses HLOOKUP to look up a monthly expenses total given a month name.

The basic lookup procedure—finding a value in a column or row and then returning an offset value—will satisfy most of your needs. However, a few operations require a more sophisticated approach that makes use of two more lookup functions: MATCH and INDEX.

The MATCH function looks through a row or column of cells for a value. If MATCH finds that value, it returns the relative position of the match in the row or column. Here's the syntax:

MATCH(lookup_value, lookup_array[, match_type])

The following table describes the MATCH function arguments.

Argument	Description
lookup_value	The value you want to find. You can use a number, string, reference, or logical value.
lookup_array	The row or column of cells you want to use for the lookup.
match_type	How you want Excel to match the *lookup_value* with the entries in the *lookup_array*. You have three choices: • 0 finds the first value that exactly matches *lookup_value*. The *lookup_array* can be in any order. • 1 finds the largest value that is less than or equal to *lookup_value* (this is the default value). The *lookup_array* must be in ascending order. • −1 finds the smallest value that is greater than or equal to *lookup_value*. The *lookup_array* must be in descending order.

Tip You can use wildcard characters within the *lookup_value* argument (provided that *match_type* is 0 and *lookup_value* is text). You can use the question mark (?) for single characters and the asterisk (*) for multiple characters.

Normally, you don't use the MATCH function by itself; you combine it with the INDEX function. INDEX returns the value of a cell at the intersection of a row and column inside a reference. Here's the syntax for INDEX:

INDEX(reference, row_num[, column_num][, area_num])

The following table describes the INDEX function arguments.

Argument	Description
reference	A reference to one or more cell ranges.
row_num	The number of the row in *reference* from which to return a value.
column_num	The number of the column in *reference* from which to return a value. You can omit *column_num* if *reference* is a single column.
area_num	If you entered more than one range for *reference*, *area_num* is the range you want to use. The first range you entered is 1 (this is the default), the second is 2, and so on.

The idea is that you use MATCH to get *row_num* and/or *column_num* (depending on how your table is laid out) and then use INDEX to return the value you need.

For example, consider a worksheet that uses a MATCH and INDEX formula in cell B2 to take the part number entered in cell B1, locate the match in the range H6:H13, and return the quantity from the range C6:C13.

The formula would look like this:

=INDEX(C6:C13, MATCH(B1, H6:H13, 0))

| B2 | ▾ | : | ✕ | ✓ | fx | =INDEX(C6:C13, MATCH(B1, H6:H13, 0)) |

◢	A	B	C	D	E	F	G	H
1	**Part Number**	D-178						
2	**Quantity**	57						
3								
4	**Parts Database**							
5	**Division**	**Description**	**Quantity**	**Cost**	**Total Cost**	**Retail**	**Gross Margin**	**Number**
6	4	Gangley Pliers	57	$ 10.47	$ 596.79	$ 17.95	71.4%	D-178
7	3	HCAB Washer	856	$ 0.12	$ 102.72	$ 0.25	108.3%	A-201
8	3	Finley Sprocket	357	$ 1.57	$ 560.49	$ 2.95	87.9%	C-098
9	2	6" Sonotube	86	$ 15.24	$ 1,310.64	$ 19.95	30.9%	B-111
10	4	Langstrom 7" Wrench	75	$ 18.69	$ 1,401.75	$ 27.95	49.5%	D-017
11	3	Thompson Socket	298	$ 3.11	$ 926.78	$ 5.95	91.3%	C-321
12	1	S-Joint	155	$ 6.85	$ 1,061.75	$ 9.95	45.3%	A-182
13	2	LAMF Valve	482	$ 4.01	$ 1,932.82	$ 6.95	73.3%	B-047

A formula that uses MATCH and INDEX to look up a quantity given a part number.

To insert a VLOOKUP or an HLOOKUP function into a formula

→ On the **Formulas** tab, in the **Function Library** group, click **Lookup & Reference**, click **VLOOKUP** or **HLOOKUP**, and then enter the arguments, as described earlier in this topic.

To insert the MATCH and INDEX functions into a formula

1. On the **Formulas** tab, in the **Function Library** group, click **Lookup & Reference**, and then click **INDEX**.

2. In the **Select Arguments** dialog box, click **reference,row_num,column_num,area_num**, then click **OK**.

3. In the **Function Arguments** dialog box, enter the INDEX function arguments, including a MATCH function for the *row_num* and/or *column_num* arguments, and then click **OK**.

Objective 3.2 practice tasks

The practice file for these tasks is located in the **MOSExcelExpert2019 \Objective3** practice file folder. The folder also contains a result file that you can use to check your work.

➤ Open the **ExcelExpert_3-2** workbook and do the following:

☐ On the **Tax Rate** worksheet, add a formula to cell B18 that uses the tax table in the range C9:F15 to look up the income entered in cell B17 and return the applicable tax rate.

☐ On the **Discount Schedule** worksheet, create formulas in the range D3:D10 that use the discount schedule in the range B13:G14 to look up the units ordered from the range A3:A10 and return the applicable discount percentage.

☐ On the **Parts** worksheet, add a formula to cell B3 that uses the range A7:H14 to look up the part number entered in cell B1 and then return the corresponding value from the field entered in cell B2.

➤ Save the workbook.

➤ Open the **ExcelExpert_3-2_results** workbook. Compare the two workbooks to check your work, and then close the open workbooks.

Objective 3.3: Apply advanced date and time functions

You can use the date and time functions in Excel to convert dates and times to serial numbers and perform operations on those numbers. This capability is useful for such things as accounts receivable aging, project scheduling, time-management applications, and much more.

Excel uses serial numbers to represent specific dates and times. To get a date serial number, Excel uses December 31, 1899, as an arbitrary starting point and then counts the number of days that have passed since then. For example, the date serial number for January 1, 1900, is 1; for January 2, 1900, it's 2; for June 6, 1944 its 16229, and so on.

To get a time serial number, Excel expresses time as a decimal fraction of the 24-hour day to return a number between 0 and 1. The starting point, midnight, is given the value 0, so noon—halfway through the day—has a serial number of 0.5, and 5:00 PM has a serial number of 0.70833. You can combine the two types of serial numbers. For example, 44196.5 represents noon on December 31, 2019.

The advantage of using serial numbers in this way is that it makes calculations involving dates and times very easy. A date or time is really just a number, so any mathematical operation you can perform on a number can also be performed on a date. This is invaluable for worksheets that track delivery times, monitor accounts receivable or accounts payable aging, and calculate invoice discount dates, for example.

Reference the date and time by using the NOW and TODAY functions

If you need a date for an expression operand or a function argument, you can enter it by hand if you have a specific date in mind. Much of the time, however, you need more flexibility, such as always entering the current date or time.

When you need to use the current date in a formula, a function, or an expression, use the TODAY function, which doesn't take any arguments. This function returns the serial number of the current date, with midnight as the assumed time. For example, on November 1, 2019, the TODAY function returns the serial number 43770.0.

The TODAY function returns the current date serial number in the date format of the cell.

Note that TODAY is a dynamic function that doesn't always return the same value. Each time you edit the formula, enter another formula, recalculate the worksheet, or reopen the workbook, TODAY updates its value to return the current system date.

When you need to use the current time in a formula, a function, or an expression, use the NOW function, which doesn't take any arguments. This function returns the serial number of the current time, with the current date as the assumed date. For example, at 11:24 AM on November 1, 2019, the NOW function returns the serial number 43770.47549.

The NOW function returns the current date and time serial number in the date/time format of the cell.

If you want only the time component of the serial number, subtract TODAY from NOW:

> *=NOW - TODAY*

Just like the TODAY function, NOW is a dynamic function that doesn't keep its initial value (that is, the time at which you entered the function). Each time you edit the formula, enter another formula, recalculate the worksheet, or reopen the workbook, NOW updates its value to return the current system time.

To insert the TODAY or NOW function in a formula

→ On the **Formulas** tab, in the **Function Library** group, click **Date & Time**, then click **TODAY** or **NOW**.

Serialize numbers by using date and time functions

The date functions in Excel work with or return date serial numbers. You can also work in the opposite direction by taking numbers that represent a specified year, month, and day, and serialize them into a valid Excel date. When you have a date serial number, you can use more Excel date functions to manipulate and perform calculations with those dates.

Similarly, the time functions work with or return time serial numbers, but you can also work in the opposite direction by taking numbers that represent a specified hour, minute, and second, and serialize them into a valid Excel time. When you have a time serial number, you can use other Excel time functions to manipulate and perform calculations with those times.

A date consists of three components: the year, month, and day. It often happens that a worksheet generates one or more of these components, and you need some way of building a proper date out of them. You can do that by using the DATE function:

   DATE(year, month, day)

The following table describes the DATE function arguments.

Argument	Description
year	The year component of the date (a number from 1900 through 9999)
month	The month component of the date (a number from 1 through 12)
day	The day component of the date (a number from 1 through 31)

IMPORTANT Different versions of Excel and even different functions within the current version of Excel interpret two-digit years differently. For example, a year entered as 30 might be interpreted as either 1930 or 2030. To avoid problems, always use a four-digit value when entering the year component of any date.

For example, the expression DATE(2020, 12, 25) returns Christmas Day in 2020.

Note, too, that DATE adjusts for wrong month and day values. For example, the expression DATE(2020, 12, 32) returns January 1, 2021. Here, DATE adds the extra day (there are 31 days in December) to return the date of the next day.

The three components of a date—year, month, and day—can also be extracted individually from a specified date. This might not seem all that interesting at first, but many useful techniques arise out of working with a date's component parts. You can extract a date's components by using the YEAR, MONTH, and DAY functions:

YEAR(serial_number) MONTH(serial_number) DAY(serial_number)

In each function, *serial_number* is the date (or a string representation of the date) you want to work with. For example, on August 23, 2020, the expression YEAR(TODAY) returns 2020.

The MONTH function returns a number between 1 and 12 that corresponds to the month component of a specified date. The DAY function returns a number between 1 and 31 that corresponds to the day component of a specified date.

B3		:	×	✓	*fx*	=MONTH(B1)	
	A	B		C	D	E	
1	Date:	August 23, 2020					
2	Year:	2020					
3	Month:	8					
4	Day:	23					

The YEAR, MONTH, and DAY functions return the year, month, and day components of a specified date.

The WEEKDAY function returns a number that corresponds to the day of the week on which a specified date falls:

WEEKDAY(serial_number[, return_type])

The following table describes the WEEKDAY function arguments.

Argument	Description
serial_number	The date (or a string representation of the date) you want to work with.
return_type	An integer that determines how the value returned by WEEKDAY corresponds to the days of the week: • A *return_type* of 1 sets the return values to 1 (Sunday) through 7 (Saturday); this is the default. • A *return_type* of 2 sets the return values to 1 (Monday) through 7 (Sunday). • A *return_type* of 3 sets the return values to 0 (Monday) through 6 (Sunday).

For example, WEEKDAY("8/23/2020") returns 1 because August 23, 2020, is a Sunday.

The WEEKDAY function returns the day of the week for a specified date.

Because Excel treats dates as serial numbers, you can calculate the difference between two dates by subtracting one date from another. However, the result includes weekends and holidays. In many business situations, you need to know the number of *workdays* between two dates. For example, when calculating the number of days an invoice is past due, it's often best to exclude weekends and holidays.

To calculate the serial number of the day that is a specified number of working days from a start date, with weekends and holidays excluded, use the WORKDAY function:

WORKDAY(start_date, days[, holidays])

The WORKDAY function returns the date that is a specified number of workdays past a starting date.

To calculate the number of workdays between two dates, use the NETWORKDAYS function (read the name as "net workdays"):

NETWORKDAYS(start_date, end_date[, holidays])

The following table describes the WORKDAYS and NETWORKDAYS function arguments.

Argument	Description
start_date	The starting date (or a string representation of the date).
days	The number of workdays after start_date.
end_date	The ending date (or a string representation of the date).

Argument	Description
holidays	A list of dates to exclude from the calculation. This can be a range of dates or an array constant—that is, a series of date serial numbers or date strings, separated by commas and surrounded by braces ({}).

The NETWORKDAYS function returns the number of workdays between two dates.

A time consists of three components: the hour, minute, and second. It often happens that a worksheet generates one or more of these components, and you need some way of building a proper time out of them. You can do that by using the TIME function:

   TIME(hour, minute, second)

The following table describes the TIME function arguments.

Argument	Description
hour	The hour component of the time (a number from 0 through 23)
minute	The minute component of the time (a number from 0 through 59)
second	The second component of the time (a number from 0 through 59)

For example, TIME(14, 45, 30) returns the time 2:45:30 PM. Like the DATE function, TIME adjusts for wrong hour, minute, and second values. For example, TIME(14, 60, 30) returns 3:00:30 PM. Here, TIME takes the extra minute and adds 1 to the hour value.

The three components of a time—hour, minute, and second—can also be extracted individually from a specified time, by using the HOUR, MINUTE, and SECOND functions:

   HOUR(serial_number)

   MINUTE(serial_number)

   SECOND(serial_number)

In each case, the *serial_number* argument is the time (or a string representation of the time) you want to work with. The HOUR function returns a number between 0 and 23 that corresponds to the hour component of a specified time. For example, HOUR(0.5) returns 12.

The MINUTE function returns a number between 0 and 59 that corresponds to the minute component of a specified time. For example, if it's currently 3:15 PM, MINUTE(NOW) returns 15.

The SECOND function returns a number between 0 and 59 that corresponds to the second component of a specified time. For example, SECOND("2:45:30 PM") returns 30.

The HOUR, MINUTE, and SECOND functions return the individual components of a specified time.

To insert a date or time function into a formula

→ On the **Formulas** tab, in the **Function Library** group, click **Date & Time**, click one of the date or time functions, and then enter the arguments, as described earlier in this chapter.

Objective 3.3 practice tasks

The practice file for these tasks is located in the **MOSExcelExpert2019 \Objective3** practice file folder. The folder also contains a result file that you can use to check your work.

➤ Open the **ExcelExpert_3-3** workbook and do the following:

☐ On the **Holidays** worksheet, for each event listed, use the values in the year (column B), the month (column C), and the day (column D) in a formula to calculate the date on which each event occurs.

☐ On the **Dates** worksheet, in cells B2:B12, create formulas that return new dates that are one year, six months, and 15 days later than the dates in A2:A12.

☐ On the **Accounts Receivable Aging** worksheet, populate the Due Date column (D4:D14) with formulas that return dates that are 60 workdays after the dates in the Invoice Date column (C4:C14).

☐ On the same worksheet, add formulas to the Past Due column (E4:E14) that calculate the number of workdays that have elapsed between the Due Date value and the date shown in cell B1.

➤ Save the workbook.

➤ Open the **ExcelExpert_3-3_results** workbook. Compare the two workbooks to check your work, then close the open workbooks.

Objective 3.4: Perform data analysis

It's often not enough to just enter data in a worksheet, build a few formulas, and add some formatting to make everything look presentable. In the business world, you're often called on to extract meaning from the jumble of numbers and formula results in your workbooks. In other words, you need to *analyze* your data to unearth conclusions, trends, and useful business knowledge. In Excel, going deeper into business data means using the program's data analysis tools.

Consolidate data

Many businesses create worksheets for specific tasks and then distribute them to various departments. The most common example is budgeting. Accounting might create a generic "budget" template that each department or division in the company must fill out and return. Similarly, you often see worksheets distributed for inventory requirements, sales forecasting, survey data, experimental results, and more.

Creating these worksheets, distributing them, and filling them in are all straightforward operations. The tricky part comes when the sheets are returned to the originating department, and all the new data must be combined into a summary report showing companywide totals. This task is called *consolidating* the data, and it's often complicated and time consuming, especially for large worksheets. Fortunately, Excel has powerful features that can take the drudgery out of consolidation.

Excel can consolidate your data by using the following methods:

- **Consolidating by position** With this method, Excel consolidates the data from several worksheets, using the same range coordinates on each sheet. You can use this method if the worksheets you're consolidating have an identical layout.

- **Consolidating by category** This method tells Excel to consolidate the data by looking for identical row and column labels in each sheet. For example, if one worksheet lists monthly Gizmo sales in row 1 and another lists monthly Gizmo sales in row 5, you can consolidate this information as long as both sheets have a "Gizmo" label at the beginning of these rows.

In both cases, you specify one or more *source ranges* (the ranges that contain the data you want to consolidate) and a *destination range* (the range where the consolidated data will appear).

If the sheets you're working with have the same layout, consolidating by position is the easiest way to go. For example, consider three workbooks—Division I Budget,

Division II Budget, and Division III Budget. Each sheet uses the same row and column labels, so they're ideal candidates for consolidation by position.

During the consolidation procedure, Excel defaults to creating links to the source data, which means it updates the consolidated data when the source data changes. To make this happen, Excel does three things:

- It adds link formulas to the destination range for each cell in the source ranges you selected.

- It consolidates the data by adding SUM functions (or whichever operation you select) that total the results of the link formulas.

- It outlines the consolidation worksheet and hides the link formulas.

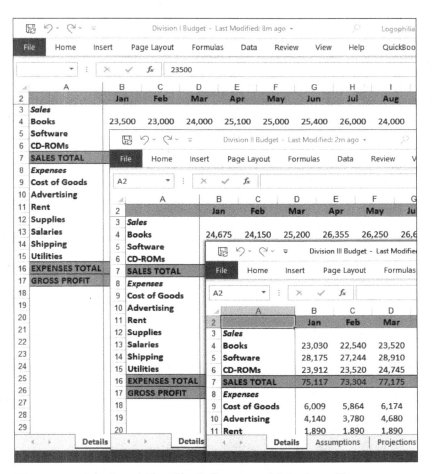

When your worksheets are laid out identically, use consolidation by position.

If you want to consolidate data from worksheets that don't use the same layout, you need to tell Excel to consolidate the data by category. In this case, Excel examines each of your source ranges and consolidates data that uses the same row or column labels.

To consolidate data by position

1. Create a new worksheet that has the same layout as the sheets you're consolidating.

2. In this new consolidation worksheet, click the upper-left corner of the destination range.

3. On the **Data** tab, in the **Data Tools** group, click **Consolidate** to open the **Consolidate** dialog box.

4. In the **Function** list, click the operation to use during the consolidation. You'll use Sum most of the time, but Excel has 10 other operations to choose from, including Count, Average, Max, and Min.

5. For each source range—not including any row and/or column labels—enter the range coordinates in the **Reference** box, then click **Add**. If the source data is open in another worksheet or workbook, you can click the range box and then select the data.

6. If you want the consolidated data to change whenever you make changes to the source data, make sure that the **Create links to source data** check box is selected.

7. Click **OK**. Excel gathers the data, consolidates it, and then adds it to the destination range.

To consolidate data by category

1. Create or select a new worksheet and click the upper-left corner of the destination range.

> **IMPORTANT** When consolidating by category, it isn't necessary to enter labels for the consolidated data because Excel does it for you automatically. If you want to see the labels in a particular order, it's okay to enter them yourself. However, if you do enter the labels yourself, make sure you spell the labels exactly as they're spelled in the source worksheets.

2. On the **Data** tab, in the **Data Tools** group, click **Consolidate** to open the **Consolidate** dialog box.

3. In the **Function** list, click the operation to use during the consolidation.

4. For each source range—including any row and/or column labels—enter the range coordinates in the **Reference** box, then click **Add**. If the source data is open in another worksheet or workbook, you can click the range box and then select the data.

5. If you want Excel to use the data labels in the top row of the selected ranges, under **Use labels in**, select the **Top row** check box. If you want Excel to use the data labels in the left column of the source ranges, select the **Left column** check box.

6. If you want the consolidated data to change whenever you make changes to the source data, make sure that the **Create links to source data** check box is selected.

7. Click **OK**. Excel gathers the data, consolidates it, and then adds it to the destination range.

Perform what-if analysis by using Goal Seek and Scenario Manager

What-if analysis is perhaps the most basic method for interrogating your worksheet data. With what-if analysis, you first calculate a formula, D, based on the input from variables A, B, and C. You then say, "What if I change variable A? Or B or C? What happens to the result?"

Data analysis is an important part of the Excel Expert exam. Besides the data analysis techniques in this objective, be sure to also study the chart, PivotTable, and PivotChart material in "Objective 4: Manage advanced charts and tables."

Perform what-if analysis by using Goal Seek

Here's a what-if question for you: What if you already know the result you want? For example, you might know that you want to have $50,000 saved to purchase new equipment five years from now, or that you have to achieve a 30 percent gross margin in your next budget. If you need to manipulate only a single variable to achieve these results, you can use the Goal Seek feature in Excel. You tell Goal Seek the final value you need and which variable to change, and it finds a solution for you (if one exists).

3

When you set up a worksheet to use Goal Seek, you usually have a formula in one cell and the formula's variable—with an initial value—in another. (Your formula can have multiple variables, but with Goal Seek you can manipulate only one variable at a time.) Goal Seek operates by using an *iterative method* to find a solution. That is, Goal Seek first tries the variable's initial value to see whether that produces the result you want. If it doesn't, Goal Seek tries different values until it converges on a solution.

Before you run Goal Seek, you need to set up your worksheet in a particular way. This means doing three things:

- Set up one cell as the *changing cell*. This is the value that Goal Seek will iteratively manipulate to attempt to reach the goal. Enter an initial value (such as 0) into the cell.

- Set up the other input values for the formula and make them proper initial values.

- Create a formula for Goal Seek to use to try to reach the goal.

For example, suppose you're a small-business owner looking to purchase new equipment worth $50,000 five years from now. Assuming your investments earn 5 percent annual interest, how much do you need to set aside every year to reach this goal? You can set up a worksheet like this to use Goal Seek:

- Make cell C5 the changing cell: the annual deposit into the fund (with an initial value of 0).

- In cells C3 and C4, enter the constants for the FV function.

- Make cell C7 the cell that contains the FV function that calculates the future value of the equipment fund. When Goal Seek is done, this cell's value should be $50,000.

C7		⋮	✕	✓	*fx*	=FV(C3, C4, C5)	
	A		B		C		D
1			*Equipment Fund Calculation*				
2							
3			**Interest Rate**		5%		
4			**Period**		5		
5			**Annual Deposit**		$0		
6							
7			**Equipment Fund**		$0		

A worksheet set up to use Goal Seek to find out how much to set aside each year to end up with a $50,000 equipment fund in five years.

To perform what-if analysis by using Goal Seek

1. On the **Data** tab, in the **Forecast** group, click **What-If Analysis**, then click **Goal Seek** to open the **Goal Seek** dialog box.

2. In the **Set cell** box, enter a reference to the cell that contains the formula you want Goal Seek to manipulate.

3. In the **To value** box, enter the final value you want for the goal cell.

4. In the **By changing cell** box, enter a reference to the changing cell.

The Goal Seek dialog box configured to perform analysis.

5. Click **OK**. Excel begins the iteration and displays the **Goal Seek Status** dialog box. When Excel finishes, the dialog box tells you whether Goal Seek found a solution.

6. If Goal Seek found a solution, you can accept the solution by clicking **OK**. To ignore the solution, click **Cancel**.

Goal Seek lets you know whether it found a solution.

Perform what-if analysis by using Scenario Manager

By definition, what-if analysis is not an exact science. All what-if models make guesses and assumptions based on history, expected events, and other factors. A particular set of guesses and assumptions that you plug into a model is called a *scenario*. Because most what-if worksheets can take a wide range of input values, you usually end up with a large number of scenarios to examine. Instead of going through the tedious chore of inserting all these values into the appropriate cells, Excel has a Scenario Manager feature that can handle the process for you.

As an example, imagine a worksheet model that analyzes a mortgage. You'd use such a model to decide how much of a down payment to make, how long the term should be, and whether to include an extra principal paydown every month.

=PMT(C4 / 12, C8 * 12, C3 - C7)		
B	C	D
Mortgage Analysis		
Fixed Cells:		
House Price	$100,000	
Interest Rate	4.00%	
Changing Cells:		
Down Payment	$15,000	
Term	25	
Paydown	($50)	
Results:	**Regular Mortgage**	**With Paydown**
Monthly Payment	($448.66)	($498.66)
Total Paid	($134,598.39)	($125,836.73)
Total Savings	#N/A	$8,761.67
Revised Term	#N/A	21.0

A worksheet model set up to analyze a mortgage.

Here are some possible questions to ask this model:

- How much will I save over the term of the mortgage if I use a shorter term, make a larger down payment, and include a monthly paydown?

- How much more will I end up paying if I extend the term, reduce the down payment, and forgo the paydown?

These are examples of scenarios that you would plug into the appropriate cells in the model. Scenario Manager helps by letting you define a scenario separately from the worksheet. You can save specific values for any or all of the model's input cells, give the scenario a name, and then recall the name (and all the input values it contains) from a list.

Before creating a scenario, you need to decide which cells in your model will be the input cells. These will be the worksheet variables—the cells that, when you change them, change the results of the model. Excel calls these the *changing cells*. You can have as many as 32 changing cells in a scenario. For best results, follow these guidelines when setting up your worksheet for scenarios:

- The changing cells should be constants. Formulas can be affected by other cells, and that can throw off the entire scenario.

- To make it easier to set up each scenario, and to make your worksheet easier to understand, group the changing cells and label them.

- For even greater clarity, assign a name to each changing cell.

To add a scenario

1. On the **Data** tab, in the **Forecast** group, click **What-If Analysis**, then click **Scenario Manager** to open the **Scenario Manager** dialog box.

2. Click **Add** to open the **Add Scenario** dialog box.

3. In the **Scenario name** box, enter a name for the scenario.

4. In the **Changing cells** box, enter references to your worksheet's changing cells. You can type in the references (be sure to separate noncontiguous cells with commas) or select the cells directly on the worksheet.

5. In the **Comment** box, enter a description for the scenario. This description appears in the **Comment** section of the **Scenario Manager** dialog box.

6. Click **OK**. Excel opens the **Scenario Values** dialog box.

7. In the **Scenario Values** dialog box, enter values for the changing cells.

8. To add more scenarios, click **Add** to return to the **Add Scenario** dialog box and repeat steps 3 through 7. Otherwise, click **OK** to return to the **Scenario Manager** dialog box.

9. Click **Close** to save the scenario and return to the worksheet.

To display a scenario

1. On the **Data** tab, in the **Forecast** group, click **What-If Analysis**, then click **Scenario Manager** to open the **Scenario Manager** dialog box.

2. In the **Scenarios** list, click the scenario you want to display.

3

3. Click **Show**. Excel enters the scenario values in the changing cells.

4. Repeat steps 2 and 3 to display other scenarios.

5. Click **Close** to return to the worksheet.

Calculate data by using financial functions

Excel is loaded with financial features that give you powerful tools for building models that manage both business and personal finances. You can use these functions to calculate such things as the monthly payment on a loan, the future value of an annuity, the internal rate of return of an investment, or the yearly depreciation of an asset.

Most of the formulas you'll work with involve three factors—the *present value* (the amount something is worth now); the *future value* (the amount something will be worth in the future); and the interest rate (or the discount rate)—plus two related factors: the *periods*, the number of payments or deposits over the term of the loan or investment, and the *payment*, the amount of money paid out or invested in each period.

Although Excel has dozens of financial functions that use many different arguments, the following table describes the arguments you'll use most frequently.

Argument	Description
rate	The fixed rate of interest over the term of the loan or investment.
nper	The number of payments or deposit periods over the term of the loan or investment.
pmt	The periodic payment or deposit.
pv	The present value of the loan (the principal) or the initial deposit in an investment.
fv	The future value of the loan or investment.
type	The type of payment or deposit. Use 0 (the default) for end-of-period payments or deposits, and use 1 for beginning-of-period payments or deposits.

When building financial formulas, you need to ask yourself the following questions:

- **Who or what is the subject of the formula?** On a mortgage analysis, for example, are you performing the analysis on behalf of yourself or the bank?

- **Which way is the money flowing with respect to the subject?** For the present value, future value, and payment, enter money that the subject receives as a positive quantity, and enter money that the subject pays out as a negative quantity. For example, if you're the subject of a mortgage analysis, the loan principal (the present value) is a positive number because it's money that you receive from the bank; the payment and the remaining principal (the future value) are negative because they're amounts that you pay to the bank.

- **What is the time unit?** The underlying unit of both the interest rate and the period must be the same. For example, if you're working with the annual interest rate, you must express the period in years. Similarly, if you're working with monthly periods, you must use a monthly interest rate.

- **When are the payments made?** Excel differentiates between payments made at the end of each period and those made at the beginning.

The following table shows the most commonly used financial functions.

Function	Returns
CUMIPMT(*rate, nper, pv, start, end, type*)	The cumulative interest paid on a loan between *start* and *end*
CUMPRINC(*rate, nper, pv, start, end, type*)	The cumulative principal paid on a loan between *start* and *end*
DB(*cost, salvage, life, period, month*)	The depreciation of an asset over a specified period using the fixed-declining balance method
DDB(*cost, salvage, life, period, factor*)	The depreciation of an asset over a specified period using the double-declining balance method
EFFECT(*nominal_rate, npery*)	The effective annual interest rate given the nominal annual interest rate and the number of yearly compounding periods
FV(*rate, nper, pmt, pv, type*)	The future value of an investment or loan
IPMT(*rate, per, nper, pv, fv, type*)	The interest payment for a specified period of a loan
IRR(*values, guess*)	The internal rate of return for a series of cash flows
MIRR(*values, finance_rate, reinvest_rate*)	The modified internal rate of return for a series of periodic cash flows

3

Function	Returns
NOMINAL(*effect_rate, npery*)	The nominal annual interest rate given the effective annual interest rate and the number of yearly compounding periods
NPER(*rate, pmt, pv, fv, type*)	The number of periods for an investment or loan based on fixed payments and interest rate
NPV(*rate, value1, value2...*)	The net present value of an investment based on a series of cash flows and a discount rate
PMT(*rate, nper, pv, fv, type*)	The periodic payment for a loan or investment
PPMT(*rate, per, nper, pv, fv, type*)	The principal payment for a specified period of a loan
PV(*rate, nper, pmt, fv, type*)	The present value of an investment
RATE(*nper, pmt, pv, fv, type, guess*)	The periodic interest rate for a loan or investment
SLN(*cost, salvage, life*)	The straight-line depreciation of an asset over one period
SYD(*cost, salvage, life, period*)	The sum-of-years' digits depreciation of an asset over a specified period

To insert a financial function into a formula

→ On the **Formulas** tab, in the **Function Library** group, click **Financial**, click the financial function you want to use, and then enter the arguments, as described earlier in this chapter.

Calculate data by using the NPER function

In some loan scenarios, you need to borrow a certain amount at the current interest rates, but you can spend only so much on each payment. If the other loan factors are fixed, the only way to adjust the payment is to adjust the term of the loan: a longer term means smaller payments, and a shorter term means larger payments.

You could figure out the term by adjusting the *nper* argument of the PMT function until you get the payment you want. However, Excel offers a more direct solution in the form of the NPER function, which returns the number of periods of a loan:

NPER(*rate, pmt, pv[, fv][, type]*)

Here, *rate* is the fixed rate of interest over the term of the loan; *pmt* is the periodic payment (a negative value, since this is money you are paying out); *pv* is the loan principal; *fv* is the optional future value of the loan (if omitted, the default is 0); and *type* is the optional type of payment (use 0, the default, for end-of-period payments or use 1 for beginning-of-period payments).

Using the NPER function to calculate a loan period.

You can also use NPER for investments. Given an investment goal, if you have an initial deposit and an amount that you can afford to deposit periodically, how long will it take to reach your goal at the prevailing market interest rate? You answer this question by using the NPER from the point of view of an investment:

NPER(rate, pmt, pv[, fv][, type])

Here, *rate* is the fixed rate of interest over the term of the investment; *pmt* is the amount invested each period payment; *pv* is the initial investment; *fv* is the optional future value of the investment (if omitted, the default is 0); and *type* is the optional type of deposit (use 0, the default, for end-of-period deposits or use 1 for beginning-of-period deposits).

To insert the NPER function into a formula

→ On the **Formulas** tab, in the **Function Library** group, click **Financial**, click **NPER**, and then enter the arguments, as described in this section.

Calculate data by using the PMT function

When negotiating a loan to purchase equipment or a mortgage for your house, the first concern that comes up is almost always the size of the payment you'll need to make each period. This is basic cash-flow management because the monthly (or whatever) payment must fit within your budget.

To return the periodic payment for a loan, use the PMT function:

PMT(rate, nper, pv[, fv][, type])

Here, *rate* is the fixed rate of interest over the term of the loan; *nper* is the number of payments over the term of the loan; *pv* is the loan principal; *fv* is the optional future value of the loan (if omitted, the default is 0); and *type* is the optional type of payment (use 0, the default, for end-of-period payments or use 1 for beginning-of-period payments).

=PMT(C2 / 12, C3 * 12, C4, -C5)	
B	C
Loan Payment Analysis	
Interest Rate (Annual)	6.00%
Periods (Years)	5
Principal	$10,000
Balloon Payment	$3,000
Monthly Payment	($150.33)

Using the PMT function to calculate a loan payment.

You can also use PMT with investment formulas. Suppose that you want to reach a future investment value goal by a certain date and that you have an initial amount to invest. Given current interest rates, how much extra do you have to periodically deposit into the investment to achieve your goal? Use the PMT function from the point of view of an investment:

   PMT(rate, nper, pv[, fv][, type])

Here, *rate* is the fixed rate of interest over the term of the investment; *nper* is the number of deposits over the term of the investment; *pv* is the initial investment; *fv* is the optional future value of the investment (if omitted, the default is 0); and *type* is the optional type of deposit (use 0, the default, for end-of-period deposits or use 1 for beginning-of-period deposits).

To insert the PMT function into a formula

→ On the **Formulas** tab, in the **Function Library** group, click **Financial**, click **PMT**, and then enter the arguments, as described in this section.

Objective 3.4 practice tasks

The practice files for these tasks are located in the **MOSExcelExpert2019 \Objective3** practice file folder. The folder also contains a result file that you can use to check your work.

➤ Open the **ExcelExpert_3-4** workbook and do the following:

❏ On the **Consolidate by Position** worksheet, consolidate the data from the **ExcelExpert_3-4a**, **ExcelExpert_3-4b**, and **ExcelExpert_3-4c** workbooks.

❏ On the **Consolidate by Category** worksheet, consolidate the data from the **ExcelExpert_3-4d**, **ExcelExpert_3-4e**, and **ExcelExpert_3-4f** workbooks.

❏ On the **Break Even** worksheet, use Goal Seek to determine the number of units that must be sold to break even (that is, generate a profit equal to 0).

❏ On the **Scenarios** worksheet, create three scenarios for the model: **Best Case** ($20,000 down payment, 20-year term, and $100 paydown); **Worst Case** ($10,000 down payment, 30-year term, and $0 paydown); and **Likeliest Case** ($15,000 down payment, 25-year term, and $50 paydown).

❏ On the **NPER** worksheet, use cell B7 to build a formula that uses the NPER function to determine the number of months of deposits that are required to reach a future value of $1,000,000 given an annual interest rate of 5%, a monthly deposit of $1,000, and an initial deposit of $50,000.

❏ On the PMT worksheet, use cell B7 to build a formula that uses the PMT function to determine the monthly deposit required to reach a future value of $50,000 given an annual interest rate of 7.5%, a term of 15 years, and no initial deposit.

➤ Save the **ExcelExpert_3-4** workbook.

➤ Open the **ExcelExpert_3-4_results** workbook. Compare the two workbooks to check your work, and then close the open workbooks.

Objective 3.5: Troubleshoot formulas

Despite your best efforts, an error might appear in your formulas from time to time. Such errors can be mathematical (for example, dividing by zero), or Excel might simply be incapable of interpreting the formula. In the latter case, problems can be caught while you're entering the formula. For example, if you try to enter a formula that has unbalanced parentheses, Excel won't accept the entry, and it displays an error message. Other errors are more insidious. For example, your formula might appear to be working—that is, it might return a value—but the result might be incorrect because the data is flawed or because your formula has referenced the wrong cell or range. Whatever the error and whatever the cause, formula woes need to be worked out because you or someone else in your company is likely depending on your models to produce accurate results.

Trace precedence and dependence

Some formula errors result from referencing other cells that contain errors or inappropriate values. The first step in troubleshooting these kinds of formula problems is to determine which cell (or group of cells) is causing an error. This is straightforward if the formula references only a single cell, but it gets progressively more difficult as the number of references increases. (Another complicating factor is the use of range names, because it won't be obvious which range each name is referencing.)

To determine which cells are wreaking havoc on your formulas, you can use Excel auditing features to visualize and trace a formula's input values and error sources. The formula-auditing features operate by creating tracers—arrows that literally point out the cells involved in a formula. You can use tracers to find two kinds of cells:

- **Precedents** These are cells that are directly or indirectly referenced in a formula. For example, suppose that cell E4 contains the formula =E2; E2 is a direct precedent of E4. Now suppose that cell E2 contains the formula =D2/2; this makes D2 a direct precedent of E2 and also an indirect precedent of cell E4.

- **Dependents** These are cells that are directly or indirectly referenced by a formula in another cell. In the preceding example, cell E2 is a direct dependent of D2, and E4 is an indirect dependent of D2.

Tracer arrows shown the precedents of cell E4.

To trace cell precedents

1. Select the cell that contains the formula whose precedents you want to trace.

2. On the **Formulas** tab, in the **Formula Auditing** group, click **Trace Precedents**. Excel adds a tracer arrow to each direct precedent.

3. Repeat step 2 to trace more levels of precedents.

Tip You also can trace precedents by double-clicking the cell if you have turned off in-cell editing. You do this by clearing the Allow Editing Directly In Cells check box on the Advanced page of the Excel Options dialog box.

To trace cell dependents

1. Select the cell whose dependents you want to trace.

2. On the **Formulas** tab, in the **Formula Auditing** group, click **Trace Dependents**. Excel adds a tracer arrow to each direct dependent.

3. Repeat step 2 to trace more levels of dependents.

Monitor cells and formulas by using the Watch Window

It is very common for a formula to refer to a precedent that resides in a different worksheet. That's a powerful technique, but it does mean that you might not be able to see the formula cell and the precedent cell at the same time. This could also happen if the precedent exists in another workbook or even elsewhere on the same sheet if you're working with a large model.

This is a problem because there's no easy way to determine the current value or formula of the unseen precedent. If you're having a problem, troubleshooting requires that you track down the far-off precedent to see if it might be the culprit. That's bad enough with a single unseen cell, but what if your formula refers to 5 or 10 such cells? And what if those cells are scattered in different worksheets and workbooks?

This level of hassle—not at all uncommon in the spreadsheet world—was no doubt the inspiration behind an elegant solution: the Watch Window. You use this window to keep track of both the value and the formula in any cell in any worksheet in any open workbook.

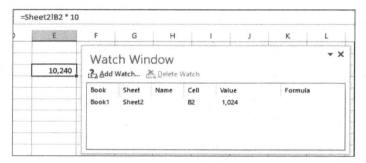

Use the Watch Window to keep track of the value or formula of a cell in any worksheet or workbook.

To add a watch

1. Go to the workbook or worksheet that contains the cell or cells you want to watch.

2. On the **Formulas** tab, in the **Formula Auditing** group, click **Watch Window** to open the **Watch Window**.

3. Click **Add Watch** to open the **Add Watch** dialog box.

4. Do either of the following:

   - In the worksheet, select the cell or cell range you want to watch.

   - In the **Select the cells that you would like to watch the value of** box, enter a reference formula for the cell or cell range (for example, =A1).

5. Click **Add** to add the cell or cells to the **Watch Window**.

To remove a watch

1. On the **Formulas** tab, in the **Formula Auditing** group, click **Watch Window** to open the **Watch Window**.

2. Click the watch you want to remove.

3. Click **Delete Watch**. Excel removes the watch.

Validate formulas by using error-checking rules

If you use Microsoft Word, you're probably familiar with the blue lines that appear under words and phrases that the grammar checker has flagged as being incorrect. The grammar checker operates by using a set of rules that determine correct grammar and syntax. As you type, the grammar checker operates in the background, constantly monitoring your writing. If something you write goes against one of the grammar checker's rules, the wavy line appears to let you know there's a problem.

Excel has a similar feature: the formula error checker. Like the grammar checker, the formula error checker uses a set of rules to determine correctness, and it operates in the background to monitor your formulas. If it detects something amiss, it displays an *error indicator*—a green triangle—in the upper-left corner of the cell containing the formula. When you select the cell with the formula error, Excel displays an icon beside the cell. If you point to the icon, a ScreenTip describes the error.

IMPORTANT You see the error indicators only if Excel's background error checking feature is turned on. On the Formulas page of the Excel Options dialog box, in the Error Checking section, make sure the Enable background error checking check box is selected. Note, too, that you can also use the Indicate errors using this color palette to select a different indicator color.

---

f_x	=F1 / (1 - F2)						
D	E	F	G	H	I	J	K
Final Price	$10.65	$21.35	$32.05				
Sales Tax	7%	7%	7%				
List Price		$22.96	$29.95				

The formula in this cell differs from the formulas in this area of the spreadsheet.

Select the cell containing the error, and then point to the icon to see a description of the error.

Clicking the icon displays the following options:

- **Corrective actions** One or more commands (depending on the type of error) that Excel suggests for either fixing the problem or helping you troubleshoot the error.

- **Help on this error** Click this option to get information on the error from the Excel Help system.

- **Ignore Error** Click this option to leave the formula as is.

- **Edit in Formula Bar** Click this option to display the formula in Edit mode in the formula bar. You can then fix the problem by editing the formula.

- **Error Checking Options** Click this option to display the Formulas page of the Excel Options dialog box (discussed next).

To run an error check on the current worksheet

→ On the **Formulas** tab in the **Formula Auditing** group, click the **Error Checking** menu, then click **Error Checking**.

Like the Word grammar checker, the Excel formula error checker has several rules that control which errors it flags. You can configure these rules on the Formulas page of the Excel Options dialog box. The following list describes each rule, including the errors each rule flags and some of the corrective actions that Excel makes available on the error-checking menu that appears when you click the error icon next to a flagged cell:

- **Cells containing formulas that result in an error** Flags formulas that evaluate to an error value such as #DIV/0! or #NAME?.

- **Inconsistent calculated column formula in tables** In calculated columns, flags any cell that contains a formula with a different structure than the other cells in the column. The error-checking menu for this error includes the Restore To Calculated Column Formula command, which you can use to update the formula so that it's consistent with the rest of the column.

- **Cells containing years represented as 2 digits** Flags formulas that contain date text strings in which the year contains only two digits (a possibly ambiguous situation because the string could refer to a date in either the 1900s or the 2000s). The error-checking menu includes two commands—Convert XX To 19XX and Convert XX To 20XX—that you can use to convert the two-digit year to a four-digit year.

- **Numbers formatted as text or preceded by an apostrophe** Flags cells that contain a number that is either formatted as text or preceded by an apostrophe. The error-checking menu includes the Convert To Number command to convert the text to its numeric equivalent.

- **Formulas inconsistent with other formulas in the region** Flags formulas that are structured differently from similar formulas in the surrounding area. The error-checking menu includes commands such as Copy Formula From Left to bring the formula into consistency with the surrounding cells.

- **Formulas which omit cells in a region** Flags formulas that omit cells that are adjacent to a range referenced in the formula. For example, suppose that the formula is =AVERAGE(C4:C21), where C4:C21 is a range of numeric values. If cell C3 also contains a numeric value, the formula error checker flags the formula to alert you to the possibility that you missed including cell C3 in the formula.

- **Unlocked cells containing formulas** Flags formulas that reside in unlocked cells. This isn't an error so much as a warning that other people could tamper with the formula even after you have protected the sheet. The error-checking menu includes the command Lock Cell to lock the cell and prevent users from changing the formula after you protect the sheet.

- **Formulas referring to empty cells** Flags formulas that reference empty cells. The error-checking menu includes the Trace Empty Cell command to help you find the empty cell. (At this point, you can either enter data in the cell or adjust the formula so that it doesn't reference the cell.)

- **Data entered in a table is invalid** Flags cells that violate a table's data-validation rules. This can happen if you set up a data-validation rule with only a Warning or Information style, in which case the user can still opt to enter the invalid data. The formula error checker flags the cells that contain invalid data. The error-checking menu includes the Display Type Information command, which shows the data-validation rule that the cell data violates.

- **Misleading number formats** Flags cells that link to another cell but that have a number format that is not only different from the linked cell's number format but that is also potentially misleading. You see this error, for example, if cell B3 is formatted as Currency, cell E4 links to B3 with the formula =B3, and E4 is formatted as Short Date. (For comparison, note that you would not see an error if cell E4 was formatted as Percentage.)

3

To configure the error-checking rules

→ On the **Formulas** page of the **Excel Options** dialog box, in the **Error checking rules** section, select or clear the check boxes to choose the rules you want to apply. Then click **OK**.

Tip You can display the Formulas page directly by clicking a cell containing an error, clicking the error checker icon, and then clicking Error Checking Options.

Evaluate formulas

If a formula produces no warnings or error values, the result might still be in error. If the result of a formula is incorrect, one method that can help you understand and fix the problem is to calculate multipart formulas one term at a time. In the formula bar, select the expression you want to calculate, then press F9. Excel converts the expression into its value. Make sure that you press the Esc key when you're done to avoid entering the formula with just the calculated values.

This is a useful technique, but it can be tedious in a long or complex formula, and there's always a danger that you might accidentally confirm a partially evaluated formula and lose your work. For complex formulas, a better solution is to use the Evaluate Formula feature in Excel. It does the same thing as the F9 technique, but it's easier and safer.

To evaluate a formula

1. Select the cell that contains the formula you want to evaluate.

2. On the **Formulas** tab, in the **Formula Auditing** group, click **Evaluate Formula** to open the **Evaluate Formula** dialog box.

3. The current term in the formula is underlined in the **Evaluation** box. At each step, select from one or more of the following buttons:

    *   **Evaluate** Click this button to display the current value of the underlined term.

    *   **Step In** Click this button to display the first dependent of the underlined term. If that dependent also has a dependent, click this button again to see it.

    *   **Step Out** Click this button to hide a dependent and evaluate its precedent.

4. Repeat step 3 until you've completed your evaluation, then click **Close**.

Objective 3.5 practice tasks

The practice file for these tasks is located in the **MOSExcelExpert2019 \Objective3** practice file folder. The folder also contains a result file that you can use to check your work.

➤ Open the **ExcelExpert_3-5** workbook, display the **Gross Margin** worksheet, and do the following:

❑ Trace the precedents of cell E4.

❑ Trace the dependents of cell G2.

➤ Display the **List Price** worksheet and do the following:

❑ Set up a watch for cell F4.

❑ Use the error checker to locate and fix the formula error on the worksheet.

➤ Return to the **Gross Margin** worksheet and do the following:

❑ Evaluate the formula in cell G4 by stepping into each of its components.

➤ Save the workbook.

➤ Open the **ExcelExpert_3-5_results** workbook. Compare the two workbooks to check your work, and then close the open workbooks.

Objective 3.6: Create and modify simple macros

One of the secrets of Excel productivity is the automation of routine tasks through the use of command macros. A *command macro* is code that performs an action that has an effect on the Excel environment. For example, the macro might insert text into a worksheet cell or change an Excel option. In general, you can think of a command macro as being akin to a ribbon command. The key is that a single macro can consist of two, three, or even a dozen or more actions, each of which is performed, in sequence, when you run the macro. Macros save time and increase efficiency in two ways:

- **For short tasks that you run frequently** Placing those tasks inside a macro is efficient because you can launch the macro with just one or two clicks or by pressing a keyboard shortcut.

- **For long tasks** Having these tasks in a macro is fast because although the entire procedure might take you several minutes manually, the macro might take only a few seconds.

Although you can create macros manually by using the Microsoft Visual Basic for Applications (VBA) Editor, it is often easier to create a macro by using the Macro Recorder. With this method, you start the recorder, then you run through the tasks you want to automate (which might include selecting cells, running ribbon commands, and choosing dialog box options). The Recorder translates everything into the appropriate Visual Basic for Applications statements and copies those statements to a macro in a module. You can then use the recorded macro to replay the entire procedure any time you want. After you have recorded a macro, you can modify it by adding a description, assigning a shortcut key, or deleting the macro.

To open the Record Macro dialog box

→ On the **Developer** tab, in the **Code** group, click **Record Macro**.

See Also For information about how to display the Developer tab, see "Copy macros between workbooks" in "Objective 1.1: Manage workbooks."

→ Near the left end of the Excel status bar, click the **Macro Recording** button. (If the button isn't on the status bar, right-click the status bar, then click **Macro Recording**.)

The Macro Recording button

You must provide a name and storage location for the macro before you record it.

To record a simple macro

1. Open the **Record Macro** dialog box.

2. In the **Macro name** box, change the name to something memorable or descriptive. You must follow these guidelines when naming your macros:

    - The name must be 255 or fewer characters.

    - The first character must be a letter or an underscore (_).

    - No spaces or periods are allowed.

3. In the **Shortcut key** box, assign an optional shortcut key to the macro.

    > **IMPORTANT** Excel shortcut keys are case-sensitive, which means that you can create separate shortcuts with uppercase and lowercase letters. Also, make sure you don't specify a shortcut key that conflicts with built-in shortcuts (such as Ctrl+B for Bold or Ctrl+C for Copy). If you use a key that clashes with an Excel shortcut, Excel overrides its own shortcut and runs your macro instead (if the workbook containing the macro is open).

4. In the **Store macro in** list, specify where the macro will reside. You can store the macro in the current workbook, a new workbook, or in the Personal Macro Workbook. If you use the Personal Macro Workbook, your macros will be available to all of your workbooks.

5. In the **Description** box, enter an optional description of the macro.

6. Click **OK** to return to the workbook and start recording.

7. Perform the tasks you want to include in the macro. Here are some things to bear in mind during the recording:

   • Excel gives you two indications that a recording is in progress: in the **Developer** tab's **Code** group, the **Record Macro** button changes to **Stop Recording**, and in the status bar the **Macro Recording** button changes to a square.

   • Excel makes the mouse available for all actions.

   • Because the **Macro Recorder** takes note of everything you do, be careful not to perform any extraneous keyboard actions or mouse clicks during the recording.

The Macro Recording
button during a recording

During a recording, the Macro Recording status bar button changes to a square.

8. When you finish the tasks, do either of the following to stop recording the macro:

   • On the **Developer** tab, in the **Code** group, click **Stop Recording**.

   • On the status bar, click the **Macro Recording** button.

To modify a macro

1. On the **Developer** tab, in the **Code** group, click **Macros** to open the **Macro** dialog box.

2. Click the macro you want to modify, then click **Options** to open the **Macro Options** dialog box.

3. Do any of the following, then click **Close** to return to the **Macro** dialog box:

   • In the **Shortcut key: Ctrl+** box, assign a shortcut key to the macro.

   • In the **Description** box, enter a description of the macro.

4. Click **Cancel** to close the **Macro** dialog box.

To run a macro

→ In the **Macro** dialog box, click the macro you want to run, then click **Run**.

→ If you assigned a shortcut key to the macro, press the shortcut key.

To delete a macro

1. In the **Macro** dialog box, click the macro you want to remove, then click **Delete**. Excel asks you to confirm.

2. Click **Yes** to delete the macro.

3

Objective 3.6 practice tasks

The practice file for these tasks is located in the **MOSExcelExpert2019 \Objective3** practice file folder. The folder also contains a result file that you can use to check your work.

➤ Open the **ExcelExpert_3-6** workbook, display the **Inventory** worksheet, and do the following:

- ❏ Select cell E2 and start recording a macro. Use the default macro name and location settings.

- ❏ Perform the following actions: apply bold, apply the Currency number format, and center the text within the cell.

- ❏ Stop the recording.

- ❏ Select cell F2 and run the macro you just recorded.

➤ Save the workbook.

➤ Open the **ExcelExpert_3-6_results** workbook. Compare the two workbooks to check your work, and then close the open workbooks.

Objective group 4

Manage advanced charts and tables

The skills tested in this section of the Microsoft Office Specialist Expert exam for Microsoft Excel 2019 relate to creating charts, PivotTables, and PivotCharts. Specifically, the following objectives are associated with this set of skills:

4.1   Create and modify advanced charts

4.2   Create and modify PivotTables

4.3   Create and modify PivotCharts

Worksheets and external databases can contain hundreds of thousands or even millions of records. Analyzing that much data can be extremely difficult without the right kinds of tools. To help you, Excel offers three powerful data analysis features: charts, PivotTables, and PivotCharts. By using these tools, you can visualize or summarize a large dataset in a concise format.

This chapter guides you in studying advanced charting techniques, including creating a chart with a second value axis and working with Excel's advanced chart types. You also learn how to create and modify PivotTables and how to use them to analyze data. Finally, you learn how to create PivotCharts that you can use to visualize and analyze your data at the same time.

4

To complete the practice tasks in this chapter, you need the practice files contained in the **MOSExcelExpert2019\Objective4** practice file folder. For more information, see "Download the practice files" in this book's introduction.

Objective 4.1: Create and modify advanced charts

This topic shows you several methods for creating advanced charts, including how to configure a chart with a second value axis and how to use Excel's advanced chart types.

Exam Strategy The information in this book assumes that you know basic Excel chart techniques, including how to create a chart, how to work with chart types, and how to select and format chart elements. If you need a refresher, see *MOS Study Guide for Microsoft Excel Exam MO-200* by Joan Lambert (Microsoft Press, 2020).

Create dual-axis charts

If you show two or more data series in a single chart, you can change the chart type for one or more series and create a combination chart. By using different chart types, you can make it easier for your readers to distinguish different categories of data shown in the same chart. For example, you can create a combination chart that shows the number of homes sold as a line chart and the average sales price as a column chart.

However, when you plot two different types of data in the same chart, the range of values can vary wildly. For example, the values for homes sold might be measured in the tens of units, whereas the values for the average sales price might be measured in the hundreds of thousands. How can you combine these two disparate data sources so that you can see both series properly? The trick is to add another vertical axis—called the *secondary axis*—and have Excel plot one of the series by using that axis. This will make it easier for the reader to see values for the associated series. In the example, you could plot average sales prices on one vertical axis and the number of homes sold on the other vertical axis.

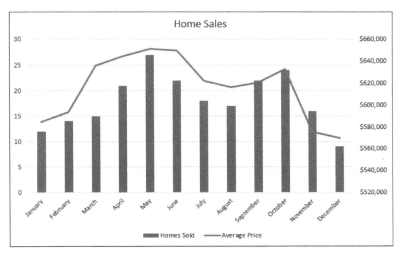

A chart of home sales with units sold on the main (left) vertical axis and average price on the secondary (right) vertical axis.

To change a selected chart to a dual-axis chart

1. Click the chart to select it.

2. On the **Chart Design** tab, in the **Type** group, click **Change Chart Type** to open the **Change Chart Type** dialog box.

3. On the **All Charts** tab, in the category list, click **Combo**.

4. For each series, in the **Chart Type** list, select the chart type you want to apply.

5. For one of the series, select the **Secondary Axis** check box.

Creating a dual-axis chart.

6. Click **OK** to close the **Change Chart Type** dialog box and return to the worksheet.

Create advanced chart types

To analyze data visually, most users turn to one of Excel's standard chart types, such as Column, Line, Pie, Bar, Area, X Y (Scatter), or Stock. These are useful chart types that get the job done most of the time, but for more technical or sophisticated scenarios, you might need to go beyond these standard types and consider one of Excel's advanced chart types:

- Box & Whisker
- Combo (see the previous section)
- Funnel
- Histogram
- Map
- Sunburst
- Treemap
- Waterfall

A Box & Whisker chart creates a display of your data that is designed to enable you to quickly visualize a variety of useful statistical details, including the mean, the median, and the percentile groupings.

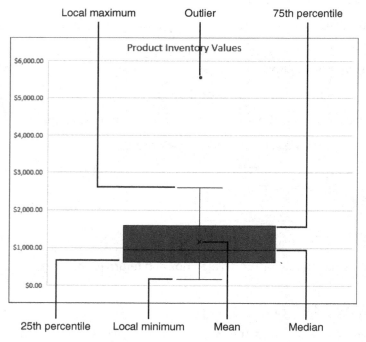

An example of a Box & Whisker chart.

A typical Box & Whisker chart has three main elements:

- **Box** The colored rectangle, which visually represents four statistical properties of the data:
  - The bottom edge of the box represents the 25th percentile, which means that the bottom 25 percent of the values lie between the local minimum and the bottom edge of the box.
  - The top edge of the box represents the 75th percentile, which means that the top 25 percent of the values lie between the top edge of the box and the local maximum.
  - The horizontal line inside the box represents the median value (also known as the 50th percentile), which means that half the values lie below this line and half the values lie above it.
  - The X inside the box represents the mean (that is, the arithmetic average of the values).
- **Whiskers** The lines that extend below and above the box, which visually represent two statistical properties of the data:
  - The horizontal line at the bottom of the lower whisker is the local minimum, meaning it's the lowest value in the dataset barring any outliers.
  - The horizontal line at the top of the upper whisker is the local maximum, meaning it's the highest value in the dataset barring any outliers.
- **Outliers** Any dots you see either above the local maximum or below the local minimum are known as outliers, which means they are exceptionally high or low values compared to the rest of the data set.

To create a Box & Whisker chart

1. Select the range of data you want to chart.
2. On the **Insert** tab, in the **Charts** group, click **Insert Statistic Chart**.
3. Click **Box & Whisker**.

A Funnel chart helps you visualize how a particular value changes over multiple stages of a process. For example, in a first-year university course, the number of students originally enrolled in the course dwindles over time, with some students dropping the course after a class or two, others after the first quiz, the first assignment, the mid-term, and so on. As the "funnel" metaphor implies, this chart type is ideally suited for visualizing values that decline over time.

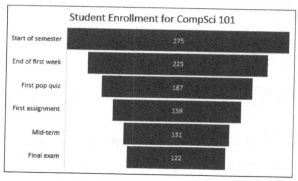

An example of a Funnel chart.

To create a Funnel chart

1. Select the range of data you want to chart.

2. On the **Insert** tab, in the **Charts** group, click **Insert Waterfall, Funnel, Stock, Surface, or Radar Chart**.

3. Click **Funnel**.

A Histogram is a chart of a *frequency distribution,* which organizes a large amount of data into numeric ranges called *bins* and then tells you the number of observations that fall within each bin. For example, when analyzing student grades, you might want to know the number of students who received grades between 90 and 100, between 80 and 89, between 70 and 79, and so on.

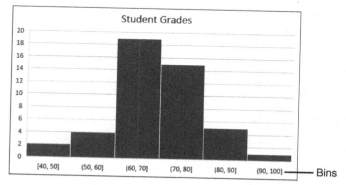

An example of a Histogram chart.

A variation on the Histogram chart is the Pareto chart, which displays the columns sorted in descending order (which is why this chart type is also known as a sorted histogram chart) as well as a line that shows the cumulative percentage of the columns.

To create a Histogram or Pareto chart

1. Select the range of data you want to chart.

2. On the **Insert** tab, in the **Charts** group, click **Insert Statistic Chart**.

3. Click **Histogram**. If you want to create a Pareto chart instead, click **Pareto**.

Tip To adjust the size of the bins in a histogram, double-click the horizontal axis to open the Format Axis pane. Under Axis Options, select the Bin Width radio button and then enter the bin size you want to use.

A Map chart visualizes geographic data by showing comparative values across regions such as countries, states, counties, or postal codes. The default Map chart is the Filled Map, so named because it applies a fill color to each map region, where the intensity of the color gives a visual indication of the relative value associated with that region (for example, the higher the value, the more intense the color).

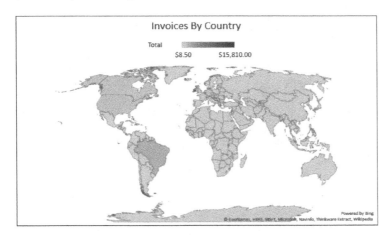

An example of a Filled Map chart.

For a Map chart to work, your data must use the Geography data type. You can convert your data to this type by selecting the data and then, on the **Data** tab, clicking **Geography** in the **Data Types** group.

To create a Map chart

1. Select the range of data you want to chart.

2. On the **Insert** tab, in the **Charts** group, click **Maps**.

3. Click **Filled Map**.

A Sunburst chart helps you visualize hierarchical data using a series of concentric circles, where the innermost circle represents the data on the top level of the hierarchy, the next circle represents the second level, and so on. Each circle has the following characteristics:

- The values in that level of the hierarchy are given segment sizes that are relative to the total of all the values in that level. For example, if a value is 50 percent of the level total, then that value's segment takes up half the circle.

- The values in the next level down are adjacent to their parent value, which enables you to easily visualize the contribution of each child value to its parent.

For example, a worksheet of technical books sales might have a number of categories, including Certification, Hardware, and Internet. Each of these categories would have one or more subcategories. For example, the Hardware category might have sub-categories such as Gadgets, Macs, and PCs. Some of those subcategories might also have one or more sub-subcategories. For example, the Gadgets subcategory might have sub-subcategories such as Smartphones, Tablets, and E-readers. A Sunburst chart for this data would have three levels: the categories would form the top level (the innermost circle), the subcategories would form the second level, and the sub-subcategories would form the third level.

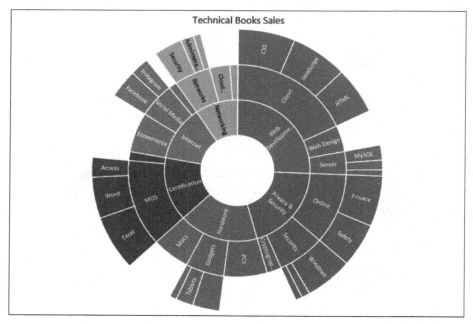

An example of a Sunburst chart.

To create a Sunburst chart

1. Select the range of data you want to chart.

2. On the **Insert** tab, in the **Charts** group, click **Insert Hierarchy Chart**.

3. Click **Sunburst**.

A Treemap chart is similar to a Sunburst chart in that it enables you to visualize hierarchical data. However, instead of organizing the hierarchy levels in concentric circles, like a Sunburst chart, a Treemap chart organizes the data using rectangles:

- The chart's largest rectangles represent the top-level hierarchical items and the rectangle sizes are relative to the total of all the values in that level. For example, if a top-level item is 25 percent of the total, then that value's rectangle takes up a quarter of the chart. This enables you to quickly visualize the contribution of each top-level item to the overall total.

- Within each top-level rectangle, the child values are shown as sub-rectangles, where the size of each sub-rectangle corresponds to the value of the child item relative to the parent value. This enables you to easily visualize the contribution of each child value to its parent.

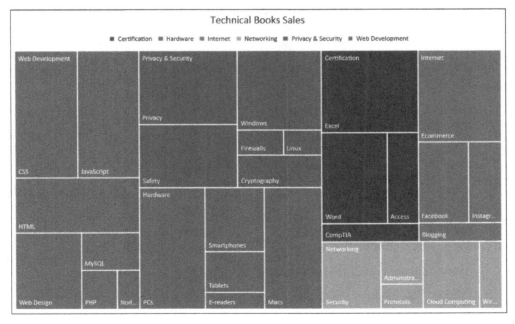

An example of a Treemap chart.

To create a Treemap chart

1. Select the range of data you want to chart.

2. On the **Insert** tab, in the **Charts** group, click **Insert Hierarchy Chart**.

3. Click **Treemap**.

A Waterfall chart enables you to visualize the cumulative effect of a series of positive and negative values. For example, a financial summary might show multiple revenue items and multiple expense items, with the bottom line being a net income value that is essentially the sum of all the revenues minus the sum of all the expenses. Along the way, the statement usually shows multiple intermediate "steps" such as net revenue, gross income, and operating income. The effect of the items that contribute to each step can be hard to visualize, but a Waterfall chart shows how each item affects the ongoing calculation.

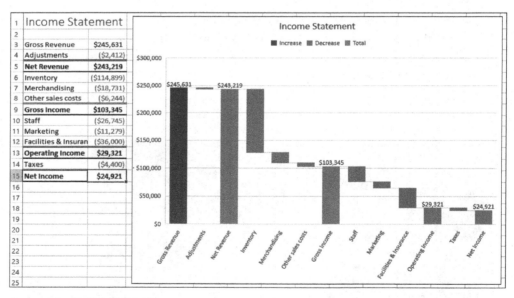

An example of a Waterfall chart.

To create a Waterfall chart

1. Select the range of data you want to chart.

2. On the **Insert** tab, in the **Charts** group, click **Insert Waterfall, Funnel, Stock, Surface, or Radar Chart**.

3. Click **Waterfall**.

Objective 4.1 practice tasks

The practice file for these tasks is located in the **MOSExcelExpert2019 \Objective4** practice file folder. The folder also contains a result file that you can use to check your work.

➤ Open the **ExcelExpert_4-1** workbook and do the following:

- ❑ On the **Box & Whisker** worksheet, create a Box & Whisker chart for the data in the Values column.

- ❑ On the **Funnel** worksheet, create a Funnel chart for the data in the Students column.

- ❑ On the **Histogram** worksheet, create a Histogram chart for the data in the Grade column.

- ❑ On the **Map** worksheet, convert the data in the Country column to the Geography data type, then create a Filled Map chart for the data in the Country and Total columns.

- ❑ On the **Sunburst** worksheet, create a Sunburst chart for the data in the Category, Subcategory, Sub-subcategory, and Sales columns.

- ❑ On the **Treemap** worksheet, create a Treemap chart for the data in the Category, Subcategory, Sub-subcategory, and Sales columns.

- ❑ On the **Waterfall** worksheet, create a Waterfall chart for the data in the range A3:B15.

➤ Save the workbook.

➤ Open the **ExcelExpert_4-1_results** workbook. Compare the two workbooks to check your work. Then close the open workbooks.

Objective 4.2: Create and modify PivotTables

As mentioned at the beginning of this chapter, Excel comes with some powerful tools that can help you analyze the hundreds—or perhaps thousands—of records that can be contained in a table or external database. One of the most powerful of these data analysis tools is the PivotTable. You can use this tool to summarize hundreds of records in a concise tabular format. You can then manipulate the layout of the table to see different views of your data.

Data analysis plays a major role in the Excel Expert exam. Therefore, besides learning the material in this objective, be sure to also study the material in "Objective 3.4: Perform data analysis."

In the simplest case, PivotTables work by summarizing the data in one field (called a *data field*) and breaking it down according to the data in another field. The unique values in the second field (called the *row field*) become the row headings. For example, consider a workbook that has a table of sales by sales representatives that also includes columns for the region and quarter. With a PivotTable, you can summarize the numbers in the Sales field (the data field) and break them down by Region (the row field). In the resulting PivotTable (on a second worksheet), Excel uses the unique items in the Region field (for example, East, Midwest, South, and West) as row headings.

B	C	D	E		A	B	C
Region ▾	**Quarter** ▾	**Sales Rep** ▾	**Sales** ▾	1			
East	1st	Steven Buchanan	$192,345	2			
West	1st	Michael Suyama	$210,880	3		**Region** ▾	**Sum of Sales**
East	1st	Margaret Peacock	$185,223	4		East	$1,463,655
South	1st	Janet Leverling	$165,778	5		Midwest	$1,365,215
Midwest	1st	Anne Dodsworth	$155,557	6		South	$1,409,544
South	1st	Nancy Davolio	$180,567	7		West	$1,477,884
West	1st	Laura Callahan	$200,767	8		**Grand Total**	**$5,716,298**
Midwest	1st	Andrew Fuller	$165,663	9			
East	2nd	Steven Buchanan	$173,493	10			
West	2nd	Michael Suyama	$200,203	11			
East	2nd	Margaret Peacock	$170,213	12			
South	2nd	Janet Leverling	$155,339	13			
Midwest	2nd	Anne Dodsworth	$148,990	14			
South	2nd	Nancy Davolio	$175,660	15			
West	2nd	Laura Callahan	$190,290	16			
Midwest	2nd	Andrew Fuller	$159,002	17			
East	3rd	Steven Buchanan	$175,776	18			

| Sales | Sales By Region | G ... ⊕ | | Sales By Region | ... ⊕ |

A PivotTable summarizes the data from the original table by showing total sales broken down by region.

Create PivotTables

PivotTables look complex to build, but creating a basic PivotTable takes just a few steps. You can also build fancier PivotTables; Excel offers a wide range of options, styles, and features.

The most common source for a PivotTable is an Excel table, although you can also use data that's set up as a regular range. You can use just about any table or range to build a PivotTable, but the best candidates for PivotTables exhibit two main characteristics:

- At least one of the fields contains *groupable* data. That is, the field contains data with a limited number of distinct text, numeric, or date values. In the Sales worksheet example, the Region field is perfect for a PivotTable because, despite having dozens of items, it has only four distinct values: East, West, Midwest, and South.
- Each field in the list must have a heading.

Excel can also put together a PivotTable even if your source data exists in an external database (for example, a Microsoft Access or SQL Server database). If you have existing data connections on your system, you can use one of them as the data source. Otherwise, you can create a new connection as needed.

Create a PivotTable by using options in the Create PivotTable dialog box.

You build a PivotTable visually by using the PivotTable Fields pane, which displays the available fields and offers four regions to which you can add one or more fields:

- **Rows** In this area, you specify the PivotTable's *row field*, which displays vertically the unique values from the field.

- **Columns** In this area, you specify the PivotTable's *column field*, which displays horizontally the unique values from the field.

- **Values** In this area, you specify the PivotTable's *data field*, which displays the results of the calculation that Excel applies to the field's numeric data.

- **Filters** In this area, you specify the PivotTable's *filter field*, which displays a list that contains the unique values from the field. When you select a value from the list, Excel filters the PivotTable results to include only the records that match the selected value.

In the PivotTable Fields pane, you drag fields into some or all of the four areas: Rows, Columns, Values, and Filters.

To create a PivotTable from an Excel table or range

1. Click inside the table or range.

2. On the **Insert** tab, in the **Tables** group, click **PivotTable** to open the **Create PivotTable** dialog box.

3. Click **Select a table or range**. The table name or the range address should already appear in the **Table/Range** box. If it does not, enter or select the table name or range address.

4. Below **Choose where you want the PivotTable report to be placed**, do either of the following:

   - Select **New Worksheet** (the default) to have Excel create a new worksheet for the PivotTable.

   - Select **Existing Worksheet** and then, in the **Location** box, enter or select the cell where you want to anchor the upper-left corner of the PivotTable.

5. Click **OK**. Excel displays the **PivotTable Fields** pane and two **PivotTable Tools** tabs: **Analyze** and **Design**.

6. Add fields to the PivotTable by doing either of the following:

   - In the **Choose fields to add to report** list, select the check box beside each field you want to add. Excel adds numeric fields to the **Values** area and text fields to the **Rows** area.

   - Drag each field and drop it inside the area where you want the field to appear.

   Tip If you're using an exceptionally large data source, it might take Excel a long time to update the PivotTable as you add each field. If this is the case, select the Defer Layout Update check box, which tells Excel not to update the PivotTable as you add each field. When you're ready to see the current PivotTable layout, click Update.

To create a PivotTable from an external data source

1. On the **Insert** tab, in the **Tables** group, click **PivotTable** to open the **Create PivotTable** dialog box.

2. Select **Use an external data source**, and then click **Choose Connection**.

3. If the connection you want to use is listed, click it, then click **Open**. Otherwise, do the following:

   Click **Browse for More** to open the **Select Data Source** dialog box.

   Click **New Source** to start the **Data Connection Wizard**.

   Click the type of data source you want, then click **Next**.

   Specify the data source. (The method depends on the type of data source. For SQL Server, you specify the server name and sign-in credentials; for an ODBC data source, such as an Access database, you specify the database file.)

   Select the database and table you want to use, then click **Next**.

   Click **Finish** to complete the **Data Connection Wizard**.

4

4. Below **Choose where you want the PivotTable report to be placed**, select **New Worksheet** or **Existing Worksheet**.

5. Click **OK** to close the dialog box and go to the PivotTable.

6. Add fields to the PivotTable as described in the procedure "To create a PivotTable from an Excel table or range" earlier in this topic.

Modify PivotTable field selections and options

A PivotTable is a powerful data analysis tool because it can take hundreds or even thousands of records and summarize them into a compact, comprehensible report. But its usefulness goes beyond simple consolidation; unlike most of the other data-analysis features in Excel, a PivotTable is not a static collection of worksheet cells. Instead, you can move the fields to different parts of the PivotTable; sort the row, column, or data field; and filter the data to show only the items you want to view.

You can move a PivotTable's fields from one area of the PivotTable to another. By doing so, you can view your data from different perspectives, which can greatly enhance the analysis of the data. Moving a field within a PivotTable is called *pivoting* the data.

The most common way to pivot the data is to move fields between the row and column areas. If your PivotTable contains just a single nondata field, moving the field between the row and column areas changes the orientation of the PivotTable between horizontal (column area) and vertical (row area). If your PivotTable contains fields in both the row and column areas, pivoting one of those fields to the other area creates multiple fields in that area. For example, pivoting a field from the column area to the row area creates two fields in the row area.

When you create a PivotTable, Excel sorts the data in ascending order based on the items in the row and column fields. For example, if the row area contains the Product field, the vertical sort order of the PivotTable is ascending according to the items in the Product field. You can change this default sort order to one that suits your needs. Excel gives you two choices: you can switch between ascending and descending, or you can sort based on a data field instead of a row or column field.

Sorting the PivotTable based on the values in a data field is useful when you want to rank the results. For example, if your PivotTable shows the sum of sales for each product, an ascending or descending sort of the product name enables you to easily find a particular product. However, if you are more interested in finding which products sold the most (or the least), you need to sort the PivotTable on the data field.

Clicking the arrow in a row or column field's header opens a menu of sort and filter options.

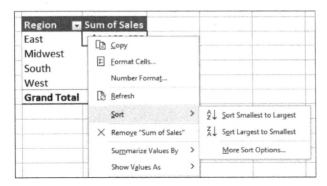

Right-clicking a data field displays a menu from which you can sort the results.

By default, each PivotTable displays a summary for all the records in your source data. This is usually what you want to see. However, there might be situations in which you need to focus more closely on some aspect of the data. You can focus on a specific item from one of the source data fields by taking advantage of the PivotTable's filter field.

For example, suppose you are dealing with a PivotTable that summarizes data from thousands of customer invoices over some period of time. A basic PivotTable might tell you the total amount sold for each product that you carry. That is interesting, but what if you want to see the total amount sold for each product in a specific country/region? If the Product field is in the PivotTable's row area, you can add the Country/Region field to the column area. However, there might be dozens of countries/regions, so that is not an efficient solution. Instead, you can add the Country/Region field to the PivotTable filter. You can then have Excel display the total sold for each product for the specific country/region that you are interested in.

Clicking the arrow in the filter field header displays possible filter values.

You can also filter a PivotTable by using a row or column field. In this case, Excel filters the PivotTable data to show only the row or column items that you add to the filter.

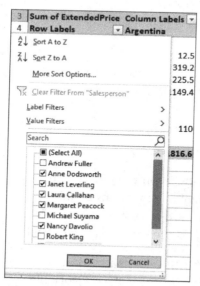

Clicking the arrow in the row or column field header displays possible filter values.

To move a field to a different area

→ In the **PivotTable Fields** pane, drag the field you want to move from its current area to the new area.

To sort a PivotTable by using a row or column field

1. In the field header for the row or column field you want to use for sorting, click the arrow.

2. Click the sort order you want to use, such as **Sort Z to A**.

To sort a PivotTable by using a data field

1. Right-click any cell in the data field.

2. In the menu, point to **Sort**, then click the sort order you want to use, such as **Sort Largest to Smallest**.

To filter PivotTable data by using the filter field

1. In the field header for the PivotTable's filter field, click the arrow.

2. Do either of the following, and then click **OK** to return to the PivotTable:

   • Click the item you want to use as the filter.

   • To apply multiple filters, select the **Select Multiple Items** check box, and then click each item you want to include in the filter.

To filter PivotTable data by using a row or column field

1. In the field header for the PivotTable's row or column field, click the arrow.

2. Clear the check box beside each item you do not want to view, then click **OK**.

Create slicers

So far in this chapter, you have learned how to filter a PivotTable either by using the filter field, which applies to the entire PivotTable, or by using row or column items, which apply only to that field. In both cases, the filter is usable only with the PivotTable in which it is defined. However, it is not unusual to require the same filter in multiple PivotTables. For example, if you are a sales manager responsible for sales in a particular set of countries/regions, you might often need to filter a PivotTable to show data from just those countries/regions. Similarly, if you work with a subset of your company's product line, you might often have to filter PivotTables to show the results from just those products.

Applying these kinds of filters to one or two PivotTables is not difficult or time con-suming, but if you have to apply the same filter over and over again, the process becomes frustrating and inefficient. To combat this, Excel offers a PivotTable feature called the *slicer*. A slicer is very similar to a filter field, except that it is independent of any PivotTable. This means that you can apply the same slicer to multiple PivotTables.

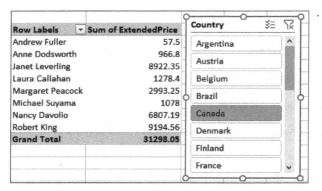

A slicer that applies a filter to any PivotTable that includes a Country/Region field.

If your PivotTable includes one or more fields with dates, you can also create a *timeline slicer*, which displays a sliding timeline that you can use to select specific days, months, or years. Excel then filters the PivotTable to show the data only for the selected time value.

Row Labels	Sum of ExtendedPrice
Alice Mutton	$1,170.00
Aniseed Syrup	$200.00
Boston Crab Meat	$551.25
Camembert Pierrot	$3,961.00
Chai	$360.00
Côte de Blaye	$8,263.36
Filo Mix	$35.00
Fløtemysost	$306.37

OrderDate

All Periods   MONTHS ▾

2020

JUN   JUL   AUG   SEP   OCT   NOV   DEC

An example of a timeline slicer.

To create and apply a slicer

1. Click a cell in a PivotTable that contains the field for which you want to create a slicer.

2. On the **PivotTable Analyze** tab, in the **Filter** group, click **Insert Slicer** to open the **Insert Slicers** dialog box.

3. Select the check box beside each field for which you want to create the slicer, then click **OK**. Excel displays one slicer for each field you selected.

4. In the slicer, click a field item that you want to include in your filter. If you want to include multiple items in your filter, hold down **Ctrl** while you click each item. Excel filters the PivotTable based on the field items you select in each slicer.

To create and apply a timeline slicer

1. Click a cell in a PivotTable that contains the field for which you want to create a slicer.

2. On the **PivotTable Analyze** tab, in the **Filter** group, click **Insert Timeline** to open the **Insert Timelines** dialog box.

3. Select the check box beside each field for which you want to create a timeline slicer, then click **OK**. Excel displays one timeline for each field you selected.

4. In the timeline's list, select a time unit: **Years**, **Quarters**, **Months**, or **Days**.

5. Click the time period you want to view. Excel filters the PivotTable based on the time period you select in each timeline.

Group PivotTable data

Most PivotTables have just a few items in the row and column fields, which makes the PivotTable easy to read and analyze. However, it is not unusual to have row or column fields that consist of dozens of items, which makes the PivotTable much more unwieldy. To make a PivotTable with a large number of row or column items easier to work with, you can group the items together. For example, you could group months into quarters, thus reducing the number of items from 12 to 4. Similarly, a PivotTable that lists dozens of countries/regions could group those countries/regions by continent, thus reducing the number of items to four or five, depending on where the countries/regions are located. Finally, if you use a numeric field in the row or column area, you might have hundreds of items, one for each numeric value. You can improve the PivotTable by creating just a few numeric ranges. In Excel, you can group three types of data: numeric, date and time, and text.

Grouping numeric values is useful when you use a numeric source for a row or column field. In Excel, you can specify numeric ranges into which the field items are grouped. For example, suppose you have a PivotTable of invoice data that shows the extended price (the row field) and the salesperson (the column field). It would be useful to group the extended prices into ranges and then count the number of invoices each salesperson processed in each range.

4

IMPORTANT The ranges that Excel creates after you apply the grouping to a numeric field are not themselves numeric values; they are, instead, text values. Unfortunately, this means it is not possible to use the AutoSort feature in Excel to switch the ranges from ascending order to descending order, because Excel sorts the items as text, not as numbers.

Count of ExtendedPrice	Column Labels			
Row Labels	Andrew Fuller	Anne Dodsworth	Janet Leverling	Laura Callahan
0-1000	83	38	156	109
1000-2000	10	4	19	13
2000-3000	7	1	6	2
3000-4000		2	1	
4000-5000	1			
5000-6000	1			
6000-7000			1	
7000-8000			1	
8000-9000				
10000-11000				
Grand Total	102	45	184	124

A PivotTable grouped in ranges of 1,000 according to the numeric values in the row field.

If your PivotTable includes a field with date or time data, you can use the grouping feature in Excel to consolidate that data into more manageable or useful groups. For example, a PivotTable based on a list of invoice data might show the total dollar amount, which is the Sum Of Extended Price in the data area, of the orders placed on each day, which is the Date field in the row area. Tracking daily sales is useful, but a manager might need a PivotTable that shows the bigger picture. In that case, you can use the Grouping feature to consolidate the dates into weeks, months, or even quarters. You can even choose multiple date groupings. For example, if you have several years' worth of invoice data, you could group the data into years, the years into quarters, and the quarters into months.

Row Labels	Sum of ExtendedPrice
Qtr1	$138,288.90
Jan	$61,258.06
Feb	$38,483.63
Mar	$38,547.21
Qtr2	$148,177.02
Apr	$53,032.95
May	$53,781.28
Jun	$36,362.79
Qtr3	$153,937.73
Jul	$51,020.83
Aug	$47,287.66
Sep	$55,629.24
Qtr4	$181,681.43
Oct	$66,749.23
Nov	$43,533.79
Dec	$71,398.41
Grand Total	$617,085.08

A PivotTable grouped by quarters, and then by months, according to the date values in the row field.

You can also group time data. For example, suppose you have data that shows the time of day that an assembly line completes each operation. If you want to analyze how the time of day affects productivity, you could set up a PivotTable that groups the data into minutes—for example, 30-minute intervals—or hours.

Finally, you can use the PivotTable Grouping feature to create custom groups from the text items in a row or column field. One common problem that arises when you work with PivotTables is that you often need to consolidate items but you have no corresponding field in the data. For example, the data might have a Country/Region field, but what if you need to consolidate the PivotTable results by continent? It is unlikely that your source data includes a Continent field. Similarly, your source data might include employee names, but you might need to consolidate the employees according to the people they report to. What do you do if your source data does not include a Supervisor field?

The solution in both cases is to use the Grouping feature to create custom groups. For the country/region data, you could create custom groups named North America, South America, Europe, and so on. For the employees, you could create a custom group for each supervisor. You select the items that you want to include in a particular group, create the custom group, and then change the new group name to reflect its content.

Sum of ExtendedPrice	Column Labels			
Row Labels	Andrew Fuller	Anne Dodsworth	Janet Leverling	Laura Callahan
⊟South America	7124.9	390.5	9575.68	9319.08
Argentina		12.5	319.2	225.5
Brazil	5524.4		3389.64	4983.6
Venezuela	1600.5	378	5866.84	4109.98
⊟Europe	46934.79	16816.59	59362.5	26543.48
Austria	6129.45	344	14595.45	5422.09
Belgium		1505.18		
Denmark	1405.2		1684.27	48.75
Finland	5292.03	1590.56		4131.8
France	5279.51	1761	8907.52	3062.57
Germany	25984.1	7800.6	22430.68	11220.47

A PivotTable grouped by continent according to the country/region names in the row field.

To group numeric data in a PivotTable

1. Click any item in the numeric field you want to group.

2. On the **PivotTable Analyze** tab, in the **Group** section, click **Group Field** to open the **Grouping** dialog box.

3. Enter the starting and ending numeric values by doing one of the following:

- In the **Starting at** box, enter the starting numeric value, and in the **Ending at** box, enter the ending numeric value.

- Select either or both of the **Starting at** and **Ending at** check boxes to have Excel extract the minimum value and the maximum value, respectively, of the numeric items, and to place that value in the corresponding box.

4. In the **By** text box, enter the size you want to use for each grouping, then click **OK** to return to the PivotTable.

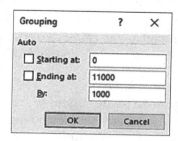

In this version of the Grouping dialog box, you can set up your numeric groupings.

To group date and time data in a PivotTable

1. Click any item in the date or time field you want to group, and open the **Grouping** dialog box.

2. Enter the starting and ending date or time values by doing one of the following:

- In the **Starting at** box, enter the starting date or time value, and in the **Ending at** box, enter the ending date or time value.

- Select either or both of the **Starting at** and **Ending at** check boxes to have Excel extract the minimum value and the maximum value, respectively, of the date or time items, and to place that value in the corresponding box.

3. In the **By** list, click the type of grouping you want. To use multiple groupings, click each type of grouping you want to use.

4. If you clicked only **Days** in step 3, in the **Number of days** box, specify the number of days to use as the group interval.

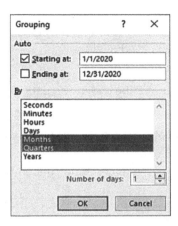

In this version of the Grouping dialog box, you can set up your date or time groupings.

5. Click **OK** to return to the PivotTable.

To group text data in a PivotTable

1. Select the items that you want to include in the group.

2. On the **Analyze** tab, in the **Group** section, click **Group Selection**. Excel creates a new group named Group*n* (where *n* means this is the *n*th group you have created) and restructures the PivotTable.

3. Click the group label, enter a new name for the group, and then press **Enter**. Excel renames the group.

4. Repeat steps 1 through 3 for the other items in the field until you have created all the groups you want.

Add calculated fields

By default, Excel uses a Sum function for calculating the data field summaries. Although Sum is the most common summary function used in PivotTables, it's not the only one. Excel offers the 11 summary functions outlined in the following table.

Function	Description
Sum	Adds the values for the underlying data
Count	Displays the total number of values in the underlying data
Average	Calculates the average of the values for the underlying data

Function	Description
Max	Returns the largest value for the underlying data
Min	Returns the smallest value for the underlying data
Product	Calculates the product of the values for the underlying data
Count Numbers	Displays the total number of numeric values in the underlying data
StdDev	Calculates the standard deviation of the values for the underlying data, treated as a sample
StdDevp	Calculates the standard deviation of the values for the underlying data, treated as a population
Var	Calculates the variance of the values for the underlying data, treated as a sample
Varp	Calculates the variance of the values for the underlying data, treated as a population

You can use summary functions to create powerful and useful PivotTables, but they don't cover every data analysis possibility. For example, suppose you have a PivotTable that uses the Sum function to summarize invoice totals by sales representative. That's useful, but you might also want to pay out a bonus to those representatives whose total sales exceed some threshold. You could use Excel's GETPIVOTDATA worksheet function to create regular worksheet formulas to calculate whether bonuses should be paid and how much they should be (assuming each bonus is a percentage of the total sales).

Tip To use the GETPIVOTDATA worksheet function, enter your formula up to the point where you want to insert the function, then click the PivotTable data field value you want to use. Excel inserts the GETPIVOTDATA function automatically.

However, this isn't very convenient. If you add sales representatives, you need to add formulas; if you remove sales representatives, existing formulas generate errors. And, in any case, one of the points of generating a PivotTable is to perform fewer worksheet calculations, not more. The solution in this case is to take advantage of the *calculated field* feature. A calculated field is a new data field based on a custom formula. For example, if your invoice's PivotTable has an Extended Price field and you want to award a 5-percent bonus to those representatives who did at least $75,000 worth of business, you'd create a calculated field based on the following formula:

*=IF('Extended Price' >= 75000, 'Extended Price' * 0.05, 0)*

IMPORTANT When you reference a field in your formula, Excel interprets this reference as the sum of that field's values. For example, if you include the logical expression 'Extended Price' >= 75000 in a calculated field formula, Excel interprets this as Sum of 'Extended Price' >= 75000. That is, it adds the values in the Extended Price field together and then compares the result with 75000.

A slightly different PivotTable problem is when a field you're using for the row or column labels doesn't contain an item you need. For example, suppose your products are organized into various categories, such as Beverages, Condiments, Confections, and Dairy Products. Suppose further that these categories are grouped into several divisions—for example, Beverages and Condiments in Division A, and Confections and Dairy Products in Division B. If the source data doesn't have a Division field, how do you see PivotTable results that apply to the divisions?

One solution is to create groups for each division, as described earlier in this objective. That works, but Excel gives you a second solution: use calculated items. A *calculated item* is a new item in a row or column where the item's values are generated by a custom formula. For example, you could create a new item named *Division A* that is based on the following formula:

=Beverages + Condiments

To change the data field summary calculation

1. Do either of the following:

   - Right-click any cell inside the data field, then point to **Summarize Values By** to display a partial list of the available summary calculations. If you see the calculation you want, click it; otherwise, click **More Options** to open the **Value Field Settings** dialog box.

   - Click any cell in the data field. Then on the **Analyze** tab, in the **Active Field** group, click **Field Settings** to open the **Value Field Settings** dialog box.

2. In the **Summarize value field by** list, click the summary calculation you want to use. Then click **OK** to return to the worksheet.

To add a calculated field

1. Click any cell inside the data field.

2. On the **PivotTable Analyze** tab, in the **Calculations** group, click **Fields, Items, & Sets** and then click **Calculated Field** to open the **Insert Calculated Field** dialog box.

3. In the **Name** box, enter a name for the calculated field.

4. In the **Formula** box, enter the formula you want to use for the calculated field.

Tip If you need to use a field name in the formula, position the cursor where you want the field name to appear, click the field name in the Fields list, and then click Insert Field.

---

5. Click **Add**, then click **OK**.

To add a calculated item

1. Click any cell inside the row or column field to which you want to add the item.

2. On the **PivotTable Analyze** tab, in the **Calculations** group, click **Fields, Items, & Sets** and then click **Calculated Item** to open the **Insert Calculated Item In "_Field_"** dialog box (where _Field_ is the name of the field you're working with).

3. In the **Name** box, enter a name for the calculated item.

4. In the **Formula** box, enter the formula you want to use for the calculated item.

5. Click **Add**, then click **OK**.

Format data

When you click any cell within a PivotTable, Excel displays the PivotTable Tools tool tabs, one of which is named _Design_. You can use the controls on the Design tool tab to perform six different PivotTable formatting tasks:

- **Configure subtotals** If you group your PivotTable values, you can configure the group subtotals to appear either at the bottom or the top of the group, or you can turn off the subtotals altogether.

- **Configure grand totals** You can set the PivotTable grand totals to appear for both rows and columns, for rows only, for columns only, or not at all.

- **Select a report layout** If you display more than one field in an area of the PivotTable, you can change the order of those fields if you want a different view of your report. When you have multiple fields in the row area, Excel displays each field in its own column, the field and subfield items all begin on the same row, and gridlines appear around every cell. This is called the _tabular layout_ and is the default PivotTable layout. Excel also comes with two other report layouts that you can use. The *outline layout* also displays each field in its own column. However, the subfield items for each field item begin one row below the field item, and no gridlines appear around the cells (except for a single gridline under each item in the outer field). The *compact layout* displays each field in a single column. The subfield items for each field item begin one row below the field item and are indented from the left. No gridlines appear around the cells (except for a single gridline under each item in the outer field).

- **Add or remove blank rows** If you have multiple fields in the row or column area, you can elect to add a blank row between each item, which can often make the PivotTable easier to read.

- **Set PivotTable style options** You can turn on or off the PivotTable row headers, column headers, banded rows, and banded columns.

- **Apply a PivotTable style** A style is a collection of formatting options—fonts, borders, and background colors—that Excel defines for different areas of a PivotTable. For example, a style might use bold, white text on a black background for labels and grand totals, and white text on a dark blue background for items and data.

To format PivotTable data

1. Click any cell inside the PivotTable.

2. On the **Design** tab, in the **Layout** group, do any of the following:

   - Click **Subtotals**, then click one of the options in the list.
   - Click **Grand Totals**, then click one of the options in the list.
   - Click **Report Layout**, then click one of the options in the list.
   - Click **Blank Rows**, then click one of the options to add or remove blank rows.

3. In the **PivotTable Style Options** group, select or clear the check boxes to turn the **Row Headers**, **Column Headers**, **Banded Rows**, and **Banded Columns** features on or off.

4. In the **PivotTable Styles** group, in the gallery, click a predefined style to apply it to the PivotTable.

4

Objective 4.2 practice tasks

The practice file for these tasks is located in the **MOSExcelExpert2019 \Objective4** practice file folder. The folder also contains a result file that you can use to check your work.

➤ Open the **ExcelExpert_4-2** workbook.

➤ From the table on the **Invoices** worksheet, create a PivotTable, place it on a new worksheet, and do the following:

❑ Rename the worksheet ***ExtendedPrice by Salesperson***.

❑ In the PivotTable, summarize the values in the ExtendedPrice field by Salesperson.

❑ Add a calculated field named ***Bonus*** that calculates a 5-percent bonus for the salespeople with sales of at least $75,000 and 0 for salespeople who sold less than that amount. (The field name will change after you create it to *Sum of Bonus*.)

➤ From the table on the **Invoices** worksheet, create a PivotTable, place it on a new worksheet, and do the following:

❑ Rename the worksheet ***Qty by Country_Region & Categ***.

❑ In the PivotTable, summarize the values in the Quantity field by both the Country/Region field (as the row field) and the Category field (as the column field).

❑ Switch the row and column fields.

❑ Create a timeline slicer based on the OrderDate field.

➤ From the table on the **Invoices** worksheet, create a PivotTable, place it on a new worksheet, and do the following:

❑ Rename the worksheet ***Quantity by Unit Price***.

❑ In the PivotTable, summarize the Quantity field by UnitPrice.

❑ Group the UnitPrice field in $10 increments from $0 to $270.

❑ In cell A1, enter ***Units sold in the lowest price range:*** in bold, and then, in cell D1, create a formula that returns the number of units sold in the *0-10* group.

➤ Save the **ExcelExpert_4-2** workbook. Open the **ExcelExpert_ 4-2_results** workbook. Compare the two workbooks to check your work. Then close the open workbooks.

Objective 4.3: Create and modify PivotCharts

A PivotChart is a graphical representation of the values in a PivotTable. However, a PivotChart goes far beyond a regular chart, because a PivotChart has many of the same capabilities as a PivotTable. These capabilities include hiding items, filtering data by using the filter field, and refreshing the PivotChart to account for changes in the underlying data. Also, if you move fields from one area of the PivotTable to another, the PivotChart changes accordingly. You also have access to most of the regular charting capabilities in Excel, so PivotCharts are a powerful addition to your data-analysis toolkit.

Create PivotCharts

Excel offers three ways to create a PivotChart:

- You can create a PivotChart directly from an existing PivotTable. This saves time because you do not have to configure the layout of the PivotChart or any other options. When you use this method, Excel uses the default chart type for the data and places the PivotChart on a new chart sheet.

- You can create a PivotChart on the same worksheet as its associated PivotTable. That way you can easily compare the PivotTable and the PivotChart. This is called *embedding* the PivotChart on the worksheet.

- If the data you want to summarize and visualize exists as an Excel table or range, you can build a PivotChart directly from that data. Note, however, that Excel does not allow you to create just a PivotChart on its own. Instead, Excel creates a PivotTable and an embedded PivotChart at the same time. If you want to analyze your data by using both a PivotTable and a PivotChart, this method will save you time because it does not require any extra steps to embed the PivotChart along with the PivotTable.

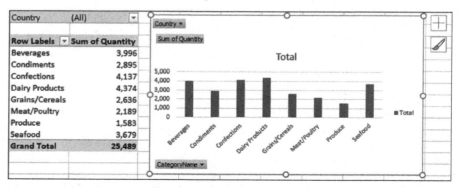

A PivotChart embedded on the same worksheet as its PivotTable.

To create a PivotChart of the default type on a new sheet from a PivotTable

→ Click any cell in the PivotTable, then press **F11**.

To embed a PivotChart on the same worksheet as a PivotTable

1. Click any cell in the PivotTable.

2. Do either of the following to open the **Insert Chart** dialog box:

   - On the **PivotTable Analyze** tab, in the **Tools** group, click **PivotChart**.

   - On the **Insert** tab, in the **Charts** group, click the **PivotChart** button (not the arrow).

3. In the category list, click the chart type you want.

   > **IMPORTANT** You can't use charts in the XY (Scatter), Stock, Treemap, Sunburst, Histogram, Box & Whisker, Waterfall, or Funnel categories to create a PivotChart from a PivotTable.

4. On the chart category page, click the chart subtype you want. Then click **OK** to close the dialog box and return to the worksheet.

To create a PivotChart from an Excel table or range

1. Click inside the table or range.

2. On the **Insert** tab, in the **Charts** group, click **PivotChart** to open the Create PivotChart dialog box.

3. Click **Select a table or range**. The table name or the range address should already appear in the **Table/Range** box. If it does not, enter or select the table name or range address.

4. Do either of the following:

   - Select **New Worksheet** (the default) to have Excel create a new worksheet for the PivotChart.

   - Select **Existing Worksheet** and then, in the **Location** box, enter or select the cell where you want to anchor the upper-left corner of the PivotChart.

5. Click **OK**. Excel creates the PivotTable and PivotChart skeletons and displays the **PivotTable Fields** pane and three PivotChart Tools tabs: **Analyze**, **Design**, and **Format**.

6. Add the fields you want to the PivotTable. As you add each field, Excel updates both the PivotTable and the PivotChart.

4

Manipulate options in existing PivotCharts

By default, each PivotChart displays a summary for all the records in your source data. This is usually what you want to see. However, there might be situations where you need to focus more closely on some aspect of the data. You can do this by changing the PivotChart's row, column, and filter options:

- Click the row field button in the lower-left corner to sort the row items, apply a filter to the row items, or hide one or more row items.

- Click the column field button just above the chart legend to sort the column items, apply a filter to the column items, or hide one or more column items.

- Click the filter field button in the upper-left corner to apply one or more filters to the entire PivotChart.

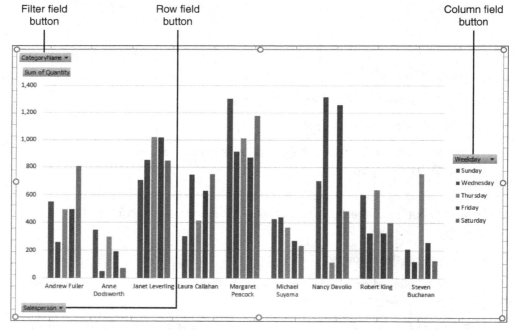

A PivotChart's row, column, and filter field headers.

To change the row, column, or filter options in a PivotChart

→ Click either the row field, column field, or report field button, then select the options you want to apply to the PivotChart.

Apply styles to PivotCharts

When you select a PivotChart, the PivotChart tool tabs appear. The Design tool tab includes several options for changing the PivotChart style:

- **Adding chart elements** You can modify the chart by adding elements such as a chart title, axis titles, data labels, a data table, and gridlines.

- **Applying a predefined chart layout** Excel offers 11 preset chart layouts that you can use to quickly display titles, gridlines, and other chart elements.

- **Changing the chart colors** You can change the color scheme that Excel applies to the chart data markers.

- **Applying a chart style** Excel offers a number of predefined styles that control the chart's colors and effects.

- **Changing the chart data** You can switch the rows and columns, and you can change the PivotTable data source.

- **Changing the chart type** You can change the current chart type to any type that supports PivotCharts.

- **Moving the chart** You can move the PivotChart to a new sheet, or you can embed the PivotChart in a different worksheet.

To apply styles to a PivotChart

1. Select the PivotChart.

2. On the **Design** tab, do any of the following:

   - In the **Chart Layouts** group, in the **Add Chart Element** list, add one or more elements to the PivotChart.

   - In the **Chart Layouts** group, in the **Quick Layout** list, apply a predefined chart layout.

   - In the **Chart Styles** group, in the **Chart Styles** gallery, apply a predefined style to the PivotChart.

   - In the **Data** group, click **Switch Row/Column** to switch the PivotChart's row and column fields.

   - In the **Data** group, click **Select Data** to choose a different PivotTable as the PivotChart's data source.

- In the **Type** group, click **Change Chart Type** to apply a new chart type to the PivotChart.

- In the **Location** group, click **Move Chart** to move the PivotChart either to a new sheet or to an existing worksheet, as an embedded object.

Drill down into PivotChart details

By definition, both a PivotTable and a PivotChart are summaries of the underlying data. This means that each data point is the highest level in a hierarchy that can include many different levels. For example, you might have a PivotChart that summarizes invoice data by showing the total quantity sold for each product category. The category is the highest level of the hierarchy. One level down in the hierarchy might be the individual products that make up each category. An example of a multilevel hierarchy would be to break down the categories into the countries/regions in which the sales occurred, then the states/provinces, and then the cities. Excel also offers the Collapse command, which you can use to move up the hierarchy to display fewer details.

To drill down into a PivotChart's details

1. Right-click the data point you want to drill down into.

2. Do one of the following:

- Click **Expand** to expand down a single level.

- Click **Expand Entire Field** to expand down all the details and see all the levels of the hierarchy.

- Click **Expand to "Field"** to expand all the details down to the field name specified by Field.

To collapse a PivotChart's details

1. Right-click the data point you want to collapse, then click **Expand/Collapse**.

2. Do one of the following:

- Click **Collapse** to collapse a single level.

- Click **Collapse Entire Field** to collapse all the details and see only the top level of the hierarchy.

- Click **Collapse to "Field"** to collapse all the details up to the field name specified by Field.

Objective 4.3 practice tasks

The practice file for these tasks is located in the **MOSExcelExpert2019 \Objective4** practice file folder. The folder also contains a result file that you can use to check your work.

➤ Open the **ExcelExpert_4-3** workbook and do the following:

❑ From the PivotTable on the **Sales by Weekday** worksheet, create a PivotChart of the default type on a new chart sheet. Rename the chart sheet *Sales by Weekday PivotChart*.

❑ From the PivotTable on the **Shippers by Location** worksheet, create a clustered column PivotChart and embed it on the same worksheet.

➤ From the table on the **Invoices** worksheet, create a PivotTable and embedded PivotChart on a new worksheet, and do the following:

❑ Rename the worksheet *Quantity Sold*.

❑ Set up the PivotTable to summarize the Quantity sold by Country/ Region (row) and Category (column).

❑ To the PivotChart, add the chart title *Quantity Sold by Category and Country/Region*.

❑ In the PivotChart, select the data point where the Country/Region is *United States* and the Category is *Seafood*, then expand this data point to drill down to the *State/Province* field.

➤ Save the workbook.

➤ Open the **ExcelExpert_4-3_results** workbook. Compare the two workbooks to check your work. Then close the open workbooks.

Index

SYMBOLS

Plug into learning at

MicrosoftPressStore.com

The Microsoft Press Store by Pearson offers:

- Free U.S. shipping

- Buy an eBook, get three formats – Includes PDF, EPUB, and MOBI to use with your computer, tablet, and mobile devices

- Print & eBook Best Value Packs

- eBook Deal of the Week – Save up to 50% on featured title

- Newsletter – Be the first to hear about new releases, announcements, special offers, and more

- Register your book – Find companion files, errata, and product updates, plus receive a special coupon* to save on your next purchase

Discounts are applied to the list price of a product. Some products are not eligible to receive additional discounts, so your discount code may not be applied to all items in your cart. Discount codes cannot be applied to products that are already discounted, such as eBook Deal of the Week, eBooks that are part of a book + eBook pack, and products with special discounts applied as part of a promotional offering. Only one coupon can be used per order.

 Pearson